Marcel Proust's continuous novel *À la Recherche du Temps Perdu* (REMEMBRANCE OF THINGS PAST) was originally published in eight parts, the titles and dates of which were: I. *Du Côté de Chez Swann* (1913); II. *À l'Ombre des Jeunes Filles en Fleurs* (1918), awarded the Prix Goncourt in 1919; III. *Le Côté de Guermantes* I (1920); IV. *Le Côté de Guermantes* II, *Sodome et Gomorrhe* I (1921); V. *Sodome et Gomorrhe* II (1922); VI. *La Prisonnière* (1923); VII. *Albertine Disparue* (1925); VIII. *Le Temps Retrouvé* (1927).

Du Côté de Chez Swann has been published in English as SWANN'S WAY: *À l'Ombre des Jeunes Filles en Fleurs* as WITHIN A BUDDING GROVE: *Le Côté de Guermantes* as THE GUERMANTES WAY: *Sodome et Gomorrhe* as CITIES OF THE PLAIN: *La Prisonnière* as THE CAPTIVE: *Albertine Disparue* as THE SWEET CHEAT GONE: and *Le Temps Retrouvé* as TIME REGAINED. The first seven parts were translated by C. K. Scott Moncrieff; the eighth by Stephen Hudson.

In the present uniform edition the volumes are as follows:—

THE MOTHER

MARCEL PROUST

SWANN'S WAY

PART ONE

Translated by
C. K. Scott Moncrieff

ILLUSTRATED BY
PHILIPPE JULLIAN

1957
CHATTO & WINDUS
LONDON

First published in English (cr. 8vo) 1922
New impressions 1923, 1924,
1925, 1928
First issued in the Phoenix Library 1929
Reprinted 1933, 1940
First issued in the Uniform Edition
(12 vols.) 1941
Reprinted 1941, 1943, 1949, 1951, 1955
Illustrated Edition 1957

To
E. J. C.

HERE, *Summer lingering, loiter I*
  When I, with Summer, should be gone . . .
Where only London lights the sky
  I go, and with me journeys "Swann"

Whose pages' dull, laborious woof
  Covers a warp of working-times,
Of firelit nights beneath your roof
  And sunlit days beneath your limes,

While, both at once or each in turn,
  Sharp-tongued but smooth, like buttered knives,
We pared, with studied unconcern,
  The problems of our private lives ;

Those tiny problems, dense yet clear,
  Like ivory balls by Chinese craft
Pierced (where each hole absorbed a tear)
  And rounded (where the assembly laughed).

Did all our laughter muffle pain,
  Our candour simulate pretence ?
Fear not.   I shall not come again
  To tease you with indifference.

Yet I may gaze for Oakham spire
  Where London suns set, watery-pale,
And dream, while tides of crimson fire
  Sweep, smoking, over Catmos vale.

Michaelmas 1921   C. K. S. M.

CONTENTS

✳

ILLUSTRATIONS

*

SWANN'S WAY

OVERTURE

FOR a long time I used to go to bed early. Sometimes, when I had put out my candle, my eyes would close so quickly that I had not even time to say " I'm going to sleep." And half an hour later the thought that it was time to go to sleep would awaken me ; I would try to put away the book which, I imagined, was still in my hands, and to blow out the light ; I had been thinking all the time, while I was asleep, of what I had just been reading, but my thoughts had run into a channel of their own, until I myself seemed actually to have become the subject of my book : a church, a quartet, the rivalry between François I and Charles V. This impression would persist for some moments after I was awake ; it did not disturb my mind, but it lay like scales upon my eyes and prevented them from registering the fact that the candle was no longer burning. Then it would begin to seem unintelligible, as the thoughts of a former existence must be to a reincarnate spirit ; the subject of my book would separate itself from me, leaving me free to choose whether I would form part of it or no ; and at the same time my sight would return and I would be astonished to find myself in a state of darkness, pleasant and restful enough for the eyes, and even more, perhaps, for my mind, to which it appeared incomprehensible, without a cause, a matter dark indeed.

I would ask myself what o'clock it could be ; I could hear the whistling of trains, which, now nearer and now farther off, punctuating the distance like the note of a bird in a forest, shewed me in perspective the deserted countryside through which a traveller would be hurrying towards the nearest station : the path that he followed being fixed for ever in his memory by the general excitement due to being in a strange place, to doing unusual things, to the last words of conversation, to farewells exchanged beneath an unfamiliar lamp which echoed still in his ears amid the silence of the night ; and to the delightful prospect of being once again at home.

I would lay my cheeks gently against the comfortable cheeks of my pillow, as plump and blooming as the cheeks of babyhood. Or I would strike a match to look at my watch. Nearly midnight. The hour when an invalid, who has been obliged to start on a journey and to sleep in a strange hotel, awakens in a moment of illness and sees with glad relief a streak of daylight shewing under his bedroom door. Oh, joy of joys ! it is morning. The servants will be about in a minute : he can ring, and some one will come to look after him. The thought of being made comfortable gives him strength to endure his pain. He is certain he heard footsteps : they come nearer, and then die away. The ray of light beneath his door is extinguished. It is midnight ; some one has turned out the gas ; the last servant has gone to bed, and he must lie all night in agony with no one to bring him any help.

I would fall asleep, and often I would be awake again for short snatches only, just long enough to hear the regular creaking of the wainscot, or to open my eyes to settle the shifting kaleidoscope of the darkness, to savour, in an instantaneous flash of perception, the sleep which lay heavy upon the furniture, the room, the whole surroundings of which I formed but an insignificant part and whose unconsciousness I should very soon return to share. Or, perhaps, while I was asleep I had returned without the least effort to an earlier stage in my life, now for ever outgrown ; and had come under the thrall of one of my childish terrors, such as that old terror of my great-uncle's pulling my curls, which was effectually dispelled on the day—the dawn of a new era to me—on which they were finally cropped from my head. I had forgotten that event during my sleep ; I remembered it again immediately I had succeeded in making myself wake up to escape my great-uncle's fingers ; still, as a measure of precaution, I would bury the whole of my head in the pillow before returning to the world of dreams.

Sometimes, too, just as Eve was created from a rib of Adam, so a woman would come into existence while I was sleeping, conceived from some strain in the position of my limbs. Formed by the appetite that I was on the point of gratifying, she it was, I imagined, who offered me that gratification. My body, conscious that its own warmth was permeating hers, would strive to become one with her, and I would awake. The rest of humanity seemed very remote in comparison with this woman whose company I had left but a moment ago : my cheek was still warm with her kiss, my body bent beneath the weight of hers. If, as would sometimes happen, she had the appearance of some woman whom I had known in waking hours, I would abandon myself altogether to the sole quest of her, like people who set out on a journey to see with their own eyes some city that they have always longed to visit, and imagine that they can taste in reality what has charmed their fancy. And then, gradually, the memory of her would dissolve and vanish, until I had forgotten the maiden of my dream.

When a man is asleep, he has in a circle round him the chain of the hours, the sequence of the years, the order of the heavenly host. Instinctively, when he awakes, he looks to these, and in an instant reads off his own position on the earth's surface and the amount of time that has elapsed during his slumbers; but this ordered procession is apt to grow confused, and to break its ranks. Suppose that, towards morning, after a night of insomnia, sleep descends upon him while he is reading, in quite a different position from that in which he normally goes to sleep, he has only to lift his arm to arrest the sun and turn it back in its course, and, at the moment of waking, he will have no idea of the time, but will conclude that he has just gone to bed. Or suppose that he gets drowsy in some even more abnormal position; sitting in an armchair, say, after dinner : then the world will fall topsy-turvy from its orbit, the magic chair will carry him at full speed through time and space, and when he opens his eyes again he will imagine that he went to sleep months earlier and in some far distant country. But for me it was enough if, in my own bed, my sleep was so heavy as completely to relax my consciousness; for then I lost all sense of the place in which I had gone to sleep, and when I awoke at midnight, not knowing where I was, I could not be sure at first who I was; I had only the most rudimentary sense of existence, such as may lurk and flicker in the depths of an animal's consciousness; I was more destitute of human qualities than the cave-dweller; but then the memory, not yet of the place in which I was, but of various other places where I had lived, and might now very possibly be, would come like a rope let down from heaven to draw me up out of the abyss of not-being, from which I could never have escaped by myself : in a flash I would traverse and surmount centuries of civilisation, and out of a half-visualised succession of oil-lamps, followed by shirts with turned-down collars, would put together by degrees the component parts of my ego.

Perhaps the immobility of the things that surround us is

forced upon them by our conviction that they are themselves,
and not anything else, and by the immobility of our concep-
tions of them. For it always happened that when I awoke
like this, and my mind struggled in an unsuccessful attempt
to discover where I was, everything would be moving round
me through the darkness : things, places, years. My body,
still too heavy with sleep to move, would make an effort to
construe the form which its tiredness took as an orientation
of its various members, so as to induce from that where the
wall lay and the furniture stood, to piece together and to give
a name to the house in which it must be living. Its memory,
the composite memory of its ribs, knees, and shoulder-blades
offered it a whole series of rooms in which it had at one time
or another slept ; while the unseen walls kept changing,
adapting themselves to the shape of each successive room that
it remembered, whirling madly through the darkness. And
even before my brain, lingering in consideration of when
things had happened and of what they had looked like, had
collected sufficient impressions to enable it to identify the
room, it, my body, would recall from each room in succession
what the bed was like, where the doors were, how daylight
came in at the windows, whether there was a passage outside,
what I had had in my mind when I went to sleep, and had
found there when I awoke. The stiffened side underneath
my body would, for instance, in trying to fix its position,
imagine itself to be lying, face to the wall, in a big bed with a
canopy ; and at once I would say to myself, " Why, I must
have gone to sleep after all, and Mamma never came to
say good night ! " for I was in the country with my grandfather, who died years ago ; and my body, the side upon which
I was lying, loyally preserving from the past an impression
which my mind should never have forgotten, brought back

5

before my eyes the glimmering flame of the night-light in its bowl of Bohemian glass, shaped like an urn and hung by chains from the ceiling, and the chimney-piece of Sienna marble in my bedroom at Combray, in my great-aunt's house, in those far distant days which, at the moment of waking, seemed present without being clearly defined, but would become plainer in a little while when I was properly awake.

Then would come up the memory of a fresh position ; the wall slid away in another direction ; I was in my room in Mme. de Saint-Loup's house in the country ; good heavens, it must be ten o'clock, they will have finished dinner ! I must have overslept myself, in the little nap which I always take when I come in from my walk with Mme. de Saint-Loup, before dressing for the evening. For many years have now elapsed since the Combray days, when, coming in from the longest and latest walks, I would still be in time to see the reflection of the sunset glowing in the panes of my bedroom window. It is a very different kind of existence at Tansonville now with Mme. de Saint-Loup, and a different kind of pleasure that I now derive from taking walks only in the evenings, from visiting by moonlight the roads on which I used to play, as a child, in the sunshine ; while the bedroom, in which I shall presently fall asleep instead of dressing for dinner, from afar off I can see it, as we return from our walk, with its lamp shining through the window, a solitary beacon in the night.

These shifting and confused gusts of memory never lasted for more than a few seconds ; it often happened that, in my spell of uncertainty as to where I was, I did not distinguish the successive theories of which that uncertainty was composed any more than, when we watch a horse running, we isolate the successive positions of its body as they appear upon a bioscope. But I had seen first one and then another of the rooms in which I had slept during my life, and in the end I would revisit them all in the long course of my waking dream: rooms in winter, where on going to bed I would at once bury my head in a nest, built up out of the most diverse materials, the corner of my pillow, the top of my blankets, a piece of a shawl, the edge of my bed, and a copy of an evening paper, all of which things I would contrive, with the infinite patience of birds building their nests, to cement into one whole ; rooms where, in a keen frost, I would feel the satisfaction of being shut in from the outer world (like the sea-swallow which builds at the end of a dark tunnel and is kept warm by the surrounding earth), and where, the fire keeping in all night, I would sleep wrapped up, as it were, in a great cloak of snug and savoury air, shot with the glow of the logs which would break out again in flame : in a sort of alcove without walls, a cave of warmth dug out of the heart of the room itself, a zone of heat whose boundaries were constantly shifting and altering in temperature as gusts of air ran across them to strike freshly upon my face, from the corners of the room, or from parts near the window or far from the fireplace which had therefore remained cold—or rooms in summer, where I would delight to feel myself a part of the warm evening, where the moonlight striking upon the half-opened shutters would throw down to the foot of my bed its enchanted ladder ; where I would fall asleep, as it might be in the open air, like a titmouse which the breeze keeps poised in the focus of a sunbeam—or sometimes the Louis XVI room, so cheerful that I could never feel really unhappy, even on my first night in it : that room where the slender columns which lightly supported its ceiling would part, ever so gracefully, to indicate where the bed was and to keep it separate ; some-

times again that little room with the high ceiling, hollowed in
the form of a pyramid out of two separate storeys, and partly
walled with mahogany, in which from the first moment my
mind was drugged by the unfamiliar scent of flowering
grasses, convinced of the hostility of the violet curtains and
of the insolent indifference of a clock that chattered on at the
top of its voice as though I were not there ; while a strange
and pitiless mirror with square feet, which stood across one
corner of the room, cleared for itself a site I had not looked to
find tenanted in the quiet surroundings of my normal field of
vision : that room in which my mind, forcing itself for hours
on end to leave its moorings, to elongate itself upwards so as
to take on the exact shape of the room, and to reach to the
summit of that monstrous funnel, had passed so many anxious
nights while my body lay stretched out in bed, my eyes staring
upwards, my ears straining, my nostrils sniffing uneasily, and
my heart beating ; until custom had changed the colour of
the curtains, made the clock keep quiet, brought an expression
of pity to the cruel, slanting face of the glass, disguised or even
completely dispelled the scent of flowering grasses, and distinctly reduced the apparent loftiness of the ceiling. Custom !
that skilful but unhurrying manager who begins by torturing the mind for weeks on end with her provisional
arrangements ; whom the mind, for all that, is fortunate
in discovering, for without the help of custom it would
never contrive, by its own efforts, to make any room seem
habitable.

Certainly I was now well awake ; my body had turned
about for the last time and the good angel of certainty had
made all the surrounding objects stand still, had set me down
under my bedclothes, in my bedroom, and had fixed, ap-
proximately in their right places in the uncertain light, my

chest of drawers, my writing-table, my fireplace, the window overlooking the street, and both the doors. But it was no good my knowing that I was not in any of those houses of which, in the stupid moment of waking, if I had not caught sight exactly, I could still believe in their possible presence ; for memory was now set in motion ; as a rule I did not attempt to go to sleep again at once, but used to spend the greater part of the night recalling our life in the old days at Combray with my great-aunt, at Balbec, Paris, Doncières, Venice, and the rest ; remembering again all the places and people that I had known, what I had actually seen of them, and what others had told me.

At Combray, as every afternoon ended, long before the time when I should have to go up to bed, and to lie there, unsleeping, far from my mother and grandmother, my bedroom became the fixed point on which my melancholy and anxious thoughts were centred. Some one had had the happy idea of giving me, to distract me on evenings when I seemed abnormally wretched, a magic lantern, which used to be set on top of my lamp while we waited for dinner-time to come : in the manner of the master-builders and glass-painters of gothic days it substituted for the opaqueness of my walls an impalpable iridescence, supernatural phenomena of many colours, in which legends were depicted, as on a shifting and transitory window. But my sorrows were only increased, because this change of lighting destroyed, as nothing else could have done, the customary impression I had formed of my room, thanks to which the room itself, but for the torture of having to go to bed in it, had become quite endurable. For now I no longer recognised it, and I became uneasy, as though I were in a room in some hotel or furnished lodging, in a place where I had just arrived, by train, for the first time.

Riding at a jerky trot, Golo, his mind filled with an infamous design, issued from the little three-cornered forest which dyed dark-green the slope of a convenient hill, and advanced by leaps and bounds towards the castle of poor Geneviève de Brabant. This castle was cut off short by a curved line which was in fact the circumference of one of the transparent ovals in the slides which were pushed into position through a slot in the lantern. It was only the wing of a castle, and in front of it stretched a moor on which Geneviève stood, lost in contemplation, wearing a blue girdle. The castle and the moor were yellow, but I could tell their colour without waiting to see them, for before the slides made their appearance the old-gold sonorous name of Brabant had given me an unmistakable clue. Golo stopped for a moment and listened sadly to the little speech read aloud by my great-aunt, which he seemed perfectly to understand, for he modified his attitude with a docility not devoid of a degree of majesty, so as to conform to the indications given in the text ; then he rode away at the same jerky trot. And nothing could arrest his slow progress. If the lantern were moved I could still distinguish Golo's horse advancing across the window-curtains, swelling out with their curves and diving into their folds. The body of Golo himself, being of the same supernatural substance as his steed's, overcame all material obstacles —everything that seemed to bar his way—by taking each as it might be a skeleton and embodying it in himself : the door-handle, for instance, over which, adapting itself at once, would float invincibly his red cloak or his pale face, never losing its nobility or its melancholy, never shewing any sign of trouble at such a transubstantiation.

And, indeed, I found plenty of charm in these bright projections, which seemed to have come straight out of a

Merovingian past, and to shed around me the reflections of
such ancient history. But I cannot express the discomfort I
felt at such an intrusion of mystery and beauty into a room
which I had succeeded in filling with my own personality
until I thought no more of the room than of myself. The
anaesthetic effect of custom being destroyed, I would begin to
think and to feel very melancholy things. The door-handle of
my room, which was different to me from all the other door-
handles in the world, inasmuch as it seemed to open of its own
accord and without my having to turn it, so unconscious had
its manipulation become ; lo and behold, it was now an astral
body for Golo. And as soon as the dinner-bell rang I would
run down to the dining-room, where the big hanging lamp,
ignorant of Golo and Bluebeard but well acquainted with
my family and the dish of stewed beef, shed the same light as
on every other evening ; and I would fall into the arms of my
mother, whom the misfortunes of Geneviève de Brabant had
made all the dearer to me, just as the crimes of Golo had
driven me to a more than ordinarily scrupulous examination
of my own conscience.

But after dinner, alas, I was soon obliged to leave Mamma,
who stayed talking with the others, in the garden if it was fine,
or in the little parlour where everyone took shelter when it
was wet. Everyone except my grandmother, who held that
" It is a pity to shut oneself indoors in the country," and used
to carry on endless discussions with my father on the very
wettest days, because he would send me up to my room with
a book instead of letting me stay out of doors. " That is not
the way to make him strong and active," she would say sadly,
" especially this little man, who needs all the strength and
character that he can get." My father would shrug his
shoulders and study the barometer, for he took an interest in

meteorology, while my mother, keeping very quiet so as not to disturb him, looked at him with tender respect, but not too hard, not wishing to penetrate the mysteries of his superior mind. But my grandmother, in all weathers, even when the rain was coming down in torrents and Françoise had rushed indoors with the precious wicker armchairs, so that they should not get soaked, you would see my grandmother pacing the deserted garden, lashed by the storm, pushing back her grey hair in disorder so that her brows might be more free to imbibe the life-giving draughts of wind and rain. She would say, "At last one can breathe!" and would run up and down the soaking paths—too straight and symmetrical for her liking, owing to the want of any feeling for nature in the new gardener, whom my father had been asking all morning if the weather were going to improve—with her keen, jerky little step regulated by the various effects wrought upon her soul by the intoxication of the storm, the force of hygiene, the stupidity of my education and of symmetry in gardens, rather than by any anxiety (for that was quite unknown to her) to save her plum-coloured skirt from the spots of mud under which it would gradually disappear to a depth which always provided her maid with a fresh problem and filled her with fresh despair.

When these walks of my grandmother's took place after dinner there was one thing which never failed to bring her back to the house : that was if (at one of those points when the revolutions of her course brought her, moth-like, in sight of the lamp in the little parlour where the liqueurs were set out on the card-table) my great-aunt called out to her : "Bathilde! Come in and stop your husband from drinking brandy!" For, simply to tease her (she had brought so foreign a type of mind into my father's family that everyone

FRANÇOISE

made a joke of it), my great-aunt used to make my grandfather, who was forbidden liqueurs, take just a few drops. My poor grandmother would come in and beg and implore her husband not to taste the brandy ; and he would become annoyed and swallow his few drops all the same, and she would go out again sad and discouraged, but still smiling, for she was so humble and so sweet that her gentleness towards others, and her continual subordination of herself and of her own troubles, appeared on her face blended in a smile which, unlike those seen on the majority of human faces, had no trace in it of irony, save for herself, while for all of us kisses seemed to spring from her eyes, which could not look upon those she loved without yearning to bestow upon them passionate caresses. The torments inflicted on her by my great-aunt, the sight of my grandmother's vain entreaties, of her in her weakness conquered before she began, but still making the futile endeavour to wean my grandfather from his liqueur-glass——all these were things of the sort to which, in later years, one can grow so well accustomed as to smile at them, to take the tormentor's side with a happy determination which deludes one into the belief that it is not, really, tormenting ; but in those days they filled me with such horror that I longed to strike my great-aunt. And yet, as soon as I heard her " Bathilde ! Come in and stop your husband from drinking brandy ! " in my cowardice I became at once a man, and did what all we grown men do when face to face with suffering and injustice ; I preferred not to see them ; I ran up to the top of the house to cry by myself in a little room beside the schoolroom and beneath the roof, which smelt of orris-root, and was scented also by a wild currant-bush which had climbed up between the stones of the outer wall and thrust a flowering branch in through the half-opened window. In-

tended for a more special and a baser use, this room, from
which, in the daytime, I could see as far as the keep of
Roussainville-le-Pin, was for a long time my place of refuge,
doubtless because it was the only room whose door I was
allowed to lock, whenever my occupation was such as required
an inviolable solitude ; reading or dreaming, secret tears or
paroxysms of desire. Alas ! I little knew that my own lack
of will-power, my delicate health, and the consequent uncertainty as to my future weighed far more heavily on my
grandmother's mind than any little breach of the rules by her
husband, during those endless perambulations, afternoon and
evening, in which we used to see passing up and down,
obliquely raised towards the heavens, her handsome face with
its brown and wrinkled cheeks, which with age had acquired
almost the purple hue of tilled fields in autumn, covered, if
she were walking abroad, by a half-lifted veil, while upon
them either the cold or some sad reflection invariably left the
drying traces of an involuntary tear.

My sole consolation when I went upstairs for the night
was that Mamma would come in and kiss me after I was in
bed. But this good night lasted for so short a time : she went
down again so soon that the moment in which I heard her
climb the stairs, and then caught the sound of her garden
dress of blue muslin, from which hung little tassels of plaited
straw, rustling along the double-doored corridor, was for me a
moment of the keenest sorrow. So much did I love that good
night that I reached the stage of hoping that it would come
as late as possible, so as to prolong the time of respite during
which Mamma would not yet have appeared. Sometimes
when, after kissing me, she opened the door to go, I longed to
call her back, to say to her " Kiss me just once again," but
I knew that then she would at once look displeased, for the

concession which she made to my wretchedness and agitation in coming up to me with this kiss of peace always annoyed my father, who thought such ceremonies absurd, and she would have liked to try to induce me to outgrow the need, the custom of having her there at all, which was a very different thing from letting the custom grow up of my asking her for an additional kiss when she was already crossing the threshold. And to see her look displeased destroyed all the sense of tranquillity she had brought me a moment before, when she bent her loving face down over my bed, and held it out to me like a Host, for an act of Communion in which my lips might drink deeply the sense of her real presence, and with it the power to sleep. But those evenings on which Mamma stayed so short a time in my room were sweet indeed compared to those on which we had guests to dinner, and therefore she did not come at all. Our 'guests' were practically limited to M. Swann, who, apart from a few passing strangers, was almost the only person who ever came to the house at Combray, sometimes to a neighbourly dinner (but less frequently since his unfortunate marriage, as my family did not care to receive his wife) and sometimes after dinner, uninvited. On those evenings when, as we sat in front of the house beneath the big chestnut-tree and round the iron table, we heard, from the far end of the garden, not the large and noisy rattle which heralded and deafened as he approached with its ferruginous, interminable, frozen sound any member of the household who had put it out of action by coming in 'without ringing,' but the double peal—timid, oval, gilded—of the visitors' bell, everyone would at once exclaim " A visitor ! Who in the world can it be ? " but they knew quite well that it could only be M. Swann. My great-aunt, speaking in a loud voice, to set an example, in a tone

which she endeavoured to make sound natural, would tell
the others not to whisper so ; that nothing could be more
unpleasant for a stranger coming in, who would be led to
think that people were saying things about him which he was
not meant to hear ; and then my grandmother would be sent
out as a scout, always happy to find an excuse for an additional
turn in the garden, which she would utilise to remove sur-
reptitiously, as she passed, the stakes of a rose-tree or two,
so as to make the roses look a little more natural, as a mother
might run her hand through her boy's hair, after the barber
had smoothed it down, to make it stick out properly round his
head.

And there we would all stay, hanging on the words which
would fall from my grandmother's lips when she brought us
back her report of the enemy, as though there had been some
uncertainty among a vast number of possible invaders, and
then, soon after, my grandfather would say : " I can hear
Swann's voice." And, indeed, one could tell him only by
his voice, for it was difficult to make out his face with its
arched nose and green eyes, under a high forehead fringed
with fair, almost red hair, dressed in the Bressant style,
because in the garden we used as little light as possible, so as
not to attract mosquitoes : and I would slip away as though
not going for anything in particular, to tell them to bring out
the syrups ; for my grandmother made a great point, thinking
it ' nicer,' of their not being allowed to seem anything out of
the ordinary, which we kept for visitors only. Although a far
younger man, M. Swann was very much attached to my
grandfather, who had been an intimate friend, in his time, of
Swann's father, an excellent but an eccentric man in whom
the least little thing would, it seemed, often check the flow
of his spirits and divert the current of his thoughts. Several

16

times in the course of a year I would hear my grandfather tell at table the story, which never varied, of the behaviour of M. Swann the elder upon the death of his wife, by whose bed-side he had watched day and night. My grandfather, who had not seen him for a long time, hastened to join him at the Swanns' family property on the outskirts of Combray, and managed to entice him for a moment, weeping profusely, out of the death-chamber, so that he should not be present when the body was laid in its coffin. They took a turn or two in the park, where there was a little sunshine. Suddenly M. Swann seized my grandfather by the arm and cried, " Oh, my dear old friend, how fortunate we are to be walking here together on such a charming day ! Don't you see how pretty they are, all these trees—my hawthorns, and my new pond, on which you have never congratulated me ? You look as glum as a night-cap. Don't you feel this little breeze ? Ah ! whatever you may say, it's good to be alive all the same, my dear Amédée ! " And then, abruptly, the memory of his dead wife returned to him, and probably thinking it too com-plicated to inquire into how, at such a time, he could have allowed himself to be carried away by an impulse of happiness, he confined himself to a gesture which he habitually em-ployed whenever any perplexing question came into his mind : that is, he passed his hand across his forehead, dried his eyes, and wiped his glasses. And he could never be consoled for the loss of his wife, but used to say to my grandfather, during the two years for which he survived her, " It's a funny thing, now ; I very often think of my poor wife, but I cannot think of her very much at any one time." " Often, but a little at a time, like poor old Swann," became one of my grandfather's favourite phrases, which he would apply to all kinds of things. And I should have assumed that this father of Swann's had been a monster if my grandfather, whom I regarded as a better judge than myself, and whose word was my law and often led me in the long run to pardon offences which I should have been inclined to condemn, had not gone on to exclaim, " But, after all, he had a heart of gold."

For many years, albeit—and especially before his marriage —M. Swann the younger came often to see them at Combray, my great-aunt and grandparents never suspected that he had entirely ceased to live in the kind of society which his family had frequented, or that, under the sort of incognito which the name of Swann gave him among us, they were harbouring—with the complete innocence of a family of honest innkeepers who have in their midst some distinguished highwayman and never know it—one of the smartest members of the Jockey Club, a particular friend of the Comte de Paris and of the Prince of Wales, and one of the men most sought after in the aristocratic world of the Faubourg Saint-Germain.

Our utter ignorance of the brilliant part which Swann was playing in the world of fashion was, of course, due in part to his own reserve and discretion, but also to the fact that middle-class people in those days took what was almost a Hindu view of society, which they held to consist of sharply defined castes, so that everyone at his birth found himself called to that station in life which his parents already occupied, and nothing, except the chance of a brilliant career or of a ' good ' marriage, could extract you from that station or admit you to a superior caste. M. Swann, the father, had been a stockbroker ; and so ' young Swann ' found himself immured for life in a caste where one's fortune, as in a list of tax-payers, varied between such and such limits of income. We knew the people with whom his father had associated, and so we knew his own associates, the people with whom he was 'in a position to mix.' If he knew other people besides, those were youthful acquaintances on whom the old friends of the family, like my relatives, shut their eyes all the more good-naturedly that Swann himself, after he was left an orphan, still came most faithfully to see us ; but we would have been ready to wager that the people outside our acquaintance whom Swann knew were of the sort to whom he would not have dared to raise his hat, had he met them while he was walking with ourselves. Had there been such a thing as a determination to apply to Swann a social coefficient peculiar to himself, as distinct from all the other sons of other stockbrokers in his father's position, his coefficient would have been rather lower than theirs, because, leading a very simple life, and having always had a craze for 'antiques' and pictures, he now lived and piled up his collections in an old house which my grandmother longed to visit, but which stood on the Quai d'Orléans, a neighbourhood in which my great-aunt thought it most degrading to be quartered. "Are you really a connoisseur, now ? " she would say to him; " I ask for your own sake, as you are likely to have 'fakes' palmed off on you by the dealers," for she did not, in fact, endow him with any critical faculty, and had no great opinion of the intelligence of a man who, in conversation, would avoid serious topics and shewed a very dull preciseness, not only when he gave us kitchen recipes, going into the most minute details, but even when my grandmother's sisters were talking to him about art. When challenged by them to give an opinion, or to express his admiration for some picture, he would remain almost impolitely silent, and would then make amends by furnishing (if he could) some fact or other about the gallery in which the picture was hung, or the date at which it had been painted. But as a rule he would content himself with trying to amuse us by telling us the story of his latest adventure—and he would have a fresh story for us on every occasion—with some one whom we ourselves knew, such as the Combray chemist, or our cook, or our coachman. These stories certainly used to make my great-aunt laugh, but she could never tell whether that was on account of the absurd parts which Swann invariably made himself play in the adventures, or of the wit that he shewed in telling us of them. " It is easy to see that you are a regular ' character,' M. Swann ! "

As she was the only member of our family who could be described as a trifle ' common,' she would always take care to remark to strangers, when Swann was mentioned, that he could easily, if he had wished to, have lived in the Boulevard Haussmann or the Avenue de l'Opéra, and that he was the son of old M. Swann who must have left four or five million francs, but that it was a fad of his. A fad which, moreover, she thought was bound to amuse other people so much that in Paris, when M. Swann called on New Year's Day bringing her a little packet of *marrons glacés*, she never failed, if there were strangers in the room, to say to him : " Well, M. Swann, and do you still live next door to the Bonded Vaults, so as to be sure of not missing your train when you go to Lyons ? " and she would peep out of the corner of her eye, over her glasses, at the other visitors.

But if anyone had suggested to my aunt that this Swann, who, in his capacity as the son of old M. Swann, was ' fully qualified ' to be received by any of the ' upper middle class,' the most respected barristers and solicitors of Paris (though he was perhaps a trifle inclined to let this hereditary privilege go into abeyance), had another almost secret existence of a wholly different kind: that when he left our house in Paris, saying that he must go home to bed, he would no sooner have turned the corner than he would stop, retrace his steps, and be off to some drawing-room on whose like no stockbroker or associate of stockbrokers had ever set eyes——that would have seemed to my aunt as extraordinary as, to a woman of wider reading, the thought of being herself on terms of intimacy with Aristaeus, of knowing that he would, when he had finished his conversation with her, plunge deep into the realms of Thetis, into an empire veiled from mortal eyes, in which Virgil depicts him as being received with open arms ; or——to be content with an image more likely to have occurred to her, for she had seen it painted on the plates we used for biscuits at Combray——as the thought of having had to dinner Ali Baba, who, as soon as he found himself alone and unobserved, would make his way into the cave, resplendent with its unsuspected treasures.

One day when he had come to see us after dinner in Paris, and had begged pardon for being in evening clothes, Françoise, when he had gone, told us that she had got it from his coachman that he had been dining " with a princess." " A pretty sort of princess," drawled my aunt ; " I know them," and she shrugged her shoulders without raising her eyes from her knitting, serenely ironical.

Altogether, my aunt used to treat him with scant ceremony. Since she was of the opinion that he ought to feel flattered by our invitations, she thought it only right and proper that he should never come to see us in summer without a basket of peaches or raspberries from his garden, and that from each of his visits to Italy he should bring back some photographs of old masters for me.

It seemed quite natural, therefore, to send to him whenever we wanted a recipe for some special sauce or for a pineapple salad for one of our big dinner-parties, to which he himself would not be invited, not seeming of sufficient importance to be served up to new friends who might be in our house for the first time. If the conversation turned upon the Princes of the House of France, " Gentlemen you and I will never know, will we, and don't want to, do we ? " my great-aunt would say tartly to Swann, who had, perhaps, a letter from Twickenham in his pocket ; she would make him play accompaniments and turn over music on evenings when my grandmother's sister sang ; manipulating this creature, so rare and refined at other times and in other places, with the rough simplicity of a child who will play with some curio from the cabinet no more carefully than if it were a penny toy. Certainly the Swann who was a familiar figure in all the clubs of those days differed hugely from the Swann created in my great-aunt's mind when, of an evening, in our little garden at Combray, after the two shy peals had sounded from the gate, she would vitalise, by injecting into it everything she had ever heard about the Swann family, the vague and unrecognisable shape which began to appear, with my grandmother in its wake, against a background of shadows, and could at last be identified by the sound of its voice. But then, even in the most insignificant details of our daily life, none of us can be said to constitute a material whole, which is identical for everyone, and need only be turned up like a page in an account-book or the record of a will ; our social personality is created by the thoughts of other people. Even the simple act which we describe as " seeing some one we know " is, to some extent, an intellectual process. We pack the physical outline of the creature we see with all the ideas we have already formed about him, and in the complete picture of him which we compose in our minds those ideas have certainly the principal place. In the end they come to fill out so completely the curve of his cheeks, to follow so exactly the line of his nose, they blend so harmoniously in the sound of his voice that these seem to be no more than a transparent envelope, so that each time we see the face or hear the voice it is our own ideas of him which we recognise and to which we listen. And so, no doubt, from the Swann they had built up for their own purposes my family had left out, in their ignorance, a whole crowd of the details of his daily life in the world of fashion, details by means of which other people, when they met him, saw all the Graces enthroned in his face and stopping at the line of his arched nose as at a natural frontier ; but they contrived also to put into a face from which its distinction had been evicted, a face vacant and roomy as an untenanted house, to plant in the depths of its unvalued eyes a lingering sense, uncertain but not unpleasing, half-memory and half-oblivion, of idle hours spent together after our weekly dinners, round the card-table or in the garden, during our companionable country life. Our friend's bodily frame had been so well lined with this sense, and with various earlier memories of his family, that their own special Swann had become to my people a complete and living creature ; so that even now I have the feeling of leaving some one I know for another quite different person when, going back in memory, I pass from the Swann whom I knew later and more intimately to this early Swann—this early Swann in whom I can distinguish the charming mistakes of my childhood, and who, incidentally, is less like his successor than he is like the other people I knew at that time, as though one's life were a series of galleries in which all the portraits of any one period had a marked family likeness, the same (so to speak) tonality—this early Swann abounding in leisure, fragrant with the scent of the great chestnut-tree, of baskets of raspberries and of a sprig of tarragon.

And yet one day, when my grandmother had gone to ask some favour of a lady whom she had known at the Sacré Cœur (and with whom, because of our caste theory, she had not cared to keep up any degree of intimacy in spite of several common interests), the Marquise de Villeparisis, of the famous house of Bouillon, this lady had said to her :

" I think you know M. Swann very well ; he is a great friend of my nephews, the des Laumes."

My grandmother had returned from the call full of praise for the house, which overlooked some gardens, and in which Mme. de Villeparisis had advised her to rent a flat ; and also for a repairing tailor and his daughter, who kept a little shop in the courtyard, into which she had gone to ask them to put a stitch in her skirt, which she had torn on the staircase. My grandmother had found these people perfectly charming : the girl, she said, was a jewel, and the tailor a most distinguished man, the finest she had ever seen. For in her eyes distinction was a thing wholly independent of social position. She was in ecstasies over some answer the tailor had made, saying to Mamma :

" Sévigné would not have said it better ! " and, by way of contrast, of a nephew of Mme. de Villeparisis whom she had met at the house :

" My dear, he is so common ! "

Now, the effect of that remark about Swann had been, not to raise him in my great-aunt's estimation, but to lower Mme. de Villeparisis. It appeared that the deference which, on my grandmother's authority, we owed to Mme. de

Villeparisis imposed on her the reciprocal obligation to do nothing that would render her less worthy of our regard, and that she had failed in her duty in becoming aware of Swann's existence and in allowing members of her family to associate with him. " How should she know Swann ? A lady who, you always made out, was related to Marshal MacMahon ! " This view of Swann's social atmosphere which prevailed in my family seemed to be confirmed later on by his marriage with a woman of the worst class, you might almost say a ' fast ' woman, whom, to do him justice, he never attempted to introduce to us, for he continued to come to us alone though he came more and more seldom ; but from whom they thought they could establish, on the assumption that he had found her there, the circle, unknown to them, in which he ordinarily moved.

But on one occasion my grandfather read in a newspaper that M. Swann was one of the most faithful attendants at the Sunday luncheons given by the Duc de X——, whose father and uncle had been among our most prominent statesmen in the reign of Louis Philippe. Now my grandfather was curious to learn all the little details which might help him to take a mental share in the private lives of men like Molé, the Duc Pasquier, or the Duc de Broglie. He was delighted to find that Swann associated with people who had known them. My great-aunt, however, interpreted this piece of news in a sense discreditable to Swann ; for anyone who chose his associates outside the caste in which he had been born and bred, outside his 'proper station,' was condemned to utter degradation in her eyes. It seemed to her that such a one abdicated all claim to enjoy the fruits of those friendly relations with people of good position which prudent parents cultivate and store up for their children's benefit, for my great-aunt had actually ceased to 'see' the son of a lawyer we had known because he had married a 'Highness' and had thereby stepped down—in her eyes—from the respectable position of a lawyer's son to that of those adventurers, upstart footmen or stable-boys mostly, to whom we read that queens have sometimes shewn their favours. She objected, therefore, to my grandfather's plan of questioning Swann, when next he came to dine with us, about these people whose friendship with him we had discovered. On the other hand, my grandmother's two sisters, elderly spinsters who shared her nobility of character but lacked her intelligence, declared that they could not conceive what pleasure their brother-in-law could find in talking about such trifles. They were ladies of lofty ambition, who for that reason were incapable of taking the least interest in what might be called the 'pinchbeck' things of life, even when they had an historic value, or, generally speaking, in anything that was not directly associated with some object aesthetically precious. So complete was their negation of interest in anything which seemed directly or indirectly a part of our everyday life that their sense of hearing—which had gradually come to understand its own futility when the tone of the conversation, at the dinner-table, became frivolous or merely mundane, without the two old ladies' being able to guide it back to the topic dear to themselves—would leave its receptive channels unemployed, so effectively that they were actually becoming atrophied. So that if my grandfather wished to attract the attention of the two sisters, he would have to make use of some such alarm signals as mad-doctors adopt in dealing with their distracted patients ; as by beating several times on a glass with the blade of a knife, fixing them at the same time with a sharp word and a compelling glance, violent methods which the said doctors are apt to bring with them into their everyday life among the sane, either from force of professional habit or because they think the whole world a trifle mad.

Their interest grew, however, when, the day before Swann was to dine with us, and when he had made them a special present of a case of Asti, my great-aunt, who had in her hand a copy of the *Figaro* in which to the name of a picture then on view in a Corot exhibition were added the words, " from the collection of M. Charles Swann," asked : " Did you see that Swann is ' mentioned ' in the *Figaro* ? "

" But I have always told you," said my grandmother, " that he had plenty of taste."

" You would, of course," retorted my great-aunt, " say anything just to seem different from *us*." For, knowing that my grandmother never agreed with her, and not being quite confident that it was her own opinion which the rest of us invariably endorsed, she wished to extort from us a wholesale condemnation of my grandmother's views, against which she hoped to force us into solidarity with her own.

But we sat silent. My grandmother's sisters having expressed a desire to mention to Swann this reference to him in the *Figaro*, my great-aunt dissuaded them. Whenever she saw in others an advantage, however trivial, which she herself lacked, she would persuade herself that it was no advantage at all, but a drawback, and would pity so as not to have to envy them.

" I don't think that would please him at all ; I know very well, I should hate to see my name printed like that, as large as life, in the paper, and I shouldn't feel at all flattered if any-one spoke to me about it."

She did not, however, put any very great pressure upon my grandmother's sisters, for they, in their horror of vulgarity, had brought to such a fine art the concealment of a personal allusion in a wealth of ingenious circumlocution, that it would often pass unnoticed even by the person to whom it was addressed. As for my mother, her only thought was of managing to induce my father to consent to speak to Swann, not of his wife, but of his daughter, whom he worshipped, and for whose sake it was understood that he had ultimately made his unfortunate marriage.

" You need only say a word ; just ask him how she is. It must be so very hard for him."

My father, however, was annoyed : " No, no ; you have the most absurd ideas. It would be utterly ridiculous."

But the only one of us in whom the prospect of Swann's arrival gave rise to an unhappy foreboding was myself. And that was because on the evenings when there were visitors, or just M. Swann in the house, Mamma did not come up to my room. I did not, at that time, have dinner with the family : I came out to the garden after dinner, and at nine I said good night and went to bed. But on these evenings I used to dine earlier than the others, and to come in afterwards and sit at table until eight o'clock, when it was understood that I must go upstairs ; that frail and precious kiss which Mamma used always to leave upon my lips when I was in bed and just going to sleep I had to take with me from the dining-room to my own, and to keep inviolate all the time that it took me to undress, without letting its sweet charm be broken, without letting its volatile essence diffuse itself and evaporate ; and just on those very evenings when I must needs take most pains to receive it with due formality, I had to snatch it, to seize it instantly and in public, without even having the time or being properly free to apply to what I was doing the punctiliousness which madmen use who compel themselves to exclude all other thoughts from their minds while they are shutting a door, so that when the sickness of uncertainty sweeps over them again they can triumphantly face and overcome it with the recollection of the precise moment in which the door was shut.

We were all in the garden when the double peal of the gate-bell sounded shyly. Everyone knew that it must be Swann, and yet they looked at one another inquiringly and sent my grandmother scouting.

"See that you thank him intelligibly for the wine," my grandfather warned his two sisters-in-law ; "you know how good it is, and it is a huge case."

"Now, don't start whispering !" said my great-aunt. "How would you like to come into a house and find everyone muttering to themselves ? "

"Ah ! There's M. Swann," cried my father. "Let's ask him if he thinks it will be fine to-morrow."

My mother fancied that a word from her would wipe out all the unpleasantness which my family had contrived to make Swann feel since his marriage. She found an opportunity to draw him aside for a moment. But I followed her : I could not bring myself to let her go out of reach of me while I felt that in a few minutes I should have to leave her in the dining-room and go up to my bed without the consoling thought, as on ordinary evenings, that she would come up, later, to kiss me.

"Now, M. Swann," she said, "do tell me about your daughter ; I am sure she shews a taste already for nice things, like her papa."

"Come along and sit down here with us all on the verandah," said my grandfather, coming up to him. My mother had to abandon the quest, but managed to extract

29

from the restriction itself a further refinement of thought, as great poets do when the tyranny of rhyme forces them into the discovery of their finest lines.

" We can talk about her again when we are by ourselves," she said, or rather whispered to Swann. " It is only a mother who can understand. I am sure that hers would agree with me."

And so we all sat down round the iron table. I should have liked not to think of the hours of anguish which I should have to spend, that evening, alone in my room, without the possibility of going to sleep : I tried to convince myself that they were of no importance, really, since I should have forgotten them next morning, and to fix my mind on thoughts of the future which would carry me, as on a bridge, across the terrifying abyss that yawned at my feet. But my mind, strained by this foreboding, distended like the look which I shot at my mother, would not allow any other impression to enter. Thoughts did, indeed, enter it, but only on the condition that they left behind them every element of beauty, or even of quaintness, by which I might have been distracted or beguiled. As a surgical patient, by means of a local anaesthetic, can look on with a clear consciousness while an operation is being performed upon him and yet feel nothing, I could repeat to myself some favourite lines, or watch my grandfather attempting to talk to Swann about the Duc d'Audriffet-Pasquier, without being able to kindle any emotion from one or amusement from the other. Hardly had my grandfather begun to question Swann about that orator when one of my grandmother's sisters, in whose ears the question echoed like a solemn but untimely silence which her natural politeness bade her interrupt, addressed the other with :

" Just fancy, Flora, I met a young Swedish governess to-day who told me some most interesting things about the co-operative movement in Scandinavia. We really must have her to dine here one evening."

" To be sure ! " said her sister Flora, " but I haven't wasted my time either. I met such a clever old gentleman at M. Vinteuil's who knows Maubant quite well, and Maubant has told him every little thing about how he gets up his parts. It is the most interesting thing I ever heard. He is a neighbour of M. Vinteuil's, and I never knew ; and he is so nice besides."

" M. Vinteuil is not the only one who has nice neighbours," cried my aunt Céline in a voice which seemed loud because she was so timid, and seemed forced because she had been planning the little speech for so long ; darting, as she spoke, what she called a ' significant glance ' at Swann. And my aunt Flora, who realised that this veiled utterance was Céline's way of thanking Swann intelligibly for the Asti, looked at him with a blend of congratulation and irony, either just because she wished to underline her sister's little epigram, or because she envied Swann his having inspired it, or merely because she imagined that he was embarrassed, and could not help having a little fun at his expense.

" I think it would be worth while," Flora went on, " to have this old gentleman to dinner. When you get him upon Maubant or Mme. Materna he will talk for hours on end."

" That must be delightful," sighed my grandfather, in whose mind nature had unfortunately forgotten to include any capacity whatsoever for becoming passionately interested in the co-operative movement among the ladies of Sweden or in the methods employed by Maubant to get up his parts, just as it had forgotten to endow my grandmother's two sisters with a grain of that precious salt which one has oneself

to 'add to taste' in order to extract any savour from a
narrative of the private life of Molé or of the Comte de Paris.

" I say ! " exclaimed Swann to my grandfather, " what I
was going to tell you has more to do than you might think
with what you were asking me just now, for in some respects
there has been very little change. I came across a passage in
Saint-Simon this morning which would have amused you.
It is in the volume which covers his mission to Spain ; not
one of the best, little more in fact than a journal, but at least
it is a journal wonderfully well written, which fairly distin-
guishes it from the devastating journalism that we feel bound
to read in these days, morning, noon and night."

" I do not agree with you : there are some days when I
find reading the papers very pleasant indeed ! " my aunt
Flora broke in, to show Swann that she had read the note
about his Corot in the *Figaro*.

" Yes," aunt Céline went one better. " When they write
about things or people in whom we are interested."

" I don't deny it," answered Swann in some bewilderment.
" The fault I find with our journalism is that it forces us to
take an interest in some fresh triviality or other every day,
whereas only three or four books in a lifetime give us anything that is of real importance. Suppose that, every morning,
when we tore the wrapper off our paper with fevered hands,
a transmutation were to take place, and we were to find inside
it—oh ! I don't know ; shall we say Pascal's *Pensées* ? "
He articulated the title with an ironic emphasis so as not to
appear pedantic. " And then, in the gilt and tooled volumes
which we open once in ten years," he went on, shewing that
contempt for the things of this world which some men of the
world like to affect, " we should read that the Queen of the
Hellenes had arrived at Cannes, or that the Princesse de Léon

had given a fancy dress ball. In that way we should arrive at the right proportion between 'information' and 'publicity.'" But at once regretting that he had allowed himself to speak, even in jest, of serious matters, he added ironically : "We are having a most entertaining conversation ; I cannot think why we climb to these lofty summits," and then, turning to my grandfather : "Well, Saint-Simon tells how Maulevrier had had the audacity to offer his hand to his sons. You remember how he says of Maulevrier, 'Never did I find in that coarse bottle anything but ill-humour, boorishness, and folly.'"

"Coarse or not, I know bottles in which there is something very different!" said Flora briskly, feeling bound to thank Swann as well as her sister, since the present of Asti had been addressed to them both. Céline began to laugh.

Swann was puzzled, but went on : "'I cannot say whether it was his ignorance or a trap,' writes Saint-Simon ; 'he wished to give his hand to my children. I noticed it in time to prevent him.'"

My grandfather was already in ecstasies over "ignorance or a trap," but Miss Céline—the name of Saint-Simon, a 'man of letters,' having arrested the complete paralysis of her sense of hearing—had grown angry.

"What ! You admire that, do you ? Well, it is clever enough ! But what is the point of it ? Does he mean that one man isn't as good as another ? What difference can it make whether he is a duke or a groom so long as he is intelligent and good ? He had a fine way of bringing up his children, your Saint-Simon, if he didn't teach them to shake hands with all honest men. Really and truly, it's abominable. And you dare to quote it ! "

And my grandfather, utterly depressed, realising how

futile it would be for him, against this opposition, to attempt
to get Swann to tell him the stories which would have amused
him, murmured to my mother : " Just tell me again that line
of yours which always comforts me so much on these occasions. Oh, yes :

What virtues, Lord, Thou makest us abhor!

Good, that is, very good."

I never took my eyes off my mother. I knew that when
they were at table I should not be permitted to stay there for
the whole of dinner-time, and that Mamma, for fear of
annoying my father, would not allow me to give her in public
the series of kisses that she would have had in my room.
And so I promised myself that in the dining-room, as they
began to eat and drink and as I felt the hour approach, I
would put beforehand into this kiss, which was bound to be
so brief and stealthy in execution, everything that my own
efforts could put into it : would look out very carefully first
the exact spot on her cheek where I would imprint it, and
would so prepare my thoughts that I might be able, thanks to
these mental preliminaries, to consecrate the whole of the
minute Mamma would allow me to the sensation of her
cheek against my lips, as a painter who can have his subject
for short sittings only prepares his palette, and from what he
remembers and from rough notes does in advance everything
which he possibly can do in the sitter's absence. But to-night,
before the dinner-bell had sounded, my grandfather said with
unconscious cruelty : " The little man looks tired ; he'ld
better go up to bed. Besides, we are dining late to-night."

And my father, who was less scrupulous than my grandmother or mother in observing the letter of a treaty, went on :
" Yes ; run along ; to bed with you."

I would have kissed Mamma then and there, but at that moment the dinner-bell rang.

"No, no, leave your mother alone. You've said good night quite enough. These exhibitions are absurd. Go on upstairs."

And so I must set forth without viaticum ; must climb each step of the staircase 'against my heart,' as the saying is, climbing in opposition to my heart's desire, which was to return to my mother, since she had not, by her kiss, given my heart leave to accompany me forth. That hateful staircase, up which I always passed with such dismay, gave out a smell of varnish which had to some extent absorbed, made definite and fixed the special quality of sorrow that I felt each evening, and made it perhaps even more cruel to my sensibility because, when it assumed this olfactory guise, my intellect was powerless to resist it. When we have gone to sleep with a maddening toothache and are conscious of it only as a little girl whom we attempt, time after time, to pull out of the water, or as a line of Molière which we repeat incessantly to ourselves, it is a great relief to wake up, so that our intelligence can disentangle the idea of toothache from any artificial semblance of heroism or rhythmic cadence. It was the precise converse of this relief which I felt when my anguish at having to go up to my room invaded my consciousness in a manner infinitely more rapid, instantaneous almost, a manner at once insidious and brutal as I breathed in—a far more poisonous thing than any moral penetration—the peculiar smell of the varnish upon that staircase.

Once in my room I had to stop every loophole, to close the shutters, to dig my own grave as I turned down the bedclothes, to wrap myself in the shroud of my nightshirt. But before burying myself in the iron bed which had been

placed there because, on summer nights, I was too hot
among the rep curtains of the four-poster, I was stirred to re-
volt, and attempted the desperate stratagem of a condemned
prisoner. I wrote to my mother begging her to come upstairs for an important reason which I could not put in
writing. My fear was that Françoise, my aunt's cook
who used to be put in charge of me when I was at Combray,
might refuse to take my note. I had a suspicion that, in her
eyes, to carry a message to my mother when there was a
stranger in the room would appear flatly inconceivable, just
as it would be for the door-keeper of a theatre to hand a letter
to an actor upon the stage. For things which might or might
not be done she possessed a code at once imperious, abundant,
subtle, and uncompromising on points themselves imperceptible or irrelevant, which gave it a resemblance to those
ancient laws which combine such cruel ordinances as the
massacre of infants at the breast with prohibitions, of exaggerated refinement, against " seething the kid in his
mother's milk," or " eating of the sinew which is upon the
hollow of the thigh." This code, if one could judge it by the
sudden obstinacy which she would put into her refusal to carry
out certain of our instructions, seemed to have foreseen such
social complications and refinements of fashion as nothing in
Françoise's surroundings or in her career as a servant in a
village household could have put into her head ; and we were
obliged to assume that there was latent in her some past
existence in the ancient history of France, noble and little
understood, just as there is in those manufacturing towns
where old mansions still testify to their former courtly days,
and chemical workers toil among delicately sculptured scenes
of the Miracle of Theophilus or the Quatre Fils Aymon.

In this particular instance, the article of her code which

made it highly improbable that—barring an outbreak of fire
—Françoise would go down and disturb Mamma when
M. Swann was there for so unimportant a person as myself
was one embodying the respect she shewed not only for
the family (as for the dead, for the clergy, or for royalty),
but also for the stranger within our gates ; a respect which I
should perhaps have found touching in a book, but which
never failed to irritate me on her lips, because of the solemn
and gentle tones in which she would utter it, and which
irritated me more than usual this evening when the sacred
character in which she invested the dinner-party might have
the effect of making her decline to disturb its ceremonial.
But to give myself one chance of success I lied without
hesitation, telling her that it was not in the least myself who
had wanted to write to Mamma, but Mamma who, on saying
good night to me, had begged me not to forget to send her an
answer about something she had asked me to find, and that
she would certainly be very angry if this note were not taken
to her. I think that Françoise disbelieved me, for, like those
primitive men whose senses were so much keener than our
own, she could immediately detect, by signs imperceptible
by the rest of us, the truth or falsehood of anything that we
might wish to conceal from her. She studied the envelope for
five minutes as though an examination of the paper itself and
the look of my handwriting could enlighten her as to the
nature of the contents, or tell her to which article of her code
she ought to refer the matter. Then she went out with an air
of resignation which seemed to imply : "What a dreadful
thing for parents to have a child like this !"

A moment later she returned to say that they were still at
the ice stage and that it was impossible for the butler to deliver
the note at once, in front of everybody ; but that when the

finger-bowls were put round he would find a way of slipping it into Mamma's hand. At once my anxiety subsided ; it was now no longer (as it had been a moment ago) until to-morrow that I had lost my mother, for my little line was going—to annoy her, no doubt, and doubly so because this contrivance would make me ridiculous in Swann's eyes—but was going all the same to admit me, invisibly and by stealth, into the same room as herself, was going to whisper from me into her ear ; for that forbidden and unfriendly dining-room, where but a moment ago the ice itself—with burned nuts in it— and the finger-bowls seemed to me to be concealing pleasures that were mischievous and of a mortal sadness because Mamma was tasting of them and I was far away, had opened its doors to me and, like a ripe fruit which bursts through its skin, was going to pour out into my intoxicated heart the gushing sweetness of Mamma's attention while she was read-ing what I had written. Now I was no longer separated from her ; the barriers were down ; an exquisite thread was binding us. Besides, that was not all, for surely Mamma would come.

As for the agony through which I had just passed, I imagined that Swann would have laughed heartily at it if he had read my letter and had guessed its purpose ; whereas, on the contrary, as I was to learn in due course, a similar anguish had been the bane of his life for many years, and no one perhaps could have understood my feelings at that moment so well as himself ; to him, that anguish which lies in knowing that the creature one adores is in some place of enjoyment where oneself is not and cannot follow—to him that anguish came through Love, to which it is in a sense predestined, by which it must be equipped and adapted ; but when, as had befallen me, such an anguish possesses one's soul before Love has yet entered into one's life, then it must drift, awaiting Love's coming, vague and free, without precise attachment, at the disposal of one sentiment to-day, of another to-morrow, of filial piety or affection for a comrade. And the joy with which I first bound myself apprentice, when Françoise returned to tell me that my letter would be delivered, Swann, too, had known well that false joy which a friend can give us, or some relative of the woman we love, when on his arrival at the house or theatre where she is to be found, for some ball or party or ' first-night ' at which he is to meet her, he sees us wandering outside, desperately awaiting some opportunity of communicating with her. He recognises us, greets us familiarly, and asks what we are doing there. And when we invent a story of having some urgent message to give to his relative or friend, he assures us that nothing could be more simple, takes us in at the door, and promises to send her down to us in five minutes. How much we love him—as at that moment I loved Françoise—the good-natured intermediary who by a single word has made supportable, human, almost propitious the inconceivable, infernal scene of gaiety in the thick of which we had been imagining swarms of enemies, perverse and seductive, beguiling away from us, even making laugh at us, the woman whom we love. If we are to judge of them by him, this relative who has accosted us and who is himself an initiate in those cruel mysteries, then the other guests cannot be so very demoniacal. Those inaccessible and torturing hours into which she had gone to taste of unknown pleasures—behold, a breach in the wall, and we are through it. Behold, one of the moments whose series will go to make up their sum, a moment as genuine as the rest, if not actually more important to ourself because our mistress is more intensely a part of it ;

we picture it to ourselves, we possess it, we intervene upon it, almost we have created it : namely, the moment in which he goes to tell her that we are waiting there below. And very probably the other moments of the party will not be essentially different, will contain nothing else so exquisite or so well able to make us suffer, since this kind friend has assured us that " Of course, she will be delighted to come down ! It will be far more amusing for her to talk to you than to be bored up there." Alas ! Swann had learned by experience that the good intentions of a third party are powerless to control a woman who is annoyed to find herself pursued even into a ball-room by a man whom she does not love. Too often, the kind friend comes down again alone.

My mother did not appear, but with no attempt to safeguard my self-respect (which depended upon her keeping up the fiction that she had asked me to let her know the result of my search for something or other) made Françoise tell me, in so many words : " There is no answer "—words I have so often, since then, heard the hall-porters in ' mansions ' and the flunkeys in gambling-clubs and the like, repeat to some poor girl, who replies in bewilderment : " What ! he's said nothing ? It's not possible. You did give him my letter, didn't you ? Very well, I shall wait a little longer." And just as she invariably protests that she does not need the extra gas which the porter offers to light for her, and sits on there, hearing nothing further, except an occasional remark on the weather which the porter exchanges with a messenger whom he will send off suddenly, when he notices the time, to put some customer's wine on the ice ; so, having declined Françoise's offer to make me some tea or to stay beside me, I let her go off again to the servants' hall, and lay down and shut my eyes, and tried not to hear the voices of my family who were drinking their coffee in the garden.

But after a few seconds I realised that, by writing that line to Mamma, by approaching—at the risk of making her angry —so near to her that I felt I could reach out and grasp the moment in which I should see her again, I had cut myself off from the possibility of going to sleep until I actually had seen her, and my heart began to beat more and more painfully as I increased my agitation by ordering myself to keep calm and to acquiesce in my ill-fortune. Then, suddenly, my anxiety subsided, a feeling of intense happiness coursed through me, as when a strong medicine begins to take effect and one's pain vanishes : I had formed a resolution to abandon all attempts to go to sleep without seeing Mamma, and had decided to kiss her at all costs, even with the certainty of being in disgrace with her for long afterwards, when she herself came up to bed. The tranquillity which followed my anguish made me extremely alert, no less than my sense of expectation, my thirst for and my fear of danger.

Noiselessly I opened the window and sat down on the foot of my bed ; hardly daring to move in case they should hear me from below. Things outside seemed also fixed in mute expectation, so as not to disturb the moonlight which, duplicating each of them and throwing it back by the extension, forwards, of a shadow denser and more concrete than its substance, had made the whole landscape seem at once thinner and longer, like a map which, after being folded up, is spread out upon the ground. What had to move—a leaf of the chestnut-tree, for instance—moved. But its minute shuddering, complete, finished to the least detail and with the utmost delicacy of gesture, made no discord with the rest of the scene, and yet was not merged in it, remaining clearly

41

outlined. Exposed upon this surface of silence, which absorbed nothing from them, the most distant sounds, those
which must have come from gardens at the far end of the
town, could be distinguished with such exact 'finish' that
the impression they gave of coming from a distance seemed
due only to their 'pianissimo' execution, like those movements on muted strings so well performed by the orchestra of
the Conservatoire that, although one does not lose a single
note, one thinks all the same that they are being played somewhere outside, a long way from the concert hall, so that all the
old subscribers, and my grandmother's sisters too, when
Swann had given them his seats, used to strain their ears as
if they had caught the distant approach of an army on the
march, which had not yet rounded the corner of the Rue de
Trévise.

I was well aware that I had placed myself in a position
than which none could be counted upon to involve me in
graver consequences at my parents' hands ; consequences far
graver, indeed, than a stranger would have imagined, and
such as (he would have thought) could follow only some
really shameful fault. But in the system of education which
they had given me faults were not classified in the same order
as in that of other children, and I had been taught to place
at the head of the list (doubtless because there was no other
class of faults from which I needed to be more carefully protected) those in which I can now distinguish the common
feature that one succumbs to them by yielding to a nervous
impulse. But such words as these last had never been uttered
in my hearing ; no one had yet accounted for my temptations
in a way which might have led me to believe that there was
some excuse for my giving in to them, or that I was actually
incapable of holding out against them. Yet I could easily

recognise this class of transgressions by the anguish of mind which preceded, as well as by the rigour of the punishment which followed them ; and I knew that what I had just done was in the same category as certain other sins for which I had been severely chastised, though infinitely more serious than they. When I went out to meet my mother as she herself came up to bed, and when she saw that I had remained up so as to say good night to her again in the passage, I should not be allowed to stay in the house a day longer, I should be packed off to school next morning ; so much was certain. Very good : had I been obliged, the next moment, to hurl myself out of the window, I should still have preferred such a fate. For what I wanted now was Mamma, and to say good night to her. I had gone too far along the road which led to the realisation of this desire to be able to retrace my steps.

I could hear my parents' footsteps as they went with Swann ; and, when the rattle of the gate assured me that he had really gone, I crept to the window. Mamma was asking my father if he had thought the lobster good, and whether M. Swann had had some more of the coffee-and-pistachio ice. "I thought it rather so-so," she was saying ; "next time we shall have to try another flavour."

"I can't tell you," said my great-aunt, "what a change I find in Swann. He is quite antiquated ! " She had grown so accustomed to seeing Swann always in the same stage of adolescence that it was a shock to her to find him suddenly less young than the age she still attributed to him. And the others too were beginning to remark in Swann that abnormal, excessive, scandalous senescence, meet only in a celibate, in one of that class for whom it seems that the great day which knows no morrow must be longer than for other men, since for such a one it is void of promise, and from its dawn the

43

moments steadily accumulate without any subsequent partition among his offspring.

" I fancy he has a lot of trouble with that wretched wife of his, who 'lives' with a certain Monsieur de Charlus, as all Combray knows. It's the talk of the town."

My mother observed that, in spite of this, he had looked much less unhappy of late. " And he doesn't nearly so often do that trick of his, so like his father, of wiping his eyes and passing his hand across his forehead. I think myself that in his heart of hearts he doesn't love his wife any more."

" Why, of course he doesn't," answered my grandfather. " He wrote me a letter about it, ages ago, to which I took care to pay no attention, but it left no doubt as to his feelings, let alone his love for his wife. Hullo ! you two ; you never thanked him for the Asti ! " he went on, turning to his sisters-in-law.

" What ! we never thanked him ? I think, between you and me, that I put it to him quite neatly," replied my aunt Flora.

" Yes, you managed it very well ; I admired you for it," said my aunt Céline.

" But you did it very prettily, too."

" Yes ; I liked my expression about ' nice neighbours.' "

" What ! Do you call that thanking him ? " shouted my grandfather. " I heard that all right, but devil take me if I guessed it was meant for Swann. You may be quite sure he never noticed it."

" Come, come ; Swann is not a fool. I am positive he appreciated the compliment. You didn't expect me to tell him the number of bottles, or to guess what he paid for them."

My father and mother were left alone and sat down for a moment ; then my father said : " Well, shall we go up to bed ? "

" As you wish, dear, though I don't feel in the least like sleeping. I don't know why ; it can't be the coffee-ice——it wasn't strong enough to keep me awake like this. But I see a light in the servants' hall : poor Françoise has been sitting up for me, so I will get her to unhook me while you go and undress."

My mother opened the latticed door which led from the hall to the staircase. Presently I heard her coming upstairs to close her window. I went quietly into the passage ; my heart was beating so violently that I could hardly move, but at least it was throbbing no longer with anxiety, but with terror and with joy. I saw in the well of the stair a light coming up-wards, from Mamma's candle. Then I saw Mamma herself : I threw myself upon her. For an instant she looked at me in astonishment, not realising what could have happened. Then her face assumed an expression of anger. She said not a single word to me ; and, for that matter, I used to go for days on end without being spoken to, for far less offences than this. A single word from Mamma would have been an admission that further intercourse with me was within the bounds of possibility, and that might perhaps have appeared to me more terrible still, as indicating that, with such a punishment as was in store for me, mere silence, and even anger, were relatively puerile.

A word from her then would have implied the false calm in which one converses with a servant to whom one has just decided to give notice ; the kiss one bestows on a son who is being packed off to enlist, which would have been denied him if it had merely been a matter of being angry with him for a few days. But she heard my father coming from the dressing-room, where he had gone to take off his clothes, and, to avoid the 'scene' which he would make if

he saw me, she said, in a voice half-stifled by her anger :
" Run away at once. Don't let your father see you standing
there like a crazy jane ! "

But I begged her again to " Come and say good night to
me ! " terrified as I saw the light from my father's candle
already creeping up the wall, but also making use of his approach as a means of blackmail, in the hope that my mother,
not wishing him to find me there, as find me he must if
she continued to hold out, would give in to me, and say :
" Go back to your room. I will come."

Too late : my father was upon us. Instinctively I murmured, though no one heard me, " I am done for ! "

I was not, however. My father used constantly to refuse
to let me do things which were quite clearly allowed by the
more liberal charters granted me by my mother and grandmother, because he paid no heed to ' Principles,' and because
in his sight there were no such things as ' Rights of Man.'
For some quite irrelevant reason, or for no reason at all, he
would at the last moment prevent me from taking some
particular walk, one so regular and so consecrated to my use
that to deprive me of it was a clear breach of faith ; or again,
as he had done this evening, long before the appointed hour
he would snap out : " Run along up to bed now ; no ex-
cuses ! " But then again, simply because he was devoid of
principles (in my grandmother's sense), so he could not,
properly speaking, be called inexorable. He looked at me for
a moment with an air of annoyance and surprise, and then
when Mamma had told him, not without some embarrass-
ment, what had happened, said to her : " Go along with him,
then ; you said just now that you didn't feel like sleep, so
stay in his room for a little. I don't need anything."

" But, dear," my mother answered timidly, " whether or

not I feel like sleep is not the point ; we must not make the child accustomed . . ."

" There's no question of making him accustomed," said my father, with a shrug of the shoulders ; " you can see quite well that the child is unhappy. After all, we aren't gaolers. You'll end by making him ill, and a lot of good that will do. There are two beds in his room ; tell Françoise to make up the big one for you, and stay beside him for the rest of the night. I'm off to bed, anyhow ; I'm not nervous like you. Good night."

It was impossible for me to thank my father ; what he called my sentimentality would have exasperated him. I stood there, not daring to move ; he was still confronting us, an immense figure in his white nightshirt, crowned with the pink and violet scarf of Indian cashmere in which, since he had begun to suffer from neuralgia, he used to tie up his head, standing like Abraham in the engraving after Benozzo Gozzoli which M. Swann had given me, telling Sarah that she must tear herself away from Isaac. Many years have passed since that night. The wall of the staircase, up which I had watched the light of his candle gradually climb, was long ago demolished. And in myself, too, many things have perished which, I imagined, would last for ever, and new structures have arisen, giving birth to new sorrows and new joys which in those days I could not have foreseen, just as now the old are difficult of comprehension. It is a long time, too, since my father has been able to tell Mamma to " Go with the child." Never again will such hours be possible for me. But of late I have been increasingly able to catch, if I listen attentively, the sound of the sobs which I had the strength to control in my father's presence, and which broke out only when I found myself alone with Mamma. Actually, their echo has never ceased : it is only because life is now growing more and more quiet round about me that I hear them afresh, like those convent bells which are so effectively drowned during the day by the noises of the streets that one would suppose them to have been stopped for ever, until they sound out again through the silent evening air.

Mamma spent that night in my room : when I had just committed a sin so deadly that I was waiting to be banished from the household, my parents gave me a far greater concession than I should ever have won as the reward of a good action. Even at the moment when it manifested itself in this crowning mercy, my father's conduct towards me was still somewhat arbitrary, and regardless of my deserts, as was characteristic of him and due to the fact that his actions were generally dictated by chance expediencies rather than based on any formal plan. And perhaps even what I called his strictness, when he sent me off to bed, deserved that title less, really, than my mother's or grandmother's attitude, for his nature, which in some respects differed more than theirs from my own, had probably prevented him from guessing, until then, how wretched I was every evening, a thing which my mother and grandmother knew well ; but they loved me enough to be unwilling to spare me that suffering, which they hoped to teach me to overcome, so as to reduce my nervous sensibility and to strengthen my will. As for my father, whose affection for me was of another kind, I doubt if he would have shewn so much courage, for as soon as he had grasped the fact that I was unhappy he had said to my mother : " Go and comfort him."

Mamma stayed all night in my room, and it seemed that she did not wish to mar by recrimination those hours, so different from anything that I had had a right to expect;

for when Françoise (who guessed that something extraordinary must have happened when she saw Mamma sitting
by my side, holding my hand and letting me cry unchecked)
said to her : "But, Madame, what is little Master crying for?"
she replied : "Why, Françoise, he doesn't know himself :
it is his nerves. Make up the big bed for me quickly and then
go off to your own." And thus for the first time my un-
happiness was regarded no longer as a fault for which I must
be punished, but as an involuntary evil which had been
officially recognised, a nervous condition for which I was in
no way responsible : I had the consolation that I need no
longer mingle apprehensive scruples with the bitterness of my
tears ; I could weep henceforward without sin. I felt no
small degree of pride, either, in Françoise's presence at this
return to humane conditions which, not an hour after Mamma had refused to come up to my room and had sent the
snubbing message that I was to go to sleep, raised me to the
dignity of a grown-up person, brought me of a sudden to a
sort of puberty of sorrow, to emancipation from tears. I
ought then to have been happy ; I was not. It struck me
that my mother had just made a first concession which must
have been painful to her, that it was a first step down from
the ideal she had formed for me, and that for the first time
she, with all her courage, had to confess herself beaten.
It struck me that if I had just scored a victory it was over her ;
that I had succeeded, as sickness or sorrow or age might have
succeeded, in relaxing her will, in altering her judgment ;
that this evening opened a new era, must remain a black date
in the calendar. And if I had dared now, I should have said to
Mamma : "No, I don't want you ; you mustn't sleep here."
But I was conscious of the practical wisdom, of what would
be called nowadays the realism with which she tempered the

I   49   C ardent idealism of my grandmother's nature, and I knew that now the mischief was done she would prefer to let me enjoy the soothing pleasure of her company, and not to disturb my father again. Certainly my mother's beautiful features seemed to shine again with youth that evening, as she sat gently holding my hands and trying to check my tears ; but, just for that reason, it seemed to me that this should not have happened ; her anger would have been less difficult to endure than this new kindness which my childhood had not known ; I felt that I had with an impious and secret finger traced a first wrinkle upon her soul and made the first white hair shew upon her head. This thought redoubled my sobs, and then I saw that Mamma, who had never allowed herself to go to any length of tenderness with me, was suddenly overcome by my tears and had to struggle to keep back her own. Then, as she saw that I had noticed this, she said to me, with a smile : " Why, my little buttercup, my little canary-boy he's going to make Mamma as silly as himself if this goes on. Look, since you can't sleep, and Mamma can't either, we mustn't go on in this stupid way ; we must do something ; I'll get one of your books." But I had none there. " Would you like me to get out the books now that your grandmother is going to give you for your birthday ? Just think it over first, and don't be disappointed if there is nothing new for you then."

I was only too delighted, and Mamma went to find a parcel of books in which I could not distinguish, through the paper in which it was wrapped, any more than its squareness and size, but which, even at this first glimpse, brief and obscure as it was, bade fair to eclipse already the paintbox of last New Year's Day and the silkworms of the year before. It contained *La Mare au Diable*, *François le Champi*, *La Petite Fadette*, and *Les Maîtres Sonneurs*. My grandmother, as I learned afterwards, had at first chosen Musset's poems, a volume of Rousseau, and *Indiana* ; for while she considered light reading as unwholesome as sweets and cakes, she did not reflect that the strong breath of genius must have upon the very soul of a child an influence at once more dangerous and less quickening than those of fresh air and country breezes upon his body. But when my father had seemed almost to regard her as insane on learning the names of the books she proposed to give me, she had journeyed back by herself to Jouy-le-Vicomte to the bookseller's, so that there should be no fear of my not having my present in time (it was a burning hot day, and she had come home so unwell that the doctor had warned my mother not to allow her again to tire herself in that way), and had there fallen back upon the four pastoral novels of George Sand.

" My dear," she had said to Mamma, " I could not allow myself to give the child anything that was not well written."

The truth was that she could never make up her mind to purchase anything from which no intellectual profit was to be derived, and, above all, that profit which good things bestowed on us by teaching us to seek our pleasures elsewhere than in the barren satisfaction of worldly wealth. Even when she had to make some one a present of the kind called ' useful,' when she had to give an armchair or some table-silver or a walking-stick, she would choose ' antiques,' as though their long desuetude had effaced from them any semblance of utility and fitted them rather to instruct us in the lives of the men of other days than to serve the common requirements of our own. She would have liked me to have in my room photographs of ancient buildings or of beautiful places. But at the moment of buying them, and for all that the subject of the picture had an aesthetic value of its own, she would find that vulgarity and utility had too prominent a part in them, through the mechanical nature of their reproduction by photography. She attempted by a subterfuge, if not to eliminate altogether their commercial banality, at least to minimise it, to substitute for the bulk of it what was art still, to introduce, as it might be, several 'thicknesses' of art; instead of photographs of Chartres Cathedral, of the Fountains of Saint-Cloud, or of Vesuvius she would inquire of Swann whether some great painter had not made pictures of them, and preferred to give me photographs of 'Chartres Cathedral' after Corot, of the 'Fountains of Saint-Cloud' after Hubert Robert, and of 'Vesuvius' after Turner, which were a stage higher in the scale of art. But although the photographer had been prevented from reproducing directly the masterpieces or the beauties of nature, and had there been replaced by a great artist, he resumed his odious position when it came to reproducing the artist's interpretation. Accordingly, having to reckon again with vulgarity, my grandmother would endeavour to postpone the moment of contact still further. She would ask Swann if the picture had not been engraved, preferring, when possible, old engravings with some interest of association apart from themselves, such, for example, as shew us a masterpiece in a state in which we can no longer see it to-day, as Morghen's print of the 'Cenacolo' of Leonardo before it was spoiled by restoration. It must be admitted that the results of this method of interpreting the art of making presents were not always happy. The idea which I formed of Venice, from a drawing by Titian which is supposed to have the lagoon in the background, was certainly far less accurate than what I have since derived from ordinary photographs. We could no longer keep count in the family (when my great-aunt tried to frame an indictment of my grandmother) of all the armchairs she had presented to married couples, young and old, which on a first attempt to sit down upon them had at once collapsed beneath the weight of their recipient. But my grandmother would have thought it sordid to concern herself too closely with the solidity of any piece of furniture in which could still be discerned a flourish, a smile, a brave conceit of the past. And even what in such pieces supplied a material need, since it did so in a manner to which we are no longer accustomed, was as charming to her as one of those old forms of speech in which we can still see traces of a metaphor whose fine point has been worn away by the rough usage of our modern tongue. In precisely the same way the pastoral novels of George Sand, which she was giving me for my birthday, were regular lumber-rooms of antique furniture, full of expressions that have fallen out of use and returned as imagery, such as one finds now only in country dialects. And my grandmother had bought them in preference to other books, just as she would have preferred to take a house that had a gothic dovecot, or some other such piece of antiquity as would have a pleasant effect on the mind, filling it with a nostalgic longing for impossible journeys through the realms of time.

Mamma sat down by my bed ; she had chosen *François le Champi*, whose reddish cover and incomprehensible title gave it a distinct personality in my eyes and a mysterious attraction. I had not then read any real novels. I had heard it said that George Sand was a typical novelist. That prepared me in advance to imagine that *François le Champi* contained something inexpressibly delicious. The course of the narrative, where it tended to arouse curiosity or melt to pity, certain modes of expression which disturb or sadden the reader, and which, with a little experience, he may recognise as

'common form' in novels, seemed to me then distinctive—
for to me a new book was not one of a number of similar
objects, but was like an individual man, unmatched, and
with no cause of existence beyond himself—an intoxicating
whiff of the peculiar essence of *François le Champi*. Beneath
the everyday incidents, the commonplace thoughts and
hackneyed words, I could hear, or overhear, an intonation,
a rhythmic utterance fine and strange. The 'action' began : to me it seemed all the more obscure because in those
days, when I read to myself, I used often, while I turned the
pages, to dream of something quite different. And to the
gaps which this habit made in my knowledge of the story
more were added by the fact that when it was Mamma who
was reading to me aloud she left all the love-scenes out.
And so all the odd changes which take place in the relations
between the miller's wife and the boy, changes which only the
birth and growth of love can explain, seemed to me plunged
and steeped in a mystery, the key to which (as I could readily
believe) lay in that strange and pleasant-sounding name of
Champi, which draped the boy who bore it, I knew not why,
in its own bright colour, purpurate and charming. If my
mother was not a faithful reader, she was, none the less
admirable when reading a work in which she found the
note of true feeling by the respectful simplicity of her interpretation and by the sound of her sweet and gentle voice.
It was the same in her daily life, when it was not works of art
but men and women whom she was moved to pity or admire :
it was touching to observe with what deference she would
banish from her voice, her gestures, from her whole conversation, now the note of joy which might have distressed
lome mother who had long ago lost a child, now the recol-
section of an event or anniversary which might have re-

minded some old gentleman of the burden of his years, now the household topic which might have bored some young man of letters. And so, when she read aloud the prose of George Sand, prose which is everywhere redolent of that generosity and moral distinction which Mamma had learned from my grandmother to place above all other qualities in life, and which I was not to teach her until much later to refrain from placing, in the same way, above all other qualities in literature ; taking pains to banish from her voice any weakness or affectation which might have blocked its channel for that powerful stream of language, she supplied all the natural tenderness, all the lavish sweetness which they demanded to phrases which seemed to have been composed for her voice, and which were all, so to speak, within her compass. She came to them with the tone that they required, with the cordial accent which existed before they were, which dictated them, but which is not to be found in the words themselves, and by these means she smoothed away, as she read on, any harshness there might be or discordance in the tenses of verbs, endowing the imperfect and the preterite with all the sweetness which there is in generosity, all the melancholy which there is in love ; guided the sentence that was drawing to an end towards that which was waiting to begin, now hastening, now slackening the pace of the syllables so as to bring them, despite their difference of quantity, into a uniform rhythm, and breathed into this quite ordinary prose a kind of life, continuous and full of feeling.

My agony was soothed ; I let myself be borne upon the current of this gentle night on which I had my mother by my side. I knew that such a night could not be repeated ; that the strongest desire I had in the world, namely, to keep my mother in my room through the sad hours of darkness, ran

too much counter to general requirements and to the wishes
of others for such a concession as had been granted me this
evening to be anything but a rare and casual exception.
To-morrow night I should again be the victim of anguish
and Mamma would not stay by my side. But when these
storms of anguish grew calm I could no longer realise their
existence ; besides, to-morrow evening was still a long way
off ; I reminded myself that I should still have time to think
about things, albeit that remission of time could bring me no
access of power, albeit the coming event was in no way
dependent upon the exercise of my will, and seemed not quite
inevitable only because it was still separated from me by this
short interval.

* * *

And so it was that, for a long time afterwards, when I
lay awake at night and revived old memories of Combray,
I saw no more of it than this sort of luminous panel, sharply
defined against a vague and shadowy background, like the
panels which a Bengal fire or some electric sign will illuminate
and dissect from the front of a building the other parts of
which remain plunged in darkness : broad enough at its base,
the little parlour, the dining-room, the alluring shadows of the
path along which would come M. Swann, the unconscious
author of my sufferings, the hall through which I would
journey to the first step of that staircase, so hard to climb,
which constituted, all by itself, the tapering ' elevation ' of
an irregular pyramid ; and, at the summit, my bedroom, with
the little passage through whose glazed door Mamma would
enter ; in a word, seen always at the same evening hour,
isolated from all its possible surroundings, detached and
solitary against its shadowy background, the bare minimum of

scenery necessary (like the setting one sees printed at the head of an old play, for its performance in the provinces) to the drama of my undressing, as though all Combray had consisted of but two floors joined by a slender staircase, and as though there had been no time there but seven o'clock at night. I must own that I could have assured any questioner that Combray did include other scenes and did exist at other hours than these. But since the facts which I should then have recalled would have been prompted only by an exercise of the will, by my intellectual memory, and since the pictures which that kind of memory shews us of the past preserve nothing of the past itself, I should never have had any wish to ponder over this residue of Combray. To me it was in reality all dead.

Permanently dead ? Very possibly.

There is a large element of hazard in these matters, and a second hazard, that of our own death, often prevents us from awaiting for any length of time the favours of the first.

I feel that there is much to be said for the Celtic belief that the souls of those whom we have lost are held captive in some inferior being, in an animal, in a plant, in some inanimate object, and so effectively lost to us until the day (which to many never comes) when we happen to pass by the tree or to obtain possession of the object which forms their prison. Then they start and tremble, they call us by our name, and as soon as we have recognised their voice the spell is broken. We have delivered them : they have overcome death and return to share our life.

And so it is with our own past. It is a labour in vain to attempt to recapture it : all the efforts of our intellect must prove futile. The past is hidden somewhere outside the realm, beyond the reach of intellect, in some material object (in the

sensation which that material object will give us) which we
do not suspect. And as for that object, it depends on chance
whether we come upon it or not before we ourselves must die.

Many years had elapsed during which nothing of Combray, save what was comprised in the theatre and the drama
of my going to bed there, had any existence for me, when one
day in winter, as I came home, my mother, seeing that I was
cold, offered me some tea, a thing I did not ordinarily take.
I declined at first, and then, for no particular reason, changed
my mind. She sent out for one of those short, plump little
cakes called 'petites madeleines,' which look as though they
had been moulded in the fluted scallop of a pilgrim's shell.
And soon, mechanically, weary after a dull day with the
prospect of a depressing morrow, I raised to my lips a spoonful
of the tea in which I had soaked a morsel of the cake. No
sooner had the warm liquid, and the crumbs with it, touched
my palate than a shudder ran through my whole body, and I
stopped, intent upon the extraordinary changes that were
taking place. An exquisite pleasure had invaded my senses,
but individual, detached, with no suggestion of its origin.
And at once the vicissitudes of life had become indifferent to
me, its disasters innocuous, its brevity illusory——this new
sensation having had on me the effect which love has of filling
me with a precious essence ; or rather this essence was not
in me, it was myself. I had ceased now to feel mediocre,
accidental, mortal. Whence could it have come to me, this
all-powerful joy ? I was conscious that it was connected with
the taste of tea and cake, but that it infinitely transcended
those savours, could not, indeed, be of the same nature as
theirs. Whence did it come ? What did it signify ? How
could I seize upon and define it ?

I drink a second mouthful, in which I find nothing more

than in the first, a third, which gives me rather less than the second. It is time to stop ; the potion is losing its magic. It is plain that the object of my quest, the truth, lies not in the cup but in myself. The tea has called up in me, but does not itself understand, and can only repeat indefinitely, with a gradual loss of strength, the same testimony ; which I, too, cannot interpret, though I hope at least to be able to call upon the tea for it again and to find it there presently, intact and at my disposal, for my final enlightenment. I put down my cup and examine my own mind. It is for it to discover the truth. But how ? What an abyss of uncertainty whenever the mind feels that some part of it has strayed beyond its own borders ; when it, the seeker, is at once the dark region through which it must go seeking, where all its equipment will avail it nothing. Seek ? More than that : create. It is face to face with something which does not so far exist, to which it alone can give reality and substance, which it alone can bring into the light of day.

And I begin again to ask myself what it could have been, this unremembered state which brought with it no logical proof of its existence, but only the sense that it was a happy, that it was a real state in whose presence other states of consciousness melted and vanished. I decide to attempt to make it reappear. I retrace my thoughts to the moment at which I drank the first spoonful of tea. I find again the same state, illumined by no fresh light. I compel my mind to make one further effort, to follow and recapture once again the fleeting sensation. And that nothing may interrupt it in its course I shut out every obstacle, every extraneous idea, I stop my ears and inhibit all attention to the sounds which come from the next room. And then, feeling that my mind is growing fatigued without having any success to report, I compel it for a change to enjoy that distraction which I have just denied it, to think of other things, to rest and refresh itself before the supreme attempt. And then for the second time I clear an empty space in front of it. I place in position before my mind's eye the still recent taste of that first mouthful, and I feel something start within me, something that leaves its resting-place and attempts to rise, something that has been embedded like an anchor at a great depth ; I do not know yet what it is, but I can feel it mounting slowly ; I can measure the resistance, I can hear the echo of great spaces traversed.

Undoubtedly what is thus palpitating in the depths of my being must be the image, the visual memory which, being linked to that taste, has tried to follow it into my conscious mind. But its struggles are too far off, too much confused ; scarcely can I perceive the colourless reflection in which are blended the uncapturable whirling medley of radiant hues, and I cannot distinguish its form, cannot invite it, as the one possible interpreter, to translate to me the evidence of its contemporary, its inseparable paramour, the taste of cake soaked in tea ; cannot ask it to inform me what special circumstance is in question, of what period in my past life.

Will it ultimately reach the clear surface of my consciousness, this memory, this old, dead moment which the magnetism of an identical moment has travelled so far to importune, to disturb, to raise up out of the very depths of my being ? I cannot tell. Now that I feel nothing, it has stopped, has perhaps gone down again into its darkness, from which who can say whether it will ever rise ? Ten times over I must essay the task, must lean down over the abyss. And each time the natural laziness which deters us from every difficult enterprise, every work of importance, has urged me to leave the thing alone, to drink my tea and to think merely of the worries of to-day and of my hopes for to-morrow, which let themselves be pondered over without effort or distress of mind.

And suddenly the memory returns. The taste was that of the little crumb of madeleine which on Sunday mornings at Combray (because on those mornings I did not go out before church-time), when I went to say good day to her in her bedroom, my aunt Léonie used to give me, dipping it first in her own cup of real or of lime-flower tea. The sight of the little madeleine had recalled nothing to my mind before I tasted it ; perhaps because I had so often seen such things in the interval, without tasting them, on the trays in pastry-cooks' windows, that their image had dissociated itself from those Combray days to take its place among others more recent ; perhaps because of those memories, so long abandoned and put out of mind, nothing now survived, everything was scattered ; the forms of things, including that of the little scallop-shell of pastry, so richly sensual under its severe, religious folds, were either obliterated or had been so long dormant as to have lost the power of expansion which would have allowed them to resume their place in my consciousness. But when from a long-distant past nothing subsists, after the people are dead, after the things are broken and scattered, still, alone, more fragile, but with more vitality, more unsubstantial, more persistent, more faithful, the smell and taste of things remain poised a long time, like souls, ready to remind us, waiting and hoping for their moment, amid the ruins of all the rest ; and bear unfaltering, in the tiny and almost impalpable drop of their essence, the vast structure of recollection.

And once I had recognised the taste of the crumb of madeleine soaked in her decoction of lime-flowers which my aunt used to give me (although I did not yet know and must long postpone the discovery of why this memory made me so happy) immediately the old grey house upon the street, where her room was, rose up like the scenery of a theatre to attach itself to the little pavilion, opening on to the garden, which had been built out behind it for my parents (the isolated panel which until that moment had been all that I could see) ; and with the house the town, from morning to night and in all weathers, the Square where I was sent before luncheon, the streets along which I used to run errands, the country roads we took when it was fine. And just as the Japanese amuse themselves by filling a porcelain bowl with water and steeping in it little crumbs of paper which until then are without character or form, but, the moment they become wet, stretch themselves and bend, take on colour and distinctive shape, become flowers or houses or people, permanent and recognisable, so in that moment all the flowers in our garden and in M. Swann's park, and the water-lilies on the Vivonne and the good folk of the village and their little dwellings and the parish church and the whole of Combray and of its surroundings, taking their proper shapes and growing solid, sprang into being, town and gardens alike, from my cup of tea.

COMBRAY at a distance, from a twenty-mile radius, as we used to see it from the railway when we arrived there every year in Holy Week, was no more than a church epitomising the town, representing it, speaking of it and for it to the horizon, and as one drew near, gathering close about its long, dark cloak, sheltering from the wind, on the open plain, as a shepherd gathers his sheep, the woolly grey backs of its flocking houses, which a fragment of its mediaeval ramparts enclosed, here and there, in an outline as scrupulously circular as that of a little town in a primitive painting. To live in, Combray was a trifle depressing, like its streets, whose houses, built of the blackened stone of the country, fronted with outside steps, capped with gables which projected long shadows downwards, were so dark that one had, as soon as the sun began to go down, to draw back the curtains in the sitting-room windows ; streets with the solemn names of Saints, not a few of whom figured in the history of the early lords of Combray, such as the Rue Saint-Hilaire, the Rue Saint-Jacques, in which my aunt's house stood, the Rue Sainte-Hildegarde, which ran past her railings, and the Rue du Saint-Esprit, on to which the little garden gate opened ; and these Combray streets exist in so remote a quarter of my memory, painted in colours so different from those in which the world is decked for me to-day, that in fact one and all of them, and the church which towered above them in the Square, seem to me now more unsubstantial than the projections of my magic-lantern ; while at times I feel that to be able to cross the Rue Saint-Hilaire again, to engage a room in the Rue de l'Oiseau, in the old hostelry of the Oiseau Flesché, from whose windows in

63

the pavement used to rise a smell of cooking which rises still in my mind, now and then, in the same warm gusts of comfort, would be to secure a contact with the unseen world more marvellously supernatural than it would be to make Golo's acquaintance and to chat with Geneviève de Brabant.

My grandfather's cousin—by courtesy my great-aunt—with whom we used to stay, was the mother of that aunt Léonie who, since her husband's (my uncle Octave's) death, had gradually declined to leave, first Combray, then her house in Combray, then her bedroom, and finally her bed ; and who now never 'came down,' but lay perpetually in an indefinite condition of grief, physical exhaustion, illness, obsessions, and religious observances. Her own room looked out over the Rue Saint-Jacques, which ran a long way further to end in the Grand-Pré (as distinct from the Petit-Pré, a green space in the centre of the town where three streets met) and which, monotonous and grey, with the three high steps of stone before almost every one of its doors, seemed like a deep furrow cut by some sculptor of gothic images in the very block of stone out of which he had fashioned a Calvary or a Crib. My aunt's life was now practically confined to two adjoining rooms, in one of which she would rest in the afternoon while they aired the other. They were rooms of that country order which (just as in certain climes whole tracts of air or ocean are illuminated or scented by myriads of protozoa which we cannot see) fascinate our sense of smell with the countless odours springing from their own special virtues, wisdom, habits, a whole secret system of life, invisible, superabundant and profoundly moral, which their atmosphere holds in solution ; smells natural enough indeed, and coloured by circumstances as are those of the neighbouring country-side, but already humanised, domesticated, confined, an exquisite, skilful, limpid jelly, blending all the fruits of the season which have left the orchard for the store-room, smells changing with the year, but plenishing, domestic smells, which compensate for the sharpness of hoar frost with the sweet savour of warm bread, smells lazy and punctual as a village clock, roving and settled, heedless and provident, linen smells, morning smells, pious smells ; rejoicing in a peace which brings only an increase of anxiety, and in a prosiness which serves as a deep source of poetry to the stranger who passes through their midst without having lived amongst them. The air of those rooms was saturated with the fine bouquet of a silence so nourishing, so succulent that I could not enter them without a sort of greedy enjoyment, particularly on those first mornings, chilly still, of the Easter holidays, when I could taste it more fully, because I had just arrived then at Combray : before I went in to wish my aunt good day I would be kept waiting a little time in the outer room, where the sun, a wintry sun still, had crept in to warm itself before the fire, lighted already between its two brick sides and plastering all the room and everything in it with a smell of soot, making the room like one of those great open hearths which one finds in the country, or one of the canopied mantelpieces in old castles under which one sits hoping that in the world outside it is raining or snowing, hoping almost for a catastrophic deluge to add the romance of shelter and security to the comfort of a snug retreat ; I would turn to and fro between the prayer-desk and the stamped velvet armchairs, each one always draped in its crocheted antimacassar, while the fire, baking like a pie the appetising smells with which the air of the room was thickly clotted, which the dewy and sunny freshness of the morning had already ' raised ' and started to ' set,' puffed them and glazed them and fluted them and swelled them into an invisible though not impalpable country cake, an immense puff-pastry, in which, barely waiting to savour the crustier, more delicate, more respectable, but also drier smells of the cupboard, the chest-of-drawers, and the patterned wall-paper I always returned with an unconfessed gluttony to bury myself in the nondescript, resinous, dull, indigestible, and fruity smell of the flowered quilt.

In the next room I could hear my aunt talking quietly to herself. She never spoke save in low tones, because she believed that there was something broken in her head and floating loose there, which she might displace by talking too loud ; but she never remained for long, even when alone, without saying something, because she believed that it was good for her throat, and that by keeping the blood there in circulation it would make less frequent the chokings and other pains to which she was liable ; besides, in the life of complete inertia which she led she attached to the least of her sensations an extraordinary importance, endowed them with a Protean ubiquity which made it difficult for her to keep them secret, and, failing a confidant to whom she might communicate them, she used to promulgate them to herself in an unceasing monologue which was her sole form of activity. Unfortunately, having formed the habit of thinking aloud, she did not always take care to see that there was no one in the adjoining room, and I would often hear her saying to herself : " I must not forget that I never slept a wink "— for " never sleeping a wink " was her great claim to distinction, and one admitted and respected in our household vocabulary ; in the morning Françoise would not ' call ' her, but would simply ' come to ' her ; during the day, when my aunt wished to take a nap, we used to say just that she wished to ' be quiet ' or to ' rest ' ; and when in conversation she so far forgot herself as to say " what made me wake up," or " I dreamed that," she would flush and at once correct herself.

After waiting a minute, I would go in and kiss her ; Françoise would be making her tea ; or, if my aunt were feeling ' upset,' she would ask instead for her ' tisane,' and it would be my duty to shake out of the chemist's little package on to a plate the amount of lime-blossom required for infusion in boiling water. The drying of the stems had twisted them into a fantastic trellis, in whose intervals the pale flowers opened, as though a painter had arranged them there, grouping them in the most decorative poses. The leaves, which had lost or altered their own appearance, assumed those instead of the most incongruous things imaginable, as though the transparent wings of flies or the blank sides of labels or the petals of roses had been collected and pounded, or interwoven as birds weave the material for their nests. A thousand trifling little details—the charming prodigality of the chemist—details which would have been eliminated from an artificial preparation, gave me, like a book in which one is astonished to read the name of a person whom one knows, the pleasure of finding that these were indeed real lime-blossoms, like those I had seen, when coming from the train, in the Avenue de la Gare, altered, but only because they were not imitations but the very same blossoms, which had grown old. And as each new character is merely a metamorphosis from something older, in these little grey balls I recognised green buds plucked before their time ; but beyond all else the rosy, moony, tender glow which lit up the blossoms among the frail forest of stems from which they hung like little golden roses—marking, as the radiance upon an old wall still marks the place of a vanished fresco, the difference between those parts of the tree which had and those which had not been ' in bloom '——shewed me that these were petals which, before their flowering-time, the chemist's package had embalmed on warm evenings of spring. That rosy candlelight was still their colour, but half-extinguished and deadened in the diminished life which was now theirs, and which may be called the twilight of a flower. Presently my aunt was able to dip in the boiling infusion, in which she would relish the savour of dead or faded blossom, a little madeleine, of which she would hold out a piece to me when it was sufficiently soft.

At one side of her bed stood a big yellow chest-of-drawers of lemon-wood, and a table which served at once as pharmacy and as high altar, on which, beneath a statue of Our Lady and a bottle of Vichy-Célestins, might be found her service-books and her medical prescriptions, everything that she needed for the performance, in bed, of her duties to soul and body, to keep the proper times for pepsin and for vespers. On the other side her bed was bounded by the window : she had the street beneath her eyes, and would read in it from morning to night to divert the tedium of her life, like a Persian prince, the daily but immemorial chronicles of Combray, which she would discuss in detail afterwards with Françoise.

I would not have been five minutes with my aunt before she would send me away in case I made her tired. She would hold out for me to kiss her sad brow, pale and lifeless, on which at this early hour she would not yet have arranged the false hair and through which the bones shone like the points of a crown of thorns or the beads of a rosary, and she would say to me : " Now, my poor child, you must go away ; go and get ready for mass ; and if you see Françoise downstairs, tell her not to stay too long amusing herself with you ; she must come up soon to see if I want anything."

Françoise, who had been for many years in my aunt's service and did not at that time suspect that she would one day be transferred entirely to ours, was a little inclined to desert my aunt during the months which we spent in her house. There had been in my infancy, before we first went to Combray, and when my aunt Léonie used still to spend the winter in Paris with her mother, a time when I knew Françoise so little that on New Year's Day, before going into my great-aunt's house, my mother put a five-franc piece in my hand and said : " Now, be careful. Don't make any mistake. Wait until you hear me say ' Good morning, Françoise,' and I touch your arm, before you give it to her." No sooner had we arrived in my aunt's dark hall than we saw in the gloom, beneath the frills of a snowy cap as stiff and fragile as if it had been made of spun sugar, the concentric waves of a smile of anticipatory gratitude. It was Françoise, motionless and erect, framed in the small doorway of the corridor like the statue of a saint in its niche. When we had grown more accustomed to this religious darkness we could discern in her features a disinterested love of all humanity, blended with a tender respect for the ' upper classes ' which raised to the most honourable quarter of her heart the hope of receiving her due reward. Mamma pinched my arm sharply and said in a loud voice : " Good morning, Françoise." At this signal my fingers parted and I let fall the coin, which found a receptacle in a confused but outstretched hand. But since we had begun to go to Combray there was no one I knew better than Françoise. We were her favourites, and in the first years at least, while she shewed the same consideration for us as for my aunt, she enjoyed us with a keener relish, because we had, in addition to our dignity as part of 'the family' (for she had for those invisible bonds by which community of blood unites the members of a family as much respect as any Greek tragedian), the fresh charm of not being her customary employers. And so with what joy would she welcome us, with what sorrow complain that the weather was still so bad for us, on the day of our arrival, just before Easter, when there was often an icy wind ; while Mamma inquired after her daughter and her nephews, and if her grandson was good-looking, and what they were going to make of him, and whether he took after his granny.

Later, when no one else was in the room, Mamma, who knew that Françoise was still mourning for her parents, who had been dead for years, would speak of them kindly, asking her endless little questions about them and their lives.

She had guessed that Françoise was not over-fond of her son-in-law, and that he spoiled the pleasure she found in visiting her daughter, as the two could not talk so freely when he was there. And so one day, when Françoise was going to their house, some miles from Combray, Mamma said to her, with a smile : " Tell me, Françoise, if Julien has had to go away, and you have Marguerite to yourself all day, you will be very sorry, but you will make the best of it, won't you ? "

And Françoise answered, laughing : " Madame knows everything ; Madame is worse than the X-rays " (she pronounced ' x ' with an affectation of difficulty and with a smile in deprecation of her, an unlettered woman's daring to employ a scientific term) " they brought here for Mme. Octave, which see what is in your heart "—and she went off, disturbed that anyone should be caring about her, perhaps anxious that we should not see her in tears : Mamma was the first person who had given her the pleasure of feeling that her

AUNT LEONTINE

peasant existence, with its simple joys and sorrows, might offer some interest, might be a source of grief or pleasure to some one other than herself.

My aunt resigned herself to doing without Françoise to some extent during our visits, knowing how much my mother appreciated the services of so active and intelligent a maid, one who looked as smart at five o'clock in the morning in her kitchen, under a cap whose stiff and dazzling frills seemed to be made of porcelain, as when dressed for churchgoing ; who did everything in the right way, who toiled like a horse, whether she was well or ill, but without noise, without the appearance of doing anything ; the only one of my aunt's maids who when Mamma asked for hot water or black coffee would bring them actually boiling ; she was one of those servants who in a household seem least satisfactory, at first, to a stranger, doubtless because they take no pains to make a conquest of him and shew him no special attention, knowing very well that they have no real need of him, that he will cease to be invited to the house sooner than they will be dismissed from it ; who, on the other hand, cling with most fidelity to those masters and mistresses who have tested and proved their real capacity, and do not look for that superficial responsiveness, that slavish affability, which may impress a stranger favourably, but often conceals an utter barrenness of spirit in which no amount of training can produce the least trace of individuality.

When Françoise, having seen that my parents had everything they required, first went upstairs again to give my aunt her pepsin and to find out from her what she would take for luncheon, very few mornings passed but she was called upon to give an opinion, or to furnish an explanation, in regard to some important event.

" Just fancy, Françoise, Mme. Goupil went by more than a quarter of an hour late to fetch her sister : if she loses any more time on the way I should not be at all surprised if she got in after the Elevation."

" Well, there'd be nothing wonderful in that," would be the answer. Or :

" Françoise, if you had come in five minutes ago, you would have seen Mme. Imbert go past with some asparagus twice the size of what mother Callot has : do try to find out from her cook where she got them. You know you've been putting asparagus in all your sauces this spring ; you might be able to get some like these for our visitors."

" I shouldn't be surprised if they came from the Curé's," Françoise would say, and :

" I'm sure you wouldn't, my poor Françoise," my aunt would reply, raising her shoulders. "From the Curé's, indeed ! You know quite well that he can never grow anything but wretched little twigs of asparagus, not asparagus at all. I tell you these ones were as thick as my arm. Not your arm, of course, but my poor arm, which has grown so much thinner again this year." Or :

" Françoise, didn't you hear that bell just now ? It split my head."

" No, Mme. Octave."

" Ah, poor girl, your skull must be very thick ; you may thank God for that. It was Maguelone come to fetch Dr. Piperaud. He came out with her at once and they went off along the Rue de l'Oiseau. There must be some child ill."

" Oh dear, dear ; the poor little creature ! " would come with a sigh from Françoise, who could not hear of any calamity befalling a person unknown to her, even in some distant part of the world, without beginning to lament. Or:

" Françoise, for whom did they toll the passing-bell just now ? Oh dear, of course, it would be for Mme. Rousseau. And to think that I had forgotten that she passed away the other night. Indeed, it is time the Lord called me home too ; I don't know what has become of my head since I lost my poor Octave. But I am wasting your time, my good girl."

" Indeed no, Mme. Octave, my time is not so precious ; whoever made our time didn't sell it to us. I am just going to see that my fire hasn't gone out."

In this way Françoise and my aunt made a critical valuation between them, in the course of these morning sessions, of the earliest happenings of the day. But sometimes these happenings assumed so mysterious or so alarming an air that my aunt felt she could not wait until it was time for Françoise to come upstairs, and then a formidable and quadruple peal would resound through the house.

" But, Mme. Octave, it is not time for your pepsin," Françoise would begin. " Are you feeling faint ? "

" No, thank you, Françoise," my aunt would reply, "that is to say, yes ; for you know well that there is very seldom a time when I don't feel faint ; one day I shall pass away like Mme. Rousseau, before I know where I am ; but that is not why I rang. Would you believe that I have just seen, as plainly as I see you, Mme. Goupil with a little girl I didn't know at all. Run and get a pennyworth of salt from Camus. It's not often that Théodore can't tell you who a person is."

" But that must be M. Pupin's daughter," Françoise would say, preferring to stick to an immediate explanation, since she had been perhaps twice already into Camus's shop that morning.

" M. Pupin's daughter ! Oh, that's a likely story, my

poor Françoise. Do you think I should not have recognised
M. Pupin's daughter ! "

" But I don't mean the big one, Mme. Octave ; I mean
the little girl, the one who goes to school at Jouy. I seem to
have seen her once already this morning."

" Oh, if that's what it is ! " my aunt would say, " she must
have come over for the holidays. Yes, that is it. No need to
ask, she will have come over for the holidays. But then we
shall soon see Mme. Sazerat come along and ring her sister's
door-bell, for her luncheon. That will be it ! I saw the
boy from Galopin's go by with a tart. You will see that the
tart was for Mme. Goupil."

" Once Mme. Goupil has anyone in the house, Mme.
Octave, you won't be long in seeing all her folk going in
to their luncheon there, for it's not so early as it was," would
be the answer, for Françoise, who was anxious to retire downstairs to look after our own meal, was not sorry to leave my
aunt with the prospect of such a distraction.

" Oh ! not before midday ! " my aunt would reply in a
tone of resignation, darting an uneasy glance at the clock,
but stealthily, so as not to let it be seen that she, who had
renounced all earthly joys, yet found a keen satisfaction in
learning that Mme. Goupil was expecting company to luncheon, though, alas, she must wait a little more than an hour
still before enjoying the spectacle. " And it will come in the
middle of my luncheon ! " she would murmur to herself.
Her luncheon was such a distraction in itself that she did not
like any other to come at the same time. " At least, you will
not forget to give me my creamed eggs on one of the flat
plates ? " These were the only plates which had pictures on
them and my aunt used to amuse herself at every meal by
reading the description on whichever might have been sent

up to her. She would put on her spectacles and spell out :
" Ali Baba and the Forty Thieves," " Aladdin, or the
Wonderful Lamp," and smile, and say " Very good
indeed."

" I may as well go across to Camus . . ." Françoise
would hazard, seeing that my aunt had no longer any intention of sending her there.

" No, no ; it's not worth while now ; it's certain to be the
Pupin girl. My poor Françoise, I am sorry to have made you
come upstairs for nothing."

But it was not for nothing, as my aunt well knew, that she
had rung for Françoise, since at Combray a person whom
one ' didn't know at all ' was as incredible a being as any
mythological deity, and it was apt to be forgotten that after
each occasion on which there had appeared in the Rue du
Saint-Esprit or in the Square one of these bewildering phenomena, careful and exhaustive researches had invariably reduced the fabulous monster to the proportions of a person
whom one ' did know,' either personally or in the abstract,
in his or her civil status as being more or less closely related
to some family in Combray. It would turn out to be Mme.
Sauton's son discharged from the army, or the Abbé Per-
dreau's niece come home from her convent, or the Curé's
brother, a tax-collector at Châteaudun, who had just retired
on a pension or had come over to Combray for the holidays.
On first noticing them you had been impressed by the thought
that there might be in Combray people whom you ' didn't
know at all,' simply because you had failed to recognise or
identify them at once. And yet long beforehand Mme.
Sauton and the Curé had given warning that they expected
their ' strangers.' In the evening, when I came in and went
upstairs to tell my aunt the incidents of our walk, if I was

rash enough to say to her that we had passed, near the Pont-
Vieux, a man whom my grandfather didn't know :

" A man grandfather didn't know at all ! " she would exclaim. " That's a likely story." None the less, she would be
a little disturbed by the news, she would wish to have the
details correctly, and so my grandfather would be summoned.
" Who can it have been that you passed near the Pont-Vieux,
uncle ? A man you didn't know at all ? "

" Why, of course I did," my grandfather would answer ;
" it was Prosper, Mme. Bouillebœuf's gardener's brother."

" Ah, well ! " my aunt would say, calm again but slightly
flushed still ; " and the boy told me that you had passed a
man you didn't know at all ! " After which I would be
warned to be more careful of what I said, and not to upset
my aunt so by thoughtless remarks. Everyone was so well
known in Combray, animals as well as people, that if my
aunt had happened to see a dog go by which she ' didn't
know at all ' she would think about it incessantly, devoting
to the solution of the incomprehensible problem all her in-
ductive talent and her leisure hours.

" That will be Mme. Sazerat's dog," Françoise would
suggest, without any real conviction, but in the hope of peace,
and so that my aunt should not ' split her head.'

" As if I didn't know Mme. Sazerat's dog ! "—for my
aunt's critical mind would not so easily admit any fresh fact.

" Ah, but that will be the new dog M. Galopin has brought
her from Lisieux."

" Oh, if that's what it is ! "

" It seems, it's a most engaging animal," Françoise would
go on, having got the story from Théodore, " as clever as a
Christian, always in a good temper, always friendly, always
everything that's nice. It's not often you see an animal so

well-behaved at that age. Mme. Octave, it's high time I left
you ; I can't afford to stay here amusing myself ; look, it's
nearly ten o'clock and my fire not lighted yet, and I've still
to dress the asparagus."

"What, Françoise, more asparagus ! It's a regular disease
of asparagus you have got this year : you will make our
Parisians sick of it."

"No, no, Mme. Octave, they like it well enough.
They'll be coming back from church soon as hungry as
hunters, and they won't eat it out of the back of their spoons,
you'll see."

"Church ! why, they must be there now ; you'd better
not lose any time. Go and look after your luncheon."

While my aunt gossiped on in this way with Françoise
I would have accompanied my parents to mass. How I loved
it : how clearly I can see it still, our church at Combray !
The old porch by which we went in, black, and full of holes
as a cullender, was worn out of shape and deeply furrowed
at the sides (as also was the holy water stoup to which it led
us) just as if the gentle grazing touch of the cloaks of peasant-
women going into the church, and of their fingers dipping
into the water, had managed by agelong repetition to acquire
a destructive force, to impress itself on the stone, to
carve ruts in it like those made by cart-wheels upon stone
gate-posts against which they are driven every day. Its
memorial stones, beneath which the noble dust of the Abbots
of Combray, who were buried there, furnished the choir with
a sort of spiritual pavement, were themselves no longer hard
and lifeless matter, for time had softened and sweetened them,
and had made them melt like honey and flow beyond their
proper margins, either surging out in a milky, frothing wave,
washing from its place a florid gothic capital, drowning the

77

white violets of the marble floor ; or else reabsorbed into
their limits, contracting still further a crabbed Latin in-
scription, bringing a fresh touch of fantasy into the arrangement of its curtailed characters, closing together two letters
of some word of which the rest were disproportionately
scattered. Its windows were never so brilliant as on days
when the sun scarcely shone, so that if it was dull outside you
might be certain of fine weather in church. One of them was
filled from top to bottom by a solitary figure, like the king
on a playing-card, who lived up there beneath his canopy of
stone, between earth and heaven ; and in the blue light of its
slanting shadow, on weekdays sometimes, at noon, when
there was no service (at one of those rare moments when the
airy, empty church, more human somehow and more luxuri-
ous with the sun shewing off all its rich furnishings, seemed to
have almost a habitable air, like the hall—all sculptured stone
and painted glass—of some mediaeval mansion), you might
see Mme. Sazerat kneel for an instant, laying down on the
chair beside her own a neatly corded parcel of little cakes
which she had just bought at the baker's and was taking
home for her luncheon. In another, a mountain of rosy snow,
at whose foot a battle was being fought, seemed to have frozen
the window also, which it swelled and distorted with its
cloudy sleet, like a pane to which snowflakes have drifted
and clung, but flakes illumined by a sunrise—the same, doubtless, which purpled the reredos of the altar with tints so fresh
that they seemed rather to be thrown on it for a moment
by a light shining from outside and shortly to be extinguished
than painted and permanently fastened on the stone. And
all of them were so old that you could see, here and there,
their silvery antiquity sparkling with the dust of centuries and
shewing in its threadbare brilliance the very cords of their

lovely tapestry of glass. There was one among them which was a tall panel composed of a hundred little rectangular windows, of blue principally, like a great game of patience of the kind planned to beguile King Charles VI ; but, either because a ray of sunlight had gleamed through it or because my own shifting vision had drawn across the window, whose colours died away and were rekindled by turns, a rare and transient fire—the next instant it had taken on all the iridescence of a peacock's tail, then shook and wavered in a flaming and fantastic shower, distilled and dropping from the groin of the dark and rocky vault down the moist walls, as though it were along the bed of some rainbow grotto of sinuous stalactites that I was following my parents, who marched before me, their prayer-books clasped in their hands ; a moment later the little lozenge windows had put on the deep transparence, the unbreakable hardness of sapphires clustered on some enormous breastplate ; but beyond which could be distinguished, dearer than all such treasures, a fleeting smile from the sun, which could be seen and felt as well here, in the blue and gentle flood in which it washed the masonry, as on the pavement of the Square or the straw of the market-place ; and even on our first Sundays, when we came down before Easter, it would console me for the blackness and bareness of the earth outside by making burst into blossom, as in some springtime in old history among the heirs of Saint Louis, this dazzling and gilded carpet of forget-me-nots in glass.

Two tapestries of high warp represented the coronation of Esther (in which tradition would have it that the weaver had given to Ahasuerus the features of one of the kings of France and to Esther those of a lady of Guermantes whose lover he had been) ; their colours had melted into one another, so as to add expression, relief, light to the pictures. A touch of red over the lips of Esther had strayed beyond their outline ; the yellow on her dress was spread with such unctuous plumpness as to have acquired a kind of solidity, and stood boldly out from the receding atmosphere ; while the green of the trees, which was still bright in silk and wool among the lower parts of the panel, but had quite ' gone ' at the top, separated in a paler scheme, above the dark trunks, the yellowing upper branches, tanned and half-obliterated by the sharp though sidelong rays of an invisible sun. All these things and, still more than these, the treasures which had come to the church from personages who to me were almost legendary figures (such as the golden cross wrought, it was said, by Saint Eloi and presented by Dagobert, and the tomb of the sons of Louis the Germanic in porphyry and enamelled copper), because of which I used to go forward into the church when we were making our way to our chairs as into a fairy-haunted valley, where the rustic sees with amazement on a rock, a tree, a marsh, the tangible proofs of the little people's supernatural passage—all these things made of the church for me something entirely different from the rest of the town ; a building which occupied, so to speak, four dimensions of space—the name of the fourth being Time—which had sailed the centuries with that old nave, where bay after bay, chapel after chapel, seemed to stretch across and hold down and conquer not merely a few yards of soil, but each successive epoch from which the whole building had emerged triumphant, hiding the rugged barbarities of the eleventh century in the thickness of its walls, through which nothing could be seen of the heavy arches, long stopped and blinded with coarse blocks of ashlar, except where, near the porch, a deep groove was furrowed into one wall by the tower-stair ; and even there the barbarity was veiled by the graceful gothic arcade which pressed coquettishly upon it, like a row of grown-up sisters who, to hide him from the eyes of strangers, arrange themselves smilingly in front of a countrified, un-mannerly and ill-dressed younger brother ; rearing into the sky above the Square a tower which had looked down upon Saint Louis, and seemed to behold him still; and thrusting down with its crypt into the blackness of a Merovingian night, through which, guiding us with groping finger-tips beneath the shadowy vault, ribbed strongly as an immense bat's wing of stone, Théodore or his sister would light up for us with a candle the tomb of Sigebert's little daughter, in which a deep hole, like the bed of a fossil, had been bored, or so it was said, " by a crystal lamp which, on the night when the Frankish princess was murdered, had left, of its own accord, the golden chains by which it was suspended where the apse is to-day and with neither the crystal broken nor the light extinguished had buried itself in the stone, through which it had gently forced its way."

And then the apse of Combray : what am I to say of that ? It was so coarse, so devoid of artistic beauty, even of the religious spirit. From outside, since the street crossing which it commanded was on a lower level, its great wall was thrust upwards from a basement of unfaced ashlar, jagged with flints, in all of which there was nothing particularly ecclesiastical ; the windows seemed to have been pierced at an abnormal height, and its whole appearance was that of a prison wall rather than of a church. And certainly in later years, were I to recall all the glorious apses that I had seen, it would never enter my mind to compare with any one of them the apse of Combray. Only, one day, turning out of a little street in some country town, I came upon three alley-ways that converged, and facing them an old wall, rubbed, worn, crumbling, and unusually high ; with windows pierced in it far overhead and the same asymmetrical appearance as the apse of Combray. And at that moment I did not say to myself, as at Chartres I might have done or at Rheims, with what strength the religious feeling had been expressed in its construction, but instinctively I exclaimed " The Church ! "

The church ! A dear, familiar friend ; close pressed in the Rue Saint-Hilaire, upon which its north door opened, by its two neighbours, Mme. Loiseau's house and the pharmacy of M. Rapin, against which its walls rested without interspace ; a simple citizen of Combray, who might have had her number in the street had the streets of Combray borne numbers, and at whose door one felt that the postman ought to stop on his morning rounds, before going into Mme. Loiseau's and after leaving M. Rapin's, there existed, for all that, between the church and everything in Combray that was not the church a clear line of demarcation which I have never succeeded in eliminating from my mind. In vain might Mme. Loiseau deck her window-sills with fuchsias, which developed the bad habit of letting their branches trail at all times and in all directions, head downwards, and whose flowers had no more important business, when they were big enough to taste the joys of life, than to go and cool their purple, congested cheeks against the dark front of the church ; to me such conduct sanctified the fuchsias not at all ; between the flowers and the blackened stones towards which they leaned, if my eyes could discern no interval, my mind preserved the impression of an abyss.

From a long way off one could distinguish and identify the steeple of Saint-Hilaire inscribing its unforgettable form upon a horizon beneath which Combray had not yet appeared ; when from the train which brought us down from Paris at Easter-time my father caught sight of it, as it slipped into every fold of the sky in turn, its little iron cock veering continually in all directions, he would say : " Come, get your wraps together, we are there." And on one of the longest walks we ever took from Combray there was a spot where the narrow road emerged suddenly on to an immense plain, closed at the horizon by strips of forest over which rose and stood alone the fine point of Saint-Hilaire's steeple, but so sharpened and so pink that it seemed to be no more than sketched on the sky by the finger-nail of a painter anxious to give to such a landscape, to so pure a piece of ' nature,' this little sign of art, this single indication of human existence. As one drew near it and could make out the remains of the square tower, half in ruins, which still stood by its side, though without rivalling it in height, one was struck, first of all, by the tone, reddish and sombre, of its stones ; and on a misty morning in autumn one would have called it, to see it rising above the violet thunder-cloud of the vineyards, a ruin of purple, almost the colour of the wild vine.

Often in the Square, as we came home, my grandmother would make me stop to look up at it. From the tower windows, placed two and two, one pair above another, with that right and original proportion in their spacing to which not only human faces owe their beauty and dignity, it released, it let fall at regular intervals flights of jackdaws which for a little while would wheel and caw, as though the ancient stones which allowed them to sport thus and never seemed to see them, becoming of a sudden uninhabitable and discharging some infinitely disturbing element, had struck them and driven them forth. Then after pattering everywhere the violet velvet of the evening air, abruptly soothed, they would return and be absorbed in the tower, deadly no longer but benignant, some perching here and there (not seeming to move, but snapping, perhaps, and swallowing some passing insect) on the points of turrets, as a seagull perches, with an angler's immobility, on the crest of a wave. Without quite knowing why, my grandmother found in the steeple of Saint-Hilaire that absence of vulgarity, pretension, and meanness which made her love—and deem rich in beneficent influences—nature itself, when the hand of man had not, as did my great-aunt's gardener, trimmed it, and the works of genius. And certainly every part one saw of the church served to distinguish the whole from any other building by a kind of general feeling which pervaded it, but it was in the steeple that the church seemed to display a consciousness of itself, to affirm its individual and responsible existence. It was the steeple which spoke for the church. I think, too, that in a confused way my grandmother found in the steeple of Combray what she prized above anything else in the world, namely, a natural air and an air of distinction. Ignorant of architecture, she would say :

"My dears, laugh at me if you like ; it is not conventionally beautiful, but there is something in its quaint old face which pleases me. If it could play the piano, I am sure it would really *play*." And when she gazed on it, when her eyes followed the gentle tension, the fervent inclination of its stony slopes which drew together as they rose, like hands joined in prayer, she would absorb herself so utterly in the outpouring of the spire that her gaze seemed to leap upwards with it ; her lips at the same time curving in a friendly smile for the worn old stones of which the setting sun now illumined no more than the topmost pinnacles, which, at the point where they entered that zone of sunlight and were softened and sweetened by it, seemed to have mounted suddenly far higher, to have become truly remote, like a song whose singer breaks into falsetto, an octave above the accompanying air.

It was the steeple of Saint-Hilaire which shaped and crowned and consecrated every occupation, every hour of the day, every point of view in the town. From my bedroom window I could discern no more than its base, which had been freshly covered with slates ; but when on Sundays I saw these, in the hot light of a summer morning, blaze like a black sun I would say to myself : " Good heavens ! nine o'clock ! I must get ready for mass at once if I am to have time to go in and kiss aunt Léonie first," and I would know exactly what was the colour of the sunlight upon the Square, I could feel the heat and dust of the market, the shade behind the blinds of the shop into which Mamma would perhaps go on her way to mass, penetrating its odour of unbleached calico, to purchase a handkerchief or something, of which the draper himself would let her see what he had, bowing from the waist : who, having made everything ready for shutting up, had just gone into the back shop to put on his Sunday coat and to wash his hands, which it was his habit, every few minutes and even on the saddest occasions, to rub one against the other with an air of enterprise, cunning, and success.

And again, after mass, when we looked in to tell Théodore to bring a larger loaf than usual because our cousins had taken advantage of the fine weather to come over from Thiberzy for luncheon, we had in front of us the steeple, which, baked and brown itself like a larger loaf still of ' holy bread,' with flakes and sticky drops on it of sunlight, pricked its sharp point into the blue sky. And in the evening, as I came in from my walk and thought of the approaching moment when I must say good night to my mother and see her no more, the steeple was by contrast so kindly, there at the close of day, that I would imagine it as being laid, like a brown velvet cushion, against—as being thrust into the pallid sky which had yielded beneath its pressure, had sunk slightly so as to make room for it, and had correspondingly risen on either side ; while the cries of the birds wheeling to and fro about it seemed to intensify its silence, to elongate its spire still further, and to invest it with some quality beyond the power of words.

Even when our errands lay in places behind the church, from which it could not be seen, the view seemed always to have been composed with reference to the steeple, which would stand up, now here, now there, among the houses, and was perhaps even more affecting when it appeared thus without the church. And, indeed, there are many others which look best when seen in this way, and I can call to mind vignettes of housetops with surmounting steeples in quite another category of art than those formed by the dreary streets of Combray. I shall never forget, in a quaint Norman town not far from Balbec, two charming eighteenth-century houses, dear to me and venerable for many reasons, between which, when one looks up at them from a fine garden which descends in terraces to the river, the gothic spire of a church (itself hidden by the houses) soars into the sky with the effect of crowning and completing their fronts, but in a material so different, so precious, so beringed, so rosy, so polished, that it is at once seen to be no more a part of them than would be a part of two pretty pebbles lying side by side, between which it had been washed on the beach, the purple, crinkled spire of some sea-shell spun out into a turret and gay with glossy colour. Even in Paris, in one of the ugliest parts of the town, I know a window from which one can see across a first, a

second, and even a third layer of jumbled roofs, street beyond
street, a violet bell, sometimes ruddy, sometimes too, in the
finest ' prints ' which the atmosphere makes of it, of an ashy
solution of black ; which is, in fact, nothing else than the
dome of Saint-Augustin, and which imparts to this view of
Paris the character of some of the Piranesi views of Rome.
But since into none of these little etchings, whatever the
taste my memory may have been able to bring to their execution, was it able to contribute an element I have long lost,
the feeling which makes us not merely regard a thing as a
spectacle, but believe in it as in a creature without parallel,
so none of them keeps in dependence on it a whole section
of my inmost life as does the memory of those aspects of the
steeple of Combray from the streets behind the church.
Whether one saw it at five o'clock when going to call for
letters at the post-office, some doors away from one, on the
left, raising abruptly with its isolated peak the ridge of
housetops ; or again, when one had to go in and ask for
news of Mme. Sazerat, one's eyes followed the line where it
ran low again beyond the farther, descending slope, and one
knew that it would be the second turning after the steeple ;
or yet again, if pressing further afield one went to the station,
one saw it obliquely, shewing in profile fresh angles and surfaces, like a solid body surprised at some unknown point in its
revolution ; or, from the banks of the Vivonne, the apse,
drawn muscularly together and heightened in perspective,
seemed to spring upwards with the effort which the steeple
made to hurl its spire-point into the heart of heaven : it was
always to the steeple that one must return, always it which
dominated everything else, summing up the houses with an
unexpected pinnacle, raised before me like the Finger of God,
Whose Body might have been concealed below among the

crowd of human bodies without fear of my confounding It, for that reason, with them. And so even to-day in any large provincial town, or in a quarter of Paris which I do not know well, if a passer-by who is 'putting me on the right road' shews me from afar, as a point to aim at, some belfry of a hospital, or a convent steeple lifting the peak of its ecclesiastical cap at the corner of the street which I am to take, my memory need only find in it some dim resemblance to that dear and vanished outline, and the passer-by, should he turn round to make sure that I have not gone astray, would see me, to his astonishment, oblivious of the walk that I had planned to take or the place where I was obliged to call, standing still on the spot, before that steeple, for hours on end, motionless, trying to remember, feeling deep within myself a tract of soil reclaimed from the waters of Lethe slowly drying until the buildings rise on it again ; and then no doubt, and then more uneasily than when, just now, I asked him for a direction, I will seek my way again, I will turn a corner . . . but . . . the goal is in my heart . .

On our way home from mass we would often meet M. Legrandin, who, detained in Paris by his professional duties as an engineer, could only (except in the regular holiday seasons) visit his home at Combray between Saturday evenings and Monday mornings. He was one of that class of men who, apart from a scientific career in which they may well have proved brilliantly successful, have acquired an entirely different kind of culture, literary or artistic, of which they make no use in the specialised work of their profession, but by which their conversation profits. More 'literary' than many 'men of letters' (we were not aware at this period that M. Legrandin had a distinct reputation as a writer, and so were greatly astonished to find that a well-known composer had set some verses of his to music), endowed with a greater ease in execution than many painters, they imagine that the life they are obliged to lead is not that for which they are really fitted, and they bring to their regular occupations either a fantastic indifference or a sustained and lofty application, scornful, bitter, and conscientious. Tall, with a good figure, a fine, thoughtful face, drooping fair moustaches, a look of disillusionment in his blue eyes, an almost exaggerated refinement of courtesy ; a talker such as we had never heard ; he was in the sight of my family, who never ceased to quote him as an example, the very pattern of a gentleman, who took life in the noblest and most delicate manner. My grandmother alone found fault with him for speaking a little too well, a little too much like a book, for not using a vocabulary as natural as his loosely knotted Lavallière neckties, his short, straight, almost schoolboyish coat. She was astonished, too, at the furious invective which he was always launching at the aristocracy, at fashionable life, and 'snobbishness'—"undoubtedly," he would say, "the sin of which Saint Paul is thinking when he speaks of the sin for which there is no forgiveness."

Worldly ambition was a thing which my grandmother was so little capable of feeling, or indeed of understanding, that it seemed to her futile to apply so much heat to its condemnation. Besides, she thought it in not very good taste that M. Legrandin, whose sister was married to a country gentleman of Lower Normandy, near Balbec, should deliver himself of such violent attacks upon the nobles, going so far as to blame the Revolution for not having guillotined them all.

"Well met, my friends !" he would say as he came towards us. "You are lucky to spend so much time here ; to-morrow I have to go back to Paris, to squeeze back into my niche.

I   89   D 2

" Oh, I admit," he went on, with his own peculiar smile, gently ironical, disillusioned and vague, " I have every useless thing in the world in my house there. The only thing wanting is the necessary thing, a great patch of open sky like this. Always try to keep a patch of sky above your life, little boy," he added, turning to me. " You have a soul in you of rare quality, an artist's nature ; never let it starve for lack of what it needs."

When, on our reaching the house, my aunt would send to ask us whether Mme. Goupil had indeed arrived late for mass, not one of us could inform her. Instead, we increased her anxiety by telling her that there was a painter at work in the church copying the window of Gilbert the Bad. Françoise was at once dispatched to the grocer's, but returned empty-handed owing to the absence of Théodore, whose dual profession of choirman, with a part in the maintenance of the fabric, and of grocer's assistant gave him not only relations with all sections of society, but an encyclopaedic knowledge of their affairs.

" Ah ! " my aunt would sigh, " I wish it were time for Eulalie to come. She is really the only person who will be able to tell me."

Eulalie was a limping, energetic, deaf spinster who had ' retired ' after the death of Mme. de la Bretonnerie, with whom she had been in service from her childhood, and had then taken a room beside the church, from which she would incessantly emerge, either to attend some service, or, when there was no service, to say a prayer by herself or to give Théodore a hand ; the rest of her time she spent in visiting sick persons like my aunt Léonie, to whom she would relate everything that had occurred at mass or vespers. She was not above adding occasional pocket-money to the little income

which was found for her by the family of her old employers
by going from time to time to look after the Curé's linen,
or that of some other person of note in the clerical world of
Combray. Above a mantle of black cloth she wore a little
white coif that seemed almost to attach her to some Order,
and an infirmity of the skin had stained part of her cheeks
and her crooked nose the bright red colour of balsam. Her
visits were the one great distraction in the life of my aunt
Léonie, who now saw hardly anyone else, except the reverend
Curé. My aunt had by degrees erased every other visitor's
name from her list, because they all committed the fatal
error, in her eyes, of falling into one or other of the two
categories of people she most detested. One group, the worse
of the two, and the one of which she rid herself first, consisted of those who advised her not to take so much care of
herself, and preached (even if only negatively and with no
outward signs beyond an occasional disapproving silence or
doubting smile) the subversive doctrine that a sharp walk in
the sun and a good red beefsteak would do her more good
(her, who had had two dreadful sips of Vichy water on her
stomach for fourteen hours !) than all her medicine bottles
and her bed. The other category was composed of people
who appeared to believe that she was more seriously ill than
she thought, in fact that she was as seriously ill as she said.
And so none of those whom she had allowed upstairs to her
room, after considerable hesitation and at Françoise's urgent
request, and who in the course of their visit had shewn how
unworthy they were of the honour which had been done
them by venturing a timid : " Don't you think that if you
were just to stir out a little on really fine days . . .? " or who,
on the other hand, when she said to them : " I am very low,
very low ; nearing the end, dear friends ! " had replied :

" Ah, yes, when one has no strength left ! Still, you may last a while yet " ; each party alike might be certain that her doors would never open to them again. And if Françoise was amused by the look of consternation on my aunt's face whenever she saw, from her bed, any of these people in the Rue du Saint-Esprit, who looked as if they were coming to see her, or heard her own door-bell ring, she would laugh far more heartily, as at a clever trick, at my aunt's devices (which never failed) for having them sent away, and at their look of discomfiture when they had to turn back without having seen her ; and would be filled with secret admiration for her mistress, whom she felt to be superior to all these other people, inasmuch as she could and did contrive not to see them. In short, my aunt stipulated, at one and the same time, that whoever came to see her must approve of her way of life, commiserate with her in her sufferings, and assure her of an ultimate recovery

In all this Eulalie excelled. My aunt might say to her twenty times in a minute : " The end is come at last, my poor Eulalie ! ", twenty times Eulalie would retort with : " Knowing your illness as you do, Mme. Octave, you will live to be a hundred, as Mme. Sazerin said to me only yesterday." For one of Eulalie's most rooted beliefs, and one that the formidable list of corrections which her experience must have compiled was powerless to eradicate, was that Mme. Sazerat's name was really Mme. Sazerin.

" I do not ask to live to a hundred," my aunt would say, for she preferred to have no definite limit fixed to the number of her days.

And since, besides this, Eulalie knew, as no one else knew, how to distract my aunt without tiring her, her visits, which took place regularly every Sunday, unless something unfore-

seen occurred to prevent them, were for my aunt a pleasure
the prospect of which kept her on those days in a state of
expectation, appetising enough to begin with, but at once
changing to the agony of a hunger too long unsatisfied if
Eulalie were a minute late in coming. For, if unduly prolonged, the rapture of waiting for Eulalie became a torture,
and my aunt would never cease from looking at the time,
and yawning, and complaining of each of her symptoms in
turn. Eulalie's ring, if it sounded from the front door at the
very end of the day, when she was no longer expecting it,
would almost make her ill. For the fact was that on Sundays
she thought of nothing else than this visit, and the moment
that our luncheon was ended Françoise would become impatient for us to leave the dining-room so that she might go
upstairs to 'occupy' my aunt. But—and this more than
ever from the day on which fine weather definitely set in at
Combray—the proud hour of noon, descending from the
steeple of Saint-Hilaire which it blazoned for a moment with
the twelve points of its sonorous crown, would long have
echoed about our table, beside the 'holy bread,' which too
had come in, after church, in its familiar way ; and we would
still be found seated in front of our Arabian Nights plates,
weighed down by the heat of the day, and even more by our
heavy meal. For upon the permanent foundation of eggs,
cutlets, potatoes, preserves, and biscuits, whose appearance on
the table she no longer announced to us, Françoise would add
—as the labour of fields and orchards, the harvest of the tides,
the luck of the markets, the kindness of neighbours, and her
own genius might provide ; and so effectively that our bill
of fare, like the quatrefoils that were carved on the porches of
cathedrals in the thirteenth century, reflected to some extent
the march of the seasons and the incidents of human life—a

brill, because the fish-woman had guaranteed its freshness;
a turkey, because she had seen a beauty in the market at
Roussainville-le-Pin ; cardoons with marrow, because she had
never done them for us in that way before; a roast leg of
mutton, because the fresh air made one hungry and there
would be plenty of time for it to 'settle down' in the seven
hours before dinner; spinach, by way of a change; apricots,
because they were still hard to get; gooseberries, because in
another fortnight there would be none left; raspberries,
which M. Swann had brought specially; cherries, the first
to come from the cherry-tree, which had yielded none for
the last two years; a cream cheese, of which in those days I
was extremely fond; an almond cake, because she had ordered
one the evening before; a fancy loaf, because it was our turn
to 'offer' the holy bread. And when all these had been
eaten, a work composed expressly for ourselves, but dedicated
more particularly to my father, who had a fondness for such
things, a cream of chocolate, inspired in the mind, created
by the hand of Françoise, would be laid before us, light and
fleeting as an 'occasional piece' of music, into which she
had poured the whole of her talent. Anyone who refused to
partake of it, saying : "No, thank you, I have finished ;
I am not hungry," would at once have been lowered to the
level of the Philistines who, when an artist makes them a
present of one of his works, examine its weight and material,
whereas what is of value is the creator's intention and his
signature. To have left even the tiniest morsel in the dish
would have shewn as much discourtesy as to rise and leave
a concert hall while the 'piece' was still being played, and
under the composer's very eyes.

At length my mother would say to me : "Now, don't
stay here all day ; you can go up to your room if you are too

hot outside, but get a little fresh air first ; don't start reading immediately after your food."

And I would go and sit down beside the pump and its trough, ornamented here and there, like a gothic font, with a salamander, which modelled upon a background of crumbling stone the quick relief of its slender, allegorical body ; on the bench without a back, in the shade of a lilac-tree, in that little corner of the garden which communicated, by a service door, with the Rue du Saint-Esprit, and from whose neglected soil rose, on two steps, an outcrop from the house itself and apparently a separate building, my aunt's back-kitchen. One could see its red-tiled floor gleaming like porphyry. It seemed not so much the cave of Françoise as a little temple of Venus. It would be overflowing with the offerings of the milkman, the fruiterer, the greengrocer, come sometimes from distant villages to dedicate here the first-fruits of their fields. And its roof was always surmounted by the cooing of a dove.

In earlier days I would not have lingered in the sacred grove which surrounded this temple, for, before going upstairs to read, I would steal into the little sitting-room which my uncle Adolphe, a brother of my grandfather and an old soldier who had retired from the service as a major, used to occupy on the ground floor, a room which, even when its opened windows let in the heat, if not actually the rays of the sun which seldom penetrated so far, would never fail to emit that vague and yet fresh odour, suggesting at once an open-air and an old-fashioned kind of existence, which sets and keeps the nostrils dreaming when one goes into a disused gun-room. But for some years now I had not gone into my uncle Adolphe's room, since he no longer came to Combray on account of a quarrel which had arisen between him and my family, by my fault, and in the following circumstances : Once or twice every month, in Paris, I used to be sent to pay him a visit, as he was finishing his luncheon, wearing a plain alpaca coat, and waited upon by his servant in a working-jacket of striped linen, purple and white. He would complain that I had not been to see him for a long time ; that he was being neglected ; he would offer me a marchpane or a tangerine, and we would cross a room in which no one ever sat, whose fire was never lighted, whose walls were picked out with gilded mouldings, its ceiling painted blue in imitation of the sky, and its furniture upholstered in satin, as at my grandparents', only yellow ; then we would enter what he called his 'study,' a room whose walls were hung with prints which shewed, against a dark background, a plump and rosy goddess driving a car, or standing upon a globe, or wearing a star on her brow ; pictures which were popular under the Second Empire because there was thought to be something about them that suggested Pompeii, which were then generally despised, and which now people are beginning to collect again for one single and consistent reason (despite any others which they may advance), namely, that they suggest the Second Empire. And there I would stay with my uncle until his man came, with a message from the coachman, to ask him at what time he would like the carriage. My uncle would then be lost in meditation, while his astonished servant stood there, not daring to disturb him by the least movement, wondering and waiting for his answer, which never varied. For in the end, after a supreme crisis of hesitation, my uncle would utter, infallibly, the words : " A quarter past two," which the servant would echo with amazement, but without disputing them : " A quarter past two ! Very good, sir . . . I will go and tell him. . . ."

At this date I was a lover of the theatre : a Platonic lover, of necessity, since my parents had not yet allowed me to enter one, and so incorrect was the picture I drew for myself of the pleasures to be enjoyed there that I almost believed that each of the spectators looked, as into a stereoscope, upon a stage and scenery which existed for himself alone, though closely resembling the thousand other spectacles presented to the rest of the audience individually.

Every morning I would hasten to the Moriss column to see what new plays it announced. Nothing could be more disinterested or happier than the dreams with which these announcements filled my mind, dreams which took their form from the inevitable associations of the words forming the title of the play, and also from the colour of the bills, still damp and wrinkled with paste, on which those words stood out. Nothing, unless it were such strange titles as the *Testament de César Girodot*, or *Œdipe-Roi*, inscribed not on the green bills of the Opéra-Comique, but on the wine-coloured bills of the Comédie-Française, nothing seemed to me to differ more profoundly from the sparkling white plume of the *Diamants de la Couronne* than the sleek, mysterious satin of the *Domino Noir* ; and since my parents had told me that, for my first visit to the theatre, I should have to choose between these two pieces, I would study exhaustively and in turn the title of one and the title of the other (for those were all that I knew of either), attempting to snatch from each a foretaste of the pleasure which it offered me, and to compare this pleasure with that latent in the other title, until in the end I had shewn myself such vivid, such compelling pictures of, on the one hand, a play of dazzling arrogance, and on the other a gentle, velvety play, that I was as little capable of deciding which play I should prefer to see as if, at the dinner-

table, they had obliged me to choose between rice *à l'impéra-
trice* and the famous cream of chocolate.

All my conversations with my playfellows bore upon
actors, whose art, although as yet I had no experience of it,
was the first of all its numberless forms in which Art itself
allowed me to anticipate its enjoyment. Between one actor's
tricks of intonation and inflection and another's, the most
trifling differences would strike me as being of an incalculable
importance. And from what I had been told of them I would
arrange them in the order of their talent in lists which I used
to murmur to myself all day long : lists which in the end
became petrified in my brain and were a source of annoyance
to it, being irremovable.

And later, in my schooldays, whenever I ventured in class,
when the master's head was turned, to communicate with
some new friend, I would always begin by asking him whether
he had begun yet to go to theatres, and if he agreed that our
greatest actor was undoubtedly Got, our second Delaunay,
and so on. And if, in his judgment, Febvre came below
Thiron, or Delaunay below Coquelin, the sudden volatility
which the name of Coquelin, forsaking its stony rigidity,
would engender in my mind, in which it moved upwards to
the second place, the rich vitality with which the name of
Delaunay would suddenly be furnished, to enable it to slip
down to fourth, would stimulate and fertilise my brain with
a sense of budding and blossoming life.

But if the thought of actors weighed so upon me, if the
sight of Maubant, coming out one afternoon from the
Théâtre-Français, had plunged me in the throes and sufferings of hopeless love, how much more did the name of a
' star,' blazing outside the doors of a theatre, how much
more, seen through the window of a brougham which passed

me in the street, the hair over her forehead abloom with roses, did the face of a woman who, I would think, was perhaps an actress, leave with me a lasting disturbance, a futile and painful effort to form a picture of her private life.

I classified, in order of talent, the most distinguished : Sarah Bernhardt, Berma, Bartet, Madeleine Brohan, Jeanne Samary ; but I was interested in them all. Now my uncle knew many of them personally, and also ladies of another class, not clearly distinguished from actresses in my mind. He used to entertain them at his house. And if we went to see him on certain days only, that was because on the other days ladies might come whom his family could not very well have met. So we at least thought ; as for my uncle, his fatal readiness to pay pretty widows (who had perhaps never been married) and countesses (whose high-sounding titles were probably no more than *noms de guerre*) the compliment of presenting them to my grandmother, or even of presenting to them some of our family jewels, had already embroiled him more than once with my grandfather. Often, if the name of some actress were mentioned in conversation, I would hear my father say, with a smile, to my mother : " One of your uncle's friends," and I would think of the weary novitiate through which, perhaps for years on end, a grown man, even a man of real importance, might have to pass, waiting on the doorstep of some such lady, while she refused to answer his letters and made her hall-porter drive him away ; and imagine that my uncle was able to dispense a little jackanapes like myself from all these sufferings by introducing me in his own home to the actress, unapproachable by all the world, but for him an intimate friend.

And so——on the pretext that some lesson, the hour of which had been altered, now came at such an awkward time that it had already more than once prevented me, and would continue to prevent me, from seeing my uncle—one day, not one of the days which he set apart for our visits, I took advantage of the fact that my parents had had luncheon earlier than usual ; I slipped out and, instead of going to read the playbills on their column, for which purpose I was allowed to go out unaccompanied, I ran all the way to his house. I noticed before his door a carriage and pair, with red carnations on the horses' blinkers and in the coachman's button-hole. As I climbed the staircase I could hear laughter and a woman's voice, and, as soon as I had rung, silence and the sound of shutting doors. The man-servant who let me in appeared embarrassed, and said that my uncle was extremely busy and probably could not see me ; he went in, however, to announce my arrival, and the same voice I had heard before said : " Oh, yes ! Do let him come in ; just for a moment ; it will be so amusing. Is that his photograph there, on your desk ? And his mother (your niece, isn't she?) beside it ? The image of her, isn't he ? I should so like to see the little chap, just for a second."

I could hear my uncle grumbling and growing angry ; finally the man-servant told me to come in.

On the table was the same plate of marchpanes that was always there ; my uncle wore the same alpaca coat as on other days ; but opposite to him, in a pink silk dress with a great necklace of pearls about her throat, sat a young woman who was just finishing a tangerine. My uncertainty whether I ought to address her as Madame or Mademoiselle made me blush, and not daring to look too much in her direction, in case I should be obliged to speak to her, I hurried across to kiss my uncle. She looked at me and smiled ; my uncle said " My nephew ! " without telling her my name or telling me hers, doubtless because, since his difficulties with my grand-father, he had endeavoured as far as possible to avoid any association of his family with this other class of acquaintance.

" How like his mother he is," said the lady.

" But you have never seen my niece, except in photo-graphs," my uncle broke in quickly, with a note of anger.

" I beg your pardon, dear friend, I passed her on the stair-case last year when you were so ill. It is true I only saw her for a moment, and your staircase is rather dark ; but I saw well enough to see how lovely she was. This young gentle-man has her beautiful eyes, and also *this*," she went on, tracing a line with one finger across the lower part of her forehead. " Tell me," she asked my uncle, " is your niece Mme. ——; is her name the same as yours ? "

" He takes most after his father," muttered my uncle, who was no more anxious to effect an introduction by proxy, in repeating Mamma's name aloud, than to bring the two together in the flesh. " He's his father all over, and also like my poor mother."

" I have not met his father, dear," said the lady in pink, bowing her head slightly, " and I never saw your poor mother. You will remember it was just after your great sorrow that we got to know one another."

I felt somewhat disillusioned, for this young lady was in no way different from other pretty women whom I had seen from time to time at home, especially the daughter of one of our cousins, to whose house I went every New Year's Day. Only better dressed ; otherwise my uncle's friend had the same quick and kindly glance, the same frank and friendly manner. I could find no trace in her of the theatrical appearance which I admired in photographs of actresses, nothing of the diabolical expression which would have been in keeping with the life she must lead. I had difficulty in believing that this was one of 'those women,' and certainly I should never have believed her one of the 'smart ones' had I not seen the carriage and pair, the pink dress, the pearl necklace, had I not been aware, too, that my uncle knew only the very best of them. But I asked myself how the millionaire who gave her her carriage and her flat and her jewels could find any pleasure in flinging his money away upon a woman who had so simple and respectable an appearance. And yet, when I thought of what her life must be like, its immorality disturbed me more, perhaps, than if it had stood before me in some concrete and recognisable form, by its secrecy and invisibility, like the plot of a novel, the hidden truth of a scandal which had driven out of the home of her middle-class parents and dedicated to the service of all mankind, which had brought to the flowering-point of her beauty, had raised to fame or notoriety this woman, the play of whose features, the intonations of whose voice, like so many others I already knew, made me regard her, in spite of myself, as a young lady of good family, her who was no longer of a family at all.

We had gone by this time into the 'study,' and my uncle, who seemed a trifle embarrassed by my presence, offered her a cigarette.

"No, thank you, dear friend," she said. "You know I only smoke the ones the Grand Duke sends me. I tell him that they make you jealous." And she drew from a case cigarettes covered with inscriptions in gold, in a foreign language. "Why, yes," she began again suddenly. "Of course I have met this young man's father with you. Isn't he your nephew? How on earth could I have forgotten? He was so nice, so charming to me," she went on, modestly

and with feeling. But when I thought to myself what must
actually have been the rude greeting (which, she made out,
had been so charming), I, who knew my father's coldness and
reserve, was shocked, as though at some indelicacy on his
part, at the contrast between the excessive recognition
bestowed on it and his never adequate geniality. It has since
struck me as one of the most touching aspects of the part
played in life by these idle, painstaking women that they devote all their generosity, all their talent, their transferable
dreams of sentimental beauty (for, like all artists, they never
seek to realise the value of those dreams, or to enclose them
in the four-square frame of everyday life), and their gold,
which counts for little, to the fashioning of a fine and precious
setting for the rubbed and scratched and ill-polished lives of
men. And just as this one filled the smoking-room, where my
uncle was entertaining her in his alpaca coat, with her
charming person, her dress of pink silk, her pearls, and the
refinement suggested by intimacy with a Grand Duke, so, in
the same way, she had taken some casual remark by my father,
had worked it up delicately, given it a 'turn,' a precious
title, set in it the gem of a glance from her own eyes, a gem
of the first water, blended of humility and gratitude ; and so
had given it back transformed into a jewel, a work of art,
into something altogether charming.

"Look here, my boy, it is time you went away," said my
uncle.

I rose ; I could scarcely resist a desire to kiss the hand of
the lady in pink, but I felt that to do so would require as
much audacity as a forcible abduction of her. My heart beat
loud while I counted out to myself " Shall I do it, shall I
not ? " and then I ceased to ask myself what I ought to do
so as at least to do something. Blindly, hotly, madly, flinging

aside all the reasons I had just found to support such action, I seized and raised to my lips the hand she held out to me.

"Isn't he delicious! Quite a ladies' man already; he takes after his uncle. He'll be a perfect 'gentleman,'" she went on, setting her teeth so as to give the word a kind of English accentuation. "Couldn't he come to me some day for 'a cup of tea,' as our friends across the channel say; he need only send me a 'blue' in the morning?"

I had not the least idea of what a 'blue' might be. I did not understand half the words which the lady used, but my fear lest there should be concealed in them some question which it would be impolite in me not to answer kept me from withdrawing my close attention from them, and I was beginning to feel extremely tired.

"No, no; it is impossible," said my uncle, shrugging his shoulders: "He is kept busy at home all day; he has plenty of work to do. He brings back all the prizes from his school," he added in a lower tone, so that I should not hear this falsehood and interrupt with a contradiction. "You can't tell; he may turn out a little Victor Hugo, a kind of Vaulabelle, don't you know."

"Oh, I love artistic people," replied the lady in pink; "there is no one like them for understanding women. Them, and really nice men like yourself. But please forgive my ignorance. Who, what is Vaulabelle? Is it those gilt books in the little glass case in your drawing-room? You know you promised to lend them to me; I will take great care of them."

My uncle, who hated lending people books, said nothing, and ushered me out into the hall. Madly in love with the lady in pink, I covered my old uncle's tobacco-stained cheeks with passionate kisses, and while he, awkwardly enough, gave me

to understand (without actually saying) that he would rather
I did not tell my parents about this visit, I assured him, with
tears in my eyes, that his kindness had made so strong an impression upon me that some day I would most certainly find
a way of expressing my gratitude. So strong an impression
had it made upon me that two hours later, after a string of
mysterious utterances which did not strike me as giving my
parents a sufficiently clear idea of the new importance with
which I had been invested, I found it simpler to let them
have a full account, omitting no detail, of the visit I had paid
that afternoon. In doing this I had no thought of causing my
uncle any unpleasantness. How could I have thought such a
thing, since I did not wish it ? And I could not suppose that
my parents would see any harm in a visit in which I myself
saw none. Every day of our lives does not some friend or other
ask us to make his apologies, without fail, to some woman to
whom he has been prevented from writing ; and do not we
forget to do so, feeling that this woman cannot attach much
importance to a silence which has none for ourselves ? I
imagined, like everyone else, that the brains of other people
were lifeless and submissive receptacles with no power of
specific reaction to any stimulus which might be applied to
them ; and I had not the least doubt that when I deposited
in the minds of my parents the news of the acquaintance I had
made at my uncle's I should at the same time transmit to them
the kindly judgment I myself had based on the introduction.
Unfortunately my parents had recourse to principles entirely
different from those which I suggested they should adopt
when they came to form their estimate of my uncle's conduct. My father and grandfather had ' words ' with him of
a violent order ; as I learned indirectly. A few days later,
passing my uncle in the street as he drove by in an open car-

riage, I felt at once all the grief, the gratitude, the remorse
which I should have liked to convey to him. Beside the immensity of these emotions I considered that merely to raise
my hat to him would be incongruous and petty, and might
make him think that I regarded myself as bound to shew him
no more than the commonest form of courtesy. I decided to
abstain from so inadequate a gesture, and turned my head
away. My uncle thought that, in doing so, I was obeying
my parents' orders ; he never forgave them ; and though he
did not die until many years later, not one of us ever set eyes
on him again.

And so I no longer used to go into the little sitting-
room (now kept shut) of my uncle Adolphe; instead, after
hanging about on the outskirts of the back-kitchen until
Françoise appeared on its threshold and announced : " I am
going to let the kitchen-maid serve the coffee and take up
the hot water ; it is time I went off to Mme. Octave,"
I would then decide to go indoors, and would go straight
upstairs to my room to read. The kitchen-maid was an abstract personality, a permanent institution to which an invariable set of attributes assured a sort of fixity and continuity
and identity throughout the long series of transitory human
shapes in which that personality was incarnate ; for we never
found the same girl there two years running. In the year in
which we ate such quantities of asparagus, the kitchen-
maid whose duty it was to dress them was a poor sickly
creature, some way ' gone ' in pregnancy when we arrived
at Combray for Easter, and it was indeed surprising that
Françoise allowed her to run so many errands in the town
and to do so much work in the house, for she was beginning to
find a difficulty in bearing before her the mysterious casket,
fuller and larger every day, whose splendid outline could be

detected through the folds of her ample smocks. These last recalled the cloaks in which Giotto shrouds some of the allegorical figures in his paintings, of which M. Swann had given me photographs. He it was who pointed out the resemblance, and when he inquired after the kitchen-maid he would say : " Well, how goes it with Giotto's Charity ? " And indeed the poor girl, whose pregnancy had swelled and stoutened every part of her, even to her face, and the vertical, squared outlines of her cheeks, did distinctly suggest those virgins, so strong and mannish as to seem matrons rather, in whom the Virtues are personified in the Arena Chapel. And I can see now that those Virtues and Vices of Padua resembled her in another respect as well. For just as the figure of this girl had been enlarged by the additional symbol which she carried in her body, without appearing to understand what it meant, without any rendering in her facial expression of all its beauty and spiritual significance, but carried as if it were an ordinary and rather heavy burden, so it is without any apparent suspicion of what she is about that the powerfully built housewife who is portrayed in the Arena beneath the label ' Caritas,' and a reproduction of whose portrait hung upon the wall of my schoolroom at Combray, incarnates that virtue, for it seems impossible that any thought of charity can ever have found expression in her vulgar and energetic face. By a fine stroke of the painter's invention she is tumbling all the treasures of the earth at her feet, but exactly as if she were treading grapes in a wine-press to extract their juice, or, still more, as if she had climbed on a heap of sacks to raise herself higher ; and she is holding out her flaming heart to God, or shall we say ' handing ' it to Him, exactly as a cook might hand up a corkscrew through the skylight of her underground kitchen to some one who had called down

to ask her for it from the ground-level above. The ' In-
vidia,' again, should have had some look on her face of envy.
But in this fresco, too, the symbol occupies so large a place
and is represented with such realism ; the serpent hissing
between the lips of Envy is so huge, and so completely fills
her wide-opened mouth that the muscles of her face are
strained and contorted, like a child's who is filling a balloon
with his breath, and that Envy, and we ourselves for that
matter, when we look at her, since all her attention and ours
are concentrated on the action of her lips, have no time,
almost, to spare for envious thoughts.

Despite all the admiration that M. Swann might profess
for these figures of Giotto, it was a long time before I could
find any pleasure in seeing in our schoolroom (where the
copies he had brought me were hung) that Charity devoid of
charity, that Envy who looked like nothing so much as a
plate in some medical book, illustrating the compression of the
glottis or uvula by a tumour in the tongue, or by the introduction of the operator's instrument, a Justice whose
greyish and meanly regular features were the very same as
those which adorned the faces of certain good and pious and
slightly withered ladies of Combray whom I used to see at
mass, many of whom had long been enrolled in the reserve
forces of Injustice. But in later years I understood that the
arresting strangeness, the special beauty of these frescoes lay
in the great part played in each of them by its symbols, while
the fact that these were depicted, not as symbols (for the
thought symbolised was nowhere expressed), but as real
things, actually felt or materially handled, added something
more precise and more literal to their meaning, something
more concrete and more striking to the lesson they imparted.
And even in the case of the poor kitchen-maid, was not our

attention incessantly drawn to her belly by the load which filled it ; and in the same way, again, are not the thoughts of men and women in the agony of death often turned towards the practical, painful, obscure, internal, intestinal aspect, towards that ' seamy side ' of death which is, as it happens, the side that death actually presents to them and forces them to feel, a side which far more closely resembles a crushing burden, a difficulty in breathing, a destroying thirst, than the abstract idea to which we are accustomed to give the name of Death ?

There must have been a strong element of reality in those Virtues and Vices of Padua, since they appeared to me to be as much alive as the pregnant servant-girl, while she herself appeared scarcely less allegorical than they. And, quite possibly, this lack (or seeming lack) of participation by a person's soul in the significant marks of its own special virtue has, apart from its aesthetic meaning, a reality which, if not strictly psychological, may at least be called physiognomical. Later on, when, in the course of my life, I have had occasion to meet with, in convents for instance, literally saintly examples of practical charity, they have generally had the brisk, decided, undisturbed, and slightly brutal air of a busy surgeon, the face in which one can discern no commiseration, no tenderness at the sight of suffering humanity, and no fear of hurting it, the face devoid of gentleness or sympathy, the sublime face of true goodness.

Then while the kitchen-maid—who, all unawares, made the superior qualities of Françoise shine with added lustre, just as Error, by force of contrast, enhances the triumph of Truth—took in coffee which (according to Mamma) was nothing more than hot water, and then carried up to our rooms hot water which was barely tepid, I would be lying stretched out on my bed, a book in my hand, in my room

which trembled with the effort to defend its frail, transparent
coolness against the afternoon sun, behind its almost closed
shutters through which, however, a reflection of the sunlight
had contrived to slip in on its golden wings, remaining
motionless, between glass and woodwork, in a corner, like a
butterfly poised upon a flower. It was hardly light enough
for me to read, and my feeling of the day's brightness and
splendour was derived solely from the blows struck down
below, in the Rue de la Cure, by Camus (whom Françoise
had assured that my aunt was not 'resting' and that he
might therefore make a noise), upon some old packing-cases
from which nothing would really be sent flying but the dust,
though the din of them, in the resonant atmosphere that ac-
companies hot weather, seemed to scatter broadcast a rain of
blood-red stars; and from the flies who performed for my
benefit, in their small concert, as it might be the chamber
music of summer; evoking heat and light quite differently
from an air of human music which, if you happen to have
heard it during a fine summer, will always bring that summer
back to your mind, the flies' music is bound to the season
by a closer, a more vital tie—born of sunny days, and not
to be reborn but with them, containing something of their
essential nature, it not merely calls up their image in our
memory, but gives us a guarantee that they do really exist,
that they are close around us, immediately accessible.

This dim freshness of my room was to the broad daylight
of the street what the shadow is to the sunbeam, that is to
say, equally luminous, and presented to my imagination the
entire panorama of summer, which my senses, if I had been
out walking, could have tasted and enjoyed in fragments
only; and so was quite in harmony with my state of repose,
which (thanks to the adventures related in my books, which

had just excited it) bore, like a hand reposing motionless in a stream of running water, the shock and animation of a torrent of activity and life.

But my grandmother, even if the weather, after growing too hot, had broken, and a storm, or just a shower, had burst over us, would come up and beg me to go outside. And as I did not wish to leave off my book, I would go on with it in the garden, under the chestnut-tree, in a little sentry-box of canvas and matting, in the farthest recesses of which I used to sit and feel that I was hidden from the eyes of anyone who might be coming to call upon the family.

And then my thoughts, did not they form a similar sort of hiding-hole, in the depths of which I felt that I could bury myself and remain invisible even when I was looking at what went on outside? When I saw any external object, my consciousness that I was seeing it would remain between me and it, enclosing it in a slender, incorporeal outline which prevented me from ever coming directly in contact with the material form ; for it would volatilise itself in some way before I could touch it, just as an incandescent body which is moved towards something wet never actually touches moisture, since it is always preceded, itself, by a zone of evaporation. Upon the sort of screen, patterned with different states and impressions, which my consciousness would quietly unfold while I was reading, and which ranged from the most deeply hidden aspirations of my heart to the wholly external view of the horizon spread out before my eyes at the foot of the garden, what was from the first the most permanent and the most intimate part of me, the lever whose incessant movements controlled all the rest, was my belief in the philosophic richness and beauty of the book I was reading, and my desire to appropriate these to myself, what-

ever the book might be. For even if I had purchased it at
Combray, having seen it outside Borange's, whose grocery
lay too far from our house for Françoise to be able to deal
there, as she did with Camus, but who enjoyed better custom
as a stationer and bookseller ; even if I had seen it, tied
with string to keep it in its place in the mosaic of monthly
parts and pamphlets which adorned either side of his doorway,
a doorway more mysterious, more teeming with suggestion
than that of a cathedral, I should have noticed and bought
it there simply because I had recognised it as a book which
had been well spoken of, in my hearing, by the schoolmaster or
the school-friend who, at that particular time, seemed to me
to be entrusted with the secret of Truth and Beauty, things
half-felt by me, half-incomprehensible, the full understanding
of which was the vague but permanent object of my thoughts.

Next to this central belief, which, while I was reading,
would be constantly in motion from my inner self to the outer
world, towards the discovery of Truth, came the emotions
aroused in me by the action in which I would be taking part,
for these afternoons were crammed with more dramatic and
sensational events than occur, often, in a whole lifetime.
These were the events which took place in the book I was
reading. It is true that the people concerned in them were
not what Françoise would have called ' real people.' But
none of the feelings which the joys or misfortunes of a
' real ' person awaken in us can be awakened except
through a mental picture of those joys or misfortunes ; and
the ingenuity of the first novelist lay in his understanding
that, as the picture was the one essential element in the
complicated structure of our emotions, so that simplification
of it which consisted in the suppression, pure and simple,
of ' real ' people would be a decided improvement. A

'real' person, profoundly as we may sympathise with him,
is in a great measure perceptible only through our senses,
that is to say, he remains opaque, offers a dead weight which
our sensibilities have not the strength to lift. If some misfortune comes to him, it is only in one small section of the
complete idea we have of him that we are capable of feeling
any emotion; indeed it is only in one small section of the
complete idea he has of himself that he is capable of feeling
any emotion either. The novelist's happy discovery was to
think of substituting for those opaque sections, impenetrable
by the human spirit, their equivalent in immaterial sections,
things, that is, which the spirit can assimilate to itself. After
which it matters not that the actions, the feelings of this new
order of creatures appear to us in the guise of truth, since we
have made them our own, since it is in ourselves that they are
happening, that they are holding in thrall, while we turn
over, feverishly, the pages of the book, our quickened breath
and staring eyes. And once the novelist has brought us to
that state, in which, as in all purely mental states, every
emotion is multiplied ten-fold, into which his book comes to
disturb us as might a dream, but a dream more lucid, and of
a more lasting impression than those which come to us in
sleep; why, then, for the space of an hour he sets free within
us all the joys and sorrows in the world, a few of which, only,
we should have to spend years of our actual life in getting to
know, and the keenest, the most intense of which would never
have been revealed to us because the slow course of their
development stops our perception of them. It is the same in
life; the heart changes, and that is our worst misfortune;
but we learn of it only from reading or by imagination; for
in reality its alteration, like that of certain natural phenomena,
is so gradual that, even if we are able to distinguish, succes-

sively, each of its different states, we are still spared the actual sensation of change.

Next to, but distinctly less intimate a part of myself than this human element, would come the view, more or less projected before my eyes, of the country in which the action of the story was taking place, which made a far stronger impression on my mind than the other, the actual landscape which would meet my eyes when I raised them from my book. In this way, for two consecutive summers I used to sit in the heat of our Combray garden, sick with a longing inspired by the book I was then reading for a land of mountains and rivers, where I could see an endless vista of sawmills, where beneath the limpid currents fragments of wood lay mouldering in beds of watercress ; and near by, rambling and clustering along low walls, purple flowers and red. And since there was always lurking in my mind the dream of a woman who would enrich me with her love, that dream in those two summers used to be quickened with the freshness and coolness of running water ; and whoever she might be, the woman whose image I called to mind, purple flowers and red would at once spring up on either side of her like complementary colours.

This was not only because an image of which we dream remains for ever distinguished, is adorned and enriched by the association of colours not its own which may happen to surround it in our mental picture ; for the scenes in the books I read were to me not merely scenery more vividly portrayed by my imagination than any which Combray could spread before my eyes but otherwise of the same kind. Because of the selection that the author had made of them, because of the spirit of faith in which my mind would exceed and anticipate his printed word, as it might be interpreting a revelation, these scenes used to give me the impression—one which I hardly ever derived from any place in which I might happen to be, and never from our garden, that undistinguished product of the strictly conventional fantasy of the gardener whom my grandmother so despised—of their being actually part of Nature herself, and worthy to be studied and explored.

Had my parents allowed me, when I read a book, to pay a visit to the country it described, I should have felt that I was making an enormous advance towards the ultimate conquest of truth. For even if we have the sensation of being always enveloped in, surrounded by our own soul, still it does not seem a fixed and immovable prison ; rather do we seem to be borne away with it, and perpetually struggling to pass beyond it, to break out into the world, with a perpetual discouragement as we hear endlessly, all around us, that unvarying sound which is no echo from without, but the resonance of a vibration from within. We try to discover in things, endeared to us on that account, the spiritual glamour which we ourselves have cast upon them ; we are disillusioned, and learn that they are in themselves barren and devoid of the charm which they owed, in our minds, to the association of certain ideas ; sometimes we mobilise all our spiritual forces in a glittering array so as to influence and subjugate other human beings who, as we very well know, are situated outside ourselves, where we can never reach them. And so, if I always imagined the woman I loved as in a setting of whatever places I most longed, at the time, to visit ; if in my secret longings it was she who attracted me to them, who opened to me the gate of an unknown world, that was not by the mere hazard of a simple association of thoughts ; no, it was because my dreams of travel and of love were only moments—which I isolate artificially to-day as though I were cutting sections, at different heights, in a jet of water, rainbow-flashing but seemingly without flow or motion—were only drops in a single, undeviating, irresistible outrush of all the forces of my life.

And then, as I continue to trace the outward course of these impressions from their close-packed intimate source in my consciousness, and before I come to the horizon of reality which envelops them, I discover pleasures of another kind, those of being comfortably seated, of tasting the good scent on the air, of not being disturbed by any visitor ; and, when an hour chimed from the steeple of Saint-Hilaire, of watching what was already spent of the afternoon fall drop by drop until I heard the last stroke which enabled me to add up the total sum, after which the silence that followed seemed to herald the beginning, in the blue sky above me, of that long part of the day still allowed me for reading, until the good dinner which Françoise was even now preparing should come to strengthen and refresh me after the strenuous pursuit of its hero through the pages of my book. And, as each hour struck, it would seem to me that a few seconds only had passed since the hour before ; the latest would inscribe itself, close to its predecessor, on the sky's surface, and I would be unable to believe that sixty minutes could be squeezed into the tiny arc of blue which was comprised between their two golden figures. Sometimes it would even happen that this precocious hour would sound two strokes more than the last ; there must then have been an hour which I had not heard strike ; something which had taken place had not taken place for me ; the fascination of my book, a magic as potent as the deepest slumber, had stopped my enchanted ears and had obliterated the sound of that golden bell from the azure surface of the enveloping silence. Sweet Sunday afternoons beneath the chestnut-tree in our Combray garden, from which I was careful to eliminate every commonplace incident of my actual life, replacing them by a career of strange adventures and ambitions in a land watered by living streams, you still recall those adventures and ambitions to my mind when I think of you, and you embody and preserve them by virtue of having little by little drawn round and enclosed them (while I went on with my book and the heat of the day declined) in the gradual crystallisation, slowly altering in form and dappled with a pattern of chestnut-leaves, of your silent, sonorous, fragrant, limpid hours.

Sometimes I would be torn from my book, in the middle of the afternoon, by the gardener's daughter, who came running like a mad thing, overturning an orange-tree in its tub, cutting a finger, breaking a tooth, and screaming out "They're coming, they're coming!" so that Françoise and I should run too and not miss anything of the show. That was on days when the cavalry stationed in Combray went out for some military exercise, going as a rule by the Rue Sainte-Hildegarde. While our servants, sitting in a row on their chairs outside the garden railings, stared at the people of Combray taking their Sunday walks and were stared at in return, the gardener's daughter, through the gap which there was between two houses far away in the Avenue de la Gare, would have spied the glitter of helmets. The servants then hurried in with their chairs, for when the troopers filed through the Rue Sainte-Hildegarde they filled it from side to side, and their jostling horses scraped against the walls of the houses, covering and drowning the pavements like banks which present too narrow a channel to a river in flood.

"Poor children," Françoise would exclaim, in tears almost before she had reached the railings; "poor boys, to be mown down like grass in a meadow. It's just shocking to think of," she would go on, laying a hand over her heart, where presumably she had felt the shock.

" A fine sight, isn't it, Mme. Françoise, all these young fellows not caring two straws for their lives ? " the gardener would ask, just to ' draw ' her. And he would not have spoken in vain.

" Not caring for their lives, is it ? Why, what in the world is there that we should care for if it's not our lives, the only gift the Lord never offers us a second time ? Oh dear, oh dear ; you're right all the same ; it's quite true, they don't care ! I can remember them in '70 ; in those wretched wars they've no fear of death left in them ; they're nothing more nor less than madmen ; and then they aren't worth the price of a rope to hang them with ; they're not men any more, they're lions." For by her way of thinking, to compare a man with a lion, which she used to pronounce ' lie-on,' was not at all complimentary to the man.

The Rue Sainte-Hildegarde turned too sharply for us to be able to see people approaching at any distance, and it was only through the gap between those two houses in the Avenue de la Gare that we could still make out fresh helmets racing along towards us, and flashing in the sunlight. The gardener wanted to know whether there were still many to come, and he was thirsty besides, with the sun beating down upon his head. So then, suddenly, his daughter would leap out, as though from a beleaguered city, would make a sortie, turn the street corner, and, having risked her life a hundred times over, reappear and bring us, with a jug of liquorice-water, the news that there were still at least a thousand of them, pouring along without a break from the direction of Thiberzy and Méséglise. Françoise and the gardener, having ' made up ' their difference, would discuss the line to be followed in case of war.

" Don't you see, Françoise," he would say, " Revolution would be better, because then no one would need to join in unless he liked."

" Oh, yes, I can see that, certainly ; it's more straightforward."

The gardener believed that, as soon as war was declared, they would stop all the railways.

" Yes, to be sure ; so that we sha'n't get away," said Françoise.

And the gardener would assent, with " Ay, they're the cunning ones," for he would not allow that war was anything but a kind of trick which the state attempted to play on the people, or that there was a man in the world who would not run away from it if he had the chance to do so.

But Françoise would hasten back to my aunt, and I would return to my book, and the servants would take their places again outside the gate to watch the dust settle on the pavement, and the excitement caused by the passage of the soldiers subside. Long after order had been restored, an abnormal tide of humanity would continue to darken the streets of Combray. And in front of every house, even of those where it was not, as a rule, ' done,' the servants, and sometimes even the masters would sit and stare, festooning their doorsteps with a dark, irregular fringe, like the border of shells and sea-weed which a stronger tide than usual leaves on the beach, as though trimming it with embroidered crape, when the sea itself has retreated.

Except on such days as these, however, I would as a rule be left to read in peace. But the interruption which a visit from Swann once made, and the commentary which he then

supplied to the course of my reading, which had brought me
to the work of an author quite new to me, called Bergotte,
had this definite result that for a long time afterwards it was
not against a wall gay with spikes of purple blossom, but on a
wholly different background, the porch of a gothic cathedral,
that I would see outlined the figure of one of the women of
whom I dreamed.

I had heard Bergotte spoken of, for the first time, by a
friend older than myself, for whom I had a strong admiration, a precious youth of the name of Bloch. Hearing me
confess my love of the *Nuit d'Octobre*, he had burst out in a
bray of laughter, like a bugle-call, and told me, by way of
warning : " You must conquer your vile taste for A. de
Musset, Esquire. He is a bad egg, one of the very worst, a
pretty detestable specimen. I am bound to admit, natheless,"
he added graciously, " that he, and even the man Racine,
did, each of them, once in his life, compose a line which is
not only fairly rhythmical, but has also what is in my eyes
the supreme merit of meaning absolutely nothing. One is

La blanche Oloossone et la blanche Camire,

and the other

La fille de Minos et de Pasiphaë.

They were submitted to my judgment, as evidence for the
defence of the two runagates, in an article by my very dear
master Father Lecomte, who is found pleasing in the sight
of the immortal gods. By which token, here is a book which
I have not the time, just now, to read, a book recommended,
it would seem, by that colossal fellow. He regards, or so
they tell me, its author, one Bergotte, Esquire, as a subtle
scribe, more subtle, indeed, than any beast of the field ; and,
albeit he exhibits on occasion a critical pacificism, a tenderness

in suffering fools, for which it is impossible to account, and hard to make allowance, still his word has weight with me as it were the Delphic Oracle. Read you then this lyrical prose, and, if the Titanic master-builder of rhythm who composed *Bhagavat* and the *Lévrier de Magnus* speaks not falsely, then, by Apollo, you may taste, even you, my master, the ambrosial joys of Olympus." It was in an ostensible vein of sarcasm that he had asked me to call him, and that he himself called me, " my master." But, as a matter of fact, we each derived a certain amount of satisfaction from the mannerism, being still at the age in which one believes that one gives a thing real existence by giving it a name.

Unfortunately I was not able to set at rest, by further talks with Bloch, in which I might have insisted upon an explanation, the doubts he had engendered in me when he told me that fine lines of poetry (from which I, if you please, expected nothing less than the revelation of truth itself) were all the finer if they meant absolutely nothing. For, as it happened, Bloch was not invited to the house again. At first, he had been well received there. It is true that my grandfather made out that, whenever I formed a strong attachment to any one of my friends and brought him home with me, that friend was invariably a Jew ; to which he would not have objected on principle—indeed his own friend Swann was of Jewish extraction—had he not found that the Jews whom I chose as friends were not usually of the best type. And so I was hardly ever able to bring a new friend home without my grandfather's humming the " O, God of our fathers " from *La Juive*, or else "`Israel, break thy chain," singing the tune alone, of course, to an " um-ti-tum-ti-tum, tra-la "; but I used to be afraid of my friend's recognising the sound, and so being able to reconstruct the words.

Before seeing them, merely on hearing their names, about which, as often as not, there was nothing particularly Hebraic, he would divine not only the Jewish origin of such of my friends as might indeed be of the chosen people, but even some dark secret which was hidden in their family.

" And what do they call your friend who is coming this evening ? "

" Dumont, grandpapa."

" Dumont ! Oh, I'm frightened of Dumont."

And he would sing :

> Archers, be on your guard !
> Watch without rest, without sound,

and then, after a few adroit questions on points of detail, he would call out " On guard ! on guard," or, if it were the victim himself who had already arrived, and had been obliged, unconsciously, by my grandfather's subtle examination, to admit his origin, then my grandfather, to shew us that he had no longer any doubts, would merely look at us, humming almost inaudibly the air of

> What ! do you hither guide the feet
> Of this timid Israelite ?

or of

> Sweet vale of Hebron, dear paternal fields,

or, perhaps, of

> Yes, I am of the chosen race.

These little eccentricities on my grandfather's part implied no ill-will whatsoever towards my friends. But Bloch had displeased my family for other reasons. He had begun by annoying my father, who, seeing him come in with wet clothes, had asked him with keen interest :

" Why, M. Bloch, is there a change in the weather ; has it been raining ? I can't understand it ; the barometer has been ' set fair.' "

Which drew from Bloch nothing more instructive than " Sir, I am absolutely incapable of telling you whether it has rained. I live so resolutely apart from physical contingencies that my senses no longer trouble to inform me of them."

" My poor boy," said my father after Bloch had gone, " your friend is out of his mind. Why, he couldn't even tell me what the weather was like. As if there could be anything more interesting ! He is an imbecile."

Next, Bloch had displeased my grandmother because, after luncheon, when she complained of not feeling very well, he had stifled a sob and wiped the tears from his eyes.

" You cannot imagine that he is sincere," she observed to me. " Why, he doesn't know me. Unless he's mad, of course."

And finally he had upset the whole household when he arrived an hour and a half late for luncheon and covered with mud from head to foot, and made not the least apology, saying merely : " I never allow myself to be influenced in the smallest degree either by atmospheric disturbances or by the arbitrary divisions of what is known as Time. I would willingly reintroduce to society the opium pipe of China or the Malayan kriss, but I am wholly and entirely without instruction in those infinitely more pernicious (besides being quite bleakly bourgeois) implements, the umbrella and the watch."

In spite of all this he would still have been received at Combray. He was, of course, hardly the friend my parents would have chosen for me ; they had, in the end, decided

that the tears which he had shed on hearing of my grandmother's illness were genuine enough ; but they knew,
either instinctively or from their own experience, that our
early impulsive emotions have but little influence over our
later actions and the conduct of our lives ; and that regard
for moral obligations, loyalty to our friends, patience in
finishing our work, obedience to a rule of life, have a surer
foundation in habits solidly formed and blindly followed than
in these momentary transports, ardent but sterile. They
would have preferred to Bloch, as companions for myself,
boys who would have given me no more than it is proper,
by all the laws of middle-class morality, for boys to give one
another, who would not unexpectedly send me a basket of
fruit because they happened, that morning, to have thought
of me with affection, but who, since they were incapable of
inclining in my favour, by any single impulse of their imagination and emotions, the exact balance of the duties and claims
of friendship, were as incapable of loading the scales to my
prejudice. Even the injuries we do them will not easily divert
from the path of their duty towards us those conventional
natures of which my great-aunt furnished a type : who, after
quarrelling for years with a niece, to whom she never spoke
again, yet made no change in the will in which she had left
that niece the whole of her fortune, because she was her next-
of-kin, and it was the ' proper thing ' to do.

But I was fond of Bloch ; my parents wished me to be
happy ; and the insoluble problems which I set myself on
such texts as the ' absolutely meaningless ' beauty of *La
fille de Minos et de Pasiphaë* tired me more and made me more
unwell than I should have been after further talks with him,
unwholesome as those talks might seem to my mother's mind.
And he would still have been received at Combray but for

one thing. That same night, after dinner, having informed me (a piece of news which had a great influence on my later life, making it happier at one time and then more unhappy) that no woman ever thought of anything but love, and that there was not one of them whose resistance a man could not overcome, he had gone on to assure me that he had heard it said on unimpeachable authority that my great-aunt herself had led a 'gay' life in her younger days, and had been notoriously 'kept.' I could not refrain from passing on so important a piece of information to my parents ; the next time Bloch called he was not admitted, and afterwards, when I met him in the street, he greeted me with extreme coldness.

But in the matter of Bergotte he had spoken truly.

For the first few days, like a tune which will be running in one's head and maddening one soon enough, but of which one has not for the moment 'got hold,' the things I was to love so passionately in Bergotte's style had not yet caught my eye. I could not, it is true, lay down the novel of his which I was reading, but I fancied that I was interested in the story alone, as in the first dawn of love, when we go every day to meet a woman at some party or entertainment by the charm of which we imagine it is that we are attracted. Then I observed the rare, almost archaic phrases which he liked to employ at certain points, where a hidden flow of harmony, a prelude contained and concealed in the work itself would animate and elevate his style ; and it was at such points as these, too, that he would begin to speak of the " vain dream of life," of the " inexhaustible torrent of fair forms," of the " sterile, splendid torture of understanding and loving," of the " moving effigies which ennoble for all time the charming and venerable fronts of our cathedrals " ; that he would express a whole system of philosophy, new to me, by the use of marvellous imagery, to the inspiration of which I would naturally have ascribed that sound of harping which began to chime and echo in my ears, an accompaniment to which that imagery added something ethereal and sublime. One of these passages of Bergotte, the third or fourth which I had detached from the rest, filled me with a joy to which the meagre joy I had tasted in the first passage bore no comparison, a joy which I felt myself to have experienced in some innermost chamber of my soul, deep, undivided, vast, from which all obstructions and partitions seemed to have been swept away. For what had happened was that, while I recognised in this passage the same taste for uncommon phrases, the same bursts of music, the same idealist philosophy which had been present in the earlier passages without my having taken them into account as the source of my pleasure, I now no longer had the impression of being confronted by a particular passage in one of Bergotte's works, which traced a purely bi-dimensional figure in outline upon the surface of my mind, but rather of the ' ideal passage ' of Bergotte, common to every one of his books, and to which all the earlier, similar passages, now becoming merged in it, had added a kind of density and volume, by which my own understanding seemed to be enlarged.

I was by no means Bergotte's sole admirer ; he was the favourite writer also of a friend of my mother's, a highly literary lady ; while Dr. du Boulbon had kept all his patients waiting until he finished Bergotte's latest volume ; and it was from his consulting room, and from a house in a park near Combray that some of the first seeds were scattered of that taste for Bergotte, a rare growth in those days, but now so universally acclimatised that one finds it flowering everywhere throughout Europe and America, and even in the tiniest villages, rare still in its refinement, but in that alone.

What my mother's friend, and, it would seem, what Dr. du Boulbon liked above all in the writings of Bergotte was just what I liked, the same flow of melody, the same old-fashioned phrases, and certain others, quite simple and familiar, but so placed by him, in such prominence, as to hint at a particular quality of taste on his part ; and also, in the sad parts of his books, a sort of roughness, a tone that was almost harsh. And he himself, no doubt, realised that these were his principal attractions. For in his later books, if he had hit upon some great truth, or upon the name of an historic cathedral, he would break off his narrative, and in an invocation, an apostrophe, a lengthy prayer, would give a free outlet to that effluence which, in the earlier volumes, remained buried beneath the form of his prose, discernible only in a rippling of its surface, and perhaps even more delightful, more harmonious when it was thus veiled from the eye, when the reader could give no precise indication of where the murmur of the current began, or of where it died away. These passages in which he delighted were our favourites also. For my own part I knew all of them by heart. I felt even disappointed when he resumed the thread of his narrative. Whenever he spoke of something whose beauty had until then remained hidden from me, of pine-forests or of hailstorms, of *Notre-Dame de Paris*, of *Athalie*, or of *Phèdre*, by some piece of imagery he would make their beauty explode and drench me with its essence. And so, dimly realising that the universe contained innumerable elements which my feeble senses would be powerless to discern, did he not bring them within my reach, I wished that I might have his opinion, some metaphor of his, upon everything in the world, and especially upon such things as I might have an opportunity, some day, of seeing for myself; and among such things, more particularly still upon some of

the historic buildings of France, upon certain views of the
sea, because the emphasis with which, in his books, he re-
ferred to these shewed that he regarded them as rich in
significance and beauty. But, alas, upon almost everything
in the world his opinion was unknown to me. I had no doubt
that it would differ entirely from my own, since his came
down from an unknown sphere towards which I was striving
to raise myself ; convinced that my thoughts would have
seemed pure foolishness to that perfected spirit, I had so
completely obliterated them all that, if I happened to find
in one of his books something which had already occurred to
my own mind, my heart would swell with gratitude and pride
as though some deity had, in his infinite bounty, restored it
to me, had pronounced it to be beautiful and right. It happened now and then that a page of Bergotte would express
precisely those ideas which I used often at night, when I was
unable to sleep, to write to my grandmother and mother, and
so concisely and well that his page had the appearance of a
collection of mottoes for me to set at the head of my letters.
And so too, in later years, when I began to compose a book
of my own, and the quality of some of my sentences seemed
so inadequate that I could not make up my mind to go on
with the undertaking, I would find the equivalent of my
sentences in Bergotte's. But it was only then, when I read
them in his pages, that I could enjoy them ; when it was I
myself who composed them, in my anxiety that they should
exactly reproduce what I seemed to have detected in my
mind, and in my fear of their not turning out ' true to life,'
I had no time to ask myself whether what I was writing
would be pleasant to read ! But indeed there was no kind of
language, no kind of ideas which I really liked, except these.
My feverish and unsatisfactory attempts were themselves a

token of my love, a love which brought me no pleasure, but was, for all that, intense and deep. And so, when I came suddenly upon similar phrases in the writings of another, that is to say stripped of their familiar accompaniment of scruples and repressions and self-tormentings, I was free to indulge to the full my own appetite for such things, just as a cook who, once in a while, has no dinner to prepare for other people, can then find time to gormandise himself. And so, when I had found, one day, in a book by Bergotte, some joke about an old family servant, to which his solemn and magnificent style added a great deal of irony, but which was in principle what I had often said to my grandmother about Françoise, and when, another time, I had discovered that he thought not unworthy of reflection in one of those mirrors of absolute Truth which were his writings, a remark similar to one which I had had occasion to make on our friend M. Legrandin (and, moreover, my remarks on Françoise and M. Legrandin were among those which I would most resolutely have sacrificed for Bergotte's sake, in the belief that he would find them quite without interest); then it was suddenly revealed to me that my own humble existence and the Realms of Truth were less widely separated than I had supposed, that at certain points they were actually in contact ; and in my new-found confidence and joy I wept upon his printed page, as in the arms of a long-lost father.

From his books I had formed an impression of Bergotte as a frail and disappointed old man, who had lost his children, and had never found any consolation. And so I would read, or rather sing his sentences in my brain, with rather more *dolce*, rather more *lento* than he himself had, perhaps, intended, and his simplest phrase would strike my ears with something peculiarly gentle and loving in its intonation. More than anything else in the world I cherished his philosophy, and had pledged myself to it in lifelong devotion. It made me impatient to reach the age when I should be eligible to attend the class at school called ' Philosophy.' I did not wish to learn or do anything else there, but simply to exist and be guided entirely by the mind of Bergotte, and, if I had been told then that the metaphysicians whom I was actually to follow there resembled him in nothing, I should have been struck down by the despair a young lover feels who has sworn lifelong fidelity, when a friend speaks to him of the other mistresses he will have in time to come.

One Sunday, while I was reading in the garden, I was interrupted by Swann, who had come to call upon my parents.

" What are you reading ? May I look ? Why, it's Bergotte ! Who has been telling you about him ? "

I replied that Bloch was responsible.

" Oh, yes, that boy I saw here once, who looks so like the Bellini portrait of Mahomet II. It's an astonishing likeness ; he has the same arched eyebrows and hooked nose and prominent cheekbones. When his beard comes he'll be Mahomet himself. Anyhow, he has good taste, for Bergotte is a charming creature." And seeing how much I seemed to admire Bergotte, Swann, who never spoke at all about the people he knew, made an exception in my favour and said : " I know him well ; if you would like him to write a few words on the title-page of your book I could ask him for you."

I dared not accept such an offer, but bombarded Swann with questions about his friend. " Can you tell me, please, who is his favourite actor ? "

"Actor? No, I can't say. But I do know this : there's not a man on the stage whom he thinks equal to Berma ; he puts her above everyone. Have you seen her ? "

" No, sir, my parents do not allow me to go to the theatre."

" That is a pity. You should insist. Berma in *Phèdre*, in the *Cid* ; well, she's only an actress, if you like, but you know that I don't believe very much in the ' hierarchy ' of the arts." As he spoke I noticed, what had often struck me before in his conversations with my grandmother's sisters, that whenever he spoke of serious matters, whenever he used an expression which seemed to imply a definite opinion upon some important subject, he would take care to isolate, to sterilise it by using a special intonation, mechanical and ironic, as though he had put the phrase or word between inverted commas, and was anxious to disclaim any personal responsibility for it ; as who should say " the ' hierarchy,' don't you know, as silly people call it." But then, if it was so absurd, why did he say the ' hierarchy ' ? A moment later he went on : " Her acting will give you as noble an inspiration as any masterpiece of art in the world, as—oh, I don't know——" and he began to laugh, " shall we say the Queens of Chartres ? " Until then I had supposed that his horror of having to give a serious opinion was something Parisian and refined, in contrast to the provincial dogmatism of my grandmother's sisters ; and I had imagined also that it was characteristic of the mental attitude towards life of the circle in which Swann moved, where, by a natural reaction from the ' lyrical ' enthusiasms of earlier generations, an excessive importance was given to small and precise facts, formerly regarded as vulgar, and anything in the nature of ' phrase-making ' was banned. But now I found myself slightly shocked by this attitude which Swann invariably adopted when face to face with generalities. He appeared unwilling to risk even having an opinion, and to be at his ease only when he could furnish, with meticulous accuracy, some precise but unimportant detail. But in so doing he did not take into account that even here he was giving an opinion, holding a brief (as they say) for something, that the accuracy of his details had an importance of its own. I thought again of the dinner that night, when I had been so unhappy because Mamma would not be coming up to my room, and when he had dismissed the balls given by the Princesse de Léon as being of no importance. And yet it was to just that sort of amusement that he was devoting his life. For what other kind of existence did he reserve the duties of saying in all seriousness what he thought about things, of formulating judgments which he would not put between inverted commas ; and when would he cease to give himself up to occupations of which at the same time he made out that they were absurd ? I noticed, too, in the manner in which Swann spoke to me of Bergotte, something which, to do him justice, was not peculiar to himself, but was shared by all that writer's admirers at that time, at least by my mother's friend and by Dr. du Boulbon. Like Swann, they would say of Bergotte : " He has a charming mind, so individual, he has a way of his own of saying things, which is a little far-fetched, but so pleasant. You never need to look for his name on the title-page, you can tell his work at once." But none of them had yet gone so far as to say " He is a great writer, he has great talent." They did not even credit him with talent at all. They did not speak, because they were not aware of it. We are very slow in recognising in the peculiar physiognomy of a new writer the type which is labelled ' great talent ' in our museum of general ideas. Simply because that physiognomy is new and strange, we can find in it no resemblance to what we are accustomed to call talent. We say rather originality, charm, delicacy, strength ; and then one day we add up the sum of these, and find that it amounts simply to talent.

" Are there any books in which Bergotte has written about Berma ? " I asked M. Swann.

" I think he has, in that little essay on Racine, but it must be out of print. Still, there has perhaps been a second impression. I will find out. Anyhow, I can ask Bergotte himself all that you want to know next time he comes to dine with us. He never misses a week, from one year's end to another. He is my daughter's greatest friend. They go about together, and look at old towns and cathedrals and castles."

As I was still completely ignorant of the different grades in the social hierarchy, the fact that my father found it impossible for us to see anything of Swann's wife and daughter had, for a long time, had the contrary effect of making me imagine them as separated from us by an enormous gulf, which greatly enhanced their dignity and importance in my eyes. I was sorry that my mother did not dye her hair and redden her lips, as I had heard our neighbour, Mme. Sazerat, say that Mme. Swann did, to gratify not her husband but M. de Charlus ; and I felt that, to her, we must be an object of scorn, which distressed me particularly on account of the daughter, such a pretty little girl, as I had heard, and one of whom I used often to dream, always imagining her with the same features and appearance, which I bestowed upon her quite arbitrarily, but with a charming effect. But from this afternoon, when I had learned that Mlle. Swann was a creature living in such rare and fortunate circumstances, bathed, as in her natural element, in such a sea of privilege that, if she should ask her parents whether anyone were coming to dinner, she would be answered in those two syllables, radiant with celestial light, would hear the name of that golden guest who was to her no more than an old friend of her family, Bergotte ; that for her the intimate conversation at table, corresponding to what my great-aunt's conversation was for me, would be the words of Bergotte upon all those subjects which he had not been able to take up in his writings, and on which I would fain have heard him utter oracles ; and that, above all, when she went to visit other towns, he would be walking by her side, unrecognised and glorious, like the gods who came down, of old, from heaven to dwell among mortal men : then I realised both the rare worth of a creature such as Mlle. Swann, and, at the same time, how coarse and ignorant I should appear to her ; and I felt so keenly how pleasant and yet how impossible it would be for me to become her friend that I was filled at once with longing and with despair. And usually, from this time forth, when I thought of her, I would see her standing before the porch of a cathedral, explaining to me what each of the statues meant, and, with a smile which was my highest commendation, presenting me, as her friend, to Bergotte. And invariably the charm of all the fancies which the thought of cathedrals used to inspire in me, the charm of the hills and valleys of the Ile-de-France and of the plains of Normandy, would radiate brightness and beauty over the picture I had formed in my mind of Mlle. Swann ; nothing more remained but to know and to love her. Once we believe that a fellow-creature has a share in some unknown existence to which that creature's love for ourselves can win us admission, that is, of all the preliminary conditions which Love exacts, the one to which he attaches most importance, the one which makes him generous or indifferent as to the rest. Even those women who pretend that they judge a man by his exterior only, see in that exterior an emanation from some special way of life. And that is why they fall in love with a soldier or a fireman, whose uniform makes them less particular about his face ; they kiss and believe that beneath the crushing breastplate there beats a heart different from the rest, more gallant, more adventurous, more tender; and so it is that a young king or a crown prince may travel in foreign countries and make the most gratifying conquests, and yet lack entirely that regular and classic profile which would be indispensable, I dare say, in an outside-broker.

While I was reading in the garden, a thing my great-aunt would never have understood my doing save on a Sunday, that being the day on which it was unlawful to indulge in any serious occupation, and on which she herself would lay aside her sewing (on a week-day she would have said, " How you can go on amusing yourself with a book ; it isn't Sunday, you know ! " putting into the word 'amusing' an implication of childishness and waste of time), my aunt Léonie would be gossiping with Françoise until it was time for Eulalie to arrive. She would tell her that she had just seen Mme. Goupil go by " without an umbrella, in the silk dress she had made for her the other day at Châteaudun. If she has far to go before vespers, she may get it properly soaked."

" Very likely " (which meant also " very likely not ") was the answer, for Françoise did not wish definitely to exclude the possibility of a happier alternative.

" There, now," went on my aunt, beating her brow, " that reminds me that I never heard if she got to church this morning before the Elevation. I must remember to ask Eulalie . . . Françoise, just look at that black cloud behind the steeple, and how poor the light is on the slates, you may be certain it will rain before the day is out. It couldn't possibly keep on like this, it's been too hot. And the sooner the better, for until the storm breaks my Vichy water won't ' go down,' " she concluded, since, in her mind, the desire to accelerate the digestion of her Vichy water was of infinitely greater importance than her fear of seeing Mme. Goupil's new dress ruined.

" Very likely."

" And you know that when it rains in the Square there's none too much shelter." Suddenly my aunt turned pale. " What, three o'clock ! " she exclaimed. " But vespers will have begun already, and I've forgotten my pepsin ! Now I know why that Vichy water has been lying on my stomach." And falling precipitately upon a prayer-book bound in purple velvet, with gilt clasps, out of which in her haste she let fall a shower of the little pictures, each in a lace fringe of yellowish paper, which she used to mark the places of the greater feasts of the church, my aunt, while she swallowed her drops, began at full speed to mutter the words of the sacred text, its meaning being slightly clouded in her brain by the uncertainty whether the pepsin, when taken so long after the Vichy, would still be able to overtake it and to ' send it down.' " Three o'clock ! It's unbelievable how time flies."

A little tap at the window, as though some missile had struck it, followed by a plentiful, falling sound, as light, though, as if a shower of sand were being sprinkled from a window overhead ; then the fall spread, took on an order, a rhythm, became liquid, loud, drumming, musical, innumerable, universal. It was the rain.

" There, Françoise, what did I tell you ? How it's coming down! But I think I heard the bell at the garden gate : go along and see who can be outside in this weather."

Françoise went and returned. " It's Mme. Amédée " (my grandmother). " She said she was going for a walk. It's raining hard, all the same."

" I'm not at all surprised," said my aunt, looking up towards the sky. " I've always said that she was not in the least like other people. Well, I'm glad it's she and not myself who's outside in all this."

" Mme. Amédée is always the exact opposite of the rest," said Françoise, not unkindly, refraining until she should be alone with the other servants from stating her belief that my grandmother was ' a bit off her head.'

" There's Benediction over ! Eulalie will never come now," sighed my aunt, " It will be the weather that's frightened her away."

" But it's not five o'clock yet, Mme. Octave, it's only half-past four."

" Only half-past four ! And here am I, obliged to draw back the small curtains, just to get a tiny streak of daylight. At half-past four ! Only a week before the Rogation-days. Ah, my poor Françoise, the dear Lord must be sorely vexed with us. The world is going too far in these days. As my poor Octave used to say, we have forgotten God too often, and He is taking vengeance upon us."

A bright flush animated my aunt's cheeks ; it was Eulalie. As ill luck would have it, scarcely had she been admitted to the presence when Françoise reappeared and, with a smile which was meant to indicate her full participation in the pleasure which, she had no doubt, her tidings would give my aunt, articulating each syllable so as to shew that, in spite of her having to translate them into indirect speech, she was repeating, as a good servant should, the very words which the new visitor had condescended to use, said : " His

reverence the Curé would be delighted, enchanted, if Mme.
Octave is not resting just now, and could see him. His
reverence does not wish to disturb Mme. Octave. His
reverence is downstairs ; I told him to go into the parlour."

Had the truth been known, the Curé's visits gave my aunt
no such ecstatic pleasure as Françoise supposed, and the air
of jubilation with which she felt bound to illuminate her face
whenever she had to announce his arrival, did not altogether
correspond to what was felt by her invalid. The Curé (an
excellent man, with whom I am sorry now that I did not
converse more often, for, even if he cared nothing for the
arts, he knew a great many etymologies), being in the habit
of shewing distinguished visitors over his church (he had
even planned to compile a history of the Parish of Combray),
used to weary her with his endless explanations, which,
incidentally, never varied in the least degree. But when his
visit synchronised exactly with Eulalie's it became frankly
distasteful to my aunt. She would have preferred to make the
most of Eulalie, and not to have had the whole of her circle
about her at one time. But she dared not send the Curé
away, and had to content herself with making a sign to
Eulalie not to leave when he did, so that she might have her
to herself for a little after he had gone.

" What is this I have been hearing, Father, that a painter
has set up his easel in your church, and is copying one of the
windows ? Old as I am, I can safely say that I have never
even heard of such a thing in all my life ! What is the world
coming to next, I wonder ! And the ugliest thing in the
whole church, too."

" I will not go so far as to say that it is quite the ugliest,
for, although there are certain things in Saint-Hilaire which
are well worth a visit, there are others that are very old now,

in my poor basilica, the only one in all the diocese that has never even been restored. The Lord knows, our porch is dirty and out of date ; still, it is of a majestic character ; take, for instance, the Esther tapestries, though personally I would not give a brass farthing for the pair of them, but experts put them next after the ones at Sens. I can quite see, too, that apart from certain details which are—well, a trifle realistic, they shew features which testify to a genuine power of observation. But don't talk to me about the windows. Is it common sense, I ask you, to leave up windows which shut out all the daylight, and even confuse the eyes by throwing patches of colour, to which I should be hard put to it to give a name, on a floor in which there are not two slabs on the same level ? And yet they refuse to renew the floor for me because, if you please, those are the tombstones of the Abbots of Combray and the Lords of Guermantes, the old Counts, you know, of Brabant, direct ancestors of the present Duc de Guermantes, and of his Duchesse also, since she was a lady of the Guermantes family, and married her cousin." (My grandmother, whose steady refusal to take any interest in ' persons ' had ended in her confusing all their names and titles, whenever anyone mentioned the Duchesse de Guermantes used to make out that she must be related to Mme. de Villeparisis. The whole family would then burst out laughing ; and she would attempt to justify herself by harking back to some invitation to a christening or funeral : " I feel sure that there was a Guermantes in it somewhere." And for once I would side with the others, and against her, refusing to admit that there could be any connection between her school-friend and the descendant of Geneviève de Brabant.)

"Look at Roussainville," the Curé went on. "It is nothing more nowadays than a parish of farmers, though in olden times the place must have had a considerable importance from its trade in felt hats and clocks. (I am not certain, by the way, of the etymology of Roussainville. I should dearly like to think that the name was originally Rouville, from *Radulfi villa*, analogous, don't you see, to Châteauroux, *Castrum Radulfi*, but we will talk about that some other time.) Very well ; the church there has superb windows, almost all quite modern, including that most imposing ' Entry of Louis-Philippe into Combray ' which would be more in keeping, surely, at Combray itself, and which is every bit as good, I understand, as the famous windows at Chartres. Only yesterday I met Dr. Percepied's brother, who goes in for these things, and he told me that he looked upon it as a most beautiful piece of work. But, as I said to this artist, who, by the way, seems to be a most civil fellow, and is a regular virtuoso, it appears, with his brush ; what on earth, I said to him, do you find so extraordinary in this window, which is, if anything, a little dingier than the rest ? "

" I am sure that if you were to ask his Lordship," said my aunt in a resigned tone, for she had begun to feel that she was going to be ' tired,' " he would never refuse you a new window."

" You may depend upon it, Mme. Octave," replied the Curé. " Why, it was just his Lordship himself who started the outcry about the window, by proving that it represented Gilbert the Bad, a Lord of Guermantes and a direct descendant of Geneviève de Brabant, who was a daughter of the House of Guermantes, receiving absolution from Saint Hilaire."

" But I don't see where Saint Hilaire comes in."

" Why yes, have you never noticed, in the corner of the window, a lady in a yellow robe ? Very well, that is Saint

Hilaire, who is also known, you will remember, in certain parts of the country as Saint Illiers, Saint Hélier, and even, in the Jura, Saint Ylie. But these various corruptions of *Sanctus Hilarius* are by no means the most curious that have occurred in the names of the blessed Saints. Take, for example, my good Eulalie, the case of your own patron, *Sancta Eulalia*; do you know what she has become in Burgundy? Saint Eloi, nothing more nor less! The lady has become a gentleman. Do you hear that, Eulalie, after you are dead they will make a man of you!"

"Father will always have his joke."

"Gilbert's brother, Charles the Stammerer, was a pious prince, but, having early in life lost his father, Pepin the Mad, who died as a result of his mental infirmity, he wielded the supreme power with all the arrogance of a man who has not been subjected to discipline in his youth, so much so that, whenever he saw a man in a town whose face he did not remember, he would massacre the whole place, to the last inhabitant. Gilbert, wishing to be avenged on Charles, caused the church at Combray to be burned down, the original church, that was, which Théodebert, when he and his court left the country residence he had near here, at Thiberzy (which is, of course, *Theodeberiacus*), to go out and fight the Burgundians, had promised to build over the tomb of Saint Hilaire if the Saint brought him victory. Nothing remains of it now but the crypt, into which Théodore has probably taken you, for Gilbert burned all the rest. Finally, he defeated the unlucky Charles with the aid of William" which the Curé pronounced 'Will'am' " the Conqueror, which is why so many English still come to visit the place. But he does not appear to have managed to win the affection of the people of Combray, for they fell upon him as he was coming out from mass, and cut off his head. Théodore has a little book, that he lends people, which tells you the whole story.

"But what is unquestionably the most remarkable thing about our church is the view from the belfry, which is full of grandeur. Certainly in your case, since you are not very strong, I should never recommend you to climb our seven and ninety steps, just half the number they have in the famous cathedral at Milan. It is quite tiring enough for the most active person, especially as you have to go on your hands and knees, if you don't wish to crack your skull, and you collect all the cobwebs off the staircase upon your clothes. In any case you should be well wrapped up," he went on, without noticing my aunt's fury at the mere suggestion that she could ever, possibly, be capable of climbing into his belfry, "for there's a strong breeze there, once you get to the top. Some people even assure me that they have felt the chill of death up there. No matter, on Sundays there are always clubs and societies, who come, some of them, long distances to admire our beautiful panorama, and they always go home charmed. Wait now, next Sunday, if the weather holds, you will be sure to find a lot of people there, for Rogation-tide. You must admit, certainly, that the view from up there is like a fairy-tale, with what you might call vistas along the plain, which have quite a special charm of their own. On a clear day you can see as far as Verneuil. And then another thing ; you can see at the same time places which you are in the habit of seeing one without the other, as, for instance, the course of the Vivonne and the ditches at Saint-Assise-lès-Combray, which are separated, really, by a screen of tall trees ; or, to take another example, there are all the canals at Jouy-le-Vicomte, which is *Gaudiacus vicecomitis*, as of course you know. Each time that I have

been to Jouy I have seen a bit of a canal in one place, and
then I have turned a corner and seen another, but when
I saw the second I could no longer see the first. I tried in
vain to imagine how they lay by one another ; it was no
good. But, from the top of Saint-Hilaire, it's quite another
matter ; the whole countryside is spread out before you like
a map. Only, you cannot make out the water ; you would
say that there were great rifts in the town, slicing it up so
neatly that it looks like a loaf of bread which still holds
together after it has been cut up. To get it all quite perfect
you would have to be in both places at once ; up here
on the top of Saint-Hilaire and down there at Jouy-le-
Vicomte."

The Curé had so much exhausted my aunt that no sooner
had he gone than she was obliged to send away Eulalie also.

" Here, my poor Eulalie," she said in a feeble voice,
drawing a coin from a small purse which lay ready to her
hand. " This is just something so that you shall not forget
me in your prayers."

" Oh, but, Mme. Octave, I don't think I ought to ; you
know very well that I don't come here for that ! " So
Eulalie would answer, with the same hesitation and the same
embarrassment, every Sunday, as though each temptation
were the first, and with a look of displeasure which enlivened
my aunt and never offended her, for if it so happened that
Eulalie, when she took the money, looked a little less sulky
than usual, my aunt would remark afterwards, " I cannot
think what has come over Eulalie ; I gave her just the trifle
I always give, and she did not look at all pleased."

" I don't think she has very much to complain of, all the
same," Françoise would sigh grimly, for she had a tendency
to regard as petty cash all that my aunt might give her for

herself or her children, and as treasure riotously squandered
on a pampered and ungrateful darling the little coins slipped,
Sunday by Sunday, into Eulalie's hand, but so discreetly passed
that Françoise never managed to see them. It was not that
she wanted to have for herself the money my aunt bestowed
on Eulalie. She already enjoyed a sufficiency of all that my
aunt possessed, in the knowledge that the wealth of the
mistress automatically ennobled and glorified the maid in the
eyes of the world ; and that she herself was conspicuous and
worthy to be praised throughout Combray, Jouy-le-Vicomte,
and other cities of men, on account of my aunt's many farms,
her frequent and prolonged visits from the Curé, and the
astonishing number of bottles of Vichy water which she
consumed. Françoise was avaricious only for my aunt ; had
she had control over my aunt's fortune (which would have
more than satisfied her highest ambition) she would have
guarded it from the assaults of strangers with a maternal
ferocity. She would, however, have seen no great harm in
what my aunt, whom she knew to be incurably generous,
allowed herself to give away, had she given only to those
who were already rich. Perhaps she felt that such persons,
not being actually in need of my aunt's presents, could not
be suspected of simulating affection for her on that account.
Besides, presents offered to persons of great wealth and position, such as Mme. Sazerat, M. Swann, M. Legrandin and
Mme. Goupil, to persons of the ' same class ' as my aunt,
and who would naturally ' mix with her,' seemed to Françoise to be included among the ornamental customs of that
strange and brilliant life led by rich people, who hunted and
shot, gave balls and paid visits, a life which she would contemplate with an admiring smile. But it was by no means
the same thing if, for this princely exchange of courtesies,

my aunt substituted mere charity, if her beneficiaries were of the class which Françoise would label " people like myself," or " people no better than myself," people whom she despised even more if they did not address her always as " Mme. Françoise," just to shew that they considered themselves to be ' not as good.' And when she saw that, despite all her warnings, my aunt continued to do exactly as she pleased, and to fling money away with both hands (or so, at least, Françoise believed) on undeserving objects, she began to find that the presents she herself received from my aunt were very tiny compared to the imaginary riches squandered upon Eulalie. There was not, in the neighbourhood of Combray, a farm of such prosperity and importance that Françoise doubted Eulalie's ability to buy it, without thinking twice, out of the capital which her visits to my aunt had ' brought in.' It must be added that Eulalie had formed an exactly similar estimate of the vast and secret hoards of Françoise. So, every Sunday, after Eulalie had gone, Françoise would mercilessly prophesy her coming downfall. She hated Eulalie, but was at the same time afraid of her, and so felt bound, when Eulalie was there, to ' look pleasant.' But she would make up for that after the other's departure; never, it is true, alluding to her by name, but hinting at her in Sibylline oracles, or in utterances of a comprehensive character, like those of Ecclesiastes, the Preacher, but so worded that their special application could not escape my aunt. After peering out at the side of the curtain to see whether Eulalie had shut the front-door behind her ; " Flatterers know how to make themselves welcome, and to gather up the crumbs ; but have patience, have patience ; our God is a jealous God, and one fine day He will be avenged upon them ! " she would declaim, with the sidelong, insinuating

glance of Joash, thinking of Athaliah alone when he says
that the

prosperity

Of wicked men runs like a torrent past,
And soon is spent.

But on this memorable afternoon, when the Curé had come
as well, and by his interminable visit had drained my aunt's
strength, Françoise followed Eulalie from the room, saying :
" Mme. Octave, I will leave you to rest ; you look utterly
tired out."

And my aunt answered her not a word, breathing a sigh
so faint that it seemed it must prove her last, and lying there
with closed eyes, as though already dead. But hardly had
Françoise arrived downstairs, when four peals of a bell,
pulled with the utmost violence, reverberated through the
house, and my aunt, sitting erect upon her bed, called out :
" Has Eulalie gone yet ? Would you believe it ; I forgot to
ask her whether Mme. Goupil arrived in church before the
Elevation. Run after her, quick ! "

But Françoise returned alone, having failed to overtake
Eulalie.

" It is most provoking," said my aunt, shaking her head.
" The one important thing that I had to ask her."

In this way life went by for my aunt Léonie, always the
same, in the gentle uniformity of what she called, with a
pretence of deprecation but with a deep tenderness, her
' little jog-trot.' Respected by all and sundry, not merely
in her own house, where every one of us, having learned the
futility of recommending any healthier mode of life, had
become gradually resigned to its observance, but in the
village as well, where, three streets away, a tradesman who
had to hammer nails into a packing-case would send first to

Françoise to make sure that my aunt was not ' resting '—
her ' little jog-trot' was, none the less, brutally disturbed on
one occasion in this same year. Like a fruit hidden among its
leaves, which has grown and ripened unobserved by man,
until it falls of its own accord, there came upon us one night
the kitchen-maid's confinement. Her pains were unbearable,
and, as there was no midwife in Combray, Françoise had to
set off before dawn to fetch one from Thiberzy. My aunt
was unable to ' rest,' owing to the cries of the girl, and as
Françoise, though the distance was nothing, was very late
in returning, her services were greatly missed. And so, in
the course of the morning, my mother said to me : " Run
upstairs, and see if your aunt wants anything."

I went into the first of her two rooms, and through the
open door of the other saw my aunt lying on her side, asleep.
I could hear her breathing, in what was almost distinguishable as a snore. I was just going to slip away when something,
probably the sound of my entry, interrupted her sleep, and
made it ' change speed,' as they say of motor-cars nowadays,
for the music of her snore broke off for a second and began
again on a lower note ; then she awoke, and half turned her
face, which I could see for the first time ; a kind of horror
was imprinted on it ; plainly she had just escaped from some
terrifying dream. She could not see me from where she was
lying, and I stood there not knowing whether I ought to go
forward or to retire ; but all at once she seemed to return to a
sense of reality, and to grasp the falsehood of the visions that
had terrified her ; a smile of joy, a pious act of thanksgiving
to God, Who is pleased to grant that life shall be less cruel
than our dreams, feebly illumined her face, and, with the
habit she had formed of speaking to herself, half-aloud, when
she thought herself alone, she murmured : " The Lord be

praised ! We have nothing to disturb us here but the kitchen-maid's baby. And I've been dreaming that my poor Octave had come back to life, and was trying to make me take a walk every day ! " She stretched out a hand towards her rosary, which was lying on the small table, but sleep was once again getting the mastery, and did not leave her the strength to reach it ; she fell asleep, calm and contented, and I crept out of the room on tiptoe, without either her or anyone's else ever knowing, from that day to this, what I had seen and heard.

When I say that, apart from such rare happenings as this confinement, my aunt's ' little jog-trot ' never underwent any variation, I do not include those variations which, repeated at regular intervals and in identical form, did no more, really, than print a sort of uniform pattern upon the greater uniformity of her life. So, for instance, every Satur-day, as Françoise had to go in the afternoon to market at Roussainville-le-Pin, the whole household would have to have luncheon an hour earlier. And my aunt had so tho-roughly acquired the habit of this weekly exception to her general habits, that she clung to it as much as to the rest. She was so well ' routined ' to it, as Françoise would say, that if, on a Saturday, she had had to wait for her luncheon until the regular hour, it would have ' upset ' her as much as if she had had, on an ordinary day, to put her luncheon forward to its Saturday time. Incidentally this acceleration of luncheon gave Saturday, for all of us, an individual character, kindly and rather attractive. At the moment when, ordinarily, there was still an hour to be lived through before meal-time sounded, we would all know that in a few seconds we should see the endives make their precocious appearance, followed by the special favour of an omelette, an unmerited steak. The return of this asymmetrical Saturday was one of those petty occurrences, intra-mural, localised, almost civic, which, in uneventful lives and stable orders of society, create a kind of national unity, and become the favourite theme for conversation, for pleasantries, for anecdotes which can be embroidered as the narrator pleases ; it would have provided a nucleus, ready-made, for a legendary cycle, if any of us had had the epic mind. At daybreak, before we were dressed, without rhyme or reason, save for the pleasure of proving the strength of our solidarity, we would call to one another good-humouredly, cordially, patriotically, "Hurry up ; there's no time to be lost ; don't forget, it's Saturday ! " while my aunt, gossiping with Françoise, and reflecting that the day would be even longer than usual, would say, "You might cook them a nice bit of veal, seeing that it's Saturday." If, at half-past ten, some one absent-mindedly pulled out a watch and said, "I say, an hour-and-a-half still before luncheon," everyone else would be in ecstasies over being able to retort at once : "Why, what are you thinking about ? Have you forgotten that it's Saturday ? " And a quarter of an hour later we would still be laughing, and reminding our-selves to go up and tell aunt Léonie about this absurd mistake, to amuse her. The very face of the sky appeared to undergo a change. After luncheon the sun, conscious that it was Saturday, would blaze an hour longer in the zenith, and when some one, thinking that we were late in starting for our walk, said, "What, only two o'clock ! " feeling the heavy throb go by him of the twin strokes from the steeple of Saint-Hilaire (which as a rule passed no one at that hour upon the highways, deserted for the midday meal or for the nap which follows it, or on the banks of the bright and ever-flowing stream, which even the angler had abandoned, and so slipped

unaccompanied into the vacant sky, where only a few loiter-
ing clouds remained to greet them) the whole family would
respond in chorus : "Why, you're forgetting ; we had
luncheon an hour earlier ; you know very well it's Saturday."

The surprise of a 'barbarian' (for so we termed everyone who was not acquainted with Saturday's special customs)
who had called at eleven o'clock to speak to my father, and
had found us at table, was an event which used to cause
Françoise as much merriment as, perhaps, anything that had
ever happened in her life. And if she found it amusing that
the nonplussed visitor should not have known, beforehand,
that we had our luncheon an hour earlier on Saturdays, it
was still more irresistibly funny that my father himself,
(fully as she sympathised, from the bottom of her heart, with
the rigid chauvinism which prompted him) should never have
dreamed that the barbarian could fail to be aware of so simple
a matter, and so had replied, with no further enlightenment
of the other's surprise at seeing us already in the dining-
room : "You see, it's Saturday." On reaching this point
in the story, Françoise would pause to wipe the tears of
merriment from her eyes, and then, to add to her own enjoyment, would prolong the dialogue, inventing a further reply
for the visitor to whom the word 'Saturday' had conveyed
nothing. And so far from our objecting to these interpolations,
we would feel that the story was not yet long enough, and
would rally her with : "Oh, but surely he said something else
as well. There was more than that, the first time you told it."

My great-aunt herself would lay aside her work, and raise
her head and look on at us over her glasses.

The day had yet another characteristic feature, namely,
that during May we used to go out on Saturday evenings
after dinner to the 'Month of Mary' devotions.

As we were liable, there, to meet M. Vinteuil, who held very strict views on "the deplorable untidiness of young people, which seems to be encouraged in these days," my mother would first see that there was nothing out of order in my appearance, and then we would set out for the church. It was in these 'Month of Mary' services that I can remember having first fallen in love with hawthorn-blossom. The hawthorn was not merely in the church, for there, holy ground as it was, we had all of us a right of entry ; but, arranged upon the altar itself, inseparable from the mysteries in whose celebration it was playing a part, it thrust in among the tapers and the sacred vessels its rows of branches, tied to one another horizontally in a stiff, festal scheme of decoration ; and they were made more lovely still by the scalloped outline of the dark leaves, over which were scattered in profusion, as over a bridal train, little clusters of buds of a dazzling whiteness. Though I dared not look at them save through my fingers, I could feel that the formal scheme was composed of living things, and that it was Nature herself who, by trimming the shape of the foliage, and by adding the crowning ornament of those snowy buds, had made the decorations worthy of what was at once a public rejoicing and a solemn mystery. Higher up on the altar, a flower had opened here and there with a careless grace, holding so unconcernedly, like a final, almost vaporous bedizening, its bunch of stamens, slender as gossamer, which clouded the flower itself in a white mist, that in following these with my eyes, in trying to imitate, somewhere inside myself, the action of their blossoming, I imagined it as a swift and thoughtless movement of the head with an enticing glance from her contracted pupils, by a young girl in white, careless and alive.

M. Vinteuil had come in with his daughter and had sat

down beside us. He belonged to a good family, and had once been music-master to my grandmother's sisters ; so that when, after losing his wife and inheriting some property, he had retired to the neighbourhood of Combray, we used often to invite him to our house. But with his intense prudishness he had given up coming, so as not to be obliged to meet Swann, who had made what he called "a most unsuitable marriage, as seems to be the fashion in these days." My mother, on hearing that he 'composed,' told him by way of a compliment that, when she came to see him, he must play her something of his own. M. Vinteuil would have liked nothing better, but he carried politeness and consideration for others to so fine a point, always putting himself in their place, that he was afraid of boring them, or of appearing egotistical, if he carried out, or even allowed them to suspect what were his own desires. On the day when my parents had gone to pay him a visit, I had accompanied them, but they had allowed me to remain outside, and as M. Vinteuil's house, Montjouvain, stood on a site actually hollowed out from a steep hill covered with shrubs, among which I took cover, I had found myself on a level with his drawing-room, upstairs, and only a few feet away from its window. When a servant came in to tell him that my parents had arrived, I had seen M. Vinteuil run to the piano and lay out a sheet of music so as to catch the eye. But as soon as they entered the room he had snatched it away and hidden it in a corner. He was afraid, no doubt, of letting them suppose that he was glad to see them only because it gave him a chance of playing them some of his compositions. And every time that my mother, in the course of her visit, had returned to the subject of his playing, he had hurriedly protested : " I cannot think who put that on the piano ; it is not the proper place for it at all," and had turned the conversation aside to other topics, simply because those were of less interest to himself.

His one and only passion was for his daughter, and she, with her somewhat boyish appearance, looked so robust that it was hard to restrain a smile when one saw the precautions her father used to take for her health, with spare shawls always in readiness to wrap round her shoulders. My grandmother had drawn our attention to the gentle, delicate, almost timid expression which might often be caught flitting across the face, dusted all over with freckles, of this otherwise stolid child. When she had spoken, she would at once take her own words in the sense in which her audience must have heard them, she would be alarmed at the possibility of a misunderstanding, and one would see, in clear outline, as though in a transparency, beneath the mannish face of the 'good sort' that she was, the finer features of a young woman in tears.

When, before turning to leave the church, I made a genuflection before the altar, I felt suddenly, as I rose again, a bitter-sweet fragrance of almonds steal towards me from the hawthorn-blossom, and I then noticed that on the flowers themselves were little spots of a creamier colour, in which I imagined that this fragrance must lie concealed, as the taste of an almond cake lay in the burned parts, or the sweetness of Mlle. Vinteuil's cheeks beneath their freckles. Despite the heavy, motionless silence of the hawthorns, these gusts of fragrance came to me like the murmuring of an intense vitality, with which the whole altar was quivering like a roadside hedge explored by living antennae, of which I was reminded by seeing some stamens, almost red in colour, which seemed to have kept the springtime virulence, the irritant power of stinging insects now transmuted into flowers.

Outside the church we would stand talking for a moment

with M. Vinteuil, in the porch. Boys would be chevying
one another in the Square, and he would interfere, taking the
side of the little ones and lecturing the big. If his daughter
said, in her thick, comfortable voice, how glad she had been
to see us, immediately it would seem as though some elder
and more sensitive sister, latent in her, had blushed at this
thoughtless, schoolboyish utterance, which had, perhaps,
made us think that she was angling for an invitation to the
house. Her father would then arrange a cloak over her
shoulders, they would clamber into a little dog-cart which
she herself drove, and home they would both go to Montjouvain. As for ourselves, the next day being Sunday, with
no need to be up and stirring before high mass, if it was a
moonlight night and warm, then, instead of taking us home
at once, my father, in his thirst for personal distinction,
would lead us on a long walk round by the Calvary, which
my mother's utter incapacity for taking her bearings, or even
for knowing which road she might be on, made her regard as
a triumph of his strategic genius. Sometimes we would go
as far as the viaduct, which began to stride on its long legs
of stone at the railway station, and to me typified all the
wretchedness of exile beyond the last outposts of civilisation,
because every year, as we came down from Paris, we would
be warned to take special care, when we got to Combray, not
to miss the station, to be ready before the train stopped, since
it would start again in two minutes and proceed across the
viaduct, out of the lands of Christendom, of which Combray,
to me, represented the farthest limit. We would return by
the Boulevard de la Gare, which contained the most attractive
villas in the town. In each of their gardens the moonlight,
copying the art of Hubert Robert, had scattered its broken
staircases of white marble, its fountains of water and gates

temptingly ajar. Its beams had swept away the telegraph office. All that was left of it was a column, half shattered, but preserving the beauty of a ruin which endures for all time. I would by now be dragging my weary limbs, and ready to drop with sleep ; the balmy scent of the lime-trees seemed a consolation which I could obtain only at the price of great suffering and exhaustion, and not worthy of the effort. From gates far apart the watchdogs, awakened by our steps in the silence, would set up an antiphonal barking, as I still hear them bark, at times, in the evenings, and it is in their custody (when the public gardens of Combray were constructed on its site) that the Boulevard de la Gare must have taken refuge, for wherever I may be, as soon as they begin their alternate challenge and acceptance, I can see it again with all its lime-trees, and its pavement glistening beneath the moon.

Suddenly my father would bring us to a standstill and ask my mother—" Where are we ? " Utterly worn out by the walk but still proud of her husband, she would lovingly confess that she had not the least idea. He would shrug his shoulders and laugh. And then, as though it had slipped, with his latchkey, from his waistcoat pocket, he would point out to us, where it stood before our eyes, the back-gate of our own garden, which had come, hand-in-hand with the familiar corner of the Rue du Saint-Esprit, to await us, to greet us at the end of our wanderings over paths unknown. My mother would murmur admiringly " You really are wonderful ! " And from that instant I had not to take another step ; the ground moved forward under my feet in that garden where, for so long, my actions had ceased to require any control, or even attention, from my will. Custom came to take me in her arms, carried me all the way up to my bed, and laid me down there like a little child.

Although Saturday, by beginning an hour earlier, and by depriving her of the services of Françoise, passed more slowly than other days for my aunt, yet, the moment it was past, and a new week begun, she would look forward with impatience to its return, as something that embodied all the novelty and distraction which her frail and disordered body was still able to endure. This was not to say, however, that she did not long, at times, for some even greater variation, that she did not pass through those abnormal hours in which one thirsts for something different from what one has, when those people who, through lack of energy or imagination, are unable to generate any motive power in themselves, cry out, as the clock strikes or the postman knocks, in their eagerness for news (even if it be bad news), for some emotion (even that of grief) ; when the heartstrings, which prosperity has silenced, like a harp laid by, yearn to be plucked and sounded again by some hand, even a brutal hand, even if it shall break them ; when the will, which has with such difficulty brought itself to subdue its impulse, to renounce its right to abandon itself to its own uncontrolled desires, and consequent sufferings, would fain cast its guiding reins into the hands of circumstances, coercive and, it may be, cruel. Of course, since my aunt's strength, which was completely drained by the slightest exertion, returned but drop by drop into the pool of her repose, the reservoir was very slow in filling, and months would go by before she reached that surplus which other people use up in their daily activities, but which she had no idea—and could never decide how to employ. And I have no doubt that then—just as a desire to have her potatoes served with béchamel sauce, for a change, would be formed, ultimately, from the pleasure she found in the daily reappearance of those mashed potatoes of which she was never

' tired '——she would extract from the accumulation of those monotonous days (on which she so much depended) a keen expectation of some domestic cataclysm, instantaneous in its happening, but violent enough to compel her to put into effect, once for all, one of those changes which she knew would be beneficial to her health, but to which she could never make up her mind without some such stimulus. She was genuinely fond of us ; she would have enjoyed the long luxury of weeping for our untimely decease ; coming at a moment when she felt ' well ' and was not in a perspiration, the news that the house was being destroyed by a fire, in which all the rest of us had already perished, a fire which, in a little while, would not leave one stone standing upon another, but from which she herself would still have plenty of time to escape without undue haste, provided that she rose at once from her bed, must often have haunted her dreams, as a prospect which combined with the two minor advantages of letting her taste the full savour of her affection for us in long years of mourning, and of causing universal stupefaction in the village when she should sally forth to conduct our obsequies, crushed but courageous, moribund but erect, the paramount and priceless boon of forcing her at the right moment, with no time to be lost, no room for weakening hesitations, to go off and spend the summer at her charming farm of Mirougrain, where there was a waterfall. Inasmuch as nothing of this sort had ever occurred, though indeed she must often have pondered the success of such a manœuvre as she lay alone absorbed in her interminable games of patience (and though it must have plunged her in despair from the first moment of its realisation, from the first of those little unforeseen facts, the first word of calamitous news, whose accents can never afterwards be expunged from

the memory, everything that bears upon it the imprint of
actual, physical death, so terribly different from the logical
abstraction of its possibility) she would fall back from time
to time, to add an interest to her life, upon imagining other,
minor catastrophes, which she would follow up with passion.
She would beguile herself with a sudden suspicion that Françoise had been robbing her, that she had set a trap to make
certain, and had caught her betrayer red-handed ; and being
in the habit, when she made up a game of cards by herself,
of playing her own and her adversary's hands at once, she
would first stammer out Françoise's awkward apologies, and
then reply to them with such a fiery indignation that any of
us who happened to intrude upon her at one of these moments
would find her bathed in perspiration, her eyes blazing, her
false hair pushed awry and exposing the baldness of her brows.
Françoise must often, from the next room, have heard these
mordant sarcasms levelled at herself, the mere framing of
which in words would not have relieved my aunt's feelings
sufficiently, had they been allowed to remain in a purely
immaterial form, without the degree of substance and reality
which she added to them by murmuring them half-aloud.
Sometimes, however, even these counterpane dramas would not
satisfy my aunt ; she must see her work staged. And so, on a
Sunday, with all the doors mysteriously closed, she would confide in Eulalie her doubts of Françoise's integrity and her determination to be rid of her, and on another day she would
confide in Françoise her suspicions of the disloyalty of
Eulalie, to whom the front-door would very soon be closed
for good. A few days more, and, disgusted with her latest
confidant, she would again be ' as thick as thieves ' with the
traitor, while, before the next performance, the two would
once more have changed their parts. But the suspicions

which Eulalie might occasionally breed in her were no more
than a fire of straw, which must soon subside for lack of fuel,
since Eulalie was not living with her in the house. It was a
very different matter when the suspect was Françoise, of
whose presence under the same roof as herself my aunt was
perpetually conscious, while for fear of catching cold, were
she to leave her bed, she would never dare go downstairs to
the kitchen to see for herself whether there was, indeed, any
foundation for her suspicions. And so on by degrees, until
her mind had no other occupation than to attempt, at every
hour of the day, to discover what was being done, what was
being concealed from her by Françoise. She would detect
the most furtive movement of Françoise's features, something
contradictory in what she was saying, some desire which she
appeared to be screening. And she would shew her that she
was unmasked, by a single word, which made Françoise turn
pale, and which my aunt seemed to find a cruel satisfaction in
driving deep into her unhappy servant's heart. And the very
next Sunday a disclosure by Eulalie—like one of those discoveries which suddenly open up an unsuspected field for
exploration to some new science which has hitherto followed
only the beaten paths—proved to my aunt that her own worst
suspicions fell a long way short of the appalling truth. " But
Françoise ought to know that," said Eulalie, " now that
you have given her a carriage."

" Now that I have given her a carriage ! " gasped my
aunt.

" Oh, but I didn't know ; I only thought so ; I saw her
go by yesterday in her open coach, as proud as Artaban, on
her way to Roussainville market. I supposed that it must be
Mme. Octave who had given it to her."

So on by degrees, until Françoise and my aunt, the quarry

and the hunter, could never cease from trying to forestall
each other's devices. My mother was afraid lest Françoise
should develop a genuine hatred of my aunt, who was
doing everything in her power to annoy her. However that
might be, Françoise had come, more and more, to pay an
infinitely scrupulous attention to my aunt's least word and
gesture. When she had to ask her for anything she would
hesitate, first, for a long time, making up her mind how best
to begin. And when she had uttered her request, she would
watch my aunt covertly, trying to guess from the expression
on her face what she thought of it, and how she would reply.
And in this way——whereas an artist who had been reading
memoirs of the seventeenth century, and wished to bring
himself nearer to the great Louis, would consider that he
was making progress in that direction when he constructed a
pedigree that traced his own descent from some historic
family, or when he engaged in correspondence with one of
the reigning Sovereigns of Europe, and so would shut his
eyes to the mistake he was making in seeking to establish
a similarity by an exact and therefore lifeless copy of mere
outward forms——a middle-aged lady in a small country town,
by doing no more than yield whole-hearted obedience to her
own irresistible eccentricities, and to a spirit of mischief
engendered by the utter idleness of her existence, could see,
without ever having given a thought to Louis XIV, the
most trivial occupations of her daily life, her morning toilet,
her luncheon, her afternoon nap, assume, by virtue of their
despotic singularity, something of the interest that was to be
found in what Saint-Simon used to call the ' machinery ' of
life at Versailles ; and was able, too, to persuade herself that
her silence, a shade of good humour or of arrogance on her
features would provide Françoise with matter for a mental

commentary as tense with passion and terror, as did the silence, the good humour or the arrogance of the King when a courtier, or even his greatest nobles had presented a petition to him, at the turning of an avenue, at Versailles.

One Sunday, when my aunt had received simultaneous visits from the Curé and from Eulalie, and had been left alone, afterwards, to rest, the whole family went upstairs to bid her good night, and Mamma ventured to condole with her on the unlucky coincidence that always brought both visitors to her door at the same time.

" I hear that things went wrong again to-day, Léonie," she said kindly, " you have had all your friends here at once."

And my great-aunt interrupted with : " Too many good things . . . " for, since her daughter's illness, she felt herself in duty bound to revive her as far as possible by always drawing her attention to the brighter side of things. But my father had begun to speak.

" I should like to take advantage," he said, " of the whole family's being here together, to tell you a story, so as not to have to begin all over again to each of you separately. I am afraid we are in M. Legrandin's bad books ; he would hardly say ' How d'ye do ' to me this morning."

I did not wait to hear the end of my father's story, for I had been with him myself after mass when we had passed M. Legrandin ; instead, I went downstairs to the kitchen to ask for the bill of fare for our dinner, which was of fresh interest to me daily, like the news in a paper, and excited me as might the programme of a coming festivity.

As M. Legrandin had passed close by us on our way from church, walking by the side of a lady, the owner of a country house in the neighbourhood, whom we knew only by sight, my father had saluted him in a manner at once friendly and reserved, without stopping in his walk ; M. Legrandin had barely acknowledged the courtesy, and then with an air of surprise, as though he had not recognised us, and with that distant look characteristic of people who do not wish to be agreeable, and who from the suddenly receding depths of their eyes seem to have caught sight of you at the far end of an interminably straight road, and at so great a distance that they content themselves with directing towards you an almost imperceptible movement of the head, in proportion to your doll-like dimensions.

Now, the lady who was walking with Legrandin was a model of virtue, known and highly respected ; there could be no question of his being out for amorous adventure, and annoyed at being detected ; and my father asked himself how he could possibly have displeased our friend.

" I should be all the more sorry to feel that he was angry with us," he said, " because among all those people in their Sunday clothes there is something about him, with his little cut-away coat and his soft neckties, so little ' dressed-up,' so genuinely simple ; an air of innocence, almost, which is really attractive."

But the vote of the family council was unanimous, that my father had imagined the whole thing, or that Legrandin, at the moment in question, had been preoccupied in thinking about something else. Anyhow, my father's fears were dissipated no later than the following evening. As we re-turned from a long walk we saw, near the Pont-Vieux, Legrandin himself, who, on account of the holidays, was spending a few days more in Combray. He came up to us with outstretched hand : " Do you know, master book-lover," he asked me, " this line of Paul Desjardins ?

Now are the woods all black, but still the sky is blue.

Is not that a fine rendering of a moment like this ? Perhaps you have never read Paul Desjardins. Read him, my boy, read him ; in these days he is converted, they tell me, into a preaching friar, but he used to have the most charming water-colour touch——

Now are the woods all black, but still the sky is blue.

May you always see a blue sky overhead, my young friend ; and then, even when the time comes, which is coming now for me, when the woods are all black, when night is fast falling, you will be able to console yourself, as I am doing, by looking up to the sky." He took a cigarette from his pocket and stood for a long time, his eyes fixed on the horizon. " Good-bye, friends ! " he suddenly exclaimed, and left us.

At the hour when I usually went downstairs to find out what there was for dinner, its preparation would already have begun, and Françoise, a colonel with all the forces of nature for her subalterns, as in the fairy-tales where giants hire themselves out as scullions, would be stirring the coals, putting the potatoes to steam, and, at the right moment, finishing over the fire those culinary masterpieces which had been first got ready in some of the great array of vessels, triumphs of the potter's craft, which ranged from tubs and boilers and cauldrons and fish kettles down to jars for game, moulds for pastry, and tiny pannikins for cream, and included an entire collection of pots and pans of every shape and size. I would stop by the table, where the kitchen-maid had shelled them, to inspect the platoons of peas, drawn up in ranks and numbered, like little green marbles, ready for a game ; but what fascinated me would be the asparagus, tinged with ultramarine and rosy pink which ran from their heads, finely stippled in mauve and azure, through a series of imperceptible changes to their white feet, still stained a little by the soil of their garden-bed : a rainbow-loveliness that was not of this world. I felt that these celestial hues indicated the presence of exquisite creatures who had been pleased to assume vegetable form, who, through the disguise which covered their firm and edible flesh, allowed me to discern in this radiance of earliest dawn, these hinted rainbows, these blue evening shades, that precious quality which I should recognise again when, all night long after a dinner at which I had partaken of them, they played (lyrical and coarse in their jesting as the fairies in Shakespeare's *Dream*) at transforming my humble chamber into a bower of aromatic perfume.

Poor Giotto's Charity, as Swann had named her, charged by Françoise with the task of preparing them for the table, would have them lying beside her in a basket ; sitting with a mournful air, as though all the sorrows of the world were heaped upon her ; and the light crowns of azure which capped the asparagus shoots above their pink jackets would be finely and separately outlined, star by star, as in Giotto's fresco are the flowers banded about the brows, or patterning the basket of his Virtue at Padua. And, meanwhile, Françoise would be turning on the spit one of those chickens, such as she alone knew how to roast, chickens which had wafted far abroad from Combray the sweet savour of her merits, and which, while she was serving them to us at table, would make the quality of kindness predominate for the moment in my private conception of her character ; the aroma of that cooked flesh, which she knew how to make so unctuous and so tender, seeming to me no more than the proper perfume of one of her many virtues.

But the day on which, while my father took counsel with his family upon our strange meeting with Legrandin, I went down to the kitchen, was one of those days when Giotto's Charity, still very weak and ill after her recent confinement, had been unable to rise from her bed ; Françoise, being without assistance, had fallen into arrears. When I went in, I saw her in the back-kitchen which opened on to the court-yard, in process of killing a chicken; by its desperate and quite natural resistance, which Françoise, beside herself with rage as she attempted to slit its throat beneath the ear, accompanied with shrill cries of " Filthy creature ! Filthy creature ! " it made the saintly kindness and unction of our servant rather less prominent than it would do, next day at dinner, when it made its appearance in a skin gold-embroidered like a chasuble, and its precious juice was poured out drop by drop as from a pyx. When it was dead Françoise mopped up its streaming blood, in which, however, she did not let her rancour drown, for she gave vent to another burst of rage, and, gazing down at the carcass of her enemy, uttered a final " Filthy creature ! "

I crept out of the kitchen and upstairs, trembling all over ; I could have prayed, then, for the instant dismissal of Fran-çoise. But who would have baked me such hot rolls, boiled me such fragrant coffee, and even—roasted me such chickens? And, as it happened, everyone else had already had to make the same cowardly reckoning. For my aunt Léonie knew (though I was still in ignorance of this) that Françoise, who, for her own daughter or for her nephews, would have given her life without a murmur, shewed a singular implacability in her dealings with the rest of the world. In spite of which my aunt still retained her, for, while conscious of her cruelty, she could appreciate her services. I began gradually to realise that Françoise's kindness, her compunction, the sum total of her virtues concealed many of these back-kitchen tragedies, just as history reveals to us that the reigns of the kings and queens who are portrayed as kneeling with clasped hands in the windows of churches, were stained by oppression and bloodshed. I had taken note of the fact that, apart from her own kinsfolk, the sufferings of humanity inspired in her a pity which increased in direct ratio to the distance separating the sufferers from herself. The tears which flowed from her in torrents when she read of the misfortunes of persons unknown to her, in a newspaper, were quickly stemmed once she had been able to form a more accurate mental picture of the victims. One night, shortly after her confinement, the kitchen-maid was seized with the most appalling pains ; Mamma heard her groans, and rose and awakened Françoise, who, quite unmoved, declared that all the outcry was mere malingering, that the girl wanted to ' play the mistress ' in the house. The doctor, who had been afraid of some such attack, had left a marker in a medical dictionary which we had, at the page on which the symptoms were described, and had told us to turn up this passage, where we would find the measures of ' first aid ' to be adopted. My mother sent Françoise to fetch the book, warning her not to let the marker drop out. An hour elapsed, and Françoise had not returned ; my mother, supposing that she had gone back to bed, grew vexed, and told me to go myself to the book-case and fetch the volume. I did so, and there found Françoise who, in her curiosity to know what the marker indicated, had begun to read the clinical account of these after-pains, and was violently sobbing, now that it was a question of a type of illness with which she was not familiar. At each painful symptom mentioned by the writer she would exclaim : " Oh, oh, Holy Virgin, is it possible that God wishes any wretched human creature to suffer so ? Oh, the poor girl ! "

But when I had called her, and she had returned to the bedside of Giotto's Charity, her tears at once ceased to flow ; she could find no stimulus for that pleasant sensation of tenderness and pity which she very well knew, having been moved to it often enough by the perusal of newspapers ; nor any other pleasure of the same kind in her sense of weariness and irritation at being pulled out of bed in the middle of the night for the kitchen-maid ; so that at the sight of those very sufferings, the printed account of which had moved her to tears, she had nothing to offer but ill-tempered mutterings, mingled with bitter sarcasm, saying, when she thought that we had gone out of earshot : " Well, she need never have done what she must have done to bring all this about ! She found that pleasant enough, I dare say ! She had better not put on any airs now. All the same, he must have been a god-forsaken young man to go after *that*. Dear, dear, it's just as they used to say in my poor mother's country :

> Snaps and snails and puppy-dogs' tails,
>   And dirty sluts in plenty,
> Smell sweeter than roses in young men's noses
>   When the heart is one-and-twenty."

Although, when her grandson had a slight cold in his head, she would set off at night, even if she were ill also, instead of going to bed, to see whether he had everything that he wanted, covering ten miles on foot before daybreak so as to be in time to begin her work, this same love for her own people, and her desire to establish the future greatness of her house on a solid foundation reacted, in her policy with regard to the other servants, in one unvarying maxim, which was never to let any of them set foot in my aunt's room ; indeed she shewed a sort of pride in not allowing anyone else to come near my aunt, preferring, when she herself was ill, to get out of bed and to administer the Vichy water in person, rather than to concede to the kitchen-maid the right of entry into her mistress's presence. There is a species of hymenoptera, observed by Fabre, the burrowing wasp, which in order to provide a supply of fresh meat for her offspring after her own decease, calls in the science of anatomy to amplify the resources of her instinctive cruelty, and, having made a collection of weevils and spiders, proceeds with marvellous knowledge and skill to pierce the nerve-centre on which their power of locomotion (but none of their other vital functions) depends, so that the paralysed insect, beside which her egg is laid, will furnish the larva, when it is hatched, with a tamed and inoffensive quarry, incapable either of flight or of resistance, but perfectly fresh for the larder : in the same way Françoise had adopted, to minister to her permanent and unfaltering resolution to render the house uninhabitable to any other servant, a series of crafty and pitiless stratagems. Many years later we discovered that, if we had been fed on asparagus day after day throughout that whole season, it was because the smell of the plants gave the poor kitchen-maid, who had to prepare them, such violent attacks of asthma that she was finally obliged to leave my aunt's service.

Alas ! we had definitely to alter our opinion of M. Legrandin. On one of the Sundays following our meeting with him on the Pont-Vieux, after which my father had been forced to confess himself mistaken, as mass drew to an end, and, with the sunshine and the noise of the outer world, something else invaded the church, an atmosphere so far from sacred that Mme. Goupil, Mme. Percepied (everyone, in fact, who a moment ago, when I arrived a little late, had

been sitting motionless, their eyes fixed on their prayer-books;
who, I might even have thought, had not seen me come in,
had not their feet moved slightly to push away the little
kneeling-desk which was preventing me from getting to my
chair) began in loud voices to discuss with us all manner of
utterly mundane topics, as though we were already outside
in the Square, we saw, standing on the sun-baked steps of the
porch, dominating the many-coloured tumult of the market,
Legrandin himself, whom the husband of the lady we had
seen with him, on the previous occasion, was just going to
introduce to the wife of another large landed proprietor of
the district. Legrandin's face shewed an extraordinary zeal
and animation ; he made a profound bow, with a subsidiary
backward movement which brought his spine sharply up
into a position behind its starting-point, a gesture in which he
must have been trained by the husband of his sister, Mme. de
Cambremer. This rapid recovery caused a sort of tense
muscular wave to ripple over Legrandin's hips, which I had
not supposed to be so fleshy ; I cannot say why, but this
undulation of pure matter, this wholly carnal fluency, with
not the least hint in it of spiritual significance, this wave lashed
to a fury by the wind of an assiduity, an obsequiousness of the
basest sort, awoke my mind suddenly to the possibility of a
Legrandin altogether different from the one whom we knew.
The lady gave him some message for her coachman, and while
he was stepping down to her carriage the impression of joy,
timid and devout, which the introduction had stamped there,
still lingered on his face. Carried away in a sort of dream, he
smiled, then he began to hurry back towards the lady ; he
was walking faster than usual, and his shoulders swayed back-
wards and forwards, right and left, in the most absurd fashion ;
altogether he looked, so utterly had he abandoned himself to

it, ignoring all other considerations, as though he were the
lifeless and wire-pulled puppet of his own happiness. Meanwhile we were coming out through the porch ; we were
passing close beside him ; he was too well bred to turn his
head away ; but he fixed his eyes, which had suddenly
changed to those of a seer, lost in the profundity of his vision,
on so distant a point of the horizon that he could not see us,
and so had not to acknowledge our presence. His face
emerged, still with an air of innocence, from his straight and
pliant coat, which looked as though conscious of having been
led astray, in spite of itself, and plunged into surroundings of
a detested splendour. And a spotted necktie, stirred by the
breezes of the Square, continued to float in front of Legrandin,
like the standard of his proud isolation, of his noble independence. Just as we reached the house my mother discovered that we had forgotten the ' Saint-Honoré,' and
asked my father to go back with me and tell them to send it
up at once. Near the church we met Legrandin, coming
towards us with the same lady, whom he was escorting to
her carriage. He brushed past us, and did not interrupt what
he was saying to her, but gave us, out of the corner of his
blue eye, a little sign, which began and ended, so to speak,
inside his eyelids, and as it did not involve the least movement
of his facial muscles, managed to pass quite unperceived by
the lady ; but, striving to compensate by the intensity of his
feelings for the somewhat restricted field in which they had
to find expression, he made that blue chink, which was set
apart for us, sparkle with all the animation of cordiality,
which went far beyond mere playfulness, and almost touched
the border-line of roguery ; he subtilised the refinements of
good-fellowship into a wink of connivance, a hint, a hidden
meaning, a secret understanding, all the mysteries of com-

plicity in a plot, and finally exalted his assurances of friendship
to the level of protestations of affection, even of a declaration
of love, lighting up for us, and for us alone, with a secret and
languid flame invisible by the great lady upon his other side,
an enamoured pupil in a countenance of ice.

Only the day before he had asked my parents to send me
to dine with him on this same Sunday evening. " Come and
bear your aged friend company," he had said to me. " Like
the nosegay which a traveller sends us from some land to which
we shall never go again, come and let me breathe from the
far country of your adolescence the scent of those flowers of
spring among which I also used to wander, many years ago.
Come with the primrose, with the canon's beard, with the
gold-cup ; come with the stone-crop, whereof are posies
made, pledges of love, in the Balzacian flora, come with that
flower of the Resurrection morning, the Easter daisy, come
with the snowballs of the guelder-rose, which begin to
embalm with their fragrance the alleys of your great-aunt's
garden ere the last snows of Lent are melted from its soil.
Come with the glorious silken raiment of the lily, apparel fit
for Solomon, and with the many-coloured enamel of the
pansies, but come, above all, with the spring breeze, still
cooled by the last frosts of winter, wafting apart, for the two
butterflies' sake, that have waited outside all morning, the
closed portals of the first Jerusalem rose."

The question was raised at home whether, all things considered, I ought still to be sent to dine with M. Legrandin.
But my grandmother refused to believe that he could have
been impolite.

" You admit yourself that he appears at church there, quite
simply dressed, and all that ; he hardly looks like a man of
fashion." She added that, in any event, even if, at the worst,

he had been intentionally rude, it was far better for us to pretend that we had noticed nothing. And indeed my father himself, though more annoyed than any of us by the attitude which Legrandin had adopted, may still have held in reserve a final uncertainty as to its true meaning. It was like every attitude or action which reveals a man's deep and hidden character ; they bear no relation to what he has previously said, and we cannot confirm our suspicions by the culprit's evidence, for he will admit nothing ; we are reduced to the evidence of our own senses, and we ask ourselves, in the face of this detached and incoherent fragment of recollection, whether indeed our senses have not been the victims of a hallucination ; with the result that such attitudes, and these alone are of importance in indicating character, are the most apt to leave us in perplexity.

I dined with Legrandin on the terrace of his house, by moonlight. " There is a charming quality, is there not," he said to me, " in this silence ; for hearts that are wounded, as mine is, a novelist, whom you will read in time to come, claims that there is no remedy but silence and shadow. And see you this, my boy, there comes in all lives a time, towards which you still have far to go, when the weary eyes can endure but one kind of light, the light which a fine evening like this prepares for us in the stillroom of darkness, when the ears can listen to no music save what the moonlight breathes through the flute of silence."

I could hear what M. Legrandin was saying ; like everything that he said, it sounded attractive ; but I was disturbed by the memory of a lady whom I had seen recently for the first time ; and thinking, now that I knew that Legrandin was on friendly terms with several of the local aristocracy, that perhaps she also was among his acquaintance, I summoned up all my courage and said to him : " Tell me, sir, do you, by any chance, know the lady—the ladies of Guermantes ? " and I felt glad because, in pronouncing the name, I had secured a sort of power over it, by the mere act of drawing it up out of my dreams and giving it an objective existence in the world of spoken things.

But, at the sound of the word Guermantes, I saw in the middle of each of our friend's blue eyes a little brown dimple appear, as though they had been stabbed by some invisible pin-point, while the rest of his pupils, reacting from the shock, received and secreted the azure overflow. His fringed eyelids darkened, and drooped. His mouth, which had been stiffened and seared with bitter lines, was the first to recover, and smiled, while his eyes still seemed full of pain, like the eyes of a good-looking martyr whose body bristles with arrows.

" No, I do not know them," he said, but instead of uttering so simple a piece of information, a reply in which there was so little that could astonish me, in the natural and con-versational tone which would have befitted it, he recited it with a separate stress upon each word, leaning forward, bowing his head, with at once the vehemence which a man gives, so as to be believed, to a highly improbable statement (as though the fact that he did not know the Guermantes could be due only to some strange accident of fortune) and with the emphasis of a man who, finding himself unable to keep silence about what is to him a painful situation, chooses to proclaim it aloud, so as to convince his hearers that the confession he is making is one that causes him no embarrass-ment, but is easy, agreeable, spontaneous, that the situation in question, in this case the absence of relations with the Guermantes family, might very well have been not forced upon, but actually designed by Legrandin himself, might arise from some family tradition, some moral principle or mystical vow which expressly forbade his seeking their society.

"No," he resumed, explaining by his words the tone in which they were uttered. "No, I do not know them ; I have never wished to know them ; I have always made a point of preserving complete independence ; at heart, as you know, I am a bit of a Radical. People are always coming to me about it, telling me I am mistaken in not going to Guermantes, that I make myself seem ill-bred, uncivilised, an old bear. But that's not the sort of reputation that can frighten me ; it's too true ! In my heart of hearts I care for nothing in the world now but a few churches, books—two or three, pictures—rather more, perhaps, and the light of the moon when the fresh breeze of youth (such as yours) wafts to my nostrils the scent of gardens whose flowers my old eyes are not sharp enough, now, to distinguish."

I did not understand very clearly why, in order to refrain from going to the houses of people whom one did not know, it should be necessary to cling to one's independence, nor how that could give one the appearance of a savage or a bear. But what I did understand was this, that Legrandin was not altogether truthful when he said that he cared only for churches, moonlight, and youth ; he cared also, he cared a very great deal for people who lived in country houses, and would be so much afraid, when in their company, of incurring their displeasure that he would never dare to let them see that he numbered, as well, among his friends middle-class people, the families of solicitors and stockbrokers, preferring, if the truth must be known, that it should be revealed in his absence, when he was out of earshot, that judgment should

go against him (if so it must) by default : in a word, he was a
snob. Of course he would never have admitted all or any
of this in the poetical language which my family and I so
much admired. And if I asked him, " Do you know the
Guermantes family ? " Legrandin the talker would reply,
" No, I have never cared to know them." But unfortunately
the talker was now subordinated to another Legrandin, whom
he kept carefully hidden in his breast, whom he would never
consciously exhibit, because this other could tell stories about
our own Legrandin and about his snobbishness which would
have ruined his reputation for ever ; and this other Legrandin
had replied to me already in that wounded look, that stiffened
smile, the undue gravity of his tone in uttering those few
words, in the thousand arrows by which our own Legrandin
had instantaneously been stabbed and sickened, like a Saint
Sebastian of snobbery :

" Oh, how you hurt me ! No, I do not know the Guermantes family. Do not remind me of the great sorrow of my
life." And since this other, this irrepressible, dominant,
despotic Legrandin, if he lacked our Legrandin's charming
vocabulary, shewed an infinitely greater promptness in
expressing himself, by means of what are called ' reflexes,'
it followed that, when Legrandin the talker attempted to
silence him, he would already have spoken, and it would be
useless for our friend to deplore the bad impression which the
revelations of his *alter ego* must have caused, since he could
do no more now than endeavour to mitigate them.

This was not to say that M. Legrandin was anything but
sincere when he inveighed against snobs. He could not (from
his own knowledge, at least) be aware that he was one also,
since it is only with the passions of others that we are ever
really familiar, and what we come to find out about our own

can be no more than what other people have shewn us. Upon ourselves they react but indirectly, through our imagination, which substitutes for our actual, primary motives other, secondary motives, less stark and therefore more decent. Never had Legrandin's snobbishness impelled him to make a habit of visiting a duchess as such. Instead, it would set his imagination to make that duchess appear, in Legrandin's eyes, endowed with all the graces. He would be drawn towards the duchess, assuring himself the while that he was yielding to the attractions of her mind, and her other virtues, which the vile race of snobs could never understand. Only his fellow-snobs knew that he was of their number, for, owing to their inability to appreciate the intervening efforts of his imagination, they saw in close juxtaposition the social activities of Legrandin and their primary cause.

At home, meanwhile, we had no longer any illusions as to M. Legrandin, and our relations with him had become much more distant. Mamma would be greatly delighted whenever she caught him red-handed in the sin, which he continued to call the unpardonable sin, of snobbery. As for my father, he found it difficult to take Legrandin's airs in so light, in so detached a spirit ; and when there was some talk, one year, of sending me to spend the long summer holidays at Balbec with my grandmother, he said : " I must, most certainly, tell Legrandin that you are going to Balbec, to see whether he will offer you an introduction to his sister. He probably doesn't remember telling us that she lived within a mile of the place."

My grandmother, who held that, when one went to the seaside, one ought to be on the beach from morning to night, to taste the salt breezes, and that one should not know anyone in the place, because calls and parties and excursions were so much time stolen from what belonged, by rights, to the sea-air, begged him on no account to speak to Legrandin of our plans ; for already, in her mind's eye, she could see his sister, Mme. de Cambremer, alighting from her carriage at the door of our hotel just as we were on the point of going out fishing, and obliging us to remain indoors all afternoon to entertain her. But Mamma laughed her fears to scorn, for she herself felt that the danger was not so threatening, and that Legrandin would shew no undue anxiety to make us acquainted with his sister. And, as it happened, there was no need for any of us to introduce the subject of Balbec, for it was Legrandin himself who, without the least suspicion that we had ever had any intention of visiting those parts, walked into the trap uninvited one evening, when we met him strolling on the banks of the Vivonne.

" There are tints in the clouds this evening, violets and blues, which are very beautiful, are they not, my friend ? " he said to my father, " especially a blue which is far more floral than atmospheric, a cineraria blue, which it is surprising to see in the sky. And that little pink cloud there, has it not just the tint of some flower, a carnation or hydrangea ? Nowhere, perhaps, except on the shores of the English Channel, where Normandy merges into Brittany, have I been able to find such copious examples of what you might call a vegetable kingdom in the clouds. Down there, close to Balbec, among all those places which are still so uncivilised, there is a little bay, charmingly quiet, where the sunsets of the Auge Valley, those red-and-gold sunsets (which, all the same, I am very far from despising) seem commonplace and insignificant ; for in that moist and gentle atmosphere these heavenly flower-beds will break into blossom, in a few moments, in the evenings, incomparably lovely, and often lasting for hours before they fade. Others shed their leaves at once, and then it is more beautiful still to see the sky strewn with the scattering of their innumerable petals, sulphurous yellow and rosy red. In that bay, which they call the Opal Bay, the golden sands appear more charming still from being fastened, like fair Andromeda, to those terrible rocks of the surrounding coast, to that funereal shore, famed for the number of its wrecks, where every winter many a brave vessel falls a victim to the perils of the sea. Balbec ! the oldest bone in the geological skeleton that underlies our soil, the true Ar-mor, the sea, the land's end, the accursed region which Anatole France—an enchanter whose works our young friend ought to read—has so well depicted, beneath its eternal fogs, as though it were indeed the land of the Cimmerians in the Odyssey. Balbec ; yes, they are building hotels there now, superimposing them upon its ancient and charming soil, which they are powerless to alter ; how delightful it is, down there, to be able to step out at once into regions so primitive and so entrancing."

"Indeed ! And do you know anyone at Balbec ? " inquired my father. "This young man is just going to spend a couple of months there with his grandmother, and my wife too, perhaps."

Legrandin, taken unawares by the question at a moment when he was looking directly at my father, was unable to turn aside his gaze, and so concentrated it with steadily increasing intensity—smiling mournfully the while—upon the eyes of his questioner, with an air of friendliness and frankness and of not being afraid to look him in the face, until he seemed to have penetrated my father's skull, as it had been a ball of glass, and to be seeing, at the moment, a long way beyond and behind it, a brightly coloured cloud, which provided him with a mental alibi, and would enable him to establish the theory that, just when he was being asked whether he knew anyone at Balbec, he had been thinking of something else, and so had not heard the question. As a rule these tactics make the questioner proceed to ask, " Why, what are you thinking about ? " But my father, inquisitive, annoyed, and cruel, repeated : " Have you friends, then, in that neighbourhood, that you know Balbec so well ? "

In a final and desperate effort the smiling gaze of Legrandin struggled to the extreme limits of its tenderness, vagueness, candour, and distraction ; then feeling, no doubt, that there was nothing left for it now but to answer, he said to us : " I have friends all the world over, wherever there are companies of trees, stricken but not defeated, which have come together to offer a common supplication, with pathetic obstinacy, to an inclement sky which has no mercy upon them."

" That is not quite what I meant," interrupted my father, obstinate as a tree and merciless as the sky. " I asked you, in case anything should happen to my mother-in-law and she wanted to feel that she was not all alone down there, at the ends of the earth, whether you knew any of the people."

" There as elsewhere, I know everyone and I know no one," replied Legrandin, who was by no means ready yet to surrender ; " places I know well, people very slightly. But, down there, the places themselves seem to me just like people, rare and wonderful people, of a delicate quality which would have been corrupted and ruined by the gift of life. Perhaps it is a castle which you encounter upon the cliff's edge ; standing there by the roadside, where it has halted to contemplate its sorrows before an evening sky, still rosy, through which a golden moon is climbing ; while the fishing-boats, homeward bound, creasing the watered silk of the Channel, hoist its pennant at their mastheads and carry its colours. Or perhaps it is a simple dwelling-house that stands alone, ugly, if anything, timid-seeming but full of romance, hiding from every eye some imperishable secret of happiness and dis-enchantment. That land which knows not truth," he continued with Machiavellian subtlety, " that land of infinite fiction makes bad reading for any boy ; and is certainly not what I should choose or recommend for my young friend here, who is already so much inclined to melancholy, for a heart already predisposed to receive its impressions. Climates that breathe amorous secrets and futile regrets may agree with an old and disillusioned man like myself ; but they must always prove fatal to a temperament which is still unformed. Believe me," he went on with emphasis, " the waters of that bay—more Breton than Norman—may exert a sedative influence, though even that is of questionable value, upon a heart which, like mine, is no longer unbroken, a heart for whose wounds there is no longer anything to compensate. But at your age, my boy, those waters are contra-indicated. . . . Good night to you, neighbours," he added, moving away from us with that evasive abruptness to which we were accustomed ; and then, turning towards us, with a physi-cianly finger raised in warning, he resumed the consultation : " No Balbec before you are fifty ! " he called out to me, " and even then it must depend on the state of the heart."

My father spoke to him of it again, as often as we met him, and tortured him with questions, but it was labour in vain : like that scholarly swindler who devoted to the fabrication of forged palimpsests a wealth of skill and knowledge and in-dustry the hundredth part of which would have sufficed to establish him in a more lucrative—but an honourable occupa-

tion, M. Legrandin, had we insisted further, would in the
end have constructed a whole system of ethics, and a celestial
geography of Lower Normandy, sooner than admit to us that,
within a mile of Balbec, his own sister was living in her own
house ; sooner than find himself obliged to offer us a letter of
introduction, the prospect of which would never have inspired
him with such terror had he been absolutely certain—as,
from his knowledge of my grandmother's character, he really
ought to have been certain—that in no circumstances whatsoever would we have dreamed of making use of it.

* * *

We used always to return from our walks in good time to
pay aunt Léonie a visit before dinner. In the first weeks of
our Combray holidays, when the days ended early, we would
still be able to see, as we turned into the Rue du Saint-Esprit,
a reflection of the western sky from the windows of the house
and a band of purple at the foot of the Calvary, which was
mirrored further on in the pond ; a fiery glow which, accompanied often by a cold that burned and stung, would
associate itself in my mind with the glow of the fire over
which, at that very moment, was roasting the chicken that
was to furnish me, in place of the poetic pleasure I had found
in my walk, with the sensual pleasures of good feeding,
warmth and rest. But in summer, when we came back to the
house, the sun would not have set ; and while we were upstairs paying our visit to aunt Léonie its rays, sinking until
they touched and lay along her window-sill, would there be
caught and held by the large inner curtains and the bands
which tied them back to the wall, and split and scattered and
filtered ; and then, at last, would fall upon and inlay with
tiny flakes of gold the lemon-wood of her chest-of-drawers,

illuminating the room in their passage with the same delicate, slanting, shadowed beams that fall among the boles of forest trees. But on some days, though very rarely, the chest-of-drawers would long since have shed its momentary adornments, there would no longer, as we turned into the Rue du Saint-Esprit, be any reflection from the western sky burning along the line of window-panes ; the pond beneath the Calvary would have lost its fiery glow, sometimes indeed had changed already to an opalescent pallor, while a long ribbon of moonlight, bent and broken and broadened by every ripple upon the water's surface, would be lying across it, from end to end. Then, as we drew near the house, we would make out a figure standing upon the doorstep, and Mamma would say to me : " Good heavens ! There is Françoise looking out for us ; your aunt must be anxious ; that means we are late."

And without wasting time by stopping to take off our ' things ' we would fly upstairs to my aunt Léonie's room to reassure her, to prove to her by our bodily presence that all her gloomy imaginings were false, that, on the contrary, nothing had happened to us, but that we had gone the ' Guermantes way,' and, good lord, when one took that walk, my aunt knew well enough that one could never say at what time one would be home.

" There, Françoise," my aunt would say, " didn't I tell you that they must have gone the Guermantes way ? Good gracious ! They must be hungry ! And your nice leg of mutton will be quite dried up now, after all the hours it's been waiting. What a time to come in ! Well, and so you went the Guermantes way ? "

" But, Léonie, I supposed you knew," Mamma would answer. " I thought that Françoise had seen us go out by the little gate, through the kitchen-garden."

For there were, in the environs of Combray, two ' ways '
which we used to take for our walks, and so diametrically op-
posed that we would actually leave the house by a different
door, according to the way we had chosen : the way towards
Méséglise-la-Vineuse, which we called also ' Swann's way,'
because, to get there, one had to pass along the boundary of
M. Swann's estate, and the ' Guermantes way.' Of
Méséglise-la-Vineuse, to tell the truth, I never knew anything more than the way there, and the strange people who
would come over on Sundays to take the air in Combray,
people whom, this time, neither my aunt nor any of us would
' know at all,' and whom we would therefore assume to be
' people who must have come over from Méséglise.' As
for Guermantes, I was to know it well enough one day, but
that day had still to come ; and, during the whole of my boy-
hood, if Méséglise was to me something as inaccessible as the
horizon, which remained hidden from sight, however far one
went, by the folds of a country which no longer bore the least
resemblance to the country round Combray; Guermantes,
on the other hand, meant no more than the ultimate goal,
ideal rather than real, of the ' Guermantes way,' a sort of
abstract geographical term like the North Pole or the Equator.
And so to ' take the Guermantes way ' in order to get to
Méséglise, or *vice versa*, would have seemed to me as non-
sensical a proceeding as to turn to the east in order to reach
the west. Since my father used always to speak of the
' Méséglise way ' as comprising the finest view of a plain
that he knew anywhere, and of the ' Guermantes way ' as
typical of river scenery, I had invested each of them, by con-
ceiving them in this way as two distinct entities, with that
cohesion, that unity which belongs only to the figments of
the mind ; the smallest detail of either of them appeared to

me as a precious thing, which exhibited the special excellence
of the whole, while, immediately beside them, in the first
stages of our walk, before we had reached the sacred soil of
one or the other, the purely material roads, at definite points
on which they were set down as the ideal view over a plain
and the ideal scenery of a river, were no more worth the
trouble of looking at them than, to a keen playgoer and lover
of dramatic art, are the little streets which may happen to run
past the walls of a theatre. But, above all, I set between them,
far more distinctly than the mere distance in miles and yards
and inches which separated one from the other, the distance
that there was between the two parts of my brain in which
I used to think of them, one of those distances of the mind
which time serves only to lengthen, which separate things
irremediably from one another, keeping them for ever upon
different planes. And this distinction was rendered still more
absolute because the habit we had of never going both ways
on the same day, or in the course of the same walk, but the
' Méséglise way ' one time and the ' Guermantes way '
another, shut them up, so to speak, far apart and unaware of
each other's existence, in the sealed vessels—between which
there could be no communication—of separate afternoons.

When we had decided to go the ' Méséglise way ' we
would start (without undue haste, and even if the sky were
clouded over, since the walk was not very long, and did not
take us too far from home), as though we were not going
anywhere in particular, by the front-door of my aunt's house,
which opened on to the Rue du Saint-Esprit. We would be
greeted by the gunsmith, we would drop our letters into the
box, we would tell Théodore, from Françoise, as we passed,
that she had run out of oil or coffee, and we would leave
the town by the road which ran along the white fence of

M. Swann's park. Before reaching it we would be met on our way by the scent of his lilac-trees, come out to welcome strangers. Out of the fresh little green hearts of their foliage the lilacs raised inquisitively over the fence of the park their plumes of white or purple blossom, which glowed, even in the shade, with the sunlight in which they had been bathed. Some of them, half-concealed by the little tiled house, called the Archers' Lodge, in which Swann's keeper lived, over-topped its gothic gable with their rosy minaret. The nymphs of spring would have seemed coarse and vulgar in comparison with these young houris, who retained, in this French garden, the pure and vivid colouring of a Persian miniature. Despite my desire to throw my arms about their pliant forms and to draw down towards me the starry locks that crowned their fragrant heads, we would pass them by without stopping, for my parents had ceased to visit Tansonville since Swann's marriage, and, so as not to appear to be looking into his park, we would, instead of taking the road which ran beside its boundary and then climbed straight up to the open fields, choose another way, which led in the same direction, but circuitously, and brought us out rather too far from home.

One day my grandfather said to my father : " Don't you remember Swann's telling us yesterday that his wife and daughter had gone off to Rheims and that he was taking the opportunity of spending a day or two in Paris ? We might go along by the park, since the ladies are not at home ; that will make it a little shorter."

We stopped for a moment by the fence. Lilac-time was nearly over ; some of the trees still thrust aloft, in tall purple chandeliers, their tiny balls of blossom, but in many places among their foliage where, only a week before, they had still been breaking in waves of fragrant foam, these were now

I   185   G 2

spent and shrivelled and discoloured, a hollow scum, dry and scentless. My grandfather pointed out to my father in what respects the appearance of the place was still the same, and how far it had altered since the walk that he had taken with old M. Swann, on the day of his wife's death ; and he seized the opportunity to tell us, once again, the story of that walk.

In front of us a path bordered with nasturtiums rose in the full glare of the sun towards the house. But to our right the park stretched away into the distance, on level ground. Overshadowed by the tall trees which stood close around it, an 'ornamental water' had been constructed by Swann's parents ; but, even in his most artificial creations, nature is the material upon which man has to work ; certain spots will persist in remaining surrounded by the vassals of their own especial sovereignty, and will raise their immemorial standards among all the 'laid-out' scenery of a park, just as they would have done far from any human interference, in a solitude which must everywhere return to engulf them, springing up out of the necessities of their exposed position, and superimposing itself upon the work of man's hands. And so it was that, at the foot of the path which led down to this artificial lake, there might be seen, in its two tiers woven of trailing forget-me-nots below and of periwinkle flowers above, the natural, delicate, blue garland which binds the luminous, shadowed brows of water-nymphs ; while the iris, its swords sweeping every way in regal profusion, stretched out over agrimony and water-growing king-cups the lilied sceptres, tattered glories of yellow and purple, of the kingdom of the lake.

The absence of Mlle. Swann, which—since it preserved me from the terrible risk of seeing her appear on one of the paths, and of being identified and scorned by this so privileged little girl who had Bergotte for a friend and used to go with

him to visit cathedrals—made the exploration of Tansonville, now for the first time permitted me, a matter of indifference to myself, seemed however to invest the property,
in my grandfather's and father's eyes, with a fresh and transient charm, and (like an entirely cloudless sky when one is
going mountaineering) to make the day extraordinarily propitious for a walk in this direction ; I should have liked to see
their reckoning proved false, to see, by a miracle, Mlle.
Swann appear, with her father, so close to us that we should
not have time to escape, and should therefore be obliged to
make her acquaintance. And so, when I suddenly noticed
a straw basket lying forgotten on the grass by the side of a line
whose float was bobbing in the water, I made a great effort
to keep my father and grandfather looking in another direction, away from this sign that she might, after all, be in
residence. Still, as Swann had told us that he ought not,
really, to go away just then, as he had some people staying
in the house, the line might equally belong to one of these
guests. Not a footstep was to be heard on any of the paths.
Somewhere in one of the tall trees, making a stage in its
height, an invisible bird, desperately attempting to make the
day seem shorter, was exploring with a long, continuous note
the solitude that pressed it on every side, but it received at
once so unanimous an answer, so powerful a repercussion of
silence and of immobility that, one would have said, it had
arrested for all eternity the moment which it had been trying
to make pass more quickly. The sunlight fell so implacably
from a fixed sky that one was naturally inclined to slip away
out of the reach of its attentions, and even the slumbering
water, whose repose was perpetually being invaded by the
insects that swarmed above its surface, while it dreamed, no
doubt, of some imaginary maelstrom, intensified the uneasi-

ness which the sight of that floating cork had wrought in me,
by appearing to draw it at full speed across the silent reaches
of a mirrored firmament ; now almost vertical, it seemed on
the point of plunging down out of sight, and I had begun to
ask myself whether, setting aside the longing and the terror
that I had of making her acquaintance, it was not actually
my duty to warn Mlle. Swann that the fish was biting—when
I was obliged to run after my father and grandfather, who
were calling me, and were surprised that I had not followed
them along the little path, climbing up hill towards the open
fields, into which they had already turned. I found the whole
path throbbing with the fragrance of hawthorn-blossom.
The hedge resembled a series of chapels, whose walls were no
longer visible under the mountains of flowers that were
heaped upon their altars ; while, underneath, the sun cast a
square of light upon the ground, as though it had shone in
upon them through a window ; the scent that swept out over
me from them was as rich, and as circumscribed in its range,
as though I had been standing before the Lady-altar, and the
flowers, themselves adorned also, held out each its little bunch
of glittering stamens with an air of inattention, fine, radiating
' nerves ' in the flamboyant style of architecture, like those
which, in church, framed the stair to the rood-loft or closed
the perpendicular tracery of the windows, but here spread out
into pools of fleshy white, like strawberry-beds in spring.
How simple and rustic, in comparison with these, would
seem the dog-roses which, in a few weeks' time, would be
climbing the same hillside path in the heat of the sun, dressed
in the smooth silk of their blushing pink bodices, which would
be undone and scattered by the first breath of wind.

But it was in vain that I lingered before the hawthorns,
to breathe in, to marshal before my mind (which knew not

GILBERTE AT COMBRAY

what to make of it), to lose in order to rediscover their invisible and unchanging odour, to absorb myself in the rhythm which disposed their flowers here and there with the light-heartedness of youth, and at intervals as unexpected as certain intervals of music ; they offered me an indefinite continuation of the same charm, in an inexhaustible profusion, but without letting me delve into it any more deeply, like those melodies which one can play over a hundred times in succession without coming any nearer to their secret. I turned away from them for a moment so as to be able to return to them with renewed strength. My eyes followed up the slope which, outside the hedge, rose steeply to the fields, a poppy that had strayed and been lost by its fellows, or a few cornflowers that had fallen lazily behind, and decorated the ground here and there with their flowers like the border of a tapestry, in which may be seen at intervals hints of the rustic theme which appears triumphant in the panel itself ; infrequent still, spaced apart as the scattered houses which warn us that we are approaching a village, they betokened to me the vast expanse of waving corn beneath the fleecy clouds, and the sight of a single poppy hoisting upon its slender rigging and holding against the breeze its scarlet ensign, over the buoy of rich black earth from which it sprang, made my heart beat as does a wayfarer's when he perceives, upon some low-lying ground, an old and broken boat which is being caulked and made sea-worthy, and cries out, although he has not yet caught sight of it, "The Sea ! "

And then I returned to my hawthorns, and stood before them as one stands before those masterpieces of painting which, one imagines, one will be better able to 'take in' when one has looked away, for a moment, at something else ; but in vain did I shape my fingers into a frame, so as to have nothing but the hawthorns before my eyes ; the sentiment which they aroused in me remained obscure and vague, struggling and failing to free itself, to float across and become one with the flowers. They themselves offered me no en-lightenment, and I could not call upon any other flowers to satisfy this mysterious longing. And then, inspiring me with that rapture which we feel on seeing a work by our favourite painter quite different from any of those that we already know, or, better still, when some one has taken us and set us down in front of a picture of which we have hitherto seen no more than a pencilled sketch, or when a piece of music which we have heard played over on the piano bursts out again in our ears with all the splendour and fullness of an orchestra, my grandfather called me to him, and, pointing to the hedge of Tansonville, said : " You are fond of hawthorns ; just look at this pink one ; isn't it pretty ? "

And it was indeed a hawthorn, but one whose flowers were pink, and lovelier even than the white. It, too, was in holiday attire, for one of those days which are the only true holidays, the holy days of religion, because they are not appointed by any capricious accident, as secular holidays are appointed, upon days which are not specially ordained for such obser-vances, which have nothing about them that is essentially festal—but it was attired even more richly than the rest, for the flowers which clung to its branches, one above an-other, so thickly as to leave no part of the tree undecorated, like the tassels wreathed about the crook of a rococo shep-herdess, were every one of them ' in colour,' and conse-quently of a superior quality, by the aesthetic standards of Combray, to the ' plain,' if one was to judge by the scale of prices at the ' stores ' in the Square, or at Camus's, where the most expensive biscuits were those whose sugar was pink.

And for my own part I set a higher value on cream cheese when it was pink, when I had been allowed to tinge it with crushed strawberries. And these flowers had chosen precisely the colour of some edible and delicious thing, or of some exquisite addition to one's costume for a great festival, which colours, inasmuch as they make plain the reason for their superiority, are those whose beauty is most evident to the eyes of children, and for that reason must always seem more vivid and more natural than any other tints, even after the child's mind has realised that they offer no gratification to the appetite, and have not been selected by the dressmaker. And, indeed, I had felt at once, as I had felt before the white blossom, but now still more marvelling, that it was in no artificial manner, by no device of human construction, that the festal intention of these flowers was revealed, but that it was Nature herself who had spontaneously expressed it (with the simplicity of a woman from a village shop, labouring at the decoration of a street altar for some procession) by burying the bush in these little rosettes, almost too ravishing in colour, this rustic ' pompadour.' High up on the branches, like so many of those tiny rose-trees, their pots concealed in jackets of paper lace, whose slender stems rise in a forest from the altar on the greater festivals, a thousand buds were swelling and opening, paler in colour, but each disclosing as it burst, as at the bottom of a cup of pink marble, its blood-red stain, and suggesting even more strongly than the full-blown flowers the special, irresistible quality of the hawthorn-tree, which, wherever it budded, wherever it was about to blossom, could bud and blossom in pink flowers alone. Taking its place in the hedge, but as different from the rest as a young girl in holiday attire among a crowd of dowdy women in everyday clothes, who are staying at home, equipped and

ready for the ' Month of Mary,' of which it seemed already
to form a part, it shone and smiled in its cool, rosy garments,
a Catholic bush indeed, and altogether delightful.

The hedge allowed us a glimpse, inside the park, of an
alley bordered with jasmine, pansies, and verbenas, among
which the stocks held open their fresh plump purses, of a pink
as fragrant and as faded as old Spanish leather, while on the
gravel-path a long watering-pipe, painted green, coiling across
the ground, poured, where its holes were, over the flowers
whose perfume those holes inhaled, a vertical and prismatic
fan of infinitesimal, rainbow-coloured drops. Suddenly I
stood still, unable to move, as happens when something appears that requires not only our eyes to take it in, but involves
a deeper kind of perception and takes possession of the whole
of our being. A little girl, with fair, reddish hair, who appeared to be returning from a walk, and held a trowel in her
hand, was looking at us, raising towards us a face powdered
with pinkish freckles. Her black eyes gleamed, and as I did
not at that time know, and indeed have never since learned
how to reduce to its objective elements any strong impression,
since I had not, as they say, enough ' power of observation '
to isolate the sense of their colour, for a long time afterwards,
whenever I thought of her, the memory of those bright eyes
would at once present itself to me as a vivid azure, since her
complexion was fair ; so much so that, perhaps, if her eyes
had not been quite so black—which was what struck one
most forcibly on first meeting her—I should not have been,
as I was, especially enamoured of their imagined blue.

I gazed at her, at first with that gaze which is not merely a
messenger from the eyes, but in whose window all the senses
assemble and lean out, petrified and anxious, that gaze which
would fain reach, touch, capture, bear off in triumph the

body at which it is aimed, and the soul with the body ; then (so frightened was I lest at any moment my grandfather and father, catching sight of the girl, might tear me away from her, by making me run on in front of them) with another, an unconsciously appealing look, whose object was to force her to pay attention to me, to see, to know me. She cast a glance forwards and sideways, so as to take stock of my grandfather and father, and doubtless the impression she formed of them was that we were all absurd people, for she turned away with an indifferent and contemptuous air, withdrew herself so as to spare her face the indignity of remaining within their field of vision ; and while they, continuing to walk on without noticing her, had overtaken and passed me, she allowed her eyes to wander, over the space that lay between us, in my direction, without any particular expression, without appearing to have seen me, but with an intensity, a half-hidden smile which I was unable to interpret, according to the instruction I had received in the ways of good breeding, save as a mark of infinite disgust ; and her hand, at the same time, sketched in the air an indelicate gesture, for which, when it was addressed in public to a person whom one did not know, the little dictionary of manners which I carried in my mind supplied only one meaning, namely, a deliberate insult.

"Gilberte, come along ; what are you doing ? " called out in a piercing tone of authority a lady in white, whom I had not seen until that moment, while, a little way beyond her, a gentleman in a suit of linen 'ducks,' whom I did not know either, stared at me with eyes which seemed to be starting from his head ; the little girl's smile abruptly faded, and, seizing her trowel, she made off without turning to look again in my direction, with an air of obedience, inscrutable and sly.

And so was wafted to my ears the name of Gilberte, bestowed on me like a talisman which might, perhaps, enable me some day to rediscover her whom its syllables had just endowed with a definite personality, whereas, a moment earlier, she had been only something vaguely seen. So it came to me, uttered across the heads of the stocks and jasmines, pungent and cool as the drops which fell from the green watering-pipe ; impregnating and irradiating the zone of pure air through which it had passed, which it set apart and isolated from all other air, with the mystery of the life of her whom its syllables designated to the happy creatures that lived and walked and travelled in her company ; unfolding through the arch of the pink hawthorn, which opened at the height of my shoulder, the quintessence of their familiarity— so exquisitely painful to myself—with her, and with all that unknown world of her existence, into which I should never penetrate.

For a moment (while we moved away, and my grandfather murmured : " Poor Swann, what a life they are leading him ; fancy sending him away so that she can be left alone with her Charlus—for that was Charlus : I recognised him at once ! And the child, too ; at her age, to be mixed up in all that ! ") the impression left on me by the despotic tone in which Gilberte's mother had spoken to her, without her replying, by exhibiting her to me as being obliged to yield obedience to some one else, as not being indeed superior to the whole world, calmed my sufferings somewhat, revived some hope in me, and cooled the ardour of my love But very soon that love surged up again in me like a reaction by which my humiliated heart was endeavouring to rise to Gilberte's level, or to draw her down to its own. I loved her ; I was sorry not to have had the time and the inspiration to insult her, to do

her some injury, to force her to keep some memory of me.
I knew her to be so beautiful that I should have liked to be
able to retrace my steps so as to shake my fist at her and shout,
" I think you are hideous, grotesque ; you are utterly dis-
gusting ! " However, I walked away, carrying with me,
then and for ever afterwards, as the first illustration of a type
of happiness rendered inaccessible to a little boy of my kind
by certain laws of nature which it was impossible to transgress, the picture of a little girl with reddish hair, and a skin
freckled with tiny pink marks, who held a trowel in her hand,
and smiled as she directed towards me a long and subtle and in-
expressive stare. And already the charm with which her
name, like a cloud of incense, had filled that archway in the
pink hawthorn through which she and I had, together, heard
its sound, was beginning to conquer, to cover, to embalm,
to beautify everything with which it had any association : her
grandparents, whom my own had been so unspeakably fortunate as to know, the glorious profession of a stockbroker, even
the melancholy neighbourhood of the Champs-Elysées, where
she lived in Paris.

" Léonie," said my grandfather on our return, " I wish
we had had you with us this afternoon. You would never
have known Tansonville. If I had had the courage I would
have cut you a branch of that pink hawthorn you used to like
so much." And so my grandfather told her the story of our
walk, either just to amuse her, or perhaps because there was
still some hope that she might be stimulated to rise from her
bed and to go out of doors. For in earlier days she had been
very fond of Tansonville, and, moreover, Swann's visits had
been the last that she had continued to receive, at a time when
she had already closed her doors to all the world. And just as,
when he called, in these later days, to inquire for her (and

she was still the only person in our household whom he would ask to see), she would send down to say that she was tired at the moment and resting, but that she would be happy to see him another time, so, this evening, she said to my grandfather, " Yes, some day when the weather is fine I shall go for a drive as far as the gate of the park." And in saying this she was quite sincere. She would have liked to see Swann and Tansonville again ; but the mere wish to do so sufficed for all that remained of her strength, which its fulfilment would have more than exhausted. Sometimes a spell of fine weather made her a little more energetic, she would rise and put on her clothes ; but before she had reached the outer room she would be ' tired ' again, and would insist on returning to her bed. The process which had begun in her—and in her a little earlier only than it must come to all of us—was the great and general renunciation which old age makes in preparation for death, the chrysalis stage of life, which may be observed wherever life has been unduly prolonged ; even in old lovers who have lived for one another with the utmost intensity of passion, and in old friends bound by the closest ties of mental sympathy, who, after a certain year, cease to make the necessary journey, or even to cross the street to see one another, cease to correspond, and know well that they will communicate no more in this world. My aunt must have been perfectly well aware that she would not see Swann again, that she would never leave her own house any more, but this ultimate seclusion seemed to be accepted by her with all the more readiness for the very reason which, to our minds, ought to have made it more unbearable ; namely, that such a seclusion was forced upon her by the gradual and steady diminution in her strength which she was able to measure daily, which, by making every action, every movement 'tiring' to her if not actually painful, gave to inaction, isolation and silence the blessed, strengthening and refreshing charm of repose.

My aunt did not go to see the pink hawthorn in the hedge, but at all hours of the day I would ask the rest of my family whether she was not going to go, whether she used not, at one time, to go often to Tansonville, trying to make them speak of Mlle. Swann's parents and grandparents, who appeared to me to be as great and glorious as gods. The name, which had for me become almost mythological, of Swann—when I talked with my family I would grow sick with longing to hear them utter it ; I dared not pronounce it myself, but I would draw them into the discussion of matters which led naturally to Gilberte and her family, in which she was involved, in speaking of which I would feel myself not too remotely banished from her company ; and I would suddenly force my father (by pretending, for instance, to believe that my grandfather's business had been in our family before his day, or that the hedge with the pink hawthorn which my aunt Léonie wished to visit was on common ground) to correct my statements, to say, as though in opposition to me and of his own accord : "No, no, the business belonged to *Swann's* father, that hedge is part of *Swann's* park." And then I would be obliged to pause for breath ; so stifling was the pressure, upon that part of me where it was for ever inscribed, of that name which, at the moment when I heard it, seemed to me fuller, more portentous than any other name, because it was burdened with the weight of all the occasions on which I had secretly uttered it in my mind. It caused me a pleasure which I was ashamed to have dared to demand from my parents, for so great was it that to have procured it for me must have involved them in an immensity of effort, and with no recompense, since for them there was no pleasure in the sound. And so I would prudently turn the conversation. And by a scruple of conscience, also. All the singular seductions which I had stored up in the sound of that word Swann, I found again as soon as it was uttered. And then it occurred to me suddenly that my parents could not fail to experience the same emotions, that they must find themselves sharing my point of view, that they perceived in their turn, that they condoned, that they even embraced my visionary longings, and I was as wretched as though I had ravished and corrupted the innocence of their hearts.

That year my family fixed the day of their return to Paris rather earlier than usual. On the morning of our departure I had had my hair curled, to be ready to face the photographer, had had a new hat carefully set upon my head, and had been buttoned into a velvet jacket ; a little later my mother, after searching everywhere for me, found me standing in tears on that steep little hillside close to Tansonville, bidding a long farewell to my hawthorns, clasping their sharp branches to my bosom, and (like a princess in a tragedy, oppressed by the weight of all her senseless jewellery) with no gratitude towards the officious hand which had, in curling those ringlets, been at pains to collect all my hair upon my forehead ; trampling underfoot the curl-papers which I had torn from my head, and my new hat with them. My mother was not at all moved by my tears, but she could not suppress a cry at the sight of my battered headgear and my ruined jacket. I did not, however, hear her. " Oh, my poor little hawthorns," I was assuring them through my sobs, " it is not you that want to make me unhappy, to force me to leave you. You, you have never done me any harm. So I shall always love you." And, drying my eyes, I promised them that, when I grew up, I would never copy the foolish example of other men, but that even in Paris, on fine spring days, instead of paying calls and listening to silly talk, I would make excursions into the country to see the first hawthorn-trees in bloom.

Once in the fields we never left them again during the rest of our Méséglise walk. They were perpetually crossed, as though by invisible streams of traffic, by the wind, which was to me the tutelary genius of Combray. Every year, on the day of our arrival, in order to feel that I really was at Combray, I would climb the hill to find it running again through my clothing, and setting me running in its wake. One always had the wind for companion when one went the ' Méséglise way,' on that swelling plain which stretched, mile beyond mile, without any disturbance of its gentle contour. I knew that Mlle. Swann used often to go and spend a few days at Laon, and, for all that it was many miles away, the distance was obviated by the absence of any intervening obstacle ; when, on hot afternoons, I would see a breath of wind emerge from the farthest horizon, bowing the heads of the corn in distant fields, pouring like a flood over all that vast expanse, and finally settling down, warm and rustling, among the clover and sainfoin at my feet, that plain which was common to us both seemed then to draw us together, to unite us ; I would imagine that the same breath had passed by her also, that there was some message from her in what it was whispering to me, without my being able to understand it, and I would catch and kiss it as it passed. On my left was a village called Champieu (*Campus Pagani*, according to the Curé). On my right I could see across the cornfields the two crocketed, rustic spires of Saint-André-des-Champs, themselves as tapering, scaly, plated, honeycombed, yellowed, and roughened as two ears of wheat.

At regular intervals, among the inimitable ornamentation of their leaves, which can be mistaken for those of no other fruit-tree, the apple-trees were exposing their broad petals of white satin, or hanging in shy bunches their unopened, blushing buds. It was while going the ' Méséglise way ' that I first noticed the circular shadow which apple-trees cast upon the sunlit ground, and also those impalpable threads of golden silk which the setting sun weaves slantingly downwards from beneath their leaves, and which I would see my father slash through with his stick without ever making them swerve from their straight path.

Sometimes in the afternoon sky a white moon would creep up like a little cloud, furtive, without display, suggesting an actress who does not have to ' come on ' for a while, and so goes ' in front ' in her ordinary clothes to watch the rest of the company for a moment, but keeps in the background, not wishing to attract attention to herself. I was glad to find her image reproduced in books and paintings, though these works of art were very different—at least in my earlier years, before Bloch had attuned my eyes and mind to more subtle harmonies—from those in which the moon seems fair to me to-day, but in which I should not have recognised her then. It might be, for instance, some novel by Saintine, some landscape by Gleyre, in which she is cut out sharply against the sky, in the form of a silver sickle, some work as unsophisticated and as incomplete as were, at that date, my own impressions, and which it enraged my grandmother's sisters to see me admire. They held that one ought to set before children, and that children shewed their own innate good taste in admiring, only such books and pictures as they would continue to admire when their minds were developed and mature. No doubt they regarded aesthetic values as material objects which an unclouded vision could not fail to discern, without needing to have their equivalent in experience of life stored up and slowly ripening in one's heart.

It was along the ' Méséglise way,' at Montjouvain, a house built on the edge of a large pond, and overlooked by a steep, shrub-grown hill, that M. Vinteuil lived. And so we used often to meet his daughter driving her dogcart at full speed along the road. After a certain year we never saw her alone, but always accompanied by a friend, a girl older than herself, with an evil reputation in the neighbourhood, who in the end installed herself permanently, one day, at Montjouvain. People said : " That poor M. Vinteuil must be blinded by love not to see what everyone is talking about, and to let his daughter—a man who is horrified if you use a *word* in the wrong sense—bring a woman like that to live under his roof. He says that she is a most superior woman, with a heart of gold, and that she would have shewn extraordinary musical talent if she had only been trained. He may be sure it is not music that she is teaching his daughter." But M. Vinteuil assured them that it was, and indeed it is remarkable that people never fail to arouse admiration of their moral qualities in the relatives of anyone with whom they are in physical intercourse. Bodily passion, which has been so unjustly decried, compels its victims to display every vestige that is in them of unselfishness and generosity, and so effectively that they shine resplendent in the eyes of all beholders. Dr. Percepied, whose loud voice and bushy eyebrows enabled him to play to his heart's content the part of ' double-dealer,' a part to which he was not, otherwise, adapted, without in the least degree compromising his unassailable and quite unmerited reputation of being a kind-hearted old curmudgeon, could make the Curé and everyone else laugh until they cried by saying in a harsh voice : " What d'ye say to this, now ? It seems that she plays music with her friend, Mlle. Vinteuil. That surprises you, does it ? Oh, I know nothing, nothing at all. It was Papa Vinteuil who told me all about it yesterday. After all, she has every right to be fond of music, that girl. I should never dream of thwarting the artistic vocation of a child ; nor Vinteuil either, it seems. And then he plays music too, with his daughter's friend. Why, gracious heavens, it must be a regular musical box, that house out there ! What are you laughing at ? I say they've been playing too much music, those people. I met Papa Vinteuil the other day, by the cemetery. It was all he could do to keep on his feet."

Anyone who, like ourselves, had seen M. Vinteuil, about this time, avoiding people whom he knew, and turning away as soon as he caught sight of them, changed in a few months into an old man, engulfed in a sea of sorrows, incapable of any effort not directly aimed at promoting his daughter's happiness, spending whole days beside his wife's grave, could hardly have failed to realise that he was gradually dying of a broken heart, could hardly have supposed that he paid no attention to the rumours which were going about. He knew, perhaps he even believed, what his neighbours were saying. There is probably no one, however rigid his virtue, who is not liable to find himself, by the complexity of circumstances, living at close quarters with the very vice which he himself has been most outspoken in condemning, without at first recognising it beneath the disguise which it assumes on entering his presence, so as to wound him and to make him suffer ; the odd words, the unaccountable attitude, one evening, of a person whom he has a thousand reasons for loving. But for a man of M. Vinteuil's sensibility it must have been far more painful than for a hardened man of the world to have to resign himself to one of those situations which are wrongly supposed to occur in Bohemian circles only ; for they are produced whenever there needs to establish itself in the security necessary to its development a vice which Nature herself has planted in the soul of a child, perhaps by no more than blending the virtues of its father and mother, as she might blend the colours of their eyes. And yet however much M. Vinteuil may have known of his daughter's conduct it did not follow that his adoration of her grew any less. The facts of life do not penetrate to the sphere in which our beliefs are cherished ; as it was not they that engendered those beliefs, so they are powerless to destroy them ; they can aim at them continual blows of contradiction and disproof without weakening them ; and an avalanche of miseries and maladies coming, one after another, without interruption into the bosom of a family, will not make it lose faith in either the clemency of its God or the capacity of its physician. But when M. Vinteuil regarded his daughter and himself from the point of view of the world, and of their reputation, when he attempted to place himself by her side in the rank which they occupied in the general estimation of their neighbours, then he was bound to give judgment, to utter his own and her social condemnation in precisely the terms which the inhabitant of Combray most hostile to him and his daughter would have employed ; he saw himself and her in ' low,' in the very ' lowest water,' inextricably stranded ; and his manners had of late been tinged with that humility, that respect for persons who ranked above him and to whom he must now look up (however far beneath him they might hitherto have been), that tendency to search for some means of rising again to their level, which is an almost mechanical result of any human misfortune.

One day, when we were walking with Swann in one of the streets of Combray, M. Vinteuil, turning out of another street, found himself so suddenly face to face with us all that he had not time to escape ; and Swann, with that almost arrogant charity of a man of the world who, amid the dissolution of all his own moral prejudices, finds in another's shame merely a reason for treating him with a friendly benevolence, the outward signs of which serve to enhance and gratify the self-esteem of the bestower because he feels that they are all the more precious to him upon whom they are bestowed, conversed at great length with M. Vinteuil, with whom for a long time he had been barely on speaking terms, and invited him, before leaving us, to send his daughter over, one day, to play at Tansonville. It was an invitation which, two years earlier, would have enraged M. Vinteuil, but which now filled him with so much gratitude that he felt himself obliged to refrain from the indiscretion of accepting. Swann's friendly regard for his daughter seemed to him to be in itself so honourable, so precious a support for his cause that he felt it would perhaps be better to make no use of it, so as to have the wholly Platonic satisfaction of keeping it in reserve.

" What a charming man ! " he said to us, after Swann had gone, with the same enthusiasm and veneration which make clever and pretty women of the middle classes fall victims to the physical and intellectual charms of a duchess, even though she be ugly and a fool. " What a charming man ! What a pity that he should have made such a deplorable marriage ! "

And then, so strong an element of hypocrisy is there in

even the most sincere of men, who cast off, while they are talking to anyone, the opinion they actually hold of him and will express when he is no longer there, my family joined with M. Vinteuil in deploring Swann's marriage, invoking principles and conventions which (all the more because they invoked them in common with him, as though we were all thorough good fellows of the same sort) they appeared to suggest were in no way infringed at Montjouvain. M. Vinteuil did not send his daughter to visit Swann, an omission which Swann was the first to regret. For constantly, after meeting M. Vinteuil, he would remember that he had been meaning for a long time to ask him about some one of the same name as himself, one of his relatives, Swann supposed. And on this occasion he determined that he would not forget what he had to say to him when M. Vinteuil should appear with his daughter at Tansonville.

Since the 'Méséglise way' was the shorter of the two that we used to take for our walks round Combray, and for that reason was reserved for days of uncertain weather, it followed that the climate of Méséglise shewed an unduly high rainfall, and we would never lose sight of the fringe of Roussainville wood, so that we could, at any moment, run for shelter beneath its dense thatch of leaves.

Often the sun would disappear behind a cloud, which impinged on its roundness, but whose edge the sun gilded in return. The brightness, though not the light of day would then be shut off from a landscape in which all life appeared to be suspended, while the little village of Roussainville carved in relief upon the sky the white mass of its gables, with a startling precision of detail. A gust of wind blew from its perch a rook, which floated away and settled in the distance, while beneath a paling sky the woods on the horizon assumed a deeper tone of blue, as though they were painted in one of those cameos which you still find decorating the walls of old houses.

But on other days would begin to fall the rain, of which we had had due warning from the little barometer-figure which the spectacle-maker hung out in his doorway. Its drops, like migrating birds which fly off in a body at a given moment, would come down out of the sky in close marching order. They would never drift apart, would make no movement at random in their rapid course, but each one, keeping in its place, would draw after it the drop which was following, and the sky would be as greatly darkened as by the swallows flying south. We would take refuge among the trees. And when it seemed that their flight was accomplished, a few last drops, feebler and slower than the rest, would still come down. But we would emerge from our shelter, for the rain was playing a game, now, among the branches, and, even when it was almost dry again underfoot, a stray drop or two, lingering in the hollow of a leaf, would run down and hang glistening from the point of it until suddenly they splashed plump upon our upturned faces from the whole height of the tree.

Often, too, we would hurry for shelter, tumbling in among all its stony saints and patriarchs, into the porch of Saint-André-des-Champs. How typically French that church was! Over its door the saints, the kings of chivalry with lilies in their hands, the wedding scenes and funerals were carved as they might have been in the mind of Françoise. The sculptor had also recorded certain anecdotes of Aristotle and Virgil, precisely as Françoise in her kitchen would break into speech about Saint Louis as though she herself had known him, generally in order to depreciate, by contrast with him, my grandparents, whom she considered less ' righteous.' One could see that the ideas which the mediaeval artist and the mediaeval peasant (who had survived to cook for us in the nineteenth century) had of classical and of early Christian history, ideas whose inaccuracy was atoned for by their honest simplicity, were derived not from books, but from a tradition at once ancient and direct, unbroken, oral, degraded, unrecognisable, and alive. Another Combray person whom I could discern also, potential and typified, in the gothic sculptures of Saint-André-des-Champs was young Théodore, the assistant in Camus's shop. And, indeed, Françoise herself was well aware that she had in him a countryman and contemporary, for when my aunt was too ill for Françoise to be able, unaided, to lift her in her bed or to carry her to her chair, rather than let the kitchen-maid come upstairs and, perhaps, ' make an impression ' on my aunt, she would send out for Théodore. And this lad, who was regarded, and quite rightly, in the town as a ' bad character,' was so abounding in that spirit which had served to decorate the porch of Saint-André-des-Champs, and particularly in the feelings of respect due, in Françoise's eyes, to all ' poor invalids,' and, above all, to her own ' poor mistress,' that he had, when he bent down to raise my aunt's head from her pillow, the same air of pre-raphaelite simplicity and zeal which the little angels in the bas-reliefs wear, who throng, with tapers in their hands, about the deathbed of Our Lady, as though those carved faces of stone, naked and grey like trees in winter, were, like them, asleep only, storing up life and waiting to flower again in countless plebeian faces, reverend and cunning as the face of Théodore, and glowing with the ruddy brilliance of ripe apples.

There, too, not fastened to the wall like the little angels, but detached from the porch, of more than human stature, erect upon her pedestal as upon a footstool, which had been placed there to save her feet from contact with the wet ground, stood a saint with the full cheeks, the firm breasts which swelled out inside her draperies like a cluster of ripe grapes inside a bag, the narrow forehead, short and stubborn nose, deep-set eyes, and strong, thick-skinned, courageous expression of the country-women of those parts. This similarity, which imparted to the statue itself a kindliness that I had not looked to find in it, was corroborated often by the arrival of some girl from the fields, come, like ourselves, for shelter beneath the porch, whose presence there—as when the leaves of a climbing plant have grown up beside leaves carved in stone—seemed intended by fate to allow us, by confronting it with its type in nature, to form a critical estimate of the truth of the work of art. Before our eyes, in the distance, a promised or an accursed land, Roussainville, within whose walls I had never penetrated, Roussainville was now, when the rain had ceased for us, still being chastised, like a village in the Old Testament, by all the innumerable spears and arrows of the storm, which beat down obliquely upon the dwellings of its inhabitants, or else had already received the forgiveness of the Almighty, Who had restored to it the light of His sun, which fell upon it in rays of uneven length, like the rays of a monstrance upon an altar.

Sometimes, when the weather had completely broken, we were obliged to go home and to remain shut up indoors. Here and there, in the distance, in a landscape which, what with the failing light and saturated atmosphere, resembled a seascape rather, a few solitary houses clinging to the lower slopes of a hill whose heights were buried in a cloudy darkness shone out like little boats which had folded their sails and would ride at anchor, all night, upon the sea. But what mattered rain or storm? In summer, bad weather is no more than a passing fit of superficial ill-temper expressed by the permanent, underlying fine weather ; a very different thing from the fluid and unstable ' fine weather' of winter, its very opposite, in fact ; for has it not (firmly established in the soil, on which it has taken solid form in dense masses of foliage over which the rain may pour in torrents without weakening the resistance offered by their real and lasting happiness) hoisted, to keep them flying throughout the season, in the village streets, on the walls of the houses and in their gardens, its silken banners, violet and white. Sitting in the little parlour, where I would pass the time until dinner with a book, I might hear the water dripping from our chestnut-trees, but I would know that the shower would only glaze and brighten the greenness of their thick, crumpled leaves, and that they themselves had undertaken to remain there, like pledges of summer, all through the rainy night, to assure me of the fine weather's continuing ; it might rain as it pleased, but to-morrow, over the white fence of Tansonville, there would surge and flow, numerous as ever, a sea of little heart-shaped leaves ; and without the least anxiety I could watch the poplar in the Rue des Perchamps praying for mercy, bowing in desperation before the storm ; without the least anxiety I could hear, at the far end of the garden, the last peals of thunder growling among our lilac-trees.

If the weather was bad all morning, my family would abandon the idea of a walk, and I would remain at home. But, later on, I formed the habit of going out by myself on such days, and walking towards Méséglise-la-Vineuse, during that autumn when we had to come to Combray to settle the division of my aunt Léonie's estate; for she had died at last, leaving both parties among her neighbours triumphant in the fact of her demise—those who had insisted that her mode of life was enfeebling and must ultimately kill her, and, equally, those who had always maintained that she suffered from some disease not imaginary, but organic, by the visible proof of which the most sceptical would be obliged to own themselves convinced, once she had succumbed to it ; causing no intense grief to any save one of her survivors, but to that one a grief savage in its violence. During the long fortnight of my aunt's last illness Françoise never went out of her room for an instant, never took off her clothes, allowed no one else to do anything for my aunt, and did not leave her body until it was actually in its grave. Then, at last, we understood that the sort of terror in which Françoise had lived of my aunt's harsh words, her suspicions and her anger, had developed in her a sentiment which we had mistaken for hatred, and which was really veneration and love. Her true mistress, whose decisions it had been impossible to foresee, from whose stratagems it had been so hard to escape, of whose good nature it had been so easy to take advantage, her sovereign, her mysterious and omnipotent monarch was no more. Compared with such a mistress we counted for very little. The time had long passed when, on our first coming to spend our holidays at Combray, we had been of equal importance, in Françoise's eyes, with my aunt.

During that autumn my parents, finding the days so fully occupied with the legal formalities that had to be gone through, and discussions with solicitors and farmers, that they had little time for walks which, as it happened, the weather made precarious, began to let me go, without them, along the ' Méséglise way,' wrapped up in a huge Highland plaid which protected me from the rain, and which I was all the more ready to throw over my shoulders because I felt that the stripes of its gaudy tartan scandalised Françoise, whom it

was impossible to convince that the colour of one's clothes
had nothing whatever to do with one's mourning for the dead,
and to whom the grief which we had shewn on my aunt's
death was wholly unsatisfactory, since we had not entertained
the neighbours to a great funeral banquet, and did not adopt
a special tone when we spoke of her, while I at times might
be heard humming a tune. I am sure that in a book—
and to that extent my feelings were closely akin to those of
Françoise—such a conception of mourning, in the manner
of the *Chanson de Roland* and of the porch of Saint-André-
des-Champs, would have seemed most attractive. But the
moment that Françoise herself approached, some evil spirit
would urge me to attempt to make her angry, and I would
avail myself of the slightest pretext to say to her that I re-
gretted my aunt's death because she had been a good woman
in spite of her absurdities, but not in the least because she was
my aunt ; that she might easily have been my aunt and yet
have been so odious that her death would not have caused me
a moment's sorrow ; statements which, in a book, would have
struck me as merely fatuous.

And if Françoise then, inspired like a poet with a flood of
confused reflections upon bereavement, grief, and family
memories, were to plead her inability to rebut my theories,
saying : " I don't know how to *espress* myself "—I would
triumph over her with an ironical and brutal common sense
worthy of Dr. Percepied ; and if she went on : " All the
same she was a *geological* relation ; there is always the respect
due to your *geology*," I would shrug my shoulders and say :
" It is really very good of me to discuss the matter with an
illiterate old woman who cannot speak her own language,"
adopting, to deliver judgment on Françoise, the mean and
narrow outlook of the pedant, whom those who are most

contemptuous of him in the impartiality of their own minds are only too prone to copy when they are obliged to play a part upon the vulgar stage of life

My walks, that autumn, were all the more delightful because I used to take them after long hours spent over a book. When I was tired of reading, after a whole morning in the house, I would throw my plaid across my shoulders and set out; my body, which in a long spell of enforced immobility had stored up an accumulation of vital energy, was now obliged, like a spinning-top wound and let go, to spend this in every direction. The walls of houses, the Tansonville hedge, the trees of Roussainville wood, the bushes against which Montjouvain leaned its back, all must bear the blows of my walking-stick or umbrella, must hear my shouts of happiness, blows and shouts being indeed no more than expressions of the confused ideas which exhilarated me, and which, not being developed to the point at which they might rest exposed to the light of day, rather than submit to a slow and difficult course of elucidation, found it easier and more pleasant to drift into an immediate outlet. And so it is that the bulk of what appear to be the emotional renderings of our inmost sensations do no more than relieve us of the burden of those sensations by allowing them to escape from us in an indistinct form which does not teach us how it should be interpreted. When I attempt to reckon up all that I owe to the ' Méséglise way,' all the humble discoveries of which it was either the accidental setting or the direct inspiration and cause, I am reminded that it was in that same autumn, on one of those walks, near the bushy precipice which guarded Montjouvain from the rear, that I was struck for the first time by this lack of harmony between our impressions and their normal forms of expression. After an hour of rain and wind, against which I had put up a brisk fight, as I came to the edge of the Montjouvain pond, and reached a little hut, roofed with tiles, in which M. Vinteuil's gardener kept his tools, the sun shone out again, and its golden rays, washed clean by the shower, blazed once more in the sky, on the trees, on the wall of the hut, and on the still wet tiles of the roof, which had a chicken perching upon its ridge. The wind pulled out sideways the wild grass that grew in the wall, and the chicken's downy feathers, both of which things let themselves float upon the wind's breath to their full extent, with the unresisting submissiveness of light and lifeless matter. The tiled roof cast upon the pond, whose reflections were now clear again in the sunlight, a square of pink marble, the like of which I had never observed before. And, seeing upon the water, where it reflected the wall, a pallid smile responding to the smiling sky, I cried aloud in my enthusiasm, brandishing my furled umbrella : " Damn, damn, damn, damn! " But at the same time I felt that I was in duty bound not to content myself with these unilluminating words, but to endeavour to see more clearly into the sources of my enjoyment.

And it was at that moment, too—thanks to a peasant who went past, apparently in a bad enough humour already, but more so when he nearly received my umbrella in his face, and who replied without any cordiality to my " Fine day, what! good to be out walking! "—that I learned that identical emotions do not spring up in the hearts of all men simultaneously, by a pre-established order. Later on I discovered that, whenever I had read for too long and was in a mood for conversation, the friend to whom I would be burning to say something would at that moment have finished indulging himself in the delights of conversation, and wanted

nothing now but to be left to read undisturbed. And if I had
been thinking with affection of my parents, and forming the
most sensible and proper plans for giving them pleasure, they
would have been using the same interval of time to discover
some misdeed that I had already forgotten, and would begin
to scold me severely, just as I flung myself upon them with a
kiss.

Sometimes to the exhilaration which I derived from being
alone would be added an alternative feeling, so that I could
not be clear in my mind to which I should give the casting
vote ; a feeling stimulated by the desire to see rise up before
my eyes a peasant-girl whom I might clasp in my arms.
Coming abruptly, and without giving me time to trace it
accurately to its source among so many ideas of a very
different kind, the pleasure which accompanied this desire
seemed only a degree superior to what was given me by my
other thoughts. I found an additional merit in everything
that was in my mind at the moment, in the pink reflection
of the tiled roof, the wild grass in the wall, the village of
Roussainville into which I had long desired to penetrate,
the trees of its wood and the steeple of its church, created in
them by this fresh emotion which made them appear more
desirable only because I thought it was they that had pro-
voked it, and which seemed only to wish to bear me more
swiftly towards them when it filled my sails with a potent,
unknown, and propitious breeze. But if this desire that a
woman should appear added for me something more exalting
than the charms of nature, they in their turn enlarged what
I might, in the woman's charm, have found too much restricted. It seemed to me that the beauty of the trees was
hers also, and that, as for the spirit of those horizons, of the
village of Roussainville, of the books which I was reading

that year, it was her kiss which would make me master of
them all ; and, my imagination drawing strength from contact with my sensuality, my sensuality expanding through all
the realms of my imagination, my desire had no longer any
bounds. Moreover—just as in moments of musing contemplation of nature, the normal actions of the mind being
suspended, and our abstract ideas of things set on one side,
we believe with the profoundest faith in the originality, in the
individual existence of the place in which we may happen
to be—the passing figure which my desire evoked seemed to
be not any one example of the general type of ' woman,'
but a necessary and natural product of the soil. For at that
time everything which was not myself, the earth and the
creatures upon it, seemed to me more precious, more important, endowed with a more real existence than they appear
to full-grown men. And between the earth and its creatures
I made no distinction. I had a desire for a peasant-girl from
Méséglise or Roussainville, for a fisher-girl from Balbec,
just as I had a desire for Balbec and Méséglise. The pleasure
which those girls were empowered to give me would have
seemed less genuine, I should have had no faith in it any
longer, if I had been at liberty to modify its conditions as I
chose. To meet in Paris a fisher-girl from Balbec or a peasant-
girl from Méséglise would have been like receiving the present of a shell which I had never seen upon the beach, or of a
fern which I had never found among the woods, would have
stripped from the pleasure which she was about to give me all
those other pleasures in the thick of which my imagination
had enwrapped her. But to wander thus among the woods of
Roussainville without a peasant-girl to embrace was to see
those woods and yet know nothing of their secret treasure,
their deep-hidden beauty. That girl whom I never saw save

dappled with the shadows of their leaves, was to me herself
a plant of local growth, only taller than the rest, and one whose
structure would enable me to approach more closely than
in them to the intimate savour of the land from which she
had sprung. I could believe this all the more readily (and also
that the caresses by which she would bring that savour to my
senses were themselves of a particular kind, yielding a pleasure
which I could never derive from any but herself) since I was
still, and must for long remain, in that period of life when one
has not yet separated the fact of this sensual pleasure from
the various women in whose company one has tasted it,
when one has not reduced it to a general idea which makes
one regard them thenceforward as the variable instruments of
a pleasure that is always the same. Indeed, that pleasure does
not exist, isolated and formulated in the consciousness, as the
ultimate object with which one seeks a woman's company,
or as the cause of the uneasiness which, in anticipation, one
then feels. Hardly even does one think of oneself, but only
how to escape from oneself. Obscurely awaited, immanent
and concealed, it rouses to such a paroxysm, at the moment
when at last it makes itself felt, those other pleasures which we
find in the tender glance, in the kiss of her who is by our side,
that it seems to us, more than anything else, a sort of trans-
port of gratitude for the kindness of heart of our companion
and for her touching predilection of ourselves, which we
measure by the benefits, by the happiness that she showers
upon us.

Alas, it was in vain that I implored the dungeon-keep of
Roussainville, that I begged it to send out to meet me some
daughter of its village, appealing to it as to the sole confidant
to whom I had disclosed my earliest desires when, from the
top floor of our house at Combray, from the little room that

smelt of orris-root, I had peered out and seen nothing but its tower, framed in the square of the half-opened window, while, with the heroic scruples of a traveller setting forth for unknown climes, or of a desperate wretch hesitating on the verge of self-destruction, faint with emotion, I explored, across the bounds of my own experience, an untrodden path which, I believed, might lead me to my death, even—until passion spent itself and left me shuddering among the sprays of flowering currant which, creeping in through the window, tumbled all about my body. In vain I called upon it now. In vain I compressed the whole landscape into my field of vision, draining it with an exhaustive gaze which sought to extract from it a female creature. I might go alone as far as the porch of Saint-André-des-Champs : never did I find there the girl whom I should inevitably have met, had I been with my grandfather, and so unable to engage her in conversation. I would fix my eyes, without limit of time, upon the trunk of a distant tree, from behind which she must appear and spring towards me ; my closest scrutiny left the horizon barren as before ; night was falling ; without any hope now would I concentrate my attention, as though to force up out of it the creatures which it must conceal, upon that sterile soil, that stale and outworn land ; and it was no longer in lightness of heart, but with sullen anger that I aimed blows at the trees of Roussainville wood, from among which no more living creatures made their appearance than if they had been trees painted on the stretched canvas background of a panorama, when, unable to resign myself to having to return home without having held in my arms the woman I so greatly desired, I was yet obliged to retrace my steps towards Combray, and to admit to myself that the chance of her appearing in my path grew smaller every moment. And if she had appeared, would I have dared to speak to her ? I felt that she would have regarded me as mad, for I no longer thought of those desires which came to me on my walks, but were never realised, as being shared by others, or as having any existence apart from myself. They seemed nothing more now than the purely subjective, impotent, illusory creatures of my temperament. They were in no way connected now with nature, with the world of real things, which from now onwards lost all its charm and significance, and meant no more to my life than a purely conventional framework, just as the action of a novel is framed in the railway carriage, on a seat of which a traveller is reading it to pass the time.

And it is perhaps from another impression which I received at Montjouvain, some years later, an impression which at that time was without meaning, that there arose, long afterwards, my idea of that cruel side of human passion called 'sadism.' We shall see, in due course, that for quite another reason the memory of this impression was to play an important part in my life. It was during a spell of very hot weather ; my parents, who had been obliged to go away for the whole day, had told me that I might stay out as late as I pleased ; and having gone as far as the Montjouvain pond, where I enjoyed seeing again the reflection of the tiled roof of the hut, I had lain down in the shade and gone to sleep among the bushes on the steep slope that rose up behind the house, just where I had waited for my parents, years before, one day when they had gone to call on M. Vinteuil. It was almost dark when I awoke, and I wished to rise and go away, but I saw Mlle. Vinteuil (or thought, at least, that I recognised her, for I had not seen her often at Combray, and then only when she was still a child, whereas she was now growing into a young woman), who probably had just come in, standing in front of me, and only a few feet away from me, in that room in which her father had entertained mine, and which she had now made into a little sitting-room for herself. The window was partly open ; the lamp was lighted ; I could watch her every movement without her being able to see me ; but, had I gone away, I must have made a rustling sound among the bushes, she would have heard me, and might have thought that I had been hiding there in order to spy upon her.

She was in deep mourning, for her father had but lately died. We had not gone to see her ; my mother had not cared to go, on account of that virtue which alone in her fixed any bounds to her benevolence—namely, modesty ; but she pitied the girl from the depths of her heart. My mother had not forgotten the sad end of M. Vinteuil's life, his complete absorption, first in having to play both mother and nursery-maid to his daughter, and, later, in the suffering which she had caused him ; she could see the tortured expression which was never absent from the old man's face in those terrible last years ; she knew that he had definitely abandoned the task of transcribing in fair copies the whole of his later work, the poor little pieces, we imagined, of an old music-master, a retired village organist, which, we assumed, were of little or no value in themselves, though we did not despise them, because they were of such great value to him and had been the chief motive of his life before he sacrificed them to his daughter ; pieces which, being mostly not even written down, but recorded only in his memory, while the rest were scribbled on loose sheets of paper, and quite illegible, must now remain unknown for ever ; my mother thought, also, of that other and still more cruel renunciation to which M. Vinteuil had been driven, that of

seeing the girl happily settled, with an honest and respectable
future ; when she called to mind all this utter and crushing
misery that had come upon my aunts' old music-master, she
was moved to very real grief, and shuddered to think of that
other grief, so different in its bitterness, which Mlle. Vinteuil
must now be feeling, tinged with remorse at having virtually
killed her father. " Poor M. Vinteuil," my mother would
say, " he lived for his daughter, and now he has died for her,
without getting his reward. Will he get it now, I wonder,
and in what form ? It can only come to him from her."

At the far end of Mlle. Vinteuil's sitting-room, on the
mantelpiece, stood a small photograph of her father which she
went briskly to fetch, just as the sound of carriage wheels
was heard from the road outside, then flung herself down on a
sofa and drew close beside her a little table on which she
placed the photograph, just as, long ago, M. Vinteuil had
' placed ' beside him the piece of music which he would have
liked to play over to my parents. And then her friend came
in. Mlle. Vinteuil greeted her without rising, clasping her
hands behind her head, and drew her body to one side of the
sofa, as though to ' make room.' But no sooner had she
done this than she appeared to feel that she was perhaps
suggesting a particular position to her friend, with an emphasis which might well be regarded as importunate. She
thought that her friend would prefer, no doubt, to sit down
at some distance from her, upon a chair ; she felt that she
had been indiscreet ; her sensitive heart took fright ; stretch-
ing herself out again over the whole of the sofa, she closed her
eyes and began to yawn, so as to indicate that it was a desire
to sleep, and that alone, which had made her lie down there.
Despite the rude and hectoring familiarity with which she
treated her companion I could recognise in her the ob-

sequious and reticent advances, the abrupt scruples and re-
straints which had characterised her father. Presently she
rose and came to the window, where she pretended to be
trying to close the shutters and not succeeding.

" Leave them open," said her friend. " I am hot."

" But it's too dreadful ! People will see us," Mlle.
Vinteuil answered. And then she guessed, probably, that her
friend would think that she had uttered these words simply
in order to provoke a reply in certain other words, which
she seemed, indeed, to wish to hear spoken, but, from prudence, would let her friend be the first to speak. And so, although I could not see her face clearly enough, I am sure
that the expression must have appeared on it which my grandmother had once found so delightful, when she hastily went
on : " When I say ' see us ' I mean, of course, see us reading.
It's so dreadful to think that in every trivial little thing you
do some one may be overlooking you."

With the instinctive generosity of her nature, a courtesy
beyond her control, she refrained from uttering the studied
words which, she had felt, were indispensable from the full
realisation of her desire. And perpetually, in the depths of her
being, a shy and suppliant maiden would kneel before that
other element, the old campaigner, battered but triumphant,
would intercede with him and oblige him to retire.

" Oh, yes, it is so extremely likely that people are looking
at us at this time of night in this densely populated district!"
said her friend, with bitter irony. " And what if they are ? "
she went on, feeling bound to annotate with a malicious yet
affectionate wink these words which she was repeating,
out of good nature, like a lesson prepared beforehand which,
she knew, it would please Mlle. Vinteuil to hear. " And
what if they are ? All the better that they should see us."

Mlle. Vinteuil shuddered and rose to her feet. In her sensitive and scrupulous heart she was ignorant what words ought to flow, spontaneously, from her lips, so as to produce the scene for which her eager senses clamoured. She reached out as far as she could across the limitations of her true character to find the language appropriate to a vicious young woman such as she longed to be thought, but the words which, she imagined, such a young woman might have uttered with sincerity sounded unreal in her own mouth. And what little she allowed herself to say was said in a strained tone, in which her ingrained timidity paralysed her tendency to freedom and audacity of speech ; while she kept on interrupting herself with : " You're sure you aren't cold ? You aren't too hot ? You don't want to sit and read by yourself ? . . .

" Your ladyship's thoughts seem to be rather ' warm ' this evening," she concluded, doubtless repeating a phrase which she had heard used, on some earlier occasion, by her friend.

In the V-shaped opening of her crape bodice Mlle. Vinteuil felt the sting of her friend's sudden kiss ; she gave a little scream and ran away ; and then they began to chase one another about the room, scrambling over the furniture, their wide sleeves fluttering like wings, clucking and crowing like a pair of amorous fowls. At last Mlle. Vinteuil fell down exhausted upon the sofa, where she was screened from me by the stooping body of her friend. But the latter now had her back turned to the little table on which the old music-master's portrait had been arranged. Mlle. Vinteuil realised that her friend would not see it unless her attention were drawn to it, and so exclaimed, as if she herself had just noticed it for the first time : " Oh ! there's my father's picture looking at us ; I can't think who can have put it there ; I'm sure I've told them twenty times, that is not the proper place for it."

I remembered the words that M. Vinteuil had used to my parents in apologising for an obtrusive sheet of music. This photograph was, of course, in common use in their ritual observances, was subjected to daily profanation, for the friend replied in words which were evidently a liturgical response : " Let him stay there. He can't trouble us any longer. D'you think he'ld start whining, d'you think he'ld pack you out of the house if he could see you now, with the window open, the ugly old monkey ? "

To which Mlle. Vinteuil replied, " Oh, please ! "—a gentle reproach which testified to the genuine goodness of her nature, not that it was prompted by any resentment at hearing her father spoken of in this fashion (for that was evidently a feeling which she had trained herself, by a long course of sophistries, to keep in close subjection at such moments), but rather because it was the bridle which, so as to avoid all appearance of egotism, she herself used to curb the gratification which her friend was attempting to procure for her. It may well have been, too, that the smiling moderation with which she faced and answered these blasphemies, that this tender and hypocritical rebuke appeared to her frank and generous nature as a particularly shameful and seductive form of that criminal attitude towards life which she was endeavouring to adopt. But she could not resist the attraction of being treated with affection by a woman who had just shewn herself so implacable towards the defenceless dead ; she sprang on to the knees of her friend and held out a chaste brow to be kissed ; precisely as a daughter would have done to her mother, feeling with exquisite joy that they would thus, between them, inflict the last turn of the screw of cruelty, in robbing M. Vinteuil, as though they were actually rifling his tomb, of the sacred rights of fatherhood. Her friend took the girl's head in her hands and placed a kiss on her brow with a docility prompted by the real affection she had for Mlle. Vinteuil, as well as by the desire to bring what distraction she could into the dull and melancholy life of an orphan.

" Do you know what I should like to do to that old horror ? " she said, taking up the photograph. She murmured in Mlle. Vinteuil's ear something that I could not distinguish.

" Oh ! You would never dare."

" Not dare to spit on it ? On that ? " shouted the friend with deliberate brutality.

I heard no more, for Mlle. Vinteuil, who now seemed weary, awkward, preoccupied, sincere, and rather sad, came back to the window and drew the shutters close ; but I knew now what was the reward that M. Vinteuil, in return for all the suffering that he had endured in his lifetime, on account of his daughter, had received from her after his death.

And yet I have since reflected that if M. Vinteuil had been able to be present at this scene, he might still, and in spite of everything, have continued to believe in his daughter's soundness of heart, and that he might even, in so doing, have been not altogether wrong. It was true that in all Mlle. Vinteuil's actions the appearance of evil was so strong and so consistent that it would have been hard to find it exhibited in such completeness save in what is nowadays called a ' sadist ' ; it is behind the footlights of a Paris theatre, and not under the homely lamp of an actual country house, that one expects to see a girl leading her friend on to spit upon the portrait of a father who has lived and died for nothing and no one but herself ; and when we find in real life a desire for melodramatic effect, it is generally the ' sadic ' instinct that is responsible for it. It is possible that, without being in the least inclined towards 'sadism,' a girl might have shewn the same outrageous cruelty as Mlle. Vinteuil in desecrating the memory and defying the wishes of her dead father, but she would not have given them deliberate expression in an act so crude in its symbolism, so lacking in subtlety ; the criminal element in her behaviour would have been less evident to other people, and even to herself, since she would not have admitted to herself that she was doing wrong. But, appearances apart, in Mlle. Vinteuil's soul, at least in the earlier stages, the evil element was probably not unmixed. A 'sadist' of her kind is an artist in evil, which a wholly wicked person could not be, for in that case the evil would not have been external, it would have seemed quite natural to her, and would not even have been distinguishable from herself ; and as for virtue, respect for the dead, filial obedience, since she would never have practised the cult of these things, she would take no impious delight in their profanation. 'Sadists' of Mlle. Vinteuil's sort are creatures so purely sentimental, so virtuous by nature, that even sensual pleasure appears to them as something bad, a privilege reserved for the wicked. And when they allow themselves for a moment to enjoy it they endeavour to impersonate, to assume all the outward appearance of wicked people, for themselves and their partners in guilt, so as to gain the momentary illusion of having escaped beyond the control of their own gentle and scrupulous natures into the inhuman world of pleasure. And I could understand how she must have longed for such an escape when I realised that it was impossible for her to effect it. At the moment when she wished to be thought the very antithesis of her father, what she atonce suggested to me were the mannerisms, in thought and speech, of the poor old music-master. Indeed, his photograph was nothing ; what she really desecrated, what she corrupted into ministering to her pleasures, but what remained between them and her and prevented her from any direct enjoyment of them, was the likeness between her face and his, his mother's blue eyes which he had handed down to her, like some trinket to be kept in the family, those little friendly movements and in-clinations which set up between the viciousness of Mlle. Vinteuil and herself a phraseology, a mentality not designed for vice, which made her regard it as not in any way different from the numberless little social duties and courtesies to which she must devote herself every day. It was not evil that gave her the idea of pleasure, that seemed to her attractive ; it was pleasure, rather, that seemed evil. And as, every time that she indulged in it, pleasure came to her attended by evil thoughts such as, ordinarily, had no place in her virtuous mind, she came at length to see in pleasure itself something diabolical, to identify it with Evil. Perhaps Mlle. Vinteuil felt that at heart her friend was not altogether bad, nor really sincere when she gave vent to those blasphemous utterances. At any rate, she had the pleasure of receiving those kisses on her brow, those smiles, those glances ; all feigned, perhaps, but akin in their base and vicious mode of expression to those which would have been discernible on the face of a creature formed not out of kindness and long-suffering, but out of self-indulgence and cruelty. She was able to delude herself for a moment into believing that she was indeed amusing herself in the way in which, with so unnatural an accomplice, a girl might amuse herself who really did experience that savage antipathy towards her father's memory. Perhaps she would not have thought of wickedness as a state so rare, so abnormal, so exotic, one which it was so refreshing to visit, had she been able to distinguish in herself, as in all her fellow-men and women, that indifference to the sufferings which they cause which, whatever names else be given it, is the one true, terrible and lasting form of cruelty.

If the ' Méséglise way ' was so easy, it was a very different matter when we took the ' Guermantes way,' for that meant a long walk, and we must make sure, first, of the weather. When we seemed to have entered upon a spell of fine days, when Françoise, in desperation that not a drop was falling upon the ' poor crops,' gazing up at the sky and seeing there only a little white cloud floating here and there upon its calm, azure surface, groaned aloud and exclaimed : " You would say they were nothing more nor less than a lot of dogfish swimming about and sticking up their snouts ! Ah, they never think of making it rain a little for the poor labourers ! And then when the corn is all ripe, down it will come, rattling all over the place, and think no more of where it is falling than if it was on the sea ! "—when my father's appeals to the gardener had met with the same encouraging answer several times in succession, then some one would say, at dinner : " To-morrow, if the weather holds, we might go the Guermantes way." And off we would set, immediately after luncheon, through the little garden gate which dropped us into the Rue des Perchamps, narrow and bent at a sharp angle, dotted with grass-plots over which two or three wasps would spend the day botanising, a street as quaint as its name, from which its odd characteristics and its personality were, I felt, derived ; a street for which one might search in vain through the Combray of to-day, for the public school now rises upon its site. But in my dreams of Combray (like those architects, pupils of Viollet-le-Duc, who, fancying that they can detect, beneath a Renaissance rood-loft and an eighteenth-century altar, traces of a Norman choir, restore the whole church to the state in which it probably was in the twelfth century) I leave not a stone of the modern edifice standing, I pierce through it and ' restore ' the Rue des Perchamps. And for such reconstruction memory furnishes me with more detailed guidance than is generally at the disposal of restorers ; the pictures which it has preserved—perhaps the last surviving in the world to-day, and soon to follow the rest into oblivion—of what Combray looked like in my childhood's days ; pictures which, simply because it was the old Combray that traced their outlines upon my mind before it vanished, are as moving—if I may compare a humble landscape with those glorious works, reproductions of which my grandmother was so fond of bestowing on me— as those old engravings of the 'Cenacolo', or that painting by Gentile Bellini, in which one sees, in a state in which they no longer exist, the masterpiece of Leonardo and the portico of Saint Mark's.

We would pass, in the Rue de l'Oiseau, before the old hostelry of the Oiseau Flesché, into whose great court-yard, once upon a time, would rumble the coaches of the Duchesses de Montpensier, de Guermantes, and de Mont-morency, when they had to come down to Combray for some litigation with their farmers, or to receive homage from them. We would come at length to the Mall, among whose tree-tops I could distinguish the steeple of Saint-Hilaire. And I should have liked to be able to sit down and spend the whole day there, reading and listening to the bells, for it was so charming there and so quiet that, when an hour struck, you would have said not that it broke in upon the calm of the day, but that it relieved the day of its superfluity, and that the steeple, with the indolent, painstaking exactitude of a person who has nothing else to do, had simply, in order to squeeze out and let fall the few golden drops which had slowly and naturally accumulated in the hot sunlight, pressed, at a given moment, the distended surface of the silence.

The great charm of the 'Guermantes way' was that we had beside us, almost all the time, the course of the Vivonne. We crossed it first, ten minutes after leaving the house, by a foot-bridge called the Pont-Vieux. And every year, when we arrived at Combray, on Easter morning, after the sermon, if the weather was fine, I would run there to see (amid all the disorder that prevails on the morning of a great festival, the gorgeous preparations for which make the everyday household utensils that they have not contrived to banish seem more sordid than ever) the river flowing past, sky-blue already between banks still black and bare, its only companions a clump of daffodils, come out before their time, a few primroses, the first in flower, while here and there burned the blue flame of a violet, its stem bent beneath the weight of the drop of perfume stored in its tiny horn. The Pont-Vieux led to a tow-path which, at this point, would be overhung in summer by the bluish foliage of a hazel, under which a fisherman in a straw hat seemed to have taken root. At Combray, where I knew everyone, and could always detect the blacksmith or grocer's boy through his disguise of a beadle's uniform or chorister's surplice, this fisherman was the only person whom I was never able to identify. He must have known my family, for he used to raise his hat when we passed ; and then I would always be just on the point of asking his name, when some one would make a sign to me to be quiet, or I would frighten the fish. We would follow the tow-path, which ran along the top of a steep bank, several feet above the stream.

The ground on the other side was lower, and stretched in a series of broad meadows as far as the village and even to the distant railway-station. Over these were strewn the remains, half-buried in the long grass, of the castle of the old Counts of Combray, who, during the Middle Ages, had had on this side the course of the Vivonne as a barrier and defence against attack from the Lords of Guermantes and Abbots of Martin-ville. Nothing was left now but a few stumps of towers, hummocks upon the broad surface of the fields, hardly visible, broken battlements over which, in their day, the bowmen had hurled down stones, the watchmen had gazed out over Nove-pont, Clairefontaine, Martinville-le-Sec, Bailleau-l'Exempt, fiefs all of them of Guermantes, a ring in which Combray was locked ; but fallen among the grass now, levelled with the ground, climbed and commanded by boys from the Christian Brothers' school, who came there in their play-time, or with lesson-books to be conned ; emblems of a past that had sunk down and well-nigh vanished under the earth, that lay by the water's edge now, like an idler taking the air, yet giving me strong food for thought, making the name of Combray connote to me not the little town of to-day only, but an historic city vastly different, seizing and holding my imagination by the remote, incomprehensible features which it half-concealed beneath a spangled veil of buttercups. For the buttercups grew past numbering on this spot which they had chosen for their games among the grass, standing singly, in couples, in whole companies, yellow as the yolk of eggs, and glowing with an added lustre, I felt, because, being powerless to consummate with my palate the pleasure which the sight of them never failed to give me, I would let it ac-cumulate as my eyes ranged over their gilded expanse. until it had acquired the strength to create in my mind a fresh example of absolute, unproductive beauty ; and so it had been from my earliest childhood, when from the tow-path I had stretched out my arms towards them, before even I could pronounce their charming name—a name fit for the Prince in some French fairy-tale ; colonists, perhaps, in some far distant century from Asia, but naturalised now for ever in the village, well satisfied with their modest horizon, rejoicing in the sunshine and the water's edge, faithful to their little glimpse of the railway-station ; yet keeping, none the less, as do some of our old paintings, in their plebeian simplicity, a poetic scintillation from the golden East.

I would amuse myself by watching the glass jars which the boys used to lower into the Vivonne, to catch minnows, and which, filled by the current of the stream, in which they themselves also were enclosed, at once 'containers' whose transparent sides were like solidified water and 'contents' plunged into a still larger container of liquid, flowing crystal, suggested an image of coolness more delicious and more provoking than the same water in the same jars would have done, standing upon a table laid for dinner, by shewing it as perpetually in flight between the impalpable water, in which my hands could not arrest it, and the insoluble glass, in which my palate could not enjoy it. I decided that I would come there again with a line and catch fish ; I begged for and obtained a morsel of bread from our luncheon basket ; and threw into the Vivonne pellets which had the power, it seemed, to bring about a chemical precipitation, for the water at once grew solid round about them in oval clusters of emaciated tadpoles, which until then it had, no doubt, been holding in solution, invisible, but ready and alert to enter the stage of crystallisation.

Presently the course of the Vivonne became choked with

water-plants. At first they appeared singly, a lily, for instance, which the current, across whose path it had unfortunately grown, would never leave at rest for a moment, so that, like a ferry-boat mechanically propelled, it would drift over to one bank only to return to the other, eternally repeating its double journey. Thrust towards the bank, its stalk would be straightened out, lengthened, strained almost to breaking-point until the current again caught it, its green moorings swung back over their anchorage and brought the unhappy plant to what might fitly be called its starting-point, since it was fated not to rest there a moment before moving off once again. I would still find it there, on one walk after another, always in the same helpless state, suggesting certain victims of neurasthenia, among whom my grandfather would have included my aunt Léonie, who present without modification, year after year, the spectacle of their odd and unaccountable habits, which they always imagine themselves to be on the point of shaking off, but which they always retain to the end ; caught in the treadmill of their own maladies and eccentricities, their futile endeavours to escape serve only to actuate its mechanism, to keep in motion the clockwork of their strange, ineluctable, fatal daily round. Such as these was the water-lily, and also like one of those wretches whose peculiar torments, repeated indefinitely throughout eternity, aroused the curiosity of Dante, who would have inquired of them at greater length and in fuller detail from the victims themselves, had not Virgil, striding on ahead, obliged him to hasten after him at full speed, as I must hasten after my parents.

But farther on the current slackened, where the stream ran through a property thrown open to the public by its owner, who had made a hobby of aquatic gardening, so that the little

ponds into which the Vivonne was here diverted were a flower
with water-lilies. As the banks at this point were thickly
wooded, the heavy shade of the trees gave the water a background which was ordinarily dark green, although sometimes, when we were coming home on a calm evening after a
stormy afternoon, I have seen in its depths a clear, crude blue
that was almost violet, suggesting a floor of Japanese cloi-
sonné. Here and there, on the surface, floated, blushing like
a strawberry, the scarlet heart of a lily set in a ring of white
petals.

Beyond these the flowers were more frequent, but paler,
less glossy, more thickly seeded, more tightly folded, and
disposed, by accident, in festoons so graceful that I would
fancy I saw floating upon the stream, as though after the
dreary stripping of the decorations used in some Watteau
festival, moss-roses in loosened garlands. Elsewhere a corner
seemed to be reserved for the commoner kinds of lily ; of a
neat pink or white like rocket-flowers, washed clean like
porcelain, with housewifely care ; while, a little farther
again, were others, pressed close together in a floating
garden-bed, as though pansies had flown out of a garden like
butterflies and were hovering with blue and burnished wings
over the transparent shadowiness of this watery border ; this
skiey border also, for it set beneath the flowers a soil of a
colour more precious, more moving than their own ; and
both in the afternoon, when it sparkled beneath the lilies in
the kaleidoscope of a happiness silent, restless, and alert, and
towards evening, when it was filled like a distant haven with
the roseate dreams of the setting sun, incessantly changing
and ever remaining in harmony, about the more permanent
colour of the flowers themselves, with the utmost profundity,
evanescence, and mystery—with a quiet suggestion of in-

finity ; afternoon or evening, it seemed to have set them
flowering in the heart of the sky.

After leaving this park the Vivonne began to flow again
more swiftly. How often have I watched, and longed to
imitate, when I should be free to live as I chose, a rower who
had shipped his oars and lay stretched out on his back, his
head down, in the bottom of his boat, letting it drift with the
current, seeing nothing but the sky which slipped quietly
above him, shewing upon his features a foretaste of happiness
and peace.

We would sit down among the irises at the water's edge.
In the holiday sky a lazy cloud streamed out to its full length.
Now and then, crushed by the burden of idleness, a carp
would heave up out of the water, with an anxious gasp.
It was time for us to feed. Before starting homewards we
would sit for a long time there, eating fruit and bread and
chocolate, on the grass, over which came to our ears, hori-
zontal, faint, but solid still and metallic, the sound of the bells
of Saint-Hilaire, which had melted not at all in the atmosphere
it was so well accustomed to traverse, but, broken piecemeal
by the successive palpitation of all their sonorous strokes,
throbbed as it brushed the flowers at our feet.

Sometimes, at the water's edge and embedded in trees,
we would come upon a house of the kind called ' pleasure
houses,' isolated and lost, seeing nothing of the world, save
the river which bathed its feet. A young woman, whose
pensive face and fashionable veils did not suggest a local
origin, and who had doubtless come there, in the popular
phrase, ' to bury herself,' to taste the bitter sweetness of
feeling that her name, and still more the name of him whose
heart she had once held, but had been unable to keep, were
unknown there, stood framed in a window from which she

had no outlook beyond the boat that was moored beside her door. She raised her eyes with an air of distraction when she heard, through the trees that lined the bank, the voices of passers-by of whom, before they came in sight, she might be certain that never had they known, nor would they know, the faithless lover, that nothing in their past lives bore his imprint, which nothing in their future would have occasion to receive. One felt that in her renunciation of life she had willingly abandoned those places in which she would at least have been able to see him whom she loved, for others where he had never trod. And I watched her, as she returned from some walk along a road where she had known that he would not appear, drawing from her submissive fingers long gloves of a precious, useless charm.

Never, in the course of our walks along the 'Guermantes way,' might we penetrate as far as the source of the Vivonne, of which I had often thought, which had in my mind so abstract, so ideal an existence, that I had been as much surprised when some one told me that it was actually to be found in the same department, and at a given number of miles from Combray, as I had been on the day when I had learned that there was another fixed point somewhere on the earth's surface, where, according to the ancients, opened the jaws of Hell. Nor could we ever reach that other goal, to which I longed so much to attain, Guermantes itself. I knew that it was the residence of its proprietors, the Duc and Duchesse de Guermantes, I knew that they were real personages who did actually exist, but whenever I thought about them I pictured them to myself either in tapestry, as was the 'Coronation of Esther' which hung in our church, or else in changing, rainbow colours, as was Gilbert the Bad in his window, where he passed from cabbage green, when I was dipping my fingers in the holy water stoup, to plum blue when I had reached our row of chairs, or again altogether impalpable, like the image of Geneviève de Brabant, ancestress of the Guermantes family, which the magic lantern sent wandering over the curtains of my room or flung aloft upon the ceiling—in short, always wrapped in the mystery of the Merovingian age, and bathed, as in a sunset, in the orange light which glowed from the resounding syllable 'antes.' And if, in spite of that, they were for me, in their capacity as a duke and a duchess, real people, though of an unfamiliar kind, this ducal personality was in its turn enormously distended, immaterialised, so as to encircle and contain that Guermantes of which they were duke and duchess, all that sunlit 'Guermantes way' of our walks, the course of the Vivonne, its water-lilies and its overshadowing trees, and an endless series of hot summer afternoons. And I knew that they bore not only the titles of Duc and Duchesse de Guermantes, but that since the fourteenth century, when, after vain attempts to conquer its earlier lords in battle, they had allied themselves by marriage, and so become Counts of Combray, the first citizens, consequently, of the place, and yet the only ones among its citizens who did not reside in it—Comtes de Combray, possessing Combray, threading it on their string of names and titles, absorbing it in their personalities, and illustrating, no doubt, in themselves that strange and pious melancholy which was peculiar to Combray ; proprietors of the town, though not of any particular house there ; dwelling, presumably, out of doors, in the street, between heaven and earth, like that Gilbert de Guermantes, of whom I could see, in the stained glass of the apse of Saint-Hilaire, only the 'other side' in dull black lacquer, if I raised my eyes to look for him, when I was going to Camus's for a packet of salt.

And then it happened that, going the ' Guermantes wav,'
I passed occasionally by a row of well-watered little gardens,
over whose hedges rose clusters of dark blossom. I would stop
before them, hoping to gain some precious addition to my
experience, for I seemed to have before my eyes a fragment
of that riverside country which I had longed so much to see
and know since coming upon a description of it by one of my
favourite authors. And it was with that story-book land, with
its imagined soil intersected by a hundred bubbling water-
courses, that Guermantes, changing its form in my mind,
became identified, after I heard Dr. Percepied speak of the
flowers and the charming rivulets and fountains that were to
be seen there in the ducal park. I used to dream that Mme.
de Guermantes, taking a sudden capricious fancy for myself,
invited me there, that all day long she stood fishing for trout
by my side. And when evening came, holding my hand in her
own, as we passed by the little gardens of her vassals, she
would point out to me the flowers that leaned their red and
purple spikes along the tops of the low walls, and would teach
me all their names. She would make me tell her, too, all
about the poems that I meant to compose. And these
dreams reminded me that, since I wished, some day, to become a writer, it was high time to decide what sort of books
I was going to write. But as soon as I asked myself the
question, and tried to discover some subject to which I could
impart a philosophical significance of infinite value, my mind
would stop like a clock, I would see before me vacuity,
nothing, would feel either that I was wholly devoid of talent,
or that, perhaps, a malady of the brain was hindering its
development. Sometimes I would depend upon my father's
arranging everything for me. He was so powerful, in such
favour with the people who ' really counted,' that he made

it possible for us to transgress laws which Françoise had
taught me to regard as more ineluctable than the laws of life
and death, as when we were allowed to postpone for a year
the compulsory repointing of the walls of our house, alone
among all the houses in that part of Paris, or when he obtained permission from the Minister for Mme. Sazerat's son,
who had been ordered to some watering-place, to take his
degree two months before the proper time, among the candi-
dates whose surnames began with ' A,' instead of having to
wait his turn as an ' S.' If I had fallen seriously ill, if I had
been captured by brigands, convinced that my father's understanding with the supreme powers was too complete, that
his letters of introduction to the Almighty were too irresistible
for my illness or captivity to turn out anything but vain
illusions, in which there was no danger actually threatening
me, I should have awaited with perfect composure the inevitable hour of my return to comfortable realities, of my
deliverance from bondage or restoration to health. Perhaps
this want of talent, this black cavity which gaped in my mind
when I ransacked it for the theme of my future writings,
was itself no more, either, than an unsubstantial illusion, and
would be brought to an end by the intervention of my father,
who would arrange with the Government and with Provi-
dence that I should be the first writer of my day. But at
other times, while my parents were growing impatient at
seeing me loiter behind instead of following them, my actual
life, instead of seeming an artificial creation by my father,
and one which he could modify as he chose, appeared, on the
contrary, to be comprised in a larger reality which had not
been created for my benefit, from whose judgments there
was no appeal, in the heart of which I was bound. helpless,
without friend or ally, and beyond which no further possi-

bilities lay concealed. It was evident to me then that I existed
in the same manner as all other men, that I must grow old,
that I must die like them, and that among them I was to be
distinguished merely as one of those who have no aptitude
for writing. And so, utterly despondent, I renounced literature for ever, despite the encouragements that had been given
me by Bloch. This intimate, spontaneous feeling, this sense
of the nullity of my intellect, prevailed against all the flatter-
ing speeches that might be lavished upon me, as a wicked man,
when everyone is loud in the praise of his good deeds, is
gnawed by the secret remorse of conscience.

One day my mother said : " You are always talking about
Mme. de Guermantes. Well, Dr. Percepied did a great deal
for her when she was ill, four years ago, and so she is coming
to Combray for his daughter's wedding. You will be able
to see her in church." It was from Dr. Percepied, as it
happened, that I had heard most about Mme. de Guermantes,
and he had even shewn us the number of an illustrated paper
in which she was depicted in the costume which she had worn
at a fancy dress ball given by the Princesse de Léon.

Suddenly, during the nuptial mass, the beadle, by moving
to one side, enabled me to see, sitting in a chapel, a lady with
fair hair and a large nose, piercing blue eyes, a billowy scarf
of mauve silk, glossy and new and brilliant, and a little spot
at the corner of her nose. And because on the surface of her
face, which was red, as though she had been very warm, I
could make out, diluted and barely perceptible, details which
resembled the portrait that had been shewn to me ; because,
more especially, the particular features which I remarked in
this lady, if I attempted to catalogue them, formulated themselves in precisely the same terms :—*a large nose, blue eyes*, as
Dr. Percepied had used when describing in my presence the

Duchesse de Guermantes, I said to myself : " This lady is like the Duchesse de Guermantes." Now the chapel from which she was following the service was that of Gilbert the Bad ; beneath its flat tombstones, yellowed and bulging like cells of honey in a comb, rested the bones of the old Counts of Brabant ; and I remembered having heard it said that this chapel was reserved for the Guermantes family, whenever any of its members came to attend a ceremony at Combray ; there was, indeed, but one woman resembling the portrait of Mme. de Guermantes who on that day, the very day on which she was expected to come there, could be sitting in that chapel : it was she ! My disappointment was immense. It arose from my not having borne in mind, when I thought of Mme. de Guermantes, that I was picturing her to myself in the colours of a tapestry or a painted window, as living in another century, as being of another substance than the rest of the human race. Never had I taken into account that she might have a red face, a mauve scarf like Mme. Sazerat ; and the oval curve of her cheeks reminded me so strongly of people whom I had seen at home that the suspicion brushed against my mind (though it was immediately banished) that this lady in her creative principle, in the molecules of her physical composition, was perhaps not substantially the Duchesse de Guermantes, but that her body, in ignorance of the name that people had given it, belonged to a certain type of femininity which included, also, the wives of doctors and tradesmen. " It is, it must be Mme. de Guermantes, and no one else ! " were the words underlying the attentive and astonished expression with which I was gazing upon this image, which, naturally enough, bore no resemblance to those that had so often, under the same title of ' Mme. de Guermantes,' appeared to me in dreams, since this one had not been, like the others, formed arbitrarily by myself, but had sprung into sight for the first time, only a moment ago, here in church ; an image which was not of the same nature, was not colourable at will, like those others that allowed themselves to imbibe the orange tint of a sonorous syllable, but which was so real that everything, even to the fiery little spot at the corner of her nose, gave an assurance of her subjection to the laws of life, as in a transformation scene on the stage a crease in the dress of a fairy, a quivering of her tiny finger, indicate the material presence of a living actress before our eyes, whereas we were uncertain, till then, whether we were not looking merely at a projection of limelight from a lantern.

Meanwhile I was endeavouring to apply to this image, which the prominent nose, the piercing eyes pinned down and fixed in my field of vision (perhaps because it was they that had first struck it, that had made the first impression on its surface, before I had had time to wonder whether the woman who thus appeared before me might possibly be Mme. de Guermantes), to this fresh and unchanging image the idea : " It is Mme. de Guermantes " ; but I succeeded only in making the idea pass between me and the image, as though they were two discs moving in separate planes, with a space between. But this Mme. de Guermantes of whom I had so often dreamed, now that I could see that she had a real existence independent of myself, acquired a fresh increase of power over my imagination, which, paralysed for a moment by contact with a reality so different from anything that it had expected, began to react and to say within me : " Great and glorious before the days of Charlemagne, the Guermantes had the right of life and death over their vassals ; the Duchesse de Guermantes descends from Geneviève de

I   I

Brabant. She does not know, nor would she consent to know, any of the people who are here to-day."

And then—oh, marvellous independence of the human gaze, tied to the human face by a cord so loose, so long, so elastic that it can stray, alone, as far as it may choose—while Mme. de Guermantes sat in the chapel above the tombs of her dead ancestors, her gaze lingered here and wandered there, rose to the capitals of the pillars, and even rested upon myself, like a ray of sunlight straying down the nave, but a ray of sunlight which, at the moment when I received its caress, appeared conscious of where it fell. As for Mme. de Guermantes herself, since she remained there motionless, sitting like a mother who affects not to notice the rude or awkward conduct of her children who, in the course of their play, are speaking to people whom she does not know, it was impossible for me to determine whether she approved or condemned the vagrancy of her eyes in the careless detachment of her heart.

I felt it to be important that she should not leave the church before I had been able to look long enough upon her, reminding myself that for years past I had regarded the sight of her as a thing eminently to be desired, and I kept my eyes fixed on her, as though by gazing at her I should be able to carry away and incorporate, to store up, for later reference, in myself the memory of that prominent nose, those red cheeks, of all those details which struck me as so much precious, authentic, unparalleled information with regard to her face. And now that, whenever I brought my mind to bear upon that face—and especially, perhaps, in my determination, that form of the instinct of self-preservation with which we guard everything that is best in ourselves, not to admit that I had been in any way deceived—I found only beauty there ; setting her once again (since they were one and the same person, this lady who sat before me and that Duchesse de Guermantes whom, until then, I had been used to conjure into an imagined shape) apart from and above that common run of humanity with which the sight, pure and simple, of her in the flesh had made me for a moment confound her, I grew indignant when I heard people saying, in the congregation round me : " She is better looking than Mme. Sazerat " or " than Mlle. Vinteuil," as though she had been in any way comparable with them. And my gaze resting upon her fair hair, her blue eyes, the lines of her neck, and overlooking the features which might have reminded me of the faces of other women, I cried out within myself, as I admired this deliberately unfinished sketch : " How lovely she is ! What true nobility ! It is indeed a proud Guermantes, the descendant of Geneviève de Brabant, that I have before me ! " And the care which I took to focus all my attention upon her face succeeded in isolating it so completely that to-day, when I call that marriage ceremony to mind, I find it impossible to visualise any single person who was present except her, and the beadle who answered me in the affirmative when I inquired whether the lady was, indeed, Mme. de Guermantes. But her, I can see her still quite clearly, especially at the moment when the procession filed into the sacristy, lighted by the intermittent, hot sunshine of a windy and rainy day, where Mme. de Guermantes found herself in the midst of all those Combray people whose names, even, she did not know, but whose inferiority proclaimed her own supremacy so loud that she must, in return, feel for them a genuine, pitying sympathy, and whom she might count on impressing even more forcibly by virtue of her simplicity and natural charm. And then, too, since she could not bring into play the deliberate glances, charged with a definite meaning, which one directs, in a crowd, towards people whom one knows, but must allow her vague thoughts to escape continually from her eyes in a flood of blue light which she was powerless to control, she was anxious not to distress in any way, not to seem to be despising those humbler mortals over whom that current flowed, by whom it was everywhere arrested. I can see again to-day, above her mauve scarf, silky and buoyant, the gentle astonishment in her eyes, to which she had added, without daring to address it to anyone in particular, but so that everyone might enjoy his share of it, the almost timid smile of a sovereign lady who seems to be making an apology for her presence among the vassals whom she loves. This smile rested upon myself, who had never ceased to follow her with my eyes. And I, remembering the glance which she had let fall upon me during the service, blue as a ray of sunlight that had penetrated the window of Gilbert the Bad, said to myself " Of course, she is thinking about me." I fancied that I had found favour in her sight, that she would continue to think of me after she had left the church, and would, perhaps, grow pensive again, that evening, at Guermantes, on my account. And at once I fell in love with her, for if it is sometimes enough to make us love a woman that she looks on us with contempt, as I supposed Mlle. Swann to have done, while we imagine that she cannot ever be ours, it is enough, also, sometimes that she looks on us kindly, as Mme. de Guermantes did then, while we think of her as almost ours already. Her eyes waxed blue as a periwinkle flower, wholly beyond my reach, yet dedicated by her to me ; and the sun, bursting out again from behind a threatening cloud and darting the full force of its rays on to the Square and into the sacristy, shed a geranium glow over the red carpet laid down for the wedding, along which Mme. de Guermantes smilingly advanced, and covered its woollen texture with a nap of rosy velvet, a bloom of light, giving it that sort of tenderness, of solemn sweetness in the pomp of a joyful celebration, which characterise certain pages of *Lohengrin*, certain paintings by Carpaccio, and make us understand how Baudelaire was able to apply to the sound of the trumpet the epithet ' delicious.'

How often, after that day, in the course of my walks along the ' Guermantes way,' and with what an intensified melancholy did I reflect on my lack of qualification for a literary career, and that I must abandon all hope of ever becoming a famous author. The regret that I felt for this, while I lingered alone to dream for a little by myself, made me suffer so acutely that, in order not to feel it, my mind of its own accord, by a sort of inhibition in the instant of pain, ceased entirely to think of verse-making, of fiction, of the poetic future on which my want of talent precluded me from counting. Then, quite apart from all those literary preoccupations, and without definite attachment to anything, suddenly a roof, a gleam of sunlight reflected from a stone, the smell of a road would make me stop still, to enjoy the special pleasure that each of them gave me, and also because they appeared to be concealing, beneath what my eyes could see, something which they invited me to approach and seize from them, but which, despite all my efforts, I never managed to discover. As I felt that the mysterious object was to be found in them, I would stand there in front of them, motionless, gazing, breathing, endeavouring to penetrate with my mind beyond the thing seen or smelt. And if I had then to hasten after my grandfather, to proceed on my way, I would still seek to recover my sense of them by closing my eyes ;

I would concentrate upon recalling exactly the line of the roof, the colour of the stone, which, without my being able to understand why, had seemed to me to be teeming, ready to open, to yield up to me the secret treasure of which they were themselves no more than the outer coverings. It was certainly not any impression of this kind that could or would restore the hope I had lost of succeeding one day in becoming an author and poet, for each of them was associated with some material object devoid of any intellectual value, and suggesting no abstract truth. But at least they gave me an unreasoning pleasure, the illusion of a sort of fecundity of mind ; and in that way distracted me from the tedium, from the sense of my own impotence which I had felt whenever I had sought a philosophic theme for some great literary work. So urgent was the task imposed on my conscience by these impressions of form or perfume or colour——to strive for a perception of what lay hidden beneath them, that I was never long in seeking an excuse which would allow me to relax so strenuous an effort and to spare myself the fatigue that it involved. As good luck would have it, my parents called me ; I felt that I had not, for the moment, the calm environment necessary for a successful pursuit of my researches, and that it would be better to think no more of the matter until I reached home, and not to exhaust myself in the meantime to no purpose. And so I concerned myself no longer with the mystery that lay hidden in a form or a perfume, quite at ease in my mind, since I was taking it home with me, protected by its visible and tangible covering, beneath which I should find it still alive, like the fish which, on days when I had been allowed to go out fishing, I used to carry back in my basket, buried in a couch of grass which kept them cool and fresh. Once in the house again I would begin to think of something else, and so my mind would become littered (as my room was with the flowers that I had gathered on my walks, or the odds and ends that people had given me) with a stone from the surface of which the sunlight was reflected, a roof, the sound of a bell, the smell of fallen leaves, a confused mass of different images, under which must have perished long ago the reality of which I used to have some foreboding, but which I never had the energy to discover and bring to light. Once, however, when we had prolonged our walk far beyond its ordinary limits, and so had been very glad to encounter, half way home, as afternoon darkened into evening, Dr. Percepied, who drove past us at full speed in his carriage, saw and recognised us, stopped, and made us jump in beside him, I received an impression of this sort which I did not abandon without having first subjected it to an examination a little more thorough. I had been set on the box beside the coachman, we were going like the wind because the Doctor had still, before returning to Combray, to call at Martinville-le-Sec, at the house of a patient, at whose door he asked us to wait for him. At a bend in the road I experienced, suddenly, that special pleasure, which bore no resemblance to any other, when I caught sight of the twin steeples of Martinville, on which the setting sun was playing, while the movement of the carriage and the windings of the road seemed to keep them continually changing their position ; and then of a third steeple, that of Vieuxvicq, which, although separated from them by a hill and a valley, and rising from rather higher ground in the distance, appeared none the less to be standing by their side.

In ascertaining and noting the shape of their spires, the changes of aspect, the sunny warmth of their surfaces, I felt that I was not penetrating to the full depth of my impression, that something more lay behind that mobility, that luminosity, something which they seemed at once to contain and to conceal.

The steeples appeared so distant, and we ourselves seemed to come so little nearer them, that I was astonished when, a few minutes later, we drew up outside the church of Martin-ville. I did not know the reason for the pleasure which I had found in seeing them upon the horizon, and the business of trying to find out what that reason was seemed to me irk-some ; I wished only to keep in reserve in my brain those converging lines, moving in the sunshine, and, for the time being, to think of them no more. And it is probable that, had I done so, those two steeples would have vanished for ever, in a great medley of trees and roofs and scents and sounds which I had noticed and set apart on account of the obscure sense of pleasure which they gave me, but without ever exploring them more fully. I got down from the box to talk to my parents while we were waiting for the Doctor to reappear. Then it was time to start ; I climbed up again to my place, turning my head to look back, once more, at my steeples, of which, a little later, I caught a farewell glimpse at a turn in the road. The coachman, who seemed little inclined for conversation, having barely acknowledged my remarks, I was obliged, in default of other society, to fall back on my own, and to attempt to recapture the vision of my steeples. And presently their outlines and their sunlit surface, as though they had been a sort of rind, were stripped apart ; a little of what they had concealed from me became ap-parent ; an idea came into my mind which had not existed for me a moment earlier, framed itself in words in my head ; and the pleasure with which the first sight of them, just now, had filled me was so much enhanced that, overpowered by a sort of intoxication, I could no longer think of anything but them. At this point, although we had now travelled a long way from Martinville, I turned my head and caught sight of them again, quite black this time, for the sun had meanwhile set. Every few minutes a turn in the road would sweep them out of sight ; then they shewed themselves for the last time, and so I saw them no more.

Without admitting to myself that what lay buried within the steeples of Martinville must be something analogous to a charming phrase, since it was in the form of words which gave me pleasure that it had appeared to me, I borrowed a pencil and some paper from the Doctor, and composed, in spite of the jolting of the carriage, to appease my conscience and to satisfy my enthusiasm, the following little fragment, which I have since discovered, and now reproduce, with only a slight revision here and there.

Alone, rising from the level of the plain, and seemingly lost in that expanse of open country, climbed to the sky the twin steeples of Martinville. Presently we saw three : springing into position, confronting them by a daring volt, a third, a dilatory steeple, that of Vieuxvicq, was come to join them. The minutes passed, we were moving rapidly, and yet the three steeples were always a long way ahead of us, like three birds perched upon the plain, motionless and conspicuous in the sunlight. Then the steeple of Vieuxvicq withdrew, took its proper distance, and the steeples of Martinville remained alone, gilded by the light of the setting sun, which, even at that distance, I could see playing and smiling upon their sloped sides. We had been so long in approaching them that I was thinking of the time that must still elapse before we could reach them when, of a sudden, the carriage, having turned a corner, set us down at their feet ; and they had flung themselves so abruptly in our path that we had barely time to stop before being dashed against the porch of the church. We resumed our course ; we had left Martinville some little time, and the village, after accompanying us for a few

seconds, had already disappeared, when, lingering alone on the
horizon to watch our flight, its steeples and that of Vieuxvicq
waved once again, in token of farewell, their sun-bathed pinnacles. Sometimes one would withdraw, so that the other two
might watch us for a moment still; then the road changed
direction, they veered in the light like three golden pivots,
and vanished from my gaze. But, a little later, when we
were already close to Combray, the sun having set meanwhile, I caught sight of them for the last time, far away,
and seeming no more now than three flowers painted upon the
sky above the low line of fields. They made me think, too,
of three maidens in a legend, abandoned in a solitary place over
which night had begun to fall; and while we drew away from
them at a gallop, I could see them timidly seeking their way,
and, after some awkward, stumbling movements of their
noble silhouettes, drawing close to one another, slipping one
behind another, shewing nothing more, now, against the still
rosy sky than a single dusky form, charming and resigned,
and so vanishing in the night.

I never thought again of this page, but at the moment
when, on my corner of the box-seat, where the Doctor's
coachman was in the habit of placing, in a hamper, the fowls
which he had bought at Martinville market, I had finished
writing it, I found such a sense of happiness, felt that it had
so entirely relieved my mind of the obsession of the steeples,
and of the mystery which they concealed, that, as though I
myself were a hen and had just laid an egg, I began to sing
at the top of my voice.

All day long, during these walks, I had been able to muse
upon the pleasure that there would be in the friendship of
the Duchesse de Guermantes, in fishing for trout, in drifting
by myself in a boat on the Vivonne; and, greedy for happiness, I asked nothing more from life, in such moments, than
that it should consist always of a series of joyous afternoons.
But when, on our way home, I had caught sight of a farm,

on the left of the road, at some distance from two other farms which were themselves close together, and from which, to return to Combray, we need only turn down an avenue of oaks, bordered on one side by a series of orchard-closes, each one planted at regular intervals with apple-trees which cast upon the ground, when they were lighted by the setting sun, the Japanese stencil of their shadows, then, sharply, my heart would begin to beat, I would know that in half an hour we should be at home, and that there, as was the rule on days when we had taken the 'Guermantes way' and dinner was, in consequence, served later than usual, I should be sent to bed as soon as I had swallowed my soup, so that my mother, kept at table, just as though there had been company to dinner, would not come upstairs to say good night to me in bed. The zone of melancholy which I then entered was totally distinct from that other zone, in which I had been bounding for joy a moment earlier, just as sometimes in the sky a band of pink is separated, as though by a line invisibly ruled, from a band of green or black. You may see a bird flying across the pink ; it draws near the border-line, touches it, enters and is lost upon the black. The longings by which I had just now been absorbed, to go to Guermantes, to travel, to live a life of happiness—I was now so remote from them that their fulfilment would have afforded me no pleasure. How readily would I have sacrificed them all, just to be able to cry, all night long, in the arms of Mamma ! Shuddering with emotion, I could not take my agonised eyes from my mother's face, which was not to appear that evening in the bedroom where I could see myself already lying, in imagination ; and wished only that I were lying dead. And this state would persist until the morrow, when, the rays of morning leaning their bars of light, as the gardener might lean his ladder,

against the wall overgrown with nasturtiums, which clam-
bered up it as far as my window-sill, I would leap out of bed
to run down at once into the garden, with no thought of
the fact that evening must return, and with it the hour when
I must leave my mother. And so it was from the ' Guermantes way' that I learned to distinguish between these
states which reigned alternately in my mind, during certain
periods, going so far as to divide every day between them,
each one returning to dispossess the other with the regularity
of a fever and ague : contiguous, and yet so foreign to one
another, so devoid of means of communication, that I could
no longer understand, or even picture to myself, in one
state what I had desired or dreaded or even done in the
other.

So the ' Méséglise way' and the ' Guermantes way'
remain for me linked with many of the little incidents of that
one of all the divers lives along whose parallel lines we are
moved, which is the most abundant in sudden reverses of
fortune, the richest in episodes ; I mean the life of the mind.
Doubtless it makes in us an imperceptible progress, and the
truths which have changed for us its meaning and its aspect,
which have opened new paths before our feet, we had for long
been preparing for their discovery ; but that preparation was
unconscious ; and for us those truths date only from the day,
from the minute when they became apparent. The flowers
which played then among the grass, the water which rippled
past in the sunshine, the whole landscape which served as
environment to their apparition lingers around the memory
of them still with its unconscious or unheeding air ; and,
certainly, when they were slowly scrutinised by this humble
passer-by, by this dreaming child—as the face of a king is
scrutinised by a petitioner lost in the crowd—that scrap of

nature, that corner of a garden could never suppose that it would be thanks to him that they would be elected to survive in all their most ephemeral details ; and yet the scent of haw-thorn which strays plundering along the hedge from which, in a little while, the dog-roses will have banished it, a sound of footsteps followed by no echo, upon a gravel path, a bubble formed at the side of a water-plant by the current, and formed only to burst—my exaltation of mind has borne them with it, and has succeeded in making them traverse all these successive years, while all around them the once-trodden ways have vanished, while those who thronged those ways, and even the memory of those who thronged those trodden ways, are dead. Sometimes the fragment of landscape thus transported into the present will detach itself in such isolation from all asso-ciations that it floats uncertainly upon my mind, like a flowering isle of Delos, and I am unable to say from what place, from what time—perhaps, quite simply, from which of my dreams—it comes. But it is pre-eminently as the deepest layer of my mental soil, as firm sites on which I still may build, that I regard the Méséglise and Guermantes ' ways.' It is because I used to think of certain things, of certain people, while I was roaming along them, that the things, the people which they taught me to know, and these alone, I still take seriously, still give me joy. Whether it be that the faith which creates has ceased to exist in me, or that reality will take shape in the memory alone, the flowers that people shew me nowadays for the first time never seem to me to be true flowers. The ' Méséglise way ' with its lilacs, its hawthorns, its cornflowers, its poppies, its apple-trees, the ' Guermantes way ' with its river full of tadpoles, its water-lilies, and its buttercups have constituted for me for all time the picture of the land in which I fain would pass my life, in which my only requirements are that I may go out fishing, drift idly in a boat, see the ruins of a gothic fortress in the grass, and find hidden among the cornfields——as Saint-André-des-Champs lay hidden——an old church, monumental, rustic, and yellow like a mill-stone ; and the cornflowers, the haw-thorns, the apple-trees which I may happen, when I go walk-ing, to encounter in the fields, because they are situated at the same depth, on the level of my past life, at once establish con-tact with my heart. And yet, because there is an element of individuality in places, when I am seized with a desire to see again the ' Guermantes way,' it would not be satisfied were I led to the banks of a river in which were lilies as fair, or even fairer than those in the Vivonne, any more than on my return home in the evening, at the hour when there awakened in me that anguish which, later on in life, transfers itself to the passion of love, and may even become its in-separable companion, I should have wished for any strange mother to come in and say good night to me, though she were far more beautiful and more intelligent than my own. No : just as the one thing necessary to send me to sleep contented (in that untroubled peace which no mistress, in later years, has ever been able to give me, since one has doubts of them at the moment when one believes in them, and never can possess their hearts as I used to receive, in her kiss, the heart of my mother, complete, without scruple or reservation, un-burdened by any liability save to myself) was that it should be my mother who came, that she should incline towards me that face on which there was, beneath her eye, something that was, it appears, a blemish, and which I loved as much as all the rest——so what I want to see again is the ' Guermantes way ' as I knew it, with the farm that stood a little apart from the two neighbouring farms, pressed so close together, at the entrance to the oak avenue ; those meadows upon whose surface, when it is polished by the sun to the mirroring radiance of a lake, are outlined the leaves of the apple-trees ; that whole landscape whose individuality sometimes, at night, in my dreams, binds me with a power that is almost fantastic, of which I can discover no trace when I awake.

No doubt, by virtue of having permanently and indissolubly combined in me groups of different impressions, for no reason save that they had made me feel several separate things at the same time, the Méséglise and Guermantes ' ways ' left me exposed, in later life, to much disillusionment, and even to many mistakes. For often I have wished to see a person again without realising that it was simply because that person recalled to me a hedge of hawthorns in blossom ; and I have been led to believe, and to make some one else believe in an aftermath of affection, by what was no more than an inclination to travel. But by the same qualities, and by their persistence in those of my impressions, to-day, to which they can find an attachment, the two ' ways ' give to those impressions a foundation, depth, a dimension lacking from the rest. They invest them, too, with a charm, a significance which is for me alone. When, on a summer evening, the resounding sky growls like a tawny lion, and everyone is complaining of the storm, it is along the ' Méséglise way ' that my fancy strays alone in ecstasy, inhaling, through the noise of falling rain, the odour of invisible and persistent lilac-trees.

* * *

And so I would often lie until morning, dreaming of the old days at Combray, of my melancholy and wakeful evenings there ; of other days besides, the memory of which had been more lately restored to me by the taste—by what would have been called at Combray the ' perfume '—of a cup of tea ; and, by an association of memories, of a story which, many years after I had left the little place, had been told me of a love affair in which Swann had been involved before I was born ; with that accuracy of detail which it is easier, often, to obtain when we are studying the lives of people who have been dead for centuries than when we are trying to chronicle those of our own most intimate friends, an accuracy which it seems as impossible to attain as it seemed impossible to speak from one town to another, before we learned of the contrivance by which that impossibility has been overcome. All these memories, following one after another, were condensed into a single substance, but had not so far coalesced that I could not discern between the three strata, between my oldest, my instinctive memories, those others, inspired more recently by a taste or ' perfume,' and those which were actually the memories of another, from whom I had acquired them at second hand—no fissures, indeed, no geological faults, but at least those veins, those streaks of colour which in certain rocks, in certain marbles, point to differences of origin, age, and formation.

It is true that, when morning drew near, I would long have settled the brief uncertainty of my waking dream, I would know in what room I was actually lying, would have reconstructed it round about me in the darkness, and—fixing my orientation by memory alone, or with the assistance of a feeble glimmer of light at the foot of which I placed the curtains and the window—would have reconstructed it complete and with its furniture, as an architect and an upholsterer might do, working upon an original, discarded plan of the doors and windows ; would have replaced the mirrors and set the chest-of-drawers on its accustomed site. But scarcely had daylight itself—and no longer the gleam from a last, dying ember on a brass curtain-rod, which I had mistaken for daylight—traced across the darkness, as with a stroke of chalk across a black-board, its first white correcting ray, when the window, with its curtains, would leave the frame of the doorway, in which I had erroneously placed it, while, to make room for it, the writing-table, which my memory had clumsily fixed where the window ought to be, would hurry off at full speed, thrusting before it the mantelpiece, and sweeping aside the wall of the passage ; the well of the courtyard would be en-throned on the spot where, a moment earlier, my dressing-room had lain, and the dwelling-place which I had built up for myself in the darkness would have gone to join all those other dwellings of which I had caught glimpses from the whirlpool of awakening ; put to flight by that pale sign traced above my window-curtains by the uplifted fore-finger of day.

SWANN IN LOVE

TO admit you to the 'little nucleus,' the 'little group,' the 'little clan' at the Verdurins', one condition sufficed, but that one was indispensable; you must give tacit adherence to a Creed one of whose articles was that the young pianist, whom Mme. Verdurin had taken under her patronage that year, and of whom she said " Really, it oughtn't to be allowed, to play Wagner as well as that ! " left both Planté and Rubinstein 'sitting'; while Dr. Cottard was a more brilliant diagnostician than Potain. Each 'new recruit' whom the Verdurins failed to persuade that the evenings spent by other people, in other houses than theirs, were as dull as ditch-water, saw himself banished forthwith. Women being in this respect more rebellious than men, more reluctant to lay aside all worldly curiosity and the desire to find out for themselves whether other drawing-rooms might not sometimes be as entertaining, and the Verdurins feeling, moreover, that this critical spirit and this demon of frivolity might, by their contagion, prove fatal to the orthodoxy of the little church, they had been obliged to expel, one after another, all those of the 'faithful' who were of the female sex.

Apart from the doctor's young wife, they were reduced almost exclusively that season (for all that Mme. Verdurin herself was a thoroughly 'good' woman, and came of a respectable middle-class family, excessively rich and wholly undistinguished, with which she had gradually and of her own accord severed all connection) to a young woman almost of a 'certain class,' a Mme. de Crécy, whom Mme. Verdurin called by her Christian name, Odette, and pronounced a 'love,' and to the pianist's aunt, who looked as though she

had, at one period, 'answered the bell' : ladies quite ignorant of the world, who in their social simplicity were so easily
led to believe that the Princesse de Sagan and the Duchesse
de Guermantes were obliged to pay large sums of money to
other poor wretches, in order to have anyone at their dinner-
parties, that if somebody had offered to procure them an
invitation to the house of either of those great dames, the
old doorkeeper and the woman of 'easy virtue' would
have contemptuously declined.

The Verdurins never invited you to dinner ; you had
your 'place laid' there. There was never any programme
for the evening's entertainment. The young pianist would
play, but only if he felt inclined, for no one was forced to do
anything, and, as M. Verdurin used to say : "We're all
friends here. Liberty Hall, you know!"

If the pianist suggested playing the Ride of the Valkyries,
or the Prelude to Tristan, Mme. Verdurin would protest,
not that the music was displeasing to her, but, on the contrary, that it made too violent an impression. "Then you
want me to have one of my headaches ? You know quite well,
it's the same every time he plays that. I know what I'm in
for. To-morrow, when I want to get up—nothing doing !"
If he was not going to play they talked, and one of the friends
—usually the painter who was in favour there that year—
would "spin," as M. Verdurin put it, "a damned funny yarn
that made 'em all split with laughter," and especially Mme.
Verdurin, for whom—so strong was her habit of taking
literally the figurative accounts of her emotions—Dr. Cottard, who was then just starting in general practice, would
"really have to come one day and set her jaw, which she had
dislocated with laughing too much."

Evening dress was barred, because you were all 'good

pals,' and didn't want to look like the ' boring people ' who were to be avoided like the plague, and only asked to the big evenings, which were given as seldom as possible, and then only if it would amuse the painter or make the musician better known. The rest of the time you were quite happy playing charades and having supper in fancy dress, and there was no need to mingle any strange element with the little 'clan.'

But just as the ' good pals ' came to take a more and more prominent place in Mme. Verdurin's life, so the ' bores,' the ' nuisances ' grew to include everybody and everything that kept her friends away from her, that made them sometimes plead ' previous engagements,' the mother of one, the professional duties of another, the ' little place in the country ' of a third. If Dr. Cottard felt bound to say good night as soon as they rose from table, so as to go back to some patient who was seriously ill ; " I don't know ; " Mme. Verdurin would say, " I'm sure it will do him far more good if you don't go disturbing him again this evening ; he will have a good night without you ; to-morrow morning you can go round early and you will find him cured." From the beginning of December it would make her quite ill to think that the ' faithful ' might fail her on Christmas and New Year's Days. The pianist's aunt insisted that he must accompany her, on the latter, to a family dinner at her mother's.

" You don't suppose she'll die, your mother," exclaimed Mme. Verdurin bitterly, " if you don't have dinner with her on New Year's Day, like people in the *provinces* ! "

Her uneasiness was kindled again in Holy Week : " Now you, Doctor, you're a sensible, broad-minded man ; you'll come, of course, on Good Friday, just like any other day ? " she said to Cottard in the first year of the little ' nucleus,' in a loud and confident voice, as though there could be no doubt of his answer. But she trembled as she waited for it, for if he did not come she might find herself condemned to dine alone.

"I shall come on Good Friday—to say good-bye to you, for we are going to spend the holidays in Auvergne."

"In Auvergne? To be eaten alive by fleas and all sorts of creatures! A fine lot of good that will do you!" And after a solemn pause : "If you had only told us, we would have tried to get up a party, and all gone there together, comfortably."

And so, too, if one of the 'faithful' had a friend, or one of the ladies a young man, who was liable, now and then, to make them miss an evening, the Verdurins, who were not in the least afraid of a woman's having a lover, provided that she had him in their company, loved him in their company and did not prefer him to their company, would say : "Very well, then, bring your friend along." And he would be put to the test, to see whether he was willing to have no secrets from Mme. Verdurin, whether he was susceptible of being enrolled in the 'little clan.' If he failed to pass, the faithful one who had introduced him would be taken on one side, and would be tactfully assisted to quarrel with the friend or mistress. But if the test proved satisfactory, the newcomer would in turn be numbered among the 'faithful.' And so when, in the course of this same year, the courtesan told M. Verdurin that she had made the acquaintance of such a charming gentleman, M. Swann, and hinted that he would very much like to be allowed to come, M. Verdurin carried the request at once to his wife. He never formed an opinion on any subject until she had formed hers, his special duty being to carry out her wishes and those of the 'faithful' generally, which he did with boundless ingenuity.

" My dear, Mme. de Crécy has something to say to you. She would like to bring one of her friends here, a M. Swann. What do you say ? "

" Why, as if anybody could refuse anything to a little piece of perfection like that. Be quiet ; no one asked your opinion. I tell you that you are a piece of perfection."

" Just as you like," replied Odette, in an affected tone, and then went on : " You know I'm not fishing for compliments."

" Very well ; bring your friend, if he's nice."

Now there was no connection whatsoever between the 'little nucleus' and the society which Swann frequented, and a purely worldly man would have thought it hardly worth his while, when occupying so exceptional a position in the world, to seek an introduction to the Verdurins. But Swann was so ardent a lover that, once he had got to know almost all the women of the aristocracy, once they had taught him all that there was to learn, he had ceased to regard those naturalisation papers, almost a patent of nobility, which the Faubourg Saint-Germain had bestowed upon him, save as a sort of negotiable bond, a letter of credit with no intrinsic value, which allowed him to improvise a status for himself in some little hole in the country, or in some obscure quarter of Paris, where the good-looking daughter of a local squire or solicitor had taken his fancy. For at such times desire, or love itself, would revive in him a feeling of vanity from which he was now quite free in his everyday life, although it was, no doubt, the same feeling which had originally prompted him towards that career as a man of fashion in which he had squandered his intellectual gifts upon frivolous amusements, and had made use of his erudition in matters of art only to advise society ladies what pictures to buy and how to decorate their houses ; and this vanity it was which made him eager to shine, in the sight of any fair unknown who had captivated him for the moment, with a brilliance which the name of Swann by itself did not emit. And he was most eager when the fair unknown was in humble circumstances. Just as it is not by other men of intelligence that an intelligent man is afraid of being thought a fool, so it is not by the great gentleman but by boors and 'bounders' that a man of fashion is afraid of finding his social value underrated. Three-fourths of the mental ingenuity displayed, of the social falsehoods scattered broadcast ever since the world began by people whose importance they have served only to diminish, have been aimed at inferiors. And Swann, who behaved quite simply and was at his ease when with a duchess, would tremble, for fear of being despised, and would instantly begin to pose, were he to meet her grace's maid.

Unlike so many people, who, either from lack of energy or else from a resigned sense of the obligation laid upon them by their social grandeur to remain moored like house-boats to a certain point on the bank of the stream of life, abstain from the pleasures which are offered to them above and below that point, that degree in life in which they will remain fixed until the day of their death, and are content, in the end, to describe as pleasures, for want of any better, those mediocre distractions, that just not intolerable tedium which is enclosed there with them ; Swann would endeavour not to find charm and beauty in the women with whom he must pass his time, but to pass his time among women whom he had already found to be beautiful and charming. And these were, as often as not, women whose beauty was of a distinctly 'common' type, for the physical qualities which attracted him instinctively, and without reason, were the direct

opposite of those that he admired in the women painted or
sculptured by his favourite masters. Depth of character, or a
melancholy expression on a woman's face would freeze his
senses, which would, however, immediately melt at the sight
of healthy, abundant, rosy human flesh.

If on his travels he met a family whom it would have been
more correct for him to make no attempt to know, but among
whom a woman caught his eye, adorned with a special charm
that was new to him, to remain on his ' high horse ' and to
cheat the desire that she had kindled in him, to substitute a
pleasure different from that which he might have tasted in
her company by writing to invite one of his former mistresses
to come and join him would have seemed to him as cowardly
an abdication in the face of life, as stupid a renunciation of a
new form of happiness as if, instead of visiting the country
where he was, he had shut himself up in his own rooms and
looked at ' views ' of Paris. He did not immure himself in
the solid structure of his social relations, but had made of
them, so as to be able to set it up afresh upon new foundations
wherever a woman might take his fancy, one of those col-
lapsible tents which explorers carry about with them. Any
part of it which was not portable or could not be adapted to
some fresh pleasure he would discard as valueless, however
enviable it might appear to others. How often had his credit
with a duchess, built up of the yearly accumulation of her
desire to do him some favour for which she had never found
an opportunity, been squandered in a moment by his calling
upon her, in an indiscreetly worded message, for a recommendation by telegraph which would put him in touch at
once with one of her agents whose daughter he had noticed
in the country, just as a starving man might barter a diamond
for a crust of bread. Indeed, when it was too late, he would

laugh at himself for it, for there was in his nature, redeemed by many rare refinements, an element of clownishness. Then he belonged to that class of intelligent men who have led a life of idleness, and who seek consolation and, perhaps, an excuse in the idea, which their idleness offers to their intelligence, of objects as worthy of their interest as any that could be attained by art or learning, the idea that ' Life ' contains situations more interesting and more romantic than all the romances ever written. So, at least, he would assure and had no difficulty in persuading the more subtle among his friends in the fashionable world, notably the Baron de Charlus, whom he liked to amuse with stories of the startling adventures that had befallen him, such as when he had met a woman in the train, and had taken her home with him, before discovering that she was the sister of a reigning monarch, in whose hands were gathered, at that moment, all the threads of European politics, of which he found himself kept informed in the most delightful fashion, or when, in the complexity of circumstances, it depended upon the choice which the Conclave was about to make whether he might or might not become the lover of somebody's cook.

It was not only the brilliant phalanx of virtuous dowagers, generals and academicians, to whom he was bound by such close ties, that Swann compelled with so much cynicism to serve him as panders. All his friends were accustomed to receive, from time to time, letters which called on them for a word of recommendation or introduction, with a diplomatic adroitness which, persisting throughout all his successive ' affairs ' and using different pretexts, revealed more glaringly than the clumsiest indiscretion, a permanent trait in his character and an unvarying quest. I used often to recall to myself when, many years later, I began to take an interest in his character because of the similarities which, in wholly different respects, it offered to my own, how, when he used to write to my grandfather (though not at the time we are now considering, for it was about the date of my own birth that Swann's great 'affair' began, and made a long interruption in his amatory practices) the latter, recognising his friend's handwriting on the envelope, would exclaim : ' Here is Swann asking for something ; on guard ! " And, either from distrust or from the unconscious spirit of devilry which urges us to offer a thing only to those who do not want it, my grandparents would meet with an obstinate refusal the most easily satisfied of his prayers, as when he begged them for an introduction to a girl who dined with us every Sunday, and whom they were obliged, whenever Swann mentioned her, to pretend that they no longer saw, although they would be wondering, all through the week, whom they could invite to meet her, and often failed, in the end, to find anyone, sooner than make a sign to him who would so gladly have accepted.

Occasionally a couple of my grandparents' acquaintance, who had been complaining for some time that they never saw Swann now, would announce with satisfaction, and perhaps with a slight inclination to make my grandparents envious of them, that he had suddenly become as charming as he could possibly be, and was never out of their house. My grandfather would not care to shatter their pleasant illusion, but would look at my grandmother, as he hummed the air of :

> What is this mystery ?
> I cannot understand it ;

or of :

> Vision fugitive . . . ;

or of :

> In matters such as this
> 'Tis best to close one's eyes.

A few months later, if my grandfather asked Swann's new friend " What about Swann ? Do you still see as much of him as ever ? " the other's face would lengthen : " Never mention his name to me again ! "

" But I thought that you were such friends . . ."

He had been intimate in this way for several months with some cousins of my grandmother, dining almost every evening at their house. Suddenly, and without any warning, he ceased to appear. They supposed him to be ill, and the lady of the house was going to send to inquire for him when, in her kitchen, she found a letter in his hand, which her cook had left by accident in the housekeeping book. In this he announced that he was leaving Paris and would not be able to come to the house again. The cook had been his mistress, and at the moment of breaking off relations she was the only one of the household whom he had thought it necessary to inform.

But when his mistress for the time being was a woman in society, or at least one whose birth was not so lowly, nor her position so irregular that he was unable to arrange for her reception in ' society,' then for her sake he would return to it, but only to the particular orbit in which she moved or into which he had drawn her. " No good depending on Swann for this evening," people would say ; " don't you remember, it's his American's night at the Opera ? " He would secure invitations for her to the most exclusive drawing-rooms, to those houses where he himself went regularly, for weekly dinners or for poker ; every evening, after a slight ' wave ' imparted to his stiffly brushed red locks had tempered with a certain softness the ardour of his bold green eyes, he would select a flower for his buttonhole and set out to meet his mistress at the house of one or other of the women of his circle ; and then, thinking of the affection and admiration which the fashionable folk, whom he always treated exactly as he pleased, would, when he met them there, lavish upon him in the presence of the woman whom he loved, he would find a fresh charm in that worldly existence of which he had grown weary, but whose substance, pervaded and warmly coloured by the flickering light which he had slipped into its midst, seemed to him beautiful and rare, now that he had incorporated in it a fresh love.

But while each of these attachments, each of these flirtations had been the realisation, more or less complete, of a dream born of the sight of a face or a form which Swann had spontaneously, and without effort on his part, found charming, it was quite another matter when, one day at the theatre, he was introduced to Odette de Crécy by an old friend of his own, who had spoken of her to him as a ravishing creature with whom he might very possibly come to an understanding ; but had made her out to be harder of conquest than she actually was, so as to appear to be conferring a special favour by the introduction. She had struck Swann not, certainly, as being devoid of beauty, but as endowed with a style of beauty which left him indifferent, which aroused in him no desire, which gave him, indeed, a sort of physical repulsion ; as one of those women of whom every man can name some, and each will name different examples, who are the converse of the type which our senses demand. To give him any pleasure her profile was too sharp, her skin too delicate, her cheek-bones too prominent, her features too tightly drawn. Her eyes were fine, but so large that they seemed to be bending beneath their own weight, strained the rest of her face and always made her appear unwell or in an ill humour. Some time after this introduction at the theatre she had written to ask Swann whether she might see his collections, which would interest her so much, she, "an ignorant woman with a taste for beautiful things," saying that she would know him better when once she had seen him in his 'home,' where she imagined him to be "so comfortable with his tea and his books"; although she had not concealed her surprise at his being in that part of the town, which must be so depressing, and was "not nearly smart enough for such a very smart man." And when he allowed her to come she had said to him as she left how sorry she was to have stayed so short a time in a house into which she was so glad to have found her way at last, speaking of him as though he had meant something more to her than the rest of the people she knew, and appearing to unite their two selves with a kind of romantic bond which had made him smile. But at the time of life, tinged already with dis-enchantment, which Swann was approaching, when a man can content himself with being in love for the pleasure of loving without expecting too much in return, this linking of hearts, if it is no longer, as in early youth, the goal towards which love, of necessity, tends, still is bound to love by so strong an association of ideas that it may well become the cause of love if it presents itself first. In his younger days a man dreams of possessing the heart of the woman whom he loves; later, the feeling that he possesses the heart of a woman may be enough to make him fall in love with her. And so, at an age when it would appear—since one seeks in love before everything else a subjective pleasure—that the taste for feminine beauty must play the larger part in its

270

procreation, love may come into being, love of the most
physical order, without any foundation in desire. At this time
of life a man has already been wounded more than once by
the darts of love ; it no longer evolves by itself, obeying its
own incomprehensible and fatal laws, before his passive and
astonished heart. We come to its aid ; we falsify it by
memory and by suggestion ; recognising one of its symptoms
we recall and recreate the rest. Since we possess its hymn,
engraved on our hearts in its entirety, there is no need of any
woman to repeat the opening lines, potent with the admiration
which her beauty inspires, for us to remember all that follows.
And if she begin in the middle, where it sings of our existing,
henceforward, for one another only, we are well enough
attuned to that music to be able to take it up and follow our
partner, without hesitation, at the first pause in her voice.

Odette de Crécy came again to see Swann ; her visits
grew more frequent, and doubtless each visit revived the
sense of disappointment which he felt at the sight of a face
whose details he had somewhat forgotten in the interval, not
remembering it as either so expressive or, in spite of her
youth, so faded ; he used to regret, while she was talking to
him, that her really considerable beauty was not of the kind
which he spontaneously admired. It must be remarked that
Odette's face appeared thinner and more prominent than it
actually was, because her forehead and the upper part of her
cheeks, a single and almost plane surface, were covered by the
masses of hair which women wore at that period, drawn
forward in a fringe, raised in crimped waves and falling
in stray locks over her ears ; while as for her figure, and she
was admirably built, it was impossible to make out its continuity (on account of the fashion then prevailing, and in
spite of her being one of the best-dressed women in Paris) for

the corset, jutting forwards in an arch, as though over an imaginary stomach, and ending in a sharp point, beneath which bulged out the balloon of her double skirts, gave a woman, that year, the appearance of being composed of different sections badly fitted together ; to such an extent did the frills, the flounces, the inner bodice follow, in complete independence, controlled only by the fancy of their designer or the rigidity of their material, the line which led them to the knots of ribbon, falls of lace, fringes of vertically hanging jet, or carried them along the bust, but nowhere attached themselves to the living creature, who, according as the architecture of their fripperies drew them towards or away from her own, found herself either strait-laced to suffocation or else completely buried.

But, after Odette had left him, Swann would think with a smile of her telling him how the time would drag until he allowed her to come again ; he remembered the anxious, timid way in which she had once begged him that it might not be very long, and the way in which she had looked at him then, fixing upon him her fearful and imploring gaze, which gave her a touching air beneath the bunches of artificial pansies fastened in the front of her round bonnet of white straw, tied with strings of black velvet. " And won't you," she had ventured, " come just once and take tea with me ? " He had pleaded pressure of work, an essay—which, in reality, he had abandoned years ago—on Vermeer of Delft. " I know that I am quite useless," she had replied, " a little wild thing like me beside a learned great man like you. I should be like the frog in the fable ! And yet I should so much like to learn, to know things, to be initiated. What fun it would be to become a regular bookworm, to bury my nose in a lot of old papers ! " she had gone on, with that self-satisfied air which a smart woman adopts when she insists that her one desire is to give herself up, without fear of soiling her fingers, to some unclean task, such as cooking the dinner, with her " hands right in the dish itself." " You will only laugh at me, but this painter who stops you from seeing me," she meant Vermeer, " I have never even heard of him ; is he alive still ? Can I see any of his things in Paris, so as to have some idea of what is going on behind that great brow which works so hard, that head which I feel sure is always puzzling away about things ; just to be able to say ' There, that's what he's thinking about ! ' What a dream it would be to be able to help you with your work."

He had sought an excuse in his fear of forming new friendships, which he gallantly described as his fear of a hopeless passion. " You are afraid of falling in love ? How funny that is, when I go about seeking nothing else, and would give my soul just to find a little love somewhere ! " she had said, so naturally and with such an air of conviction that he had been genuinely touched. " Some woman must have made you suffer. And you think that the rest are all like her. She can't have understood you : you are so utterly different from ordinary men. That's what I liked about you when I first saw you ; I felt at once that you weren't like everybody else."

" And then, besides, there's yourself———— " he had continued, " I know what women are ; you must have a whole heap of things to do, and never any time to spare."

" I ? Why, I have never anything to do. I am always free, and I always will be free if you want me. At whatever hour of the day or night it may suit you to see me, just send for me, and I shall be only too delighted to come. Will you do that ? Do you know what I should really like—to introduce you

to Mme. Verdurin, where I go every evening. Just fancy
my finding you there, and thinking that it was a little for my
sake that you had gone."

No doubt, in thus remembering their conversations, in
thinking about her thus when he was alone, he did no more
than call her image into being among those of countless other
women in his romantic dreams ; but if, thanks to some accidental circumstance (or even perhaps without that assistance,
for the circumstance which presents itself at the moment
when a mental state, hitherto latent, makes itself felt, may
well have had no influence whatsoever upon that state), the
image of Odette de Crécy came to absorb the whole of his
dreams, if from those dreams the memory of her could no
longer be eliminated, then her bodily imperfections would no
longer be of the least importance, nor would the conformity
of her body, more or less than any other, to the requirements
of Swann's taste ; since, having become the body of her whom
he loved, it must henceforth be the only one capable of causing
him joy or anguish.

It so happened that my grandfather had known—which
was more than could be said of any of their actual acquaintance
—the family of these Verdurins. But he had entirely
severed his connection with what he called " young Verdurin," taking a general view of him as one who had fallen—
though without losing hold of his millions—among the riff-
raff of Bohemia. One day he received a letter from Swann
asking whether my grandfather could put him in touch with
the Verdurins : " On guard ! on guard ! " he exclaimed
as he read it, " I am not at all surprised ; Swann was bound
to finish up like this. A nice lot of people ! I cannot do what
he asks, because, in the first place, I no longer know the
gentleman in question. Besides, there must be a woman in

it somewhere, and I don't mix myself up in such matters. Ah, well, we shall see some fun if Swann begins running after the little Verdurins."

And on my grandfather's refusal to act as sponsor, it was Odette herself who had taken Swann to the house.

The Verdurins had had dining with them, on the day when Swann made his first appearance, Dr. and Mme. Cottard, the young pianist and his aunt, and the painter then in favour, while these were joined, in the course of the evening, by several more of the ' faithful.'

Dr. Cottard was never quite certain of the tone in which he ought to reply to any observation, or whether the speaker was jesting or in earnest. And so in any event he would embellish all his facial expressions with the offer of a conditional, a provisional smile whose expectant subtlety would exonerate him from the charge of being a simpleton, if the remark addressed to him should turn out to have been facetious. But as he must also be prepared to face the alternative, he never dared to allow this smile a definite expression on his features, and you would see there a perpetually flickering uncertainty, in which you might decipher the question that he never dared to ask : " Do you really mean that ? " He was no more confident of the manner in which he ought to conduct himself in the street, or indeed in life generally, than he was in a drawing-room ; and he might be seen greeting passers-by, carriages, and anything that occurred with a malicious smile which absolved his subsequent behaviour of all impropriety, since it proved, if it should turn out unsuited to the occasion, that he was well aware of that, and that if he had assumed a smile, the jest was a secret of his own.

On all those points, however, where a plain question appeared to him to be permissible, the Doctor was unsparing in his endeavours to cultivate the wilderness of his ignorance and uncertainty and so to complete his education.

So it was that, following the advice given him by a wise mother on his first coming up to the capital from his provincial home, he would never let pass either a figure of speech or a proper name that was new to him without an effort to secure the fullest information upon it.

As regards figures of speech, he was insatiable in his thirst for knowledge, for often imagining them to have a more definite meaning than was actually the case, he would want to know what, exactly, was intended by those which he most frequently heard used: 'devilish pretty,' 'blue blood,' 'a cat and dog life,' 'a day of reckoning,' 'a queen of fashion,' 'to give a free hand,' 'to be at a deadlock,' and so forth ; and in what particular circumstances he himself might make use of them in conversation. Failing these, he would adorn it with puns and other 'plays upon words' which he had learned by rote. As for the names of strangers which were uttered in his hearing, he used merely to repeat them to himself in a questioning tone, which, he thought, would suffice to furnish him with explanations for which he would not ostensibly seek.

As the critical faculty, on the universal application of which he prided himself, was, in reality, completely lacking, that refinement of good breeding which consists in assuring some one whom you are obliging in any way, without expecting to be believed, that it is really yourself that is obliged to him, was wasted on Cottard, who took everything that he heard in its literal sense. However blind she may have been to his faults, Mme. Verdurin was genuinely annoyed, though she still continued to regard him as brilliantly clever, when, after she had invited him to see and hear Sarah Bernhardt from a

stage box, and had said politely : " It is very good of you to
have come, Doctor, especially as I'm sure you must often
have heard Sarah Bernhardt ; and besides, I'm afraid we're
rather too near the stage," the Doctor, who had come into
the box with a smile which waited before settling upon or
vanishing from his face until some one in authority should
enlighten him as to the merits of the spectacle, replied : " To
be sure, we are far too near the stage, and one is getting sick
of Sarah Bernhardt. But you expressed a wish that I should
come. For me, your wish is a command. I am only too glad
to be able to do you this little service. What would one not
do to please you, you are so good." And he went on, " Sarah
Bernhardt ; that's what they call the Voice of Gold, ain't
it ? You see, often, too, that she ' sets the boards on fire.'
That's an odd expression, ain't it ? " in the hope of an
enlightening commentary, which, however, was not forth-
coming.

" D'you know," Mme. Verdurin had said to her husband,
" I believe we are going the wrong way to work when we
depreciate anything we offer the Doctor. He is a scientist
who lives quite apart from our everyday existence ; he knows
nothing himself of what things are worth, and he accepts
everything that we say as gospel."

" I never dared to mention it," M. Verdurin had answered,
" but I've noticed the same thing myself." And on the following New Year's Day, instead of sending Dr. Cottard a ruby
that cost three thousand francs, and pretending that it was
a mere trifle, M. Verdurin bought an artificial stone for three
hundred, and let it be understood that it was something
almost impossible to match.

When Mme. Verdurin had announced that they were to
see M. Swann that evening ; " Swann ! " the Doctor had

exclaimed in a tone rendered brutal by his astonishment, for the smallest piece of news would always take utterly unawares this man who imagined himself to be perpetually in readiness for anything. And seeing that no one answered him, " Swann ! Who on earth is Swann ? " he shouted, in a frenzy of anxiety which subsided as soon as Mme. Verdurin had explained, " Why, Odette's friend, whom she told us about."

" Ah, good, good ; that's all right, then," answered the Doctor, at once mollified. As for the painter, he was over-joyed at the prospect of Swann's appearing at the Verdurins', because he supposed him to be in love with Odette, and was always ready to assist at lovers' meetings. " Nothing amuses me more than match-making," he confided to Cottard ; " I have been tremendously successful, even with women ! "

In telling the Verdurins that Swann was extremely ' smart,' Odette had alarmed them with the prospect of another ' bore.' When he arrived, however, he made an excellent impression, an indirect cause of which, though they did not know it, was his familiarity with the best society. He had, indeed, one of those advantages which men who have lived and moved in the world enjoy over others, even men of intelligence and refinement, who have never gone into society, namely that they no longer see it transfigured by the longing or repulsion with which it fills the imagination, but regard it as quite unimportant. Their good nature, freed from all taint of snobbishness and from the fear of seeming too friendly, grown independent, in fact, has the ease, the grace of movement of a trained gymnast each of whose supple limbs will carry out precisely the movement that is required without any clumsy participation by the rest of his body. The simple and elementary gestures used by a man of the

world when he courteously holds out his hand to the unknown
youth who is being introduced to him, and when he bows discreetly before the Ambassador to whom he is being introduced, had gradually pervaded, without his being conscious
of it, the whole of Swann's social deportment, so that in the
company of people of a lower grade than his own, such as the
Verdurins and their friends, he instinctively shewed an
assiduity, and made overtures with which, by their account,
any of their ' bores ' would have dispensed. He chilled,
though for a moment only, on meeting Dr. Cottard ; for
seeing him close one eye with an ambiguous smile, before
they had yet spoken to one another (a grimace which Cottard
styled " letting 'em all come "), Swann supposed that the
Doctor recognised him from having met him already somewhere, probably in some house of ' ill-fame,' though these
he himself very rarely visited, never having made a habit of
indulging in the mercenary sort of love. Regarding such
an allusion as in bad taste, especially before Odette, whose
opinion of himself it might easily alter for the worse, Swann
assumed his most icy manner. But when he learned that the
lady next to the Doctor was Mme. Cottard, he decided that
so young a husband would not deliberately, in his wife's
hearing, have made any allusion to amusements of that order,
and so ceased to interpret the Doctor's expression in the sense
which he had at first suspected. The painter at once invited
Swann to visit his studio with Odette, and Swann found him
very pleasant. " Perhaps you will be more highly favoured
than I have been," Mme. Verdurin broke in, with mock
resentment of the favour, " perhaps you will be allowed to
see Cottard's portrait " (for which she had given the painter
a commission). " Take care, Master Biche," she reminded
the painter, whom it was a time-honoured pleasantry to

address as ' Master,' " to catch that nice look in his eyes, that witty little twinkle. You know, what I want to have most of all is his smile ; that's what I've asked you to paint— the portrait of his smile." And since the phrase struck her as noteworthy, she repeated it very loud, so as to make sure that as many as possible of her guests should hear it, and even made use of some indefinite pretext to draw the circle closer before she uttered it again. Swann begged to be introduced to everyone, even to an old friend of the Verdurins, called Saniette, whose shyness, simplicity and good-nature had deprived him of all the consideration due to his skill in palaeography, his large fortune, and the distinguished family to which he belonged. When he spoke, his words came with a confusion which was delightful to hear because one felt that it indicated not so much a defect in his speech as a quality of his soul, as it were a survival from the age of innocence which he had never wholly outgrown. All the consonants which he did not manage to pronounce seemed like harsh utterances of which his gentle lips were incapable. By asking to be made known to M. Saniette, Swann made M. Verdurin reverse the usual form of introduction (saying, in fact, with emphasis on the distinction : " M. Swann, pray let me present to you our friend Saniette ") but he aroused in Saniette himself a warmth of gratitude, which, however, the Ver- durins never disclosed to Swann, since Saniette rather annoyed them, and they did not feel bound to provide him with friends. On the other hand the Verdurins were extremely touched by Swann's next request, for he felt that he must ask to be introduced to the pianist's aunt. She wore a black dress, as was her invariable custom, for she believed that a woman always looked well in black, and that nothing could be more distinguished ; but her face was exceedingly red, as it always was for some time after a meal. She bowed to Swann with deference, but drew herself up again with great dignity. As she was entirely uneducated, and was afraid of making mistakes in grammar and pronunciation, she used purposely to speak in an indistinct and garbling manner, thinking that if she should make a slip it would be so buried in the surrounding confusion that no one could be certain whether she had actually made it or not ; with the result that her talk was a sort of continuous, blurred expectoration, out of which would emerge, at rare intervals, those sounds and syllables of which she felt positive. Swann supposed himself entitled to poke a little mild fun at her in conversation with M. Verdurin, who, however, was not at all amused.

°" She is such an excellent woman ! " he rejoined. " I grant you that she is not exactly brilliant ; but I assure you that she can talk most charmingly when you are alone with her."

" I am sure she can," Swann hastened to conciliate him. " All I meant was that she hardly struck me as 'distinguished,' " he went on, isolating the epithet in the inverted commas of his tone, " and, after all, that is something of a compliment."

" Wait a moment," said M. Verdurin, " now, this will surprise you ; she writes quite delightfully. You have never heard her nephew play ? It is admirable ; eh, Doctor ? Would you like me to ask him to play something, M. Swann ? "

" I should count myself most fortunate . . . " Swann was beginning, a trifle pompously, when the Doctor broke in derisively. Having once heard it said, and never having forgotten that in general conversation emphasis and the use of formal expressions were out of date, whenever he heard a solemn word used seriously, as the word 'fortunate' had been used just now by Swann, he at once assumed that the speaker was being deliberately pedantic. And if, moreover, the same word happened to occur, also, in what he called an old 'tag' or 'saw,' however common it might still be in current usage, the Doctor jumped to the conclusion that the whole thing was a joke, and interrupted with the remaining words of the quotation, which he seemed to charge the speaker with having intended to introduce at that point, although in reality it had never entered his mind.

"Most fortunate for France!" he recited wickedly, shooting up both arms with great vigour. M. Verdurin could not help laughing.

"What are all those good people laughing at over there? there's no sign of brooding melancholy down in your corner," shouted Mme. Verdurin. "You don't suppose I find it very amusing to be stuck up here by myself on the stool of repentance," she went on peevishly, like a spoiled child.

Mme. Verdurin was sitting upon a high Swedish chair of waxed pinewood, which a violinist from that country had given her, and which she kept in her drawing-room, although in appearance it suggested a school 'form,' and 'swore,' as the saying is, at the really good antique furniture which she had besides; but she made a point of keeping on view the presents which her 'faithful' were in the habit of making her from time to time, so that the donors might have the pleasure of seeing them there when they came to the house. She tried to persuade them to confine their tributes to flowers and sweets, which had at least the merit of mortality; but she was never successful, and the house was gradually filled with a collection of foot-warmers, cushions, clocks, screens, barometers and vases, a constant repetition and a boundless incongruity of useless but indestructible objects.

From this lofty perch she would take her spirited part in the conversation of the 'faithful,' and would revel in all their fun ; but, since the accident to her jaw, she had abandoned the effort involved in real hilarity, and had substituted a kind of symbolical dumb-show which signified, without endangering or even fatiguing her in any way, that she was 'laughing until she cried.' At the least witticism aimed by any of the circle against a 'bore,' or against a former member of the circle who was now relegated to the limbo of 'bores '—and to the utter despair of M. Verdurin, who had always made out that he was just as easily amused as his wife, but who, since his laughter was the 'real thing,' was out of breath in a moment, and so was overtaken and vanquished by her device of a feigned but continuous hilarity—she would utter a shrill cry, shut tight her little bird-like eyes, which were beginning to be clouded over by a cataract, and quickly, as though she had only just time to avoid some indecent sight or to parry a mortal blow, burying her face in her hands, which completely engulfed it, and prevented her from seeing anything at all, she would appear to be struggling to suppress, to eradicate a laugh which, were she to give way to it, must inevitably leave her inanimate. So, stupefied with the gaiety of the 'faithful,' drunken with comradeship, scandal and asseveration, Mme. Verdurin, perched on her high seat like a cage-bird whose biscuit has been steeped in mulled wine, would sit aloft and sob with fellow-feeling.

Meanwhile M. Verdurin, after first asking Swann's permission to light his pipe (" No ceremony here, you understand ; we're all pals ! "), went and begged the young musician to sit down at the piano.

" Leave him alone ; don't bother him ; he hasn't come

here to be tormented," cried Mme. Verdurin. " I won't have him tormented."

" But why on earth should it bother him ? " rejoined M. Verdurin. " I'm sure M. Swann has never heard the sonata in F sharp which we discovered ; he is going to play us the pianoforte arrangement."

" No, no, no, not my sonata ! " she screamed, " I don't want to be made to cry until I get a cold in the head, and neuralgia all down my face, like last time ; thanks very much, I don't intend to repeat that performance ; you are all very kind and considerate ; it is easy to see that none of you will have to stay in bed for a week."

This little scene, which was re-enacted as often as the young pianist sat down to play, never failed to delight the audience, as though each of them were witnessing it for the first time, as a proof of the seductive originality of the ' Mistress ' as she was styled, and of the acute sensitiveness of her musical ' ear.' Those nearest to her would attract the attention of the rest, who were smoking or playing cards at the other end of the room, by their cries of ' Hear, hear!' which, as in Parliamentary debates, shewed that something worth listening to was being said. And next day they would commiserate with those who had been prevented from coming that evening, and would assure them that the ' little scene ' had never been so amusingly done.

" Well, all right, then," said M. Verdurin, " he can play just the *andante*."

" Just the *andante* ! How you do go on," cried his wife. " As if it weren't ' just the *andante* ' that breaks every bone in my body. The ' Master ' is really too priceless ! Just as though, 'in the Ninth,' he said 'we need only have the *finale*,' or ' just the overture ' of the *Meistersingers*."

The Doctor, however, urged Mme. Verdurin to let the pianist play, not because he supposed her to be malingering when she spoke of the distressing effects that music always had upon her, for he recognised the existence of certain neurasthenic states—but from his habit, common to many doctors, of at once relaxing the strict letter of a prescription as soon as it appeared to jeopardise, what seemed to him far more important, the success of some social gathering at which he was present, and of which the patient whom he had urged for once to forget her dyspepsia or headache formed an essential factor.

" You won't be ill this time, you'll find," he told her, seeking at the same time to subdue her mind by the magnetism of his gaze. " And, if you are ill, we will cure you."

" Will you, really ? " Mme. Verdurin spoke as though, with so great a favour in store for her, there was nothing for it but to capitulate. Perhaps, too, by dint of saying that she was going to be ill, she had worked herself into a state in which she forgot, occasionally, that it was all only a ' little scene,' and regarded things, quite sincerely, from an invalid's point of view. For it may often be remarked that invalids grow weary of having the frequency of their attacks depend always on their own prudence in avoiding them, and like to let themselves think that they are free to do everything that they most enjoy doing, although they are always ill after doing it, provided only that they place themselves in the hands of a higher authority which, without putting them to the least inconvenience, can and will, by uttering a word or by administering a tabloid, set them once again upon their feet.

Odette had gone to sit on a tapestry-covered sofa near the piano, saying to Mme. Verdurin, " I have my own little corner, haven't I ? "

And Mme. Verdurin, seeing Swann by himself upon a chair, made him get up : " You're not at all comfortable there ; go along and sit by Odette ; you can make room for M. Swann there, can't you, Odette ? "

" What charming Beauvais ! " said Swann, stopping to admire the sofa before he sat down on it, and wishing to be polite.

" I am glad you appreciate my sofa," replied Mme. Verdurin, " and I warn you that if you expect ever to see another like it you may as well abandon the idea at once. They never made any more like it. And these little chairs, too, are perfect marvels. You can look at them in a moment. The emblems in each of the bronze mouldings correspond to the subject of the tapestry on the chair ; you know, you combine amusement with instruction when you look at them ;—I can promise you a delightful time, I assure you. Just look at the little border round the edges ; here, look, the little vine on a red background in this one, the Bear and the Grapes. Isn't it well drawn ? What do you say ? I think they knew a thing or two about design ! Doesn't it make your mouth water, this vine ? My husband makes out that I am not fond of fruit, because I eat less than he does. But not a bit of it, I am greedier than any of you, but I have no need to fill my mouth with them when I can feed on them with my eyes. What are you all laughing at now, pray ? Ask the Doctor ; he will tell you that those grapes act on me like a regular purge. Some people go to Fontainebleau for cures ; I take my own little Beauvais cure here. But, M. Swann, you mustn't run away without feeling the little bronze mouldings on the backs. Isn't it an exquisite surface ? No, no, not with your whole hand like that ; feel them properly ! "

" If Mme. Verdurin is going to start playing about with

her bronzes," said the painter, " we shan't get any music to-night."

" Be quiet, you wretch ! And yet we poor women," she went on, " are forbidden pleasures far less voluptuous than this. There is no flesh in the world as soft as these. None. When M Verdurin did me the honour of being madly jealous . . . come, you might at least be polite. Don't say that you never have been jealous ! "

" But, my dear, I have said absolutely nothing. Look here, Doctor, I call you as a witness ; did I utter a word ? "

Swann had begun, out of politeness, to finger the bronzes, and did not like to stop.

" Come along ; you can caress them later ; now it is you that are going to be caressed, caressed in the ear ; you'll like that, I think. Here's the young gentleman who will take charge of that."

After the pianist had played, Swann felt and shewed more interest in him than in any of the other guests, for the following reason :

The year before, at an evening party, he had heard a piece of music played on the piano and violin. At first he had appreciated only the material quality of the sounds which those instruments secreted. And it had been a source of keen pleasure when, below the narrow ribbon of the violin-part, delicate, unyielding, substantial and governing the whole, he had suddenly perceived, where it was trying to surge upwards in a flowing tide of sound, the mass of the piano-part, multiform, coherent, level, and breaking everywhere in melody like the deep blue tumult of the sea, silvered and charmed into a minor key by the moonlight. But at a given moment, without being able to distinguish any clear outline, or to give a name to what was pleasing him, suddenly enraptured, he had tried to collect, to treasure in his memory the phrase or harmony—he knew not which—that had just been played, and had opened and expanded his soul, just as the fragrance of certain roses, wafted upon the moist air of evening, has the power of dilating our nostrils. Perhaps it was owing to his own ignorance of music that he had been able to receive so confused an impression, one of those that are, notwithstanding, our only purely musical impressions, limited in their extent, entirely original, and irreducible into any other kind. An impression of this order, vanishing in an instant, is, so to speak, an impression *sine materia*. Presumably the notes which we hear at such moments tend to spread out before our eyes, over surfaces greater or smaller according to their pitch and volume ; to trace arabesque designs, to give us the sensation of breadth or tenuity, stability or caprice. But the notes themselves have vanished before these sensations have developed sufficiently to escape submersion under those which the following, or even simultaneous notes have already begun to awaken in us. And this indefinite perception would continue to smother in its molten liquidity the *motifs* which now and then emerge, barely discernible, to plunge again and disappear and drown ; recognised only by the particular kind of pleasure which they instil, impossible to describe, to recollect, to name ; ineffable ;—if our memory, like a labourer who toils at the laying down of firm foundations beneath the tumult of the waves, did not, by fashioning for us facsimiles of those fugitive phrases, enable us to compare and to contrast them with those that follow. And so, hardly had the delicious sensation, which Swann had experienced, died away, before his memory had furnished him with an immediate transcript, summary, it is true, and provisional, but one on which he had kept his eyes fixed while the playing continued, so effectively

that, when the same impression suddenly returned, it was no
longer uncapturable. He was able to picture to himself its
extent, its symmetrical arrangement, its notation, the strength
of its expression ; he had before him that definite object
which was no longer pure music, but rather design, architecture, thought, and which allowed the actual music to be
recalled. This time he had distinguished, quite clearly, a
phrase which emerged for a few moments from the waves of
sound. It had at once held out to him an invitation to partake of intimate pleasures, of whose existence, before hearing
it, he had never dreamed, into which he felt that nothing but
this phrase could initiate him ; and he had been filled with
love for it, as with a new and strange desire.

With a slow and rhythmical movement it led him here,
there, everywhere, towards a state of happiness noble, unintelligible, yet clearly indicated. And then, suddenly, having
reached a certain point from which he was prepared to follow
it, after pausing for a moment, abruptly it changed its direction, and in a fresh movement, more rapid, multiform,
melancholy, incessant, sweet, it bore him off with it towards
a vista of joys unknown. Then it vanished. He hoped, with
a passionate longing, that he might find it again, a third time.
And reappear it did, though without speaking to him more
clearly, bringing him, indeed, a pleasure less profound. But
when he was once more at home he needed it, he was like a
man into whose life a woman, whom he has seen for a
moment passing by, has brought a new form of beauty, which
strengthens and enlarges his own power of perception, without his knowing even whether he is ever to see her again
whom he loves already, although he knows nothing of her,
not even her name.

Indeed this passion for a phrase of music seemed, in the

first few months, to be bringing into Swann's life the possibility of a sort of rejuvenation. He had so long since ceased to direct his course towards any ideal goal, and had confined himself to the pursuit of ephemeral satisfactions, that he had come to believe, though without ever formally stating his belief even to himself, that he would remain all his life in that condition, which death alone could alter. More than this, since his mind no longer entertained any lofty ideals, he had ceased to believe in (although he could not have expressly denied) their reality. He had grown also into the habit of taking refuge in trivial considerations, which allowed him to set on one side matters of fundamental importance. Just as he had never stopped to ask himself whether he would not have done better by not going into society, knowing very well that if he had accepted an invitation he must put in an appearance, and that afterwards, if he did not actually call, he must at least leave cards upon his hostess ; so in his con-versation he took care never to express with any warmth a personal opinion about a thing, but instead would supply facts and details which had a value of a sort in themselves, and excused him from shewing how much he really knew. He would be extremely precise about the recipe for a dish, the dates of a painter's birth and death, and the titles of his works. Sometimes, in spite of himself, he would let himself go so far as to utter a criticism of a work of art, or of some one's interpretation of life, but then he would cloak his words in a tone of irony, as though he did not altogether associate himself with what he was saying. But now, like a confirmed invalid whom, all of a sudden, a change of air and surround-ings, or a new course of treatment, or, as sometimes happens, an organic change in himself, spontaneous and unaccountable, seems to have so far recovered from his malady that he begins

to envisage the possibility, hitherto beyond all hope, of
starting to lead—and better late than never—a wholly
different life, Swann found in himself, in the memory of the
phrase that he had heard, in certain other sonatas which he
had made people play over to him, to see whether he might
not, perhaps, discover his phrase among them, the presence
of one of those invisible realities in which he had ceased to
believe, but to which, as though the music had had upon the
moral barrenness from which he was suffering a sort of
recreative influence, he was conscious once again of a desire,
almost, indeed, of the power to consecrate his life. But, never
having managed to find out whose work it was that he had
heard played that evening, he had been unable to procure a
copy, and finally had forgotten the quest. He had indeed, in
the course of the next few days, encountered several of the
people who had been at the party with him, and had questioned
them ; but most of them had either arrived after or left before
the piece was played ; some had indeed been in the house,
but had gone into another room to talk, and those who had
stayed to listen had no clearer impression than the rest. As
for his hosts, they knew that it was a recently published work
which the musicians whom they had engaged for the evening
had asked to be allowed to play ; but, as these last were now
on tour somewhere, Swann could learn nothing further.
He had, of course, a number of musical friends, but, vividly
as he could recall the exquisite and inexpressible pleasure
which the little phrase had given him, and could see, still,
before his eyes the forms that it had traced in outline, he was
quite incapable of humming over to them the air. And so,
at last, he ceased to think of it.

But to-night, at Mme. Verdurin's, scarcely had the little
pianist begun to play when, suddenly, after a high note held

on through two whole bars, Swann saw it approaching, stealing forth from underneath that resonance, which was prolonged and stretched out over it, like a curtain of sound, to veil the mystery of its birth—and recognised, secret, whispering, articulate, the airy and fragrant phrase that he had loved. And it was so peculiarly itself, it had so personal a charm, which nothing else could have replaced, that Swann felt as though he had met, in a friend's drawing-room, a woman whom he had seen and admired, once, in the street, and had despaired of ever seeing again. Finally the phrase withdrew and vanished, pointing, directing, diligent among the wandering currents of its fragrance, leaving upon Swann's features a reflection of its smile. But now, at last, he could ask the name of his fair unknown (and was told that it was the *andante* movement of Vinteuil's sonata for the piano and violin), he held it safe, could have it again to himself, at home, as often as he would, could study its language and acquire its secret.

And so, when the pianist had finished, Swann crossed the room and thanked him with a vivacity which delighted Mme. Verdurin.

" Isn't he charming ? " she asked Swann, " doesn't he just understand it, his sonata, the little wretch ? You never dreamed, did you, that a piano could be made to express all that ? Upon my word, there's everything in it except the piano ! I'm caught out every time I hear it ; I think I'm listening to an orchestra. Though it's better, really, than an orchestra, more complete."

The young pianist bent over her as he answered, smiling and underlining each of his words as though he were making an epigram : " You are most generous to me."

And while Mme. Verdurin was saying to her husband,

" Run and fetch him a glass of orangeade ; it's well earned ! "
Swann began to tell Odette how he had fallen in love with
that little phrase. When their hostess, who was a little way
off, called out, " Well ! It looks to me as though some one
was saying nice things to you, Odette ! " she replied, " Yes,
very nice," and he found her simplicity delightful. Then he
asked for some information about this Vinteuil ; what else
he had done, and at what period in his life he had composed
the sonata ;—what meaning the little phrase could have had
for him, that was what Swann wanted most to know.

But none of these people who professed to admire this
musician (when Swann had said that the sonata was really
charming Mme. Verdurin had exclaimed, " I quite believe
it ! Charming, indeed ! But you don't dare to confess that
you don't know Vinteuil's sonata ; you have no right not
to know it ! "—and the painter had gone on with, " Ah,
yes, it's a very fine bit of work, isn't it ? Not, of course, if
you want something ' obvious,' something ' popular,' but,
I mean to say, it makes a very great impression on us artists "),
none of them seemed ever to have asked himself these questions, for none of them was able to reply.

Even to one or two particular remarks made by Swann on
his favourite phrase, " D'you know, that's a funny thing ;
I had never noticed it ; I may as well tell you that I don't
much care about peering at things through a microscope, and
pricking myself on pin-points of difference ; no ; we don't
waste time splitting hairs in this house ; why not ? well,
it's not a habit of ours, that's all," Mme. Verdurin replied,
while Dr. Cottard gazed at her with open-mouthed admiration, and yearned to be able to follow her as she skipped
lightly from one stepping-stone to another of her stock of
ready-made phrases. Both he, however, and Mme. Cottard,

with a kind of common sense which is shared by many people
of humble origin, would always take care not to express an
opinion, or to pretend to admire a piece of music which they
would confess to each other, once they were safely at home,
that they no more understood than they could understand
the art of ' Master ' Biche. Inasmuch as the public cannot
recognise the charm, the beauty, even the outlines of nature
save in the stereotyped impressions of an art which they have
gradually assimilated, while an original artist starts by re-
jecting those impressions, so M. and Mme. Cottard, typical,
in this respect, of the public, were incapable of finding, either
in Vinteuil's sonata or in Biche's portraits, what constituted
harmony, for them, in music or beauty in painting. It appeared to them, when the pianist played his sonata, as though
he were striking haphazard from the piano a medley of notes
which bore no relation to the musical forms to which they
themselves were accustomed, and that the painter simply
flung the colours haphazard upon his canvas. When, on one
of these, they were able to distinguish a human form, they
always found it coarsened and vulgarised (that is to say lacking
all the elegance of the school of painting through whose
spectacles they themselves were in the habit of seeing the
people—real, living people, who passed them in the streets)
and devoid of truth, as though M. Biche had not known how
the human shoulder was constructed, or that a woman's hair
was not, ordinarily, purple.

And yet, when the 'faithful' were scattered out of earshot,
the Doctor felt that the opportunity was too good to be missed,
and so (while Mme. Verdurin was adding a final word of
commendation of Vinteuil's sonata) like a would-be swimmer
who jumps into the water, so as to learn, but chooses a
moment when there are not too many people looking on :

" Yes, indeed ; he's what they call a musician *di primo cartello!*" he exclaimed, with sudden determination.

Swann discovered no more than that the recent publication of Vinteuil's sonata had caused a great stir among the most advanced school of musicians, but that it was still unknown to the general public.

" I know some one, quite well, called Vinteuil," said Swann, thinking of the old music-master at Combray who had taught my grandmother's sisters.

" Perhaps that's the man ! " cried Mme. Verdurin.

" Oh, no ! " Swann burst out laughing. " If you had ever seen him for a moment you wouldn't put the question."

" Then to put the question is to solve the problem ? " the Doctor suggested.

" But it may well be some relative ; " Swann went on. " That would be bad enough ; but, after all, there is no reason why a genius shouldn't have a cousin who is a silly old fool. And if that should be so, I swear there's no known or unknown form of torture I wouldn't undergo to get the old fool to introduce me to the man who composed the sonata ; starting with the torture of the old fool's company, which would be ghastly."

The painter understood that Vinteuil was seriously ill at the moment, and that Dr. Potain despaired of his life.

" What ! " cried Mme. Verdurin, " Do people still call in Potain ? "

" Ah ! Mme. Verdurin," Cottard simpered, " you forget that you are speaking of one of my colleagues—I should say, one of my masters."

The painter had heard, somewhere, that Vinteuil was threatened with the loss of his reason. And he insisted that signs of this could be detected in certain passages in the sonata.

This remark did not strike Swann as ridiculous ; rather, it puzzled him. For, since a purely musical work contains none of those logical sequences, the interruption or confusion of which, in spoken or written language, is a proof of insanity, so insanity diagnosed in a sonata seemed to him as mysterious a thing as the insanity of a dog or a horse, although instances may be observed of these.

" Don't speak to me about ' your masters ' ; you know ten times as much as he does ! " Mme. Verdurin answered Dr. Cottard, in the tone of a woman who has the courage of her convictions, and is quite ready to stand up to anyone who disagrees with her. " Anyhow, you don't kill your patients ! "

" But, Madame, he is in the Academy." The Doctor smiled with bitter irony. " If a sick person prefers to die at the hands of one of the Princes of Science. . . It is far more smart to be able to say, ' Yes, I have Potain.' "

" Oh, indeed ! More smart, is it ? " said Mme. Verdurin. " So there are fashions, nowadays, in illness, are there ? I didn't know that. . . . Oh, you do make me laugh ! " she screamed, suddenly, burying her face in her hands. " And here was I, poor thing, talking quite seriously, and never seeing that you were pulling my leg."

As for M. Verdurin, finding it rather a strain to start laughing again over so small a matter, he was content with puffing out a cloud of smoke from his pipe, while he reflected sadly that he could never again hope to keep pace with his wife in her Atalanta-flights across the field of mirth.

" D'you know ; we like your friend so very much," said Mme. Verdurin, later, when Odette was bidding her good night. " He is so unaffected, quite charming. If they're all like that, the friends you want to bring here, by all means bring them."

M. Verdurin remarked that Swann had failed, all the same, to appreciate the pianist's aunt.

" I dare say he felt a little strange, poor man," suggested Mme. Verdurin. " You can't expect him to catch the tone of the house the first time he comes ; like Cottard, who has been one of our little ' clan ' now for years. The first time doesn't count ; it's just for looking round and finding out things. Odette, he understands all right, he's to join us to-morrow at the Châtelet. Perhaps you might call for him and bring him."

" No, he doesn't want that."

" Oh, very well ; just as you like. Provided he doesn't fail us at the last moment."

Greatly to Mme. Verdurin's surprise, he never failed them. He would go to meet them, no matter where, at restaurants outside Paris, (not that they went there much at first, for the season had not yet begun) and more frequently at the play, in which Mme. Verdurin delighted. One evening, when they were dining at home, he heard her complain that she had not one of those permits which would save her the trouble of waiting at doors and standing in crowds, and say how useful it would be to them at first-nights, and gala performances at the Opera, and what a nuisance it had been, not having one, on the day of Gambetta's funeral. Swann never spoke of his distinguished friends, but only of such as might be regarded as detrimental, whom, therefore, he thought it snobbish, and in not very good taste to conceal ; while he frequented the Faubourg Saint-Germain he had come to include, in the latter class, all his friends in the official world of the Third Republic, and so broke in, without thinking : " I'll see to that, all right. You shall have it in time for the *Danicheff* revival. I shall be lunching

297

with the Prefect of Police to-morrow, as it happens, at the Elysée."

" What's that ? The Elysée ? " Dr. Cottard roared in a voice of thunder.

" Yes, at M. Grévy's," replied Swann, feeling a little awkward at the effect which his announcement had produced.

" Are you often taken like that ? " the painter asked Cottard, with mock-seriousness.

As a rule, once an explanation had been given, Cottard would say : " Ah, good, good ; that's all right, then," after which he would shew not the least trace of emotion. But this time Swann's last words, instead of the usual calming effect, had that of heating, instantly, to boiling-point his astonishment at the discovery that a man with whom he himself was actually sitting at table, a man who had no official position, no honours or distinction of any sort, was on visiting terms with the Head of the State.

" What's that you say ? M. Grévy ? Do you know M. Grévy ? " he demanded of Swann, in the stupid and incredulous tone of a constable on duty at the palace, when a stranger has come up and asked to see the President of the Republic ; until, guessing from his words and manner what, as the newspapers say, ' it is a case of,' he assures the poor lunatic that he will be admitted at once, and points the way to the reception ward of the police infirmary.

" I know him slightly ; we have some friends in common " (Swann dared not add that one of these friends was the Prince of Wales). " Anyhow, he is very free with his invitations, and, I assure you, his luncheon-parties are not the least bit amusing ; they're very simple affairs, too, you know ; never more than eight at table," he went on, trying desperately to cut out everything that seemed to shew off his relations with the President in a light too dazzling for the Doctor's eyes.

Whereupon Cottard, at once conforming in his mind to the literal interpretation of what Swann was saying, decided that invitations from M. Grévy were very little sought after, were sent out, in fact, into the highways and hedgerows. And from that moment he never seemed at all surprised to hear that Swann, or anyone else, was 'always at the Elysée'; he even felt a little sorry for a man who had to go to luncheon-parties which, he himself admitted, were a bore.

"Ah, good, good; that's quite all right, then," he said, in the tone of a customs official who has been suspicious up to now, but, after hearing your explanations, stamps your passport and lets you proceed on your journey without troubling to examine your luggage.

"I can well believe you don't find them amusing, those parties; indeed, it's very good of you to go to them!" said Mme. Verdurin, who regarded the President of the Republic only as a 'bore' to be especially dreaded, since he had at his disposal means of seduction, and even of compulsion, which, if employed to captivate her 'faithful,' might easily make them 'fail.' "It seems, he's as deaf as a post; and eats with his fingers."

"Upon my word! Then it can't be much fun for you, going there." A note of pity sounded in the Doctor's voice; and then struck by the number—only eight at table—"Are these luncheons what you would describe as 'intimate'?" he inquired briskly, not so much out of idle curiosity as in his linguistic zeal.

But so great and glorious a figure was the President of the French Republic in the eyes of Dr. Cottard that neither the modesty of Swann nor the spite of Mme. Verdurin could ever wholly efface that first impression, and he never sat down to dinner with the Verdurins without asking anxiously, " D'you think we shall see M. Swann here this evening ? He is a personal friend of M. Grévy's. I suppose that means he's what you'ld call a ' gentleman ' ? " He even went to the length of offering Swann a card of invitation to the Dental Exhibition.

" This will let you in, and anyone you take with you," he explained, " but dogs are not admitted. I'm just warning you, you understand, because some friends of mine went there once, who hadn't been told, and there was the devil to pay."

As for M. Verdurin, he did not fail to observe the distressing effect upon his wife of the discovery that Swann had influential friends of whom he had never spoken.

If no arrangement had been made to ' go anywhere,' it was at the Verdurins' that Swann would find the ' little nucleus ' assembled, but he never appeared there except in the evenings, and would hardly ever accept their invitations to dinner, in spite of Odette's entreaties.

" I could dine with you alone somewhere, if you'ld rather," she suggested.

" But what about Mme. Verdurin ? "

" Oh, that's quite simple. I need only say that my dress wasn't ready, or that my cab came late. There is always some excuse."

" How charming of you."

But Swann said to himself that, if he could make Odette feel (by consenting to meet her only after dinner) that there were other pleasures which he preferred to that of her company, then the desire that she felt for his would be all the longer in reaching the point of satiety. Besides, as he infinitely preferred to Odette's style of beauty that of a little

working girl, as fresh and plump as a rose, with whom he
happened to be simultaneously in love, he preferred to spend
the first part of the evening with her, knowing that he was
sure to see Odette later on. For the same reason, he would
never allow Odette to call for him at his house, to take him
on to the Verdurins' The little girl used to wait, not far
from his door, at a street corner ; Rémi, his coachman,
knew where to stop ; she would jump in beside him, and
hold him in her arms until the carriage drew up at the
Verdurins'. He would enter the drawing-room ; and there,
while Mme. Verdurin, pointing to the roses which he had
sent her that morning, said : " I am furious with you ! " and
sent him to the place kept for him, by the side of Odette,
the pianist would play to them—for their two selves, and for
no one else—that little phrase by Vinteuil which was, so to
speak, the national anthem of their love. He began, always,
with a sustained *tremolo* from the violin part, which, for
several bars, was unaccompanied, and filled all the foreground;
until suddenly it seemed to be drawn aside, and—just as in
those interiors by Pieter de Hooch, where the subject is set
back a long way through the narrow framework of a half-
opened door—infinitely remote, in colour quite different,
velvety with the radiance of some intervening light, the little
phrase appeared, dancing, pastoral, interpolated, episodic,
belonging to another world. It passed, with simple and immortal movements, scattering on every side the bounties of
its grace, smiling ineffably still ; but Swann thought that he
could now discern in it some disenchantment. It seemed to be
aware how vain, how hollow was the happiness to which it
shewed the way. In its airy grace there was, indeed, something definitely achieved, and complete in itself, like the mood
of philosophic detachment which follows an outburst of vain

regret. But little did that matter to him ; he looked upon the sonata less in its own light—as what it might express, had, in fact, expressed to a certain musician, ignorant that any Swann or Odette, anywhere in the world, existed, when he composed it, and would express to all those who should hear it played in centuries to come—than as a pledge, a token of his love, which made even the Verdurins and their little pianist think of Odette and, at the same time, of himself— which bound her to him by a lasting tie ; and at that point he had (whimsically entreated by Odette) abandoned the idea of getting some ' professional ' to play over to him the whole sonata, of which he still knew no more than this one passage. "Why do you want the rest ? " she had asked him, " Our little bit ; that's all we need." He went farther ; agonised by the reflection, at the moment when it passed by him, so near and yet so infinitely remote, that, while it was addressed to their ears, it knew them not, he would regret, almost, that it had a meaning of its own, an intrinsic and un-alterable beauty, foreign to themselves, just as in the jewels given to us, or even in the letters written to us by a woman with whom we are in love, we find fault with the ' water ' of a stone, or with the words of a sentence because they are not fashioned exclusively from the spirit of a fleeting intimacy and of a ' lass unparallel'd.'

It would happen, as often as not, that he had stayed so long outside, with his little girl, before going to the Verdurins' that, as soon as the little phrase had been rendered by the pianist, Swann would discover that it was almost time for Odette to go home. He used to take her back as far as the door of her little house in the Rue La Pérouse, behind the Arc de Triomphe. And it was perhaps on this account, and so as not to demand the monopoly of her favours, that he sacrificed the pleasure (not so essential to his well-being) of seeing her earlier in the evening, of arriving with her at the Verdurins', to the exercise of this other privilege, for which she was grateful, of their leaving together ; a privilege which he valued all the more because, thanks to it, he had the feeling that no one else would see her, no one would thrust himself between them, no one could prevent him from remaining with her in spirit, after he had left her for the night.

Printed in Great Britain by R. & R. CLARK, LIMITED, *Edinburgh.*